PENGUIN BOOKS

barely breathing

USA Today bestselling author Rebecca Donovan has been a writer most of her life, but has just recently been deemed an author. Her debut novels, *Reason to Breathe* and the follow-up *Barely Breathing*, have resonated with readers around the world. Rebecca is currently working on the third and final instalment of the Breathing series, *Out of Breath*. She graduated from the University of Missouri–Columbia and currently lives in a small town in Massachusetts.

Books by Rebecca Donovan

REASON TO BREATHE

BARELY BREATHING

Coming soon

OUT OF BREATH

barely breathing

REBECCA DONOVAN

PENGUIN BOOKS

PENGUIN BOOKS

Published by the Penguin Group

Penguin Books Ltd, 80 Strand, London WC2R ORL, England

Penguin Group (USA) Inc., 375 Hudson Street, New York, New York 10014, USA

Penguin Group (Canada), 90 Eglinton Avenue East, Suite 700, Toronto, Ontario, Canada M4P 2Y3
(a division of Pearson Penguin Canada Inc.)

Penguin Ireland, 25 St Stephen's Green, Dublin 2, Ireland (a division of Penguin Books Ltd)

Penguin Group (Australia), 707 Collins Street, Melbourne, Victoria 3008, Australia
(a division of Pearson Australia Group Pty Ltd)

Penguin Books India Pvt Ltd, 11 Community Centre, Panchsheel Park, New Delhi – 110 017, India

Penguin Group (NZ), 67 Apollo Drive, Rosedale, Auckland 0632, New Zealand
(a division of Pearson New Zealand Ltd)

Penguin Books (South Africa) (Pty) Ltd, Block D, Rosebank Office Park,
181 Jan Smuts Avenue, Parktown North, Gauteng 2193, South Africa

Penguin Books Ltd, Registered Offices: 80 Strand, London WC2R ORL, England

www.penguin.com

First published as an electronic edition by Penguin Books Ltd 2012
This edition published 2013
001

Set in 12.5/14.75pt Garamond MT Std
Typeset by Jouve (UK), Milton Keynes
Printed in Great Britain by Clays Ltd, St Ives plc

British Library Cataloguing in Publication Data
A CIP catalogue record for this book is available from the British Library

ISBN: 978-0-141-34845-2

www.greenpenguin.co.uk

Penguin Books is committed to a sustainable
future for our business, our readers and our planet.
This book is made from Forest Stewardship
Council™ certified paper.

ALWAYS LEARNING   **PEARSON**

For my gifted friend, Elizabeth
~ my search of words led me to you,
where I found the perfect partnership and a beautiful friendship ~

Contents

Prologue

Six months ago, I was dead. My heart didn't beat within my chest. Breath did not pass between my lips. Everything was gone, and I was dead.

It's not easy to think about, not existing – despite how much I fought to be forgettable all those years. So I've chosen not to think of it at all.

My therapist asked me to write down my thoughts and feelings in this journal. After months of avoiding the assignment, I figured I should try it once – then maybe I could finally get some sleep. I'm doubtful, but I'll try anything.

I don't honestly remember what happened that night. I get glimpses and moments of panic in my nightmares, but the details evade me. And I'm not looking to fill in the blanks.

I woke up in a hospital bed, barely able to talk, with dark bruises on my neck. There were bandages wrapped around my wrists to protect the raw skin. A sling supported my dislocated shoulder, and a cast concealed my ankle after reconstructive surgery. I don't know what I went through to end up that way. All I care about is that I'm breathing.

The police asked questions. The doctors asked questions. The lawyers asked questions. Whenever they'd start to talk about the details, I'd close them off, or leave the room. Evan and Sara had promised to keep the details from me as well. They weren't there that night, but they were in the courtroom for the entire trial — as brief as it was.

Carol . . .

It's so hard to even write her name. She pleaded guilty. I didn't have to see her. I didn't have to testify. I didn't have to listen to the witnesses' testimonies. They summoned Sara and Evan, and I couldn't be there for that either — even though the lawyers requested my presence.

And George . . . from what little I've overheard, he was there that night. He was the one who called the ambulance. They didn't press charges. I begged them not to. Leyla and Jack need their dad. And now . . . Now I don't even know where they are. ~~I hope they remember how much~~ Sorry. I can't. It hurts too much to think about them.

Sara and Evan have barely left my side since that night. I've tried to assure them that I'm okay, but they just have to look at the circles under my eyes to know that I'm not. In truth, I don't want to be alone.

There was some press coverage, but it was a closed trial, and the records are sealed because I'm a minor (I'm pretty sure Sara's father had some influence over that too) — so there wasn't much for the papers to write about.

The town exploded with news of the attempted murder, and you can only imagine what it was like to return to school, or to be seen anywhere in Weslyn. Whispers. Pointing. Eyes following me everywhere. I've become a morbid celebrity – the girl who survived death.

Even the teachers treat me differently, like they're waiting for me to shatter. The small group who confronted me that day are especially wary. Their interference is what put the whole ordeal in motion. They'd made a call to the authorities before speaking with me, and then called George when I left the school.

Carol must have found out about their call to George, or maybe someone from the state contacted her to look into the allegations. Either way, she was desperate for me to disappear – forever. But it doesn't matter what made her do it. She can't hurt me now.

I do hurt. I'm not going to deny that. Especially since no one will ever see this journal. My ankle will probably never be the same, and will remain a constant reminder of what I went through. I fought to recover, and despite the anticipated out-come, I returned to the soccer field four months later. At the beginning, I would cry in the shower after each practice and game. The pain was almost unbearable. But now I barely notice it.

Nothing looks the same any more. Nothing feels the same. I'm not sure how to explain this to Sara and Evan. I don't know if they'd understand. I'm not sure that I do.

She wanted me dead.

I keep telling myself that's she's gone. She's in prison where she can stay for as long as forever, as far as I'm concerned. But I don't feel safe. Especially when I close my eyes each night and she's right there waiting for me.

I need to get out of Weslyn. Away from the stares. Away from the shadows that continue to haunt me. Away from the pain that paralyses me when I least expect it. Six more months and all of it will be gone. I get to start again, with the two people I love most in the world.

Then again, my life is anything but predictable, and a lot can happen in six months.

I

Try Again

IT'S JUST A DREAM. I RECOGNIZED THE thought, trying to pull me out of the hands that dragged me to the darkest depths of the water. But panic overshadowed the rational thought, and I kicked as hard as I could. *It's just a dream*, my voice echoed through my head again, trying to wake me.

I looked down into the murky water, my breath burning in my lungs. The hands were now long, jagged claws, and as I kicked, one claw pierced my ankle, anchoring me under the water. A dark cloud surrounded me as the blood oozed around its nails. I struggled against it, but it only tore deeper into me. A rush of air bubbled around me as I screamed in pain. I was about to inhale my death when something pressed against my face.

It didn't feel like a dream any more.

I shot up with a gasp, the pillow falling from my face. Disoriented and panting, I searched the room. Sara stood frozen by her bed, her eyes wide and mouth open.

'I'm so sorry,' she muttered. 'I thought I heard you talking. I thought you were awake.'

'I'm awake,' I said, exhaling quickly. With a deep breath, I pushed the panic away. Sara remained stunned even after I'd recovered.

'I shouldn't have thrown the pillow on your head. I'm really sorry,' she frowned guiltily.

'What are you talking about?' I brushed off her apology. 'It was just a dream. I'm fine.' After another deep breath to ease the shaking, I pulled back the covers. They clung to the layer of sweat covering my body.

'Good morning, Sara,' I said as normally as I could.

'Good morning, Emma,' she finally replied, forced out of her guilt-ridden stupor. And just like that, it was over, thankfully. 'I'm going to take a shower. We have to hurry. We're leaving in an hour.' She grabbed her things and disappeared.

I'd been trying to prepare myself for this day for over a month. It didn't matter. I was still freaked just thinking about it. And now it was here.

I collapsed back on the bed and stared up at the white glowing skylights that lined the ceiling, the morning sun hidden behind the snow.

I looked around the room that had no true connection to me – the large flat-screen hanging on the wall, and a vanity in the corner, lined with make-up that had seen way too many makeovers at my expense. There were pictures of laughing friends taped to the mirror, and vibrant art adorned the walls. No reminder of my life before I came here. It was the place where I'd been hiding – hiding from the judgements, whispers and stares.

Why was I here? I knew the answer. If I had the choice, I'd never leave. It's not like I had anywhere else to go, and the McKinleys wouldn't turn their backs on me. They were the only family I had, and for that I would always be grateful. But that wasn't completely the truth. They *weren't* the only family I had.

So when the phone rang while Sara was in the shower, I sucked in all the courage I could gather, put the phone to my ear and said, 'Hi.'

'Oh! You're there,' my mother exclaimed, completely taken by surprise. 'I'm so glad I was finally able to catch you. How are you?'

'I'm fine,' I replied, my heart stammering in my chest. 'Um, so you have plans tonight?'

'Just a party with some friends,' she replied, sounding just as awkward as I felt. 'Listen. I was hoping we could try, you know . . . I mean, I live pretty much in Weslyn now if you ever decide you'd like to . . .'

'Yeah, sure,' I blurted, before I lost my nerve, 'I'll live with you.'

'Oh, um, okay,' she responded in strained excitement. 'Really?'

'Sure,' I answered, trying to sound sincere. 'I mean, I'm leaving for college soon, so better reconnect now than when I'm across the country, right?'

She was silent, probably digesting that I'd just invited myself to move in. 'Uh, yeah, that sounds great. When are you thinking?'

'Since I go back to school on Monday, how about Sunday?'

'Meaning, *this* Sunday? As in, three days from now?'

There was no hiding the panic in her voice. My heart skipped a beat. She wasn't ready to take me back, was she?

'Would that be okay? I mean, I don't need anything, just a bed, or even a couch. But if it's too much . . . Sorry, I shouldn't have –'

'No . . . no, that's perfect,' she stumbled. 'Um, I have time to get your room ready, so . . . sure, Sunday it is. I live on Decatur Street. I'll text you the address.'

'Okay. I'll see you Sunday then.'

'Yup,' my mother replied, the shock still lingering in her tone. 'Happy New Year, Emily.'

'You too,' I returned before hanging up the phone. I stared up at the ceiling. *What did I just do?! What was I thinking?*

I grabbed my things and walked past Sara into the bathroom, trying to control the panic rising inside me. By the time I emerged, I had come to terms with it. It was what I had to do.

'So, I have something to tell you,' I began, sitting on the stool next to Sara while her mother, Anna, poured herself a cup of coffee. 'I spoke to my mother this morning –'

'It's about time,' Sara interrupted. 'You've only been ignoring her for like six months.'

'What did she have to say?' Anna encouraged, ignoring Sara's outburst.

'Well . . . I'm moving in with her this Sunday.' I held my breath as I watched the news sink in.

Sara's spoon clanged inside the cereal bowl, but she didn't say a word.

'What made you decide that was the best thing to do?'

Anna asked calmly, diverting attention from Sara's silent disapproval.

'She's my mother,' I shrugged. 'I'm leaving for college soon, and I don't think I'll have another opportunity to try to fix us. I haven't exactly been fair to her, and she keeps trying to connect, so I thought this was the best way to do it.'

Anna nodded, considering my explanation. Sara stood up and briskly walked to the sink to drop her bowl in, still unable to look at me.

'Well, Carl and I will need to talk about it since we were given guardianship until you're eighteen. And I'd really like to meet her before anything's final. Okay?'

I nodded, not having expected Anna's answer. I wasn't used to having a parent actually care about me, so I didn't really know what to say.

'I understand why you want to do this,' Anna assured me with a soft smile. 'Let us just talk about it first, that's all.'

'Thanks.' I smiled weakly. 'It would mean a lot to get to know my mother again.'

Sara stormed up the stairs without a single word. I exhaled deeply before following her up the stairs.

'Okay, say it,' I demanded flatly while Sara shoved items into her overnight bag.

'I don't have anything to say,' Sara retorted. But she did; it just took a three-hour car ride to the hotel and a day of primping before it came out.

After a day of being prepped and primped from head to toe in Newport, I was exhausted, and we hadn't even been to the party yet. Or maybe it was the drama of the impromptu decision to move in with my mother that drained my energy. Either way, I was having a hard time looking forward to tonight.

'I don't understand why you're moving in with her,' Sara reprimanded me out of nowhere as she smoothed the brush over my lids. 'Couldn't you start with . . . uh . . . *talking* first? I just don't like it. She left you, Em. Why go back?'

'Sara, please,' I implored her quietly, 'I need to do this. I know it seems messed up to you, but it's important to me. It's not like you're losing me or anything. And if it's *horrible*, I'll move back in with you. I feel like I should give her another chance.'

Sara sighed dramatically. 'I still don't think it's a good idea, but . . .' She paused a moment. 'You're one of the most stubborn people I know, and if this is what you want to do, I know I won't be able to talk you out of it. Um, you can open your eyes now.'

I stretched my eyes open and blinked, the mascara sticking along my lashes.

She deliberated, finally conceding with a roll of her eyes, 'Fine. Live with her. But she'd better not do anything monumentally stupid like she did when she left you with *Psycho*.'

I grinned, adoring Sara's protectiveness. 'Thank you. So . . . how do I look?'

'Amazing, of course,' Sara gloated, taking in her masterpiece. 'I'm going to put my dress on, and then we'll be ready to meet the guys in the lobby.'

I picked up the note that had been waiting for us when we returned to the hotel and ran my thumb over the elegant script.

Dear Emily and Sara,

I am thrilled that you have arrived safely and hope you enjoy your afternoon together. I am looking forward to seeing you this evening for dinner. I have arranged for the car to pick you up along with Evan and Jared at 6.45 p.m. for our 7.00 p.m. reservation.

I have no doubt that you will enjoy all that has been planned this evening!

Sincerely,
Vivian Mathews

'I hope I don't embarrass her,' I hollered through the bathroom door.

'Stop being so nervous,' Sara returned. 'Vivian really wants you there. This is important to her. She even convinced Jared to take me so I could be here with you.'

I grinned, knowing that Jared didn't need much convincing.

'What do you think? You haven't said anything about how you look.'

'Oh, uh,' I stepped in front of the full-length mirror, and my lips curled up naturally. There was a slight resemblance to the girl who preferred jeans and a ponytail, the girl who still couldn't conquer applying make-up on her own. Her light brown eyes glistened under a shimmer of pink and dark lashes. Those were her flushed cheeks, and her full lips veiled with gloss, smiling back at me.

I turned to the side and the layers of chiffon flowed around me. My fingers traced the soft pink embroidered design on the champagne corseted top. Sara had chosen the same shade of pink to weave in my hair, resembling an inset headband, and a pile of soft curls was artistically stacked at the nape of my neck. I picked up the finishing touch from the dresser and secured it around my neck, allowing my fingertips to brush the sparkling diamond as I had the day he'd given it to me.

As Sara stepped out of the bathroom, I turned towards the door with my cheeks aglow, ready to thank her for her ingenious transformation, but I was held speechless at the sight of her. The sapphire-blue dress skimmed her body, brushing her curves in a shimmering dance. Large curls of red draped over her right shoulder. She looked ... worshipable.

'Jared is in so much trouble,' I gaped. 'Sara, you look amazing.' I wasn't sure why I was so in awe. She was the most desirable girl in school for a reason, but I guess I forgot that most of the time because she was just *Sara* to me. There was no denying her modelesque figure and Hellenic beauty now.

Sara smiled vibrantly, revealing perfect white teeth behind her glossy red lips. 'Maybe he is.'

'Sara, please don't tell me you're going to sleep with him,' I begged.

'Relax. I won't,' she said with a roll of her eyes. 'But that doesn't mean we can't have fun.'

My phone beeped, distracting me from her comment. *Spoke with Carl and we called Rachel. She's sweet, and I believe she wants this too. Meeting her on Saturday, but it looks like everything's all set for Sunday.*

Sara handed me my jacket and the bag that held Evan's gift. 'Your parents are letting me move in with her,' I announced.

'Well, then I guess it's official.' Sara held the door open for me to follow.

'I guess so,' I returned, my stomach flipping with the realization.

I thought my knees might give way when we rounded the corner into the main lobby and I saw the back of the black tailored jacket. My eyes trailed to find his usually tousled light brown hair neatly swept to the side in a more distinguished look. He was caught up in a conversation with his brother and didn't notice us as we approached.

Evan stopped mid-sentence when Jared's mouth dropped open. Jared *was* in trouble, and it was written all over his face as Sara sauntered towards him.

I couldn't feel my legs moving as Evan turned around. My heart stopped at the sight of his smoky blue eyes, and a rush of heat filled my cheeks when his mouth formed that perfect smile. It had only been two weeks since he'd left for his skiing trip, but for some reason it was like I was seeing him for the first time all over again.

'Hi,' I whispered. He stepped up to take my hand, our connection unbroken from the moment our eyes first met.

'Hi,' he responded, still smiling. He tilted his head down to kiss me, but Sara interrupted.

'We need to go or we'll be late.'

'Sure,' Evan replied, instantly snapping us back to the bustling lobby of formally dressed people, most likely attending the same event. He helped me slip on my jacket. I slid on black leather gloves in preparation for January's freeze and took his hand again.

'What's that?' Evan asked, gesturing towards the bag.

'A surprise,' I grinned, having waited so long to give it to him it was killing me.

'I have one of those too,' he smirked, holding the door open for me.

'One what?'

'A surprise,' he revealed, smiling wider and sending another rush of colour to my cheeks.

I ducked into the limo and slid in beside Sara, since she was sitting across from Jared. Evan was forced to sit next to his brother, leaving my hand empty. I glanced across at him, and we silently exchanged the *I wish I were sitting next to you too* look.

The limo pulled into a circular cobblestone driveway, and the driver came around to open the door. The restaurant resembled a mansion more than a dining establishment, with multiple eaves and glowing windows on each level.

We were escorted to a private patio that was glassed in for the winter season, offering a spectacular view of the dark rolling ocean.

'Wonderful! You're here,' Vivian greeted us brightly with open arms. She gripped each of her sons by the shoulders as they bent to kiss her on the cheek, then admired Sara and me after the guys had helped remove our jackets.

'Exquisite,' she declared, wrapping each of us in her

signature brief embrace with a brush of her lips on our cheeks. 'Come. Sit down.'

Stuart remained unmoved. He had not given us a glance since our arrival. He stoically gazed out at the ocean holding a glass of ice, filled with caramel-coloured liquor.

At Vivian's insistence, we each found a seat. I made certain to sit next to Evan at the rectangular table, with Jared and Sara across from us and Vivian and Stuart at each end. Evan took my hand under the draped table, instantly calming my nerves.

The polite small talk began. I tried my best not to participate unless a question or comment was directed my way, and of course each time it was, I usually had my mouth full or was in mid-gulp. Sara pressed her lips together to keep from laughing, which only made me squirm uncomfortably.

After surviving the anxiety-inducing dinner, I excused myself to use the restroom and promised to meet Evan in the foyer.

It was a struggle to hold the chiffon over my head so it wouldn't fall in the toilet. I was standing outside the bathroom door, smoothing the layers back in place, when I heard, 'I don't want to talk about this again.'

I remained still. Not sure if I should continue around the corner, or wait until they were done, I was thankful that I'd decided not walk in on, 'She's not your future, Evan. It's about time you realized that. I won't allow you to pass up Yale to follow a girl, especially *that* one, across the country.'

'It's not your choice to make for me, Dad,' Evan bit back. 'I don't expect *you* to understand.'

'Stuart, what are you doing?' Vivian beckoned from afar. 'We're going to be late.'

I remained still, having collapsed flat against the restroom door with my heart pounding and my mind racing. What just happened? I knew Stuart was withdrawn, but I had no idea it was because he didn't approve of me. His reaction sank in, and my lip quivered.

I bit my lip, taking a deep breath to compose myself. Then I walked around the corner and forced a smile when I saw Evan waiting for me with my jacket over his arm.

'Are you okay?' he asked, inspecting my face. I pushed my smile wider with a nod of my head. I slipped my arms into the jacket with my back towards Evan, afraid he could see right through me.

Evan held the door open and allowed me to lead the way to the limo. Sara and Jared were across from us, lost in conversation about who they deemed to be the best guitarist.

Evan took my hand. 'Are you shaking?'

'It's cold,' I lied, wanting to roll my eyes at my involuntary reaction. Evan wrapped his arm around me to warm me up. I eased away the nerves, nuzzling into him.

'Wow,' Sara admired the uplit mansion as the limo slowly crept in line with the others. A streak of nerves twisted my stomach. I felt like I was nearing the head of the line for a death-defying roller coaster ride.

'They're just people,' Evan assured me in a whisper, probably noticing I wasn't breathing. I exhaled to relax my shoulders, squeezing his hand.

Just people soaked in jewels of every colour or poised in tailored tuxedoes, full of judgement and snide comments.

We made our way through the glitz-covered bodies shimmering in the candlelight. The voices swirled in time with the smooth jazz band in the ballroom.

Everywhere I looked, I was struck by more brilliance.

'Mrs Mathews, this is incredible,' Sara gawked. 'I've never seen anything so beautiful.'

'I'm not so sure my sons would agree,' Vivian replied with a sparkling smile. My cheeks grew warm when Evan squeezed my hand. 'This did turn out more spectacular than I could have hoped. I am so happy to have you all here with me. I need to greet a few more guests, but I will be expecting a dance later, Evan.' The corner of her mouth rose as she met her son's eyes, and she glided away in the antique ivory dress that floated around her. Vivian was the picture of sophistication with her blonde hair swept back into a French twist. I admired how collected she always remained, even in a setting that was completely overwhelming to me.

'What was that about?' Sara demanded, looking at Evan. 'Do you have some crazy dance moves or something?'

Jared laughed, and Evan shot him a warning glance. 'Evan's Mom's *dance partner*. My father refuses to dance, and I failed the lessons –'

'You took lessons?' Sara laughed, interrupting Jared.

'Yes,' Evan finally admitted. 'My mother loves to dance. And I seem to be the only one who can keep up with her without stepping on her toes.' He glared at Jared, who sneered mockingly back at him.

'I can't wait to see this,' Sara smirked.

We found a lounge set in a corner away from the

stifling conversations, and immersed ourselves in the details of Evan and Jared's skiing trip in France.

'Oh, Em, did you tell Evan about the news?' Sara burst out. It took me a moment to remember what she was talking about, hoping she wasn't about to ruin the surprise I had wrapped in the box.

'No,' I said slowly, then remembered with a slight nod. 'Oh, I'm moving in with my mother this weekend,' I confessed casually, like I had just announced I was buying a new pair of shoes.

Jared had no idea why this was big news, but Evan narrowed his eyes. 'You're doing what?' he asked.

'Your mother's looking for you,' Stuart interrupted from behind us. Evan turned around to view Vivian scanning the crowd. She raised her hand when she located him.

'I'll be right back,' Evan announced, rising to escort his mother to the dance floor. I turned towards Sara, but she and Jared were already making their way through the crowd, not wanting to miss the spectacle. I was left alone in Stuart's shadow.

Feeling I couldn't just walk away without appearing completely rude, I fumbled for something intelligent to say. Instead I said, 'This is quite the party, huh?'

He peered down at me as if I'd spoken in a foreign tongue, shook his head slightly and walked away.

'Okay then,' I mumbled under my breath, glancing around to see if anyone had witnessed my humiliation. I pinballed my way through the crowd to the ballroom. The dance floor was full of couples, but one couple stood out among them. They floated around with ease and grace to the cool rhythms of the Sinatra song sung by a lanky crooner.

'Omigod,' Sara gasped next to me with a glass of champagne in her hand. 'They can really *dance*.' My mouth popped open at the sight of Evan leading Vivian in a perfect stance, cradling her hand in his. Her eyes sparkled as they twirled around the dance floor, their feet in perfect unison.

'Told you,' Jared interjected. 'Kinda scary good, right?'

'Very,' I floundered, finding that there were way too many things about Evan I still didn't know.

The song concluded, and there was an overwhelming burst of applause. Evan appeared uncomfortable, while Vivian smiled brightly. At that moment a woman with short white hair in a long-sleeved black dress stepped up to the mic. Stuart joined Vivian, and Evan spotted the three of us on the opposite side of the dance floor.

Wow, I mouthed when he slid his arm around my waist. He shrugged, abashed, and redirected his attention to the speaker.

The woman went on to recognize Vivian's philanthropic achievements over the years, acknowledging her success and dedication to each cause and organization. She'd invested not only time, but her passion. I listened intently, completely astounded by all that Vivian had done. The presentation concluded with a roar of applause, and the white-haired woman handed Vivian an award made of crystal, giving her a kiss on her cheek.

The music picked up again, and we met Vivian, along with every other person in the audience, congratulating her affectionately. Evan hugged his mother, followed by Jared and Sara. I went to congratulate her as well. She wrapped her arms around me tighter and longer than she'd ever done before and whispered into my ear, 'I'm so glad you're here with us.'

My eyes watered instantly, understanding the intended meaning of her words. She released me and was pulled in another direction, with more words of praise.

Evan took my hand and led me away from the crowd. I was still caught up in the moment, my head buzzing with emotion.

'Let's get out of here,' Evan said in my ear.

'What? You want to leave?' I searched his face, baffled by his request.

'Yeah. I want to show you something.'

'Okay,' I responded, still so very confused. We retrieved our coats, and Evan escorted me out the door without saying goodbye to anyone.

2

Fireworks

Evan led me down the long driveway lined with limousines and town cars. We approached the parking lot, and I recognized Evan's BMW.

'When did your car get here?' I asked suspiciously.

'I drove it here earlier,' he shared with a crooked grin. That's when I realized this was part of his plan, the *surprise* he'd mentioned when we left the hotel.

He opened the passenger-side door and pulled out a backpack. He unzipped it and handed me a pair of sneakers. I eyed him apprehensively, recognizing the shoes that were supposed to be at Sara's – which meant Sara was in on this too.

'I figured they would be more comfortable than the heels,' he explained, tossing his black dress shoes on the floor of the car, along with his tux jacket and tie, and lacing up a pair of sneakers. I sat on the passenger seat, switching my shoes.

I had tried to figure out his plans in the past with little success, so I'd learned just to go along with them without too many questions – unless he walked us to the edge of a cliff and asked me to jump. Then I would have something to say.

Evan found my hand again, and we continued towards the cobblestoned street lined with lanterns. My shoulder brushed against him as we walked with the crisp air swirling around us. The sky was clear, allowing the full moon to follow us like a spotlight.

We hadn't walked very far when Evan pulled me between two hedges that lined the bordering property.

'Evan, where are we going?' I demanded in a panic, fearing we were trespassing and about to get caught.

'They're not home,' he assured me, our feet crunching in the glistening layer of untouched snow. I looked up to find a tall mansion with dramatic peaks. The windows were dark.

'But I'm sure they have an alarm system or something,' I argued, looking around nervously, anticipating the arrival of flashing lights. I continued after him, faltering on the collapsing surface. I was forced to lift my layers out of the ankle-deep snow to keep from tripping.

'Stop worrying,' he laughed, supporting me by my elbow. 'My mother knows the people who live here and even invited them to the party tonight. They're in Brazil. I spoke with them myself about what I wanted to do, and they couldn't care less. We're not going into their house or anything.'

'Really?' I questioned, slightly doubtful.

'Really,' Evan confirmed again with a smile. 'Trust me.'

We walked beneath the long shadows of the mansion

to the back terrace. I stopped in my tracks at the sight of a flickering light. 'I thought you said no one was home.'

Evan laughed again, amused by my overly panicked state. 'They're *not*. This is for us. I paid the limo driver to start the fire and bring over our bags.'

'Oh.'

It was a charming setting, with two Adirondack chairs set before a fireplace on the stone terrace, sheltered by an overhang. A portable Bose system and my gift were set on a small table off to the side. 'I like this,' I beamed up at him.

We walked over to the small fireplace and stood in front of the crackling fire, absorbing its warmth. Evan stepped behind me and slid his arms around my waist, holding me against him. I turned to face him with a ridiculous smile spread across my face. 'I've missed you.'

'I've missed you, too.' Evan bent down to find me. His nose was cold against my cheek, but his breath on my lips instantly warmed my entire body. He pressed his firm mouth softly against mine, and lingered there just long enough for me to lose my breath before pulling away. My eyes remained closed, savouring the buzz on my lips.

'I'm glad you came tonight,' he said, hovering inches away. 'I know it was hard for you. But it meant a lot to my mother.'

'I'm glad I came too. I wouldn't have wanted to miss hearing all that was said about Vivian. She's amazing; I had no idea.'

Evan leaned over and kissed me, running his hand down the side of my face.

'Do you want your present?' Evan asked when he

pulled back. I began to smile, but faltered. Confusion flashed across his face. 'You don't?'

All I could hear were Stuart Mathews' disapproving words, and I wasn't so sure I was excited to give him my gift any longer. 'Can we wait?' I requested awkwardly.

'Uh, no,' Evan responded with his brows pulled together, retrieving the small rectangular box from the table. 'But, you can open yours first if it makes you feel better.'

I took it from his hands nervously.

'Go on, open it,' he encouraged me impatiently. I tore the silver paper to find a long rectangular box that looked expensive. I held my breath when I opened it. A gleaming smile spread across my face when I pulled out two concert tickets.

'Evan!' I jumped up to wrap my arms around his neck. 'Yes! This is the perfect gift. Thank you.'

'You're welcome,' Evan replied, hugging me back. 'I wanted to be the one to take you to your first concert.'

'When is it?' I inspected the ticket for the date. 'The end of the month. Great. I won't have to wait too long.'

'I almost bought a third one for Sara because I know how much she loves the band, but I decided this was just for us.'

I laughed, already hearing Sara's groan in my head when I showed her the tickets to the sold-out show she'd been dying to see.

I put the tickets back in the box and tucked it into the inside pocket of my coat. Evan looked at me in anticipation. I pressed my lips together, fighting the urge to make up some reason not to give him his gift – but I knew I had to.

'So, I hope you like it.' I removed the shiny, green-wrapped box from the bag and handed it to him, holding my breath as he opened it. He took off the lid and looked from what was inside to me, then back down again.

'Does this mean?' His eyes lit up and his mouth curled into a stunning smile as he set the box on the chair. Despite my reservations, I couldn't help but smile back – his excitement was too contagious. 'You got in!' He swept his arms around my waist and picked me up. I yelled out in surprise, laughing. 'Em, I'm so happy for you.' He kissed and hugged me again.

'When did you find out?' Evan couldn't stop smiling.

'Ten days ago,' I confessed as he set me back on the ground.

'Wow. That must have been hard not to tell anyone,' he said, impressed, knowing how much I'd wanted this. 'Stanford. You totally deserve this. You didn't even tell me that you'd applied for early admission.'

I averted my eyes sheepishly. 'It was hard. But I did tell Sara – sorry.'

'When I said *anyone*, I didn't count her. She's a given.' The excitement continued to seep in. 'Now I just have to find out which school accepts me so I can join you.'

My smile faltered again.

'What?' Evan asked, his brow furrowed in confusion.

I opened my mouth to speak, but then immediately closed it.

'Say it,' he demanded. 'Let me into that head of yours before you start thinking things you shouldn't.'

'Too late,' I confessed with a guilty shrug. I paused again before I revealed, 'I heard your dad.' Evan opened his mouth, about to spew some not so happy words, when I interrupted, 'He's right.'

He stopped and stared at me. 'About what?'

'You can't make one of the biggest decisions of your life based on a girl.'

Evan smirked. Not the reaction I expected. 'Okay.' My eyes widened at his casual response. He continued to wear his infamous amused grin as he added, 'Because Stanford and Berkeley are *horrible* schools, and I'd be jeopardizing my whole future if I went to California. You're right. We should just break up now since there's no point in us considering each other in any decisions we make about our futures.'

'Evan!' I balled up the wrapping paper and threw it at him. He laughed and batted it into the fire as if he'd planned it. 'That's not what I meant,' I huffed.

'I know,' he chuckled, pulling me towards him, 'but you can't listen to my father. He only *thinks* he knows what's best for me, when in fact he has no idea who I am.' He kissed the top of my head and added, 'I would never make such a huge decision based on a girl.' He paused long enough for a jolt of panic to make my back tense, before completing with, 'But you're not just any girl. I'm . . . *We're* going to California.'

I buried my face in his chest and squeezed my arms around him. 'Yale's the best law school in the country,' I reminded him without conviction.

'And who said I wanted to be a lawyer?' he responded, squeezing me back. Suddenly, he pulled away and declared, 'I want to teach you how to dance.'

My heart stopped. 'You what?'

Evan laughed.

'I can't dance.'

He laughed again. 'I know. That's why I'm going to teach you.'

I groaned and clenched my teeth in dread as he approached the Bose system. I was trying to figure out how to conjure up an ounce of grace as he inserted his iPhone and scrolled through the song selections. I scanned the empty terrace, scouting for potential tripping hazards. Then I took in the puddle of chiffon around my sneakers and exhaled in defeat – this was going to be a disaster.

My head popped up at the sudden strum of a guitar followed by a round of drums. Evan started nodding his head to the beat, walking slowly over to me. He reached for me, cradling my hips in his hands and rocking me to the punk song.

'Ready?' he asked, taking my hand and spinning me around as I laughed. When I turned back to face him, he started bouncing up and down, forcing me up with him. The thumping energy surged through me and I found myself jumping alongside him. He smiled in approval and proceeded to thrash his head in time with the thumping bass. I rocked from side to side and jumped in a circle, swinging my arms – my skirt swirling around me.

We pogoed around the terrace for another song until I finally collapsed into an Adirondack, giddy and out of breath.

'You're amazing.'

Evan stood in front of me, admiring me with flushed cheeks.

'I'm sure I don't look so amazing now,' I noted, blowing

the strand of hair stuck to my nose as a line of sweat ran down my temple.

'That's not what I said,' he corrected. 'You *are* amazing.'

I could feel my cheeks changing colour, and my lips stretched into an embarrassed smile. 'What did I do?'

'Just you, everything about you – you're amazing,' he stated simply.

'You just love that I'm such a great dancer,' I teased, making him chuckle.

Evan pulled me to my feet and met me with a kiss that set off a thousand fireworks through my entire body. Wait. Those *were* fireworks. I turned to witness a sprinkling of red sparks in the sky. We stepped out from under the terrace to watch the brilliant spectacle.

'Happy New Year,' Evan said into my ear, pulling me around to kiss me before I could say the same.

It was the most dazzling fireworks display I'd ever seen; I could feel my heart beating in my chest with each explosion. The sparks felt like they were going to sprinkle down upon us. Every so often, I'd glance up at Evan to find him watching me adoringly. Then he'd redirect his attention towards the fire in the sky.

When it was over, my toes were numb from standing in the snow and I was shivering. The fireworks had been so mesmerizing, I hadn't registered that the temperature had dropped until now.

'Let's get going,' Evan said, rubbing my arms when he noticed me shaking. 'You're about to freeze into a lawn ornament.' I followed him to the terrace where the fire had become a heap of glowing embers. Evan walked to the side of the house and returned with a couple of gallons of water to douse the remaining heat in the fireplace. I packed up Evan's package and speaker system while he put the fire out.

When we neared the front of the house, Evan's black BMW was idling in the driveway.

'The limo driver?'

'Is awesome,' Evan declared in pleasure. When we ducked into the warm car, I pulled off my gloves and thawed my hands in front of the blowing heater vent. 'Now where?'

'Hotel?' I suggested, trying to sound nonchalant.

Evan grinned knowingly. 'Mine or yours?'

The question suddenly made me think of Sara. I wondered how her night had gone, and where she and Jared were right now.

'Where do you think they are?' Evan asked, as if reading my mind.

'You don't think they . . .' I questioned.

'He was excited to see her again,' he said with a shrug, 'and she looked incredible tonight . . .'

'I know, right?!' I agreed emphatically. 'But you don't think they would . . . do you?'

Evan shrugged again. 'Let's just pick a room and hope it's empty.' He leaned over and found me waiting. What started as a soft kiss pressed into a more urgent one, coated with want. The nervousness that shot through me at the thought of going to the hotel room was quickly replaced with a need to get there as fast as we could.

Evan pulled back, breathing heavily, 'Yours.' He buckled his seat belt and put the car in gear, speeding out of the driveway. That's when we met the line of slow-moving limos pulling out of the mansion's driveway and were practically forced to stop. 'No way,' Evan groaned, banging his head against his headrest in frustration. I laughed.

While we patiently waited to move more than twenty feet a minute, Evan stated, 'I think this is going to be a great year, Em.'

'I hope so,' I squeezed his hand that rested on my lap and thought, *It can't be any worse than last year.*

'It's going to be different, that's for sure,' he continued, 'especially since you're moving in with your mother. Where did that come from anyway?'

I shrugged. 'I figured now was a better time than any to recognize I have a mother.'

'Okay,' he noted slowly with a nod of his head. 'But this weekend? All in, huh?'

'What do you mean?'

'If you're going to do something, you're going to give it everything you have. You've decided to reconnect with your mother, so why not move in with her?'

I shrugged again, never consciously recognizing that this was one of my character traits. But he was right. I was an overachiever, needing to excel in everything I did – so why not this?

'What's your therapist going to say about your decision?' he asked, and then shook his head when I wouldn't answer. 'You stopped seeing her, didn't you?' I still wouldn't say anything, knowing how he felt about the therapy. 'How come?'

'I'm fine,' I defended. 'I don't see the point. Besides,

Sara's a better therapist than anyone with a PhD, and she doesn't force me to write down my feelings.'

Evan chuckled. 'That's probably true.' His laugh tapered off and he became serious. 'You know if you ever need to talk . . .'

'I'm not much of a talker.' I directed my attention out the window, not wanting to stir the emotions I'd made a point of shutting off.

He accepted this. 'I know,' he said softly. After a moment of silence, he added, 'This year will be better at school, too.'

I glanced at him sceptically.

'Really,' he assured me. 'You know something stupid had to have happened over the break. Somebody got a nose job or slept with their best friend's girlfriend. They have short memories.' Evan squeezed my hand, and I hoped more than anything that he was right.

My stomach fluttered with nerves when we pulled up to the hotel. While we waited for the valet attendant, Evan said, 'Let's not go into this with expectations. We can do whatever comes naturally.'

I stared at him. 'Are you serious? Of course I have expectations. I've *expected* to have sex with you for about six months now.'

'Okay then,' Evan replied with a smile. 'We obviously have the same expectations.' I laughed, easing the nervous tension.

We left the car in the hands of the valet and made our way to the elevator. Evan held my hand the entire time, and my whole body was jittering so much that I couldn't find anything to say.

Before I opened the door, Evan turned me around and said, 'Close your eyes.' I obeyed. 'Deep breath.' I inhaled deeply and relaxed my shoulders with the exhale. I awaited my next instruction but felt his lips upon mine instead. Their touch surprised me. My calm breath faltered and my knees weakened. I opened my mouth to the rhythm of his, feeling the warmth of his tongue on mine. Fumbling in my pocket for the key, I tried to open the door while remaining connected. It didn't work.

I pulled away long enough to insert the key and open the door. Then I tugged Evan towards me, finding his lips again. Evan started to unbutton his jacket as I backed into the room. That's when I heard, 'You're here!' I pushed away from Evan mid-kiss and spun around, slamming the door in his face.

'Sara, hi,' I fumbled, trying to catch my breath. I cracked the door open to find Evan rubbing his forehead. 'So, Sara's here. Umm, I guess I'll see you in the morning.'

'Uh, okay,' Evan said slowly, looking at me like I was acting weird – only because I was. 'I guess I'll see you in the morning.' I shut the door before he could even kiss me goodnight.

'What's wrong with you?' Sara demanded. 'You could've let him in.'

'No, it's late,' I said in a rush, taking off my jacket and tossing it on the chair, my face on fire.

'Oh, wait,' she shot out. 'You two thought you'd have the room to yourselves. Oh, Em!' She started laughing hysterically.

'Sara,' I scowled. 'It's not funny.'

'Oh, it is,' she countered. 'For the first time ever, I like a guy and don't sleep with him. And you were finally about to have sex and didn't get to. Oh that's so fucking funny. Em, I'm so sorry.'

I groaned and collapsed next to her on the king-sized bed. 'This had better not be an indication of how this year's going to be.'

Sara rested her head on my shoulder and draped her arm across my stomach. 'It's the end of our senior year. Then we're off to college. It's going to be the best year of our lives. Believe me.'

I groaned, not sharing her optimism.

3

Still Loved

'CAN WE TALK ABOUT WHAT HAPPENED LAST night?' I asked Sara after leaving the small restaurant where we had eaten a greasy breakfast with Jared and Evan, surrounded by people who looked like they wished they'd never seen the New Year.

'What? That you were planning on losing your virginity *finally*, but I screwed it up?'

'No, I'm definitely not talking about that,' I retorted. 'You mentioned *liking* Jared. What happened between you two?'

'I'd rather not talk about it.'

Something was off. Avoiding a conversation about a guy was not like Sara at all.

'I'm confused.'

'Em, he lives in New York. I'm still in high school, forget about the fact that we're moving to California,' she explained, void of emotion. 'I can't keep torturing myself. I need to forget about him . . . again.'

I glanced over at her. She kept texting and wouldn't look at me.

'Thanks for driving,' she said, slipping the phone into her purse. 'I'm going to sleep most of the way if you don't mind.'

'Sure,' I responded, concerned by her reaction.

The quiet drive gave me time to think – which wasn't necessarily a good thing. Being trapped in my head for almost three hours could be a bit overwhelming – even scary. But at the end of it, I was content with my internal discussion. Whether moving in with my mother was the right thing to do or not, I was committed to trying.

'Let's just do nothing today and watch movies,' Sara proposed as we unloaded our bags from the car.

'Sounds perfect.'

Evan had to drive Jared back to school, so it was just Sara and me in front of the television the entire New Year's Day. I forced myself to get sucked into the sappy romantic comedies and awkward teenage humiliation.

Sara responded to a beeping text. 'Em, do you want to go to a party tonight?'

'Yeah, I don't think so,' I answered without thinking twice.

'Are you ever going to go to another party again?'

'I don't know,' I sighed. 'I just don't want to hear it if someone gets too drunk and then asks me the wrong thing. I don't want to be the freak any more.'

'They need to get over it, and so do you,' Sara argued. 'You can't stay locked away forever because you're afraid someone's going to say the wrong thing. Someone *always* says the wrong thing eventually, so fuck them. Who cares?'

I grinned, knowing she was right. 'Just not tonight, okay?'

'Okay,' Sara shrugged. I knew she was disappointed. I hadn't been to a party with her in over six months.

'But why don't you go?' I suggested. 'I don't want to, but there's no reason you shouldn't.'

'Are you sure?' she questioned cautiously.

'Of course,' I replied adamantly.

Sara's face lit up. She went back to her phone and began texting the masses to get the details.

Anna hollered up the stairs, 'Girls, we're home. Come down and tell us about the party.'

Sara jumped up and hopped down the stairs. I followed behind, still not accustomed to this family sharing thing that Sara had going on. Anna and Carl were so patient with me, not prying too much. But even the slightest questions about my day caught me off guard – questions that were so very natural to them.

Sara sat in her usual spot, cross-legged on their king-sized bed, and I sat down on the edge of the bed, very much a spectator. Anna was unpacking while Carl flipped through the mail. He pulled an envelope from the stack. 'Emma, this is for you.'

'Thanks.' I replied, as I took it from his hand.

I examined the plain business envelope with no return address while Sara completely recreated every detail of the evening – from the decor, to Vivian's award, to the fireworks display.

I was running my finger over the Boca Raton, Florida,

postmark when I heard, 'How did Evan react when you told him about Stanford, Emma?'

I flipped my eyes up on hearing my name. All three were eagerly awaiting my response, making me realize that Sara and I hadn't talked about it either.

'He's excited,' I replied awkwardly.

They waited a second longer, and when they recognized that this was the extent of my account, Anna said, 'I'm looking forward to meeting your mom in the morning.'

I nodded, my stomach tensing at the thought.

'Then I thought you, Sara and I might go shopping after.'

'Mom, you should know by now that Emma dreads shopping. But I'm in,' Sara answered on my behalf.

Carl looked over at me knowingly and offered, 'College football?' I nodded in relief.

'What are you doing tonight?' Anna questioned. 'Isn't Marissa Fleming having a party?' I shouldn't have been shocked that Anna knew this. She seemed to know the social schedule of just about everyone in town.

Sara's face flashed with excitement. 'Yes, and I'm going with the girls.'

'What about you, Emma?' Anna asked, hanging a dress in the closet.

'I'm just going to hang out here and read,' I answered feebly.

Sara slid off the bed. 'You have to help me pick out something to wear.'

Knowing I wouldn't really have any input in this decision, I answered, 'Sure,' anyway.

I saw Sara off to the party, with several assurances that I would be fine. I was then able to redirect my attention to the mysterious envelope, while sitting on the pile of pillows beneath Sara's floor-to-ceiling bookshelves.

I tried to recall if I was expecting something from Florida. It didn't look official enough for college correspondence; it was simply a plain white envelope with small handwriting addressed to me at the McKinleys'.

When I pulled out the folded paper, my heart stopped. I unfolded it with shaking hands to find it streaked with crayon. On the front was a rudimentary picture of a boy, a girl, a man and a woman with grey hair standing by a pink Christmas tree. I opened the paper to find, 'Merry Christmas Emma. We miss you!' slanted across the page in a child's oversized handwriting. The message concluded on the back with, 'Love always, Leyla and Jack.'

I stared at the words, tears trailing down my cheeks, and swallowed against the knot in my throat. But the large red smiles and the mountain of presents under the festive tree were comforting. The man was undeniably George, but I couldn't figure out who the woman was supposed to be. I wanted to believe it was Carol's mother, Janet, but she didn't have grey hair.

I dismissed it, thinking it must be a teacher or someone they'd met in Florida. I guess I knew where they were now – it wasn't like I'd ever see them again, though.

That did it. That sent me over the edge. I collapsed into the pillows and cried until I felt a hand brush against my back and I raised my head in surprise. Anna was kneeling next to me, her eyes glassy as she offered me a comforting smile. She noticed the picture in my hand and settled in next to me.

'They look happy,' she noted, gently tucking my hair behind my ear. 'That's all you ever wanted for them, right?' It became clear to me that Sara had confided in her mother after everything that had happened last May. How could she not? Anna would have insisted on knowing why Sara hadn't come to her, probably feeling betrayed and hurt. So, of course Sara had had to tell her that I'd stayed to prevent Leyla and Jack from being taken from their parents. Well . . . at least they still had one of their parents.

'Yes,' I choked, my voice hoarse.

'It was nice that he sent that to you.' She continued to console me. 'It means the kids still really love you.'

I knew she was trying to take away my pain, but thinking of them missing me tightened my chest, and hot tears flowed freely. Anna pulled me into her arms and hugged me tightly, and I let her without tensing. I inhaled her warm floral fragrance with each gasp of air and allowed myself to miss them.

Once I had control over the pain and was quiet again, Anna released me. I sat up, wiping my wet cheeks.

'I understand why you want to move in with your mother,' Anna finally said. 'And I want more than anything for the two of you to find the connection you've missed out on over the years. But if for any reason it doesn't work, this is your home first, and we'll always do what's best for you. We're not going to say anything to the social worker, since that will open a whole realm of paperwork that isn't necessary and you'll be eighteen soon. We'll just let her continue to do her periodic check-ins by phone. Okay?'

I nodded, unable to find my voice.

Anna hesitated before adding, 'I love you, Emma. We all do. And I am very serious when I say that we will do anything for you; you only need to ask. Do you understand?'

My breath faltered with her emotional declaration, and I replied, 'I understand. Thank you.'

Anna's mouth spread into the smile that Sara had inherited, lighting up her kind blue eyes, instantly changing the seriousness of the moment with, 'Let's get some ice cream.'

I couldn't help but smile in return, and allowed her to help me up from the heap of pillows to follow her down the stairs to the kitchen.

'Is that everything?' Carl asked, examining the backpack and two duffle bags in the back of Anna's SUV.

'I don't own much,' I stated.

Anna and Sara got into the car while I turned to Carl. 'Thank you for everything.'

'It's been great having you here, Emma,' he said in return, and without warning, wrapped his arms around me and pulled me to his chest. 'I'll keep in touch with Stanford for you, but I'm sure you'll be over before I know it.' Then he released me and walked to the house without looking back. I remained still, not having been quite prepared for the departing hug.

'Ready?' Sara hollered from the open car window.

'Sure,' I answered, heading towards my car.

When I pulled out of the driveway, I glanced up one more time at the large house with a twinge of sadness. Although I had never felt like I completely belonged there, I had certainly felt safe, which was something I hadn't experienced very often in my life.

4

'Home'

I TRIED TO PAY ATTENTION TO THE ROADS we turned down as I followed Anna in my Honda, knowing I'd need to find my way back to Sara's on my own eventually. At least now I'd be able to drive the car that Carl had helped me pick out a few months ago, after I'd *finally* got my licence. There hadn't been any need to drive when Sara and Evan chauffeured me every day. But now I was going to be responsible for getting myself to school.

It took about twenty minutes for us to reach the outskirts of Weslyn where my mother was renting a house. We veered way down an interwoven maze of streets within the disorganized neighbourhood. Unlike Sara's neighbourhood, a grid of large homes all lined up neatly, this swirling road map had much smaller houses. Kids ran from one snow-covered yard into another, since most of the properties overlapped their neighbours' without a bordering fence.

Anna pulled into the driveway of a house at the tail end of the maze. With only one neighbour, it was isolated at the dead end, across from the stark woods that surrounded the neighbourhood. I pulled up alongside the kerb so Anna could back out when she left.

The small yellow two-storey house was quaint, with white shutters framing the windows and a weathered white porch welcoming us to enter. The front door opened, and my mother appeared, propping the screen door open with her hip. She waited for us to each grab a bag with her arms crossed, shivering from the winter air.

I didn't make eye contact as I passed her going into the house, fearful that her clear blue eyes would reveal something other than the words that came out of her mouth. 'Hi, Emily. I'm glad you're here.'

'Thanks for letting me stay with you,' I replied awkwardly.

'Of course,' she answered, her voice coated with nerves. 'This is your house too now. You even have your own room.'

'You have to see it,' Sara burst out, taking me by the hand and dragging me up the wide wooden staircase set in the middle of the small hall. Anna laughed, making me suspect that they had done more than shop yesterday.

At the top of the stairs was a small landing. Straight ahead was an open door that led into a bathroom, and two closed doors flanked the stairs. Sara opened the door to the right and flipped the light on. I slowly followed her.

Stepping into the room, I let my eyes trace all four walls, three of them white, and the wall where the door stood open, solid black. I turned in a circle to take it all in, inhaling the lingering fumes of fresh paint. My lips curled up.

A full-sized bed sat across from the door, covered with a black-and-white baroque duvet, accented with white pillows bordered in black. Above the bed was a three-dimensional art piece that looked like a hundred black butterflies were bursting out of the white wall, tethered by black wires.

Two small windows to the left of the bed were framed dramatically by thick black curtains. A white chest of drawers rested against the black wall next to a full-length white-framed mirror tilting on a stand.

On the opposite side of the room was a desk; its glass top was stencilled with black flowers and butterflies and set upon two white bookcases. A cloth-covered board with the same black-and-white baroque pattern hung on the wall above it. There was a note pinned to the board that read, 'Welcome Home, Emma,' in Sara's undeniable scrawl.

'Do you love it?' Sara demanded in anticipation.

I turned to find Anna and my mother in the doorway awaiting my reaction.

'I can't believe you did this,' I gasped. 'Thank you so much.'

'Of course,' Anna replied. My mother stood a few steps behind Anna, watching.

'Do you want something to drink?' she asked Anna when Sara started unzipping the duffle bags to put my minimal possessions in their places. The two women disappeared down the stairs, Anna's voice drifting away as they neared the bottom.

'Sara, really, thank you.'

Sara paused with a stack of shirts clasped between her hands, recognizing the sincerity in my voice.

'I knew you were nervous about moving in with her,' she explained, setting the shirts in the opened drawer, 'even if you wouldn't admit it. My mom wanted to get to know Rachel too, so this seemed like the best idea. We spent the day together yesterday – shopping, painting and decorating. Emma, I don't think you have anything to worry about. In fact, Rachel's probably more nervous than you are.'

I wasn't sure if that was possible.

When Sara was finally pleased with her work – having put away my clothes, arranged my books and set up the laptop and router that I'd received from Anna and Carl for Christmas, she announced, 'I think you're all set.' Nerves shot through me, realizing she was preparing to go.

I tried to think of a way to delay her, but then Anna hollered up the stairs, 'Sara, are you ready?'

The truth was, I wasn't ready to be alone with my mother. And I gathered from her fidgety body language that she wasn't ready to be left with me either.

We said goodbye and lingered on the porch until they pulled away, inevitably leaving us alone. I walked back into the house and the awkwardness hit me in the face.

'So . . . you can look around if you want,' she offered hesitantly, closing the thick wooden door, the pane of glass in the middle rattling when she clicked it shut.

'Uh, okay,' I replied, veering right and stepping through the arched entrance of the kitchen. My mother remained outside the room in the hall, watching me intently.

Besides a layer of soft yellow paint, the kitchen probably hadn't been updated since the house was built. The doors on the wooden cabinets hung slightly askew above a scarred countertop. A deep porcelain double sink sat below a window that looked out at the woods. A refrigerator that was smaller than me hummed loudly in the corner, with a white gas stove sticking out next to it. There wasn't a lot of room for much else in the kitchen except for a small round table with four mismatched chairs. One of the chairs was pinned against the wall to allow room to pass to the entrance.

'Help yourself to whatever,' she said from the doorway. The tight space didn't allow two people to avoid each other. I peered into the refrigerator to find condiments and left over Chinese food that looked like it had been in there a while.

'Thanks,' I replied, closing the door.

'Guess we need to go shopping, huh?' she noted with a nervous laugh.

My mother stepped back with her hands in the back pockets of her jeans, giving me room to walk across the hall to the living room. I could feel her eyes following me, adding to the mounting anxiety. I felt like I should say something, to make an attempt at some sort of conversation, but I had no idea where to start.

So I stood in the middle of the living room, playing nervously with my fingers, taking in the brown couch and love seat in front of the television. A spindled rocking chair rested in front of the front window. I paused in my tentative inspection.

It took me a moment before I realized where I knew it from. It had been in my bedroom when I'd lived with her and my father.

The sight of it caused my chest to tighten. I wasn't

prepared for the sudden flash of memories. I wanted to go over and touch it, hoping that by running my fingers along the carved arms I'd be filled with the happiness of the memories stored within its frame. Stories told while wrapped in strong arms, rocking back and forth. Whispered words of love and promises as I drifted to sleep to the thumps of his heart against my ear. I could feel her staring at me as I remained motionless, my eyes locked on the chair.

'I have a ton of movies.' Her voice crashed through my reverie, bringing me back to the present. It took me a moment to connect with what she'd said. I nodded at the built-in bookshelf next to the window that was lined with DVD cases.

'Oh, that's great.'

On the other side of the living room was a large sideboard displaying a sound system surrounded by an array of framed pictures. I walked over to them. I couldn't say I was expecting pictures of me, but my stomach hollowed when I didn't see *any*. I glanced around for any indication that I existed, or that she'd had a life with my father – only to find the room filled with strangers.

'Pictures of my friends,' she explained briefly without going into any further detail. I nodded, fearing that my voice would reveal the hurt.

'So, you have school tomorrow? Ready to go back?' my mother asked as I thumbed through the CDs she had stacked in another built-in nook in the corner.

'Not really,' I answered honestly, recognizing she was trying to have a conversation to which I was doing a lousy job of contributing.

'When's your next basketball game?'

'Friday,' I responded, scanning the room.

'Would you mind if I came?' She sounded nervous. The unease in her voice drew my attention.

'You can come,' I answered, finally looking at her with an awkward smile. The tension in her blue eyes slowly melted away.

'Great. Thank you.' That one answer changed everything. The next thing I knew, she was pointing to people in the pictures and talking about where they were and what was going on. She pulled out a couple of CDs, insisting I listen to them because they were life altering.

I didn't say much. I didn't think I could have gotten a word in if I wanted to. Her nervous chatter flowed without pause as she sat in front of the player and spread CDs across the floor. I tried to relax as I listened to her stories, inspecting the woman before me and trying to connect with her as my mother. It felt like a million years since I'd actually had one. I had no idea how to act around her, or what to say.

'So do you really like your room?' she asked after slipping a CD into the player.

'I really do,' I admitted honestly.

'I was pretty useless in designing it. I just let Anna and Sara pick out everything,' my mother confessed, her cheeks reddening.

A knock at the door interrupted her search for the song that reminded her of her trip to New Orleans last year. I watched as she answered it. She appeared puzzled. 'Um, hello?'

'Hi, Mrs Thomas. I'm Evan. I'm looking for Emma.'

I jumped up from my cross-legged position on the floor and practically ran to the door.

'Hi,' I greeted him in a rush before my mother could say anything. Evan peeked around the door and his signature smile crept over his face, causing my heart to stutter. I was beyond relieved to see him.

'Well, come on in, Evan.' He stepped into the hall to allow my mother to close the door. 'I'm Rachel. It would completely freak me out if you called me Mrs Thomas. Mrs Thomas was Derek's mother, and she didn't like me very much. Besides my last name is Walace, so if anything I would be Ms Walace, but I really would prefer Rachel.' Evan and I were stilled by the burst of information that spewed from her mouth in a single breath. Her cheeks reddened and she laughed awkwardly when she found us staring at her. 'Wow. I have no idea why I just said all that. I'm not usually this nervous. Okay, yes I am.' She reacted to our stunned faces and said, 'I'm so sorry.'

'That's okay,' I assured her – all too familiar with being possessed by nervousness. 'Why don't I show Evan around?'

'Uh, sure,' she agreed, returning to the living room to put away the CDs that were spread over the floor.

I didn't bother showing Evan the downstairs, since all he had to do was turn in a circle to see the entire layout. I took his hand and led him to my room, closing the door behind us.

'Nice room,' Evan admired, ducking under the slanted ceiling to sit on my bed. 'How's it going? She seems nice.'

'Yeah,' I said hesitantly, not knowing how to answer him. 'It's fine . . . I mean, she's great.'

'You're nervous too, huh?' he acknowledged with a small laugh. 'I guess I can see who you get your red cheeks from.'

'Funny,' I returned sarcastically. Nervous was just the tip of what I was feeling. I couldn't begin to describe the panic that slithered inside me. Maybe when it all came down to it, I was afraid she was going to tell me that she couldn't do this – that she didn't want to be a part of my life again. And that thought kept me from being able to relax long enough to appreciate that I was here, with her. 'I guess I am kinda nervous.'

'You're going to be fine,' Evan assured me, giving my hand a squeeze. 'Oh, I have something for your room.'

Evan reached inside his jacket and pulled out a large envelope, handing it to me. I opened it and pulled out a stack of pictures. I smiled as I flipped through the images Evan had captured with his camera. Action shots of me playing soccer, feral and intense. Still moments of Sara and me laughing. Another of me sitting on his front porch, lost in thought, oblivious to his camera. There were even a few shots of the two of us posing, his arm around my shoulder, that were taken during a picnic last fall.

I leaned over and kissed him. 'Exactly what my room needs.' I removed the sign from the board above the desk and tucked the pictures under the black ribbon that criss-crossed over its surface.

A soft knock rapped on my door. Before I could say anything, my mother slowly opened it and poked her head in. 'I was going to order a pizza. Are you hungry?'

'That sounds great. Thank you,' Evan responded for the two of us. I pressed my lips together and nodded.

I remained silent at the kitchen table, listening to my mother's nervous chatter. She interrogated Evan about . . . well, everything. I think focusing on him was her way of keeping the awkwardness between us at bay. If we were both desperately focused on every word that came out of Evan's mouth, we wouldn't have to figure out what to say to each other. Evan handled the pressure calmly, as usual. He didn't give a hint that the atmosphere was heavily laced with anxiety. But after he'd left, the uneasy tension was crushing.

'Do you want to watch a movie?' she asked as I wrapped the leftover pizza to place it in the bare refrigerator.

'I actually have a paper I need to work on that's due tomorrow,' I lied. She nodded slowly, and I feared she could tell I wasn't being honest.

'Okay,' she finally said, looking disappointed. A pang of guilt shot through me as I retreated to my room. But I really needed to be alone.

I lay down on my bed with my arms crossed behind my head and stared up at the freshly painted ceiling. I had so many strange emotions swirling inside me. I needed a moment to sort them out.

I hadn't said more than a half dozen words to this woman in five years, and now I was her room-mate. Well, that's what it felt like. She told stories about her friends and the trips she'd taken as if she were sharing them with someone she'd just met, not her daughter. They made me think about what I was doing while she was having so much fun, and I felt ill.

While I'd been in the darkest depths of hell, my mother had been travelling, drinking and living a carefree life.

I wanted to throw up just thinking about it. She hadn't once mentioned leaving me, or my time with Carol and George and what they'd done to me. It was as if that time had never happened, and we were starting anew – with a big black hole in between. I guess *I* was having a hard time moving past it.

To be honest, I hadn't considered what it would be like to live with her. It's not like I had expected to rekindle a relationship that had never been there in the first place, but I wasn't expecting to discover that I'd been completely absent from her life both physically and emotionally for the past five years.

I stayed in my room for the rest of the night, finally going into the bathroom – that was pretty much the size of a large closet – to get ready for bed around midnight. The television was on in the living room. 'Goodnight.' I hollered down the stairs and heard her talking and laughing in the kitchen, evidently on the phone. I shut my door without waiting for her to respond and slipped under the crisp new white sheets, pulling the duvet under my chin.

My phone chimed next to me, and I picked it up to read, *Goodnight. Hope you sleep well in your new room!* from Sara. I didn't respond and clicked off the bedside lamp.

I stared into the dark, still trying to wrap my head around the fact that I was here, living with my mother. The windows rattled as a gust of wind howled outside. I closed my eyes, but within minutes they snapped open. The boards creaked on the stairs. I tried to relax, realizing it was just my mother. I followed her footsteps as each board gave beneath her, until she shut the bathroom door.

I wish I could say that I drifted off to sleep, but it appeared the boards didn't need anyone walking on them to creak. I was restless throughout the night, continually awakened by the groans of the house. The cold air whistled through the rattling panes of the windows, just like the scattered thoughts that whirled through my head.

5

People Change

'GOOD MORNING,' EVAN GREETED ME FROM the slick walkway. I closed the door behind me, leaving my mother in the shower getting ready for work.

'Hi,' I replied flatly, adjusting my backpack over my shoulder as I took calculated steps towards his car.

'You have something against mornings, don't you?' Evan teased, opening the passenger door. I smirked before kissing him briefly on the lips and ducking into the car.

When he'd closed his door I explained, 'Sorry, I didn't sleep well. This house is super creaky.' Considering my weariness, I was glad he'd offered to pick me up on our first day back after the break.

'What are you doing after practice tonight? Do you want to come over?'

'Sure,' I answered automatically, and then quickly countered with, 'I can't.'

Evan appeared confused.

'I'm going grocery shopping with my mother,' I explained. 'She's not sure what I eat, so she wants me to go with her.'

'Okay,' Evan replied. 'How was it after I left last night? You two were pretty funny at dinner – she talks when she's nervous, and you don't say anything.'

'That was torture for you, wasn't it?'

'I was fine,' he chuckled. 'I'm pretty sure it was worse for you.'

'I . . . I don't know what to talk to her about,' I confessed.

'I think you could just let her do all the talking,' Evan advised comically.

I stared out the window in a daze. I didn't realize we had pulled into the school parking lot until the car stopped. A wave of dread consumed me as I watched the students getting out of their cars.

Evan acknowledged this, reading my thoughts. 'I know you don't want to be here,' he said, 'but I'm convinced it'll be different.' I didn't say anything and got out of the car.

I used to look forward to coming to school – not for the social life, but to escape the oppression at home. After everything that had happened, my safe place had become the place I dreaded most.

When I'd started the school year, I'd kept my head bowed, trying to retract further into my shell – not only in the halls but in the classroom as well. I'd refused to participate other than to complete the assignments. Sara and Evan eventually gave up trying to encourage me, promising that it wasn't as bad as I thought.

I stared at the brick building and took a deep breath before closing the car door. I pulled my backpack over my shoulder, preparing myself for the scrutiny. Evan took my hand, his warmth comforting me. Sara was waiting for us by the back door, smiling brightly as usual, and greeting just about everyone passing her by.

'Good morning,' she beamed. Then her brows dipped into a scowl. 'You didn't sleep well, huh?'

'Wow,' I responded to her bluntness. 'Do I look that bad?'

'No,' Evan countered quickly before Sara could utter the truthful words on the tip of her tongue.

'Liar,' Sara and I chimed in unison. I met her eyes and we started laughing. The sound of my laughter had the strangest effect, like waking a sleepy village from a curse. All of a sudden I heard, 'Hi, Emma.'

I turned my head to find Jill standing next to us. 'How was your New Year?' Before any of us could respond, or shake off the stupefied looks on our faces, she continued, 'Did you hear about the party at Michaela's? Her parents came home in the middle of it, and of course everyone was drunk. But the worst part was when they found Nick and Tara having sex on their bed. Michaela is so screwed.'

And just like that, it was as if the past seven months had never happened. Jill and Sara continued talking about the party while Evan and I followed behind. Evan wore an 'I told you so' smile on his face, and I smirked at the sight of it. As we continued down the hall, I realized the stares were gone, and no one was whispering as I passed them. Every so often, someone would acknowledge us with a 'hi' or 'good morning'. It was freaking me out. Everyone was letting it go . . . or pretending to anyway.

'Good to see you survived over vacation,' a voice cut through the crowd. Evidently not *everyone* had gotten over it.

Evan stiffened as the jeering words found us. My chest tightened in response. Evan spun around and pinned a guy against a locker with his forearm across his chest. I looked on in complete shock, and everyone in the hallway froze.

'What did you say?' But it wasn't Evan asking the question. Several other seniors were surrounding the guy who, by the size of him, must have been a freshman. Joel Rederick leaned in closer as Evan kept the guy immobilized. The freshman stared back in complete panic, sweat beading along his forehead.

'Nothing,' he choked.

'That's what I thought,' another senior threatened.

'Don't bother walking down the senior halls again,' Evan seethed.

'What's going on here?' an authoritative voice questioned from behind the crowd. Evan released the freshman, and the seniors began to part. The guy scurried away in search of the small pack who had abandoned him.

'Dick,' Jill snapped from behind me. Everyone continued on their way, and the talking resumed. No one looked twice at me as I remained still, attempting to digest what had just happened.

'Sorry about that,' Evan offered, taking my hand once again.

'It's okay,' I replied slowly, recovering from my befuddlement. 'Thank you.'

He studied me with eyebrows raised, not expecting my reaction, then grinned before leaning down to kiss me.

'Ahh, you're in the middle of the hall,' Sara stated with an undertone of *omigod*. Evan pulled back, and I looked at her oddly.

Sara and I continued to our lockers, and I asked, 'Since when do you care if Evan kisses me in the hall?'

'You don't like to draw attention, remember?' Sara stated from within her locker.

'Sara, is there something wrong?' I questioned, sensing she was still not right.

'No, I'm fine,' she replied, closing her locker with a smile.

I watched her walk off, knowing she wasn't being honest with me.

After basketball practice, I arrived home to find my mother at the kitchen table writing down a list of what we needed – which was practically everything from the looks of it.

'Hi,' she greeted. 'I think I have some ideas for meals. Is there anything you don't like?'

'I'm pretty open to trying anything . . . except for meatballs,' I told her with an inadvertent shiver. 'But you don't have to do anything crazy. Besides, I usually come home late because of basketball.'

'We'll pick out some easy things. How's that?' she offered, scanning her list again. 'That way you can throw something together for yourself if you come home late or if I have to stay at work.'

The thought of preparing anything beyond a sandwich was intimidating. 'What?' she questioned anxiously, when she saw my scrunched face.

'Um, I'm not exactly adept in the kitchen,' I confessed sheepishly.

'You can't cook?' she clarified in shock.

'Does oatmeal count?' I shrugged in embarrassment.

My mother laughed. 'Well . . . I guess we'll be shopping in the frozen-food section, too.'

We got into her car and drove to the grocery store in the next town over. She spent the ride reviewing the list and asking for my input. I'd never really had a say before, so I didn't contribute much. When I'd lived with Carol and George, I would write the basics of what I needed on the grocery list – cereal, granola bars and the like – since I wasn't allowed to eat it unless I'd asked for it. But for the most part, I ate what was put in front of me, no questions asked – even when it made me violently ill.

We ultimately decided to make up the list as we went along. Which was pretty much our approach to everything – including our relationship.

'You know I'm not exactly very good at this mother thing, right?' my mother said, picking through a pile of apples and putting a few that met her approval in a produce bag.

I didn't know how to respond. It was the start of a conversation I'd never expected to have in a grocery store.

'I mean, I don't want you to think that I'm expecting to walk back into your life and take charge or anything,' she continued, her voice laced with apprehension. 'I just want . . . I think it would be nice if we were . . . friends. You know, instead of . . .' She looked at me with her lips pressed together. 'I just want to get to know you. Does that make sense?'

My shoulders eased in relief. I had no idea where the conversation was headed, but this was a welcome surprise. I wasn't exactly sure how to be her daughter any more than I expected her to be my mother.

'Yes,' I agreed with a smile. 'I'd like that.'

'So, would you be okay with calling me Rachel then?' she asked cautiously. '*Mom* feels a little weird to be honest.'

I let out an uncomfortable laugh, slightly surprised by the request. 'I can try.'

She smiled softly and released her nervousness with a quick breath. 'Great. Now, what do you eat for lunch?'

I continued behind her, pushing the grocery cart around as she held up items and waited for me to nod or shake my head before placing them in the cart or putting them back. By the time we were done, there was more food in the cart than two people could eat in a month. Thankfully, a good portion of it was frozen.

'Do you want to learn how to cook?' my mother asked as she set the items on the belt. 'I could teach you.'

I smiled warmly at her offer. 'Uh, sure,' I replied, not having the heart to tell her that Evan had already made several attempts to teach me, and each had ended disastrously. She seemed eager to be able to do something with me – I would at least *try*.

'So, how long have you and Evan been together?' she asked after we had loaded the groceries into the car and were driving home.

'Officially,' I calculated, 'about ten months.'

'What does *officially* mean?'

'Well,' I fumbled, not sure how to explain how we'd felt for each other from pretty much day one, and how due to misunderstandings and hurt feelings, it had taken forever before we'd finally ended up together. 'I guess I don't know how to answer that. Let's just say we started dating last March.'

'Okay,' she said with a confused nod. 'He seems really nice.'

'Yes,' I agreed. My face glowed. 'He is.'

'I'm still looking,' she said with a sigh. 'I'll never find anyone like Derek again.'

My heart faltered. I knew we had agreed to be *friends*, but she was still my mother. And having her talk so casually about finding the next best thing to my dead father knocked me back a bit.

'Do you want to help me with dinner tonight?'

'Huh?' I stumbled, still trying to get over her comment.

'Want to start your cooking lessons?' she clarified.

'Can I take a pass on tonight?' I begged. 'I think I want to wait a bit before revealing how terrible I am.'

She laughed. 'You can't be *that* bad.'

'You have no idea,' I grumbled, making her laugh again.

'Okay. Maybe another night.'

I sat in the kitchen with her while she explained what she was doing as she filled the pork chops with stuffing. I just nodded like I was paying attention, knowing it was useless. I could figure out the most complex equations, or understand the workings of the nervous system, but asking me to baste or julienne anything caused anxiety beyond explanation.

My mother set the plates down on the table I'd set for two, the one thing I *could* do.

'Thank you,' I said, sitting down with a glass of water.

'Sure,' she responded, sitting across from me.

When I looked up from my plate to praise her for the meal, I found her watching me. It was like she was examining every inch of my face, so intently that it made me want to sink under the table.

'I forgot how much you look like him.' Her eyes were glassy and distant – she was looking at me but *not* at the same time. I bowed my head to escape her sorrowful gaze.

'So, Sara seems like she's an amazing friend,' my mother said, her voice suddenly back to normal. I glanced up as she pierced the cut pork chop with her fork.

'Uh, yeah,' I responded, shaking off the haunted look in her eye. 'She's my best friend.'

'I have one of those,' my mother smiled. 'Sharon.' She let out a laugh just thinking about her. 'We've done *everything* together. She usually gets me into trouble, but I have the best stories because of her.'

I nodded, trying to remember this woman who seemed to be such a huge part of her life – but came up blank. I realized there wasn't much about my mother that I knew, even from the twelve years she had technically been in my life.

It wasn't the howling of the wind or the boards groaning that drew me from my bed that night. Yes, they were the reasons I was still awake, but I was brought to my feet by the clatter of metal crashing outside my door. I found my mother kneeling on the floor with her back to me, trying to stack the framed photographs that were scattered across the hallway.

As I got closer, I could hear her mumbling to herself, clumsily setting one frame on top of the other. When I bent down to help her pick them up, I realized that she was crying.

'Are you okay?' I asked tentatively.

'Huh?' Her head shot up. 'Oh, Emily, I'm sorry.' She sniffled and wiped her red cheeks with her sleeve. 'I woke you up.'

She blinked heavily, and I sank to the floor when it struck me . . . she was drunk. I spotted the bottle of vodka resting next to the top step and swallowed hard against the disappointment that rose in my throat.

'I was . . . I was just remembering,' she stuttered. She was crouching, trying to balance the stack of frames, when she clumsily plopped down to sit.

'Fuck,' she muttered, blowing a stray hair from her eye, her arm still wrapped around the frames as she reached for the bottle. It was just out of her reach, so she scooted over to grab it and repositioned herself so her feet rested on the top steps. She took a swig and ran her arm across her forehead, frustrated with the floating hairs that kept falling in her face. She looked like she'd just travelled through a tunnel of blankets.

I held the remaining frames that she couldn't quite manage and settled next to her. I noticed they were all pictures of my father.

My mother shuffled through the stack that teetered on her lap and sent one slipping and sliding down the stairs. 'Fuck.'

Big wet tears streamed down her face as she held a photo up. It was of her and my father sitting on a sailboat.

'I know you were looking for these,' she blubbered, swiping the back of her hand across her nose. 'I had to dig them out of the back of the closet. But I can't . . .'

She couldn't continue. Her eyes were smeared with mascara, bloodshot and half-open. Behind her inebriation was a sadness that was consuming her, and my heart ached at the sight of it.

'You remind me of him.'

'I'm sorry,' I whispered, not knowing how to comfort her.

'I forgot how much I missed him,' she slurred, slouching against the banister. Another frame slid from her lap and crashed down the stairs.

'Fuck!' she screamed. In one sudden motion, she picked up her pile and threw the pictures down the stairs. I jumped at her outburst. Glass splintered along the staircase as the frames collided with each step.

'Why? Why? Why?' she bellowed in agony, crumpling to the floor. I remained paralysed beside her, my back tense. I took in the destruction at the bottom of the stairs, and then the woman who was disintegrating before my eyes.

'It's okay,' I whispered, my heart beating frantically. I doubted she could hear me.

She pushed herself up to sit and reached for the bottle to take another swig. She flopped back against the post, barely able to keep her eyes open. The bottle tilted in her hand as she attempted to rest it on the floor. I grabbed for it, setting it down next to me before it joined the carnage at the bottom of the stairs.

'Let me help you to bed,' I offered softly. Releasing the stack of frames that I still gripped tightly and setting them on the floor, I slid closer to her so I could put her arm around my shoulder.

'Huh?' my mother groaned, unable to hold her head up.

'There you go,' I encouraged, slowly getting her to her feet. 'Easy.' She wobbled under my support. I focused on the bedroom door and hoped we'd make it inside before she toppled over. I had a good five inches on her, but if she fell, we'd both go down.

I guided her to her bed, and she collapsed face first. She drew in heavy breaths with a slight snore as I pulled the blanket over her. Leaving her in her induced peace, I shut the door behind me.

I stood on the top step and surveyed the mess below, exhaling deeply and shaking my head. Picking up the bottle that had instigated this disaster, my jaw tightened. I blinked away the tears, not wanting to feel anything. With a weight in my chest, I trudged down the stairs and dumped the bottle's contents down the kitchen sink. I blew out an exhausted sigh before slowly picking up the shattered pieces.

I hadn't exactly been waiting for it, but I should've known. I was never convinced after seeing her sober one night a year ago in front of my school that sobriety was going to take. She may not have had a drink *that night*, but it didn't mean she hadn't every night after. I knew was this going to happen . . . I just wanted to be wrong.

I picked up the picture of her and my father on the sailboat, and the lump tightened in the back of my throat. I closed my eyes and took a deep breath to suppress the storm that was brewing in my chest. I breathed out once more before opening them.

After stacking the photos on the stairs, I filled the trash bag with the broken glass and busted frames and swept up the remnants. When I returned from taking the bag to the barrel outside, I brought the memories back to my room, where I tucked them under the sweatshirts on my shelf in the closet. I wasn't ready to face them either.

I slipped back under the covers and lay staring at the ceiling. The tears silently slid along my temples and were absorbed into my hair. I let them flow, but I kept the lump lodged in my throat, pushing away the pain and sorrow I'd seen in my mother's eyes.

6

Lifestyles

By THE TIME I STUMBLED OUT OF BED THE next morning, tired and bleary-eyed, my mother had already left for work. There was a text waiting for me. *So sorry about last night. You shouldn't have seen that. Dinner tonight?*

I responded with, *See you tonight.*

But when I arrived home after practice, I found her rushing around, slipping earrings into her ears. She wore a short skirt and a flowy blouse, and her dark hair was flipped and curled in an abundance of volume.

'Hi,' she said, out of breath, hopping into one of her heels and almost falling over. 'Um, I hope you don't mind, but I forgot I had plans tonight. I made them a while ago, you know, before I knew that you'd be here.' She stopped, awaiting my reaction with her face scrunched in apology. 'But I could cancel them. I mean . . . I could stay.'

'No, go,' I encouraged her. 'I'll be okay, really.'

'Are you sure?' she asked again, battling with her decision.

'Yeah, I have a ton of homework to do,' I said, exaggerating in an attempt to make her feel better. 'Have a good time.'

'Okay,' she replied, staggering on one foot to pull up the strap of her heel as she grabbed her purse. 'Well, help yourself to the freezer, I guess.' She took out a mini Altoids mints tin and opened it, popping a small white pill down her throat with a toss of her head.

'Don't wait up,' she advised, removing her jacket from the hall closet next to the stairs. 'I'll probably be pretty late.' Before I could even unzip my jacket, she was out the front door. I shook my head in befuddlement and took in the vacant house with a heavy breath.

The door flew open behind me. I turned with a start. 'Uh . . . can you move your car?'

'Oh, yeah. Sorry.' I followed her back out the door.

'Sorry that I'm running off so fast,' she attempted to explain as we walked down the driveway. 'I'm so late and my friends hate waiting on me.'

'It's okay,' I replied to . . . no one. She was already in her car, anxiously waiting for me to back up. I watched her speed away before pulling back into the driveway.

I put my things in my room and went down to the kitchen to prepare something to eat. I pulled out a frozen lasagne and followed the instructions to heat it in the microwave.

As I sat in the silent house, watching television and eating the lasagne, I realized I'd never been alone like this before. As much as I'd felt alone most of my life, emotionally isolating myself from . . . well, everyone, I'd never really been by myself. Before I lived with Sara, I wasn't allowed to be home alone. But I was usually involved in something at school that kept me occupied anyway. And now that I was alone, I didn't like the stillness. It made the thoughts in my head too loud.

I ventured upstairs a couple of hours later, leaving the table lamp turned on at the bottom of the stairs, along with the light on the porch. After getting ready for bed, I kept myself busy with homework as best I could. But with every creak, my head jerked to attention and my heartbeat faltered. When the wind picked up outside, rattling the windows in their peeling wooden frames, I opted to drown out the creepiness with music.

Eventually, I crawled into bed, leaving the music playing so I wouldn't be kept awake by every groaning board in the house. I took a deep breath and stared at the black door across from me, hesitating before shutting off the light. The door and the entire wall disappeared with the click of the lamp.

I shot up in the bed, gasping and covered in sweat, flipping on the light to disperse the figure at my door. The black door remained closed, mocking me.

My eyes twitched as I listened for movement. I wasn't sure if I'd screamed out loud since my mother hadn't rushed into the room. That's when I heard the deadbolt click open at the bottom of the stairs followed by laughter and a deep voice. It was after two in the morning. I blinked at the clock, wondering where she could've been and who she was with now.

I shut off my light, so she wouldn't think I was waiting up for her, and pulled the covers over me. The wind screeched against the windows, rustling the black curtains with each frigid gust. The old house couldn't keep out the cold that seeped in through its bowed boards. I pulled the covers up to my nose, waiting for sleep.

'That was quite the storm last night, wasn't it, Mary?' the radio personality chuckled, his voice forcing its way into my ears. I rolled over and hit snooze, fighting the urge to pull the covers up over my head and go back to sleep. I lay on my back and stared up at the ceiling, dreading the chill that awaited me once I flipped back the blankets.

My phone beeped. *Snow Day!* was displayed under Sara's name. Good. That meant I could stay in bed until my mother turned up the heat.

Coming to get you in a few hours, appeared on my phone a moment later under Evan's name. I responded with an affirmative, feeling much too awake to find sleep again. Footsteps fell across the unforgiving boards leading to the bathroom, and seconds later the pipes thumped and squealed with the sound of water rushing through them. 'Fine,' I huffed out loud, 'I'm getting up.'

I threw my hair up in a pile of twists on top of my head and slid on socks to protect my feet from the icy floorboards before plodding down the stairs. Pulling a box of cereal from the cabinet, I poured myself a bowl to take into the living room. I adjusted the thermostat to a warmer temperature so I would no longer have to see my breath.

I flipped on the sports channel and started eating the cereal. The sound of the door opening and feet banging against the wood on the porch stopped me mid-bite. I peeked over to find a guy brushing snow from his jacket and shoving off his boots by the door. My heart pounded; I knew what I looked like and did not want to be seen by whoever it was entering like he belonged here.

I watched with wide eyes as a guy with messy dark hair walked into the living room with a bowl of cereal of his own. I pulled my knees up to cover my chest, very aware that I didn't have anything on under my long-sleeved shirt. He had a muscular build and a youthful face – making me question exactly who he was. He didn't look that much older than Jared.

'Hey,' he greeted me with a nod, sitting next to me on the couch like he'd known me for years.

'Hi,' I replied, not moving a muscle.

'I'm Chris,' he offered before shovelling a mound of cereal into his mouth, the milk dribbling down his chin. He wiped it off with his sleeve while his eyes remained glued to the television. He glanced over at me again and said, 'It's a shitty mess out there.'

I nodded, not really wanting to have a conversation with this strange guy sitting next to me.

'Chris, are you still here?' my mother yelled from the top of the stairs, sounding like she hadn't expected him to be.

'Yeah,' he bellowed in return.

'I thought you were leaving to get to class,' she replied in confusion.

'Got cancelled,' he answered, still staring at the TV.

'Um . . . could you start my car for me?'

'Yeah, sure.'

Without complaint, Chris put his bowl down on the coffee table and walked out of the room. I listened to the jangling of keys and the click of the door. I'd hoped to disappear before he returned, but I was met with the door flinging open as he rushed in, out of breath, to escape the cold.

'What are you up to today?' he asked, using his toes to remove his snow-covered boots.

'Not sure,' I answered with my arms crossed over my chest.

'My friend's having a party tonight if you and Rachel want to come by,' he stated.

'Oh,' was all that I could find to say.

'Emily, you're up,' my mother noted in surprise as she walked down the stairs in a long black skirt, black leather dress boots and a fitted green turtleneck sweater. 'I thought school was cancelled.'

'Don't you look all sexy in your work clothes,' Chris interrupted before I could answer. She flashed an embarrassed glance my way and laughed uncomfortably. He grabbed her when she reached the bottom step, burying his face in her neck. She giggled awkwardly and pushed him away, walking past him to the kitchen.

'So, will I see you when I get back from school in a few weeks?' he asked, following her.

'Umm . . . we'll see,' she replied reluctantly, her cheeks bright red. 'Want some coffee?' He followed her into the kitchen, and I hopped up the stairs two at a time to escape to my room. I stayed in there until I heard them leave. A few minutes later a text appeared. *I'm so, so sorry about that. Thought he'd be gone by the time you got up.* I didn't respond. I didn't even know what to say.

I wish I could say that Chris was a fluke and it never

72

happened again. Although she attempted to hide the guys, I could hear her coming home giggling on the nights she stayed out late after work – presumably after drinking a little too much. I didn't usually see them, nor could I confirm if she was in fact drunk – I just had a feeling. Every so often, I'd bump into one of the guys on my way to the bathroom in the morning. I probably wouldn't have known most of them were there at all if I actually slept.

She never provided an explanation or apologized for their presence. Perhaps she didn't realize I knew. They'd come in after I was in bed, and she'd sneak them out early, before I got up. It's not like it happened every night, but it happened enough that I always made sure I had a sports bra on before I left my room.

I hadn't exactly been prepared for her lifestyle. And she hadn't exactly been prepared for mine either.

A creak pulled me from my sleep. I remained still with my eyes closed, listening to the wind push against the house and the groans of the old building fighting against it. I opened my eyes, staring into the dark with my ears at attention. There was another creak, closer to my room.

My unblinking eyes slowly adjusted to the light, as little as there was. But it didn't matter how much I stared at the door, I couldn't see into the black paint. I might as well have been looking into an abyss. I only knew where it was because a sliver of light seeped in under its uneven edge. Another board let out a creak right outside the door.

I wanted to call out for my mother, hoping it was her. But I remained paralysed in my bed. The only thing that moved was my heart racing in my chest. I heard the handle jiggle, and the hinges shrieked open. The silhouette stood in the door's frame, unmoving.

I opened my mouth to ask who it was, but I could barely breathe. The person stepped forward, allowing just enough light to make out the angular features of her face and the sneer on her lips. I looked down at her hand and she was holding something long and hard. It reflected the light enough for me to know that whatever it was, it was going to hurt.

'You don't deserve to live,' she grunted, raising her arm over her head.

'Emily?!' another voice screamed. My eyes shot open. I remained frozen, breathing heavily, trying to orient myself. The door flung open and my mother rushed in, in a panic. 'What's wrong?' She stood just inside the door, flipping on the light, her hand over her heart.

My shoulders relaxed and I took a deep breath to ease the racing beats in my chest. 'It was just a dream,' I explained, from my startled seated position.

'Holy shit, Emily,' she declared, letting out a long breath. 'You just about gave me a heart attack.'

'Sorry.' I ran my hand over my brow, erasing the lingering sweat that clung to my skin. 'I'm fine.'

She hesitated before leaving, like she wanted to say something. She looked me over again and finally said, 'Well . . . goodnight,' then walked out, shutting off the light and closing the door behind her.

I clicked on the lamp next to my bed, to keep out the dark, and settled into my pillow with my arms wrapped tightly across my body. The dream lingered. It felt so real, I was afraid to close my eyes again.

My mother came into my room only a couple of times after that night, panicked by my screams. But then she stopped, probably realizing there wasn't anything she could do.

I felt guilty for waking her, especially when I saw her slumped over her coffee each morning. I knew I wasn't easy to live with. I'd often found Sara on the couch of her entertainment room where she'd gone in an attempt to escape me.

My therapist had prescribed sleeping pills, but they didn't take the nightmares away. They only kept me trapped, thrashing inside them.

'I'm sorry,' I offered one morning. My mother looked up from her coffee. 'About keeping you awake.'

She shrugged. 'You can't help it.'

We didn't talk about it after that.

7

Social Life

'So, I just started dating this guy,' my mother blurted one morning while I was buttering toast. I paused before turning around, not prepared for the confession – especially after all the guys she'd hidden in the past month since my 'breakfast' with Chris.

I took a breath and turned to face her. 'Really?' I tried to remember the last time I'd heard a visitor and narrowed it down to about a week or week and a half ago.

'Except –' she hesitated with a breath – 'he's . . . younger. *A lot* younger, and I'm not sure how I feel about it.' She appeared troubled, clearly looking to me for advice.

'How old is he?' I asked, attempting to fill the role.

'Twenty-eight,' she grimaced, waiting for me to pass judgement. I didn't react. He was older than I'd expected, to be honest.

'How old was Chris?' I asked, without thinking.

Her face changed to a hue of red. 'He was . . . young, but I had no interest in *dating* him.'

'Right,' I nodded, flushing uncomfortably. 'So, do you like him?'

'Yes,' she answered, her eyes lighting up. 'He's *so* nice, and smart, and amazingly hot and confident,' she gushed, 'but . . . he's *so* young, Emily. I have no idea what I'm doing.'

'Who cares,' I offered with a shrug, taking on my role with a little more gusto. 'You obviously like him, and if the age difference doesn't bother him, then . . . date him. I mean, is it serious?'

'Not really,' she admitted. 'Not yet, anyway. We've only been on a couple of dates. But we have so much fun together, and he keeps asking to see me again.'

'Then do it,' I urged her, completely freaking out on the inside that I was encouraging my mother to date a younger guy, or to date at all. She beamed at my acceptance.

'You're going to the concert with Evan tonight, right?' She took a sip of her coffee, unable to keep the smile from her face.

'Yes,' I replied, eyeing her jovial expression apprehensively.

'Shit, I'm going to be late,' she exclaimed suddenly, glancing at the clock on the microwave and jumping up from the chair. She looked to me and tensed excitedly, and before I knew it, she threw her arms around me and squeezed. I was too stunned to move. 'Thank you,' she squealed.

As I was walking into school alongside Evan and Sara, my mother texted me. *Going out with him again tonight! So excited!* I couldn't help but laugh.

'What's so funny?' Evan asked.

'My mother's *dating*,' I explained with a shake of my head, 'and she's more nervously excited about it than most girls at our school.'

Evan raised his eyebrows. 'That's got to be interesting.'

'You have no idea,' I responded, rolling my eyes.

'She has more of a social life than *I* do,' Sara added, having heard my spiels about my mother's late nights and the sleepovers she'd hosted.

'Does she go out a lot?' Evan asked, not knowing any of it. I shot Sara a wide-eyed glance.

'Sometimes,' I replied casually.

When Evan was out of earshot, Sara stated, 'I didn't know you hadn't told him about how much Rachel goes out.'

'I was afraid of how it would sound to him,' I explained.

'Who cares,' Sara countered. 'It's not like it's you who's bringing home strange men.'

'Yeah,' I explained, 'but I don't want him worrying about me being in the same house as the *strange men*.'

Sara nodded, understanding how that would rouse Evan's protective side.

'Besides,' I continued, 'she really seems to like this guy. So maybe the string of one-nighters is over.'

'Em, you never saw the guys. Maybe it was the same guy each night.'

I flipped my eyes towards her and shook my head. 'Don't think so.'

'Oh,' Sara said with a shocked look of understanding. 'Well, let's hope he's a keeper.'

*

The sweat had barely dried from my skin, and my tank top and hair were still damp from the exertion when I ran into the house, slamming the door behind me and flying up the stairs. Of all the nights for Coach to torture us with sprints. It's not like we lost by that much in yesterday afternoon's game.

I glanced at the clock as I pulled jeans from the closet and a long-sleeved shirt from the dresser, tossing them on the bed. I had twenty minutes to get ready. From the quiet, I could tell I was alone in the house. She was probably on her date.

I kicked off my sneakers and tore at my socks, then pulled my shirt over my head and dropped my shorts somewhere along the way to the bathroom. My urgency didn't help cool my skin. I turned on the shower and made myself calm down long enough to wash – and hopefully stop sweating.

Wrapped in a towel, I scampered out of the bathroom towards my room, and I heard the front door open. Shit. I hadn't been fast enough.

'I'll be right . . .' I started to holler, peering down the stairs. At the same time, the guy at the bottom hollered, 'Rach –'

We both froze and stared at each other. Neither of us had anticipated seeing the other – especially me in just a towel. It didn't seem to faze him that I was standing in front of him half naked.

'Whoa,' he exclaimed in surprise. 'You're not Rachel.'

'Uh, she's not home,' I answered, but he'd probably already figured that out. I remained still. My instinct was to rush into my room and shut the door, but I couldn't move.

'I knocked.' He looked up at me apologetically. 'Sorry. I shouldn't have just walked in like that.' It didn't seem to faze him that I was dripping wet, half naked. He didn't avert his dark eyes. 'I'm Jonathan.'

I widened my eyes, dumbfounded by his casualness. 'Emma,' I uttered.

'Well, it's nice to meet you, Emma,' he responded with a smile, still looking me in the eye. 'I guess I'll just call her. Have a good night.' Before I could say another word, he was out the front door. Within seconds I unglued myself from the floor and was right behind him, securing the deadbolt while exhaling the breath I'd been holding at the sight of him.

It took a moment for me to remember what I was *supposed* to be doing, and I ran back up the stairs, nearly falling on my face as I slid across the wet boards at the top.

I heard the knock on the front door just as I was tying my shoes.

'Hi.' I smiled brightly when I opened the door, finally able to get excited about tonight. 'Wasn't sure what to wear.'

Evan closed the door behind him, examining my selection. 'You look great, except you might want to wear short sleeves. It's going to get pretty hot, especially near the stage.'

'Right,' I concurred, turning back up the stairs. Evan was about to follow me when I noticed my abandoned clothes leading to the bathroom. 'I'll be right down,' I said, stopping him on the second step. I scooped up my sweaty clothes and brought them into the room with me. I re-emerged from my room, readjusting my ponytail after sliding on a black *Newbury Comics* T-shirt.

'Much better,' Evan pronounced. 'Are you ready?'

'Definitely.' I bounded down the steps to grab the jacket he held out for me.

When we arrived at the concert, there was a long line on the sidewalk. We walked to the back, awaiting entry with everyone else. Evan stood behind me, wrapping his arms around me to help keep me warm while we waited. I hadn't noticed the cold, too distracted by the anticipation. We continued to shuffle forward until we finally reached the guys in the bright yellow jackets checking IDs. We received large black 'X's on the back of our right hands, branding us underage. After they'd scanned our tickets and we'd been frisked by blue-gloved hands, we were finally released into the rolling energy of the venue.

Evan held my hand tightly, steering us through the crowd. I let the bottled-up excitement seep in, accepting it with a grin on my face. Evan looked back and smiled when his eyes connected with mine. I knew he'd been concerned about how I'd react to being engulfed by so many people.

This was different. These people didn't know who I was, nor did they care. We were instantly bonded by the music blaring on the stage as the opening act continued its set. They were pretty good, although I'd never heard of them before. A group leaning against the metal barriers along the front seemed to know exactly who they were as they rocked their heads and hollered out the lyrics.

We excused our way to the front, continuing along the perimeter and stopping at the steps that descended into the pit. Those standing directly in front of the large stage were already sweating. Their intertwining bodies jostled for position to get closer. I was instantly captivated by the bare skin, backwards baseball caps, tank tops with bra straps revealed, oversized T-shirts hanging over baggy pants – as their heads bobbed in unison.

I turned towards Evan and yelled, 'This is so great.'

'It will only get better,' he bellowed in my ear.

And it did. The sea of bodies dispersed slightly in between the opener and the headliner, but as soon as the roadies started tuning the guitars and pounding the bass, the hollering began and the crowd swarmed together even tighter than before. Within a few minutes the band members started filing onto the stage, taking their positions, acknowledging the crowd with a wave. The masses ignited into a trembling roar.

The opening song was recognized by just about everyone. Heads started rocking, the massive crowd cresting with jumping bodies and hands thrust into the air. The storm of energy was contagious, and I found my head nodding in time with the beat. Before I knew it, Evan and I were jumping and screaming out the lyrics along with everyone else. The bass and guitar riffs exploded in my chest.

I was a sweaty mess by the end, but I could've sworn I was floating. The crowd only enhanced the experience, bodies surfing across hands, voices bellowing the words, fists pumping in time – I was addicted. It released me from everything. I was overtaken by every note, until finally, nothing else mattered.

'Thank you,' I rasped, my voice lost from screaming. I wrapped my slick arms around Evan's neck and pulled him towards me. I could taste the salt on his lips as I expressed my gratitude.

'Watching you tonight, jumping around and getting lost in the music – you were more entertaining than the band. I'm glad I got to see it.' He squeezed my hand as we followed the crowd that was still riding the experience. We were released into a bitter cold that licked at the sweat on our skin, triggering a chill down my spine.

'Don't tell Sara, but I'm happy I went with you.'

The buzz of the music echoed in my ears when I found my way to the front door, still floating from the entire night, and his parting kiss.

My mother burst into the room after I'd released a blood-curdling scream. She appeared dishevelled and bleary-eyed when she flipped on the light.

'What is wrong with you?' she yelled. 'You'd think someone was killing you or something.' Then she slammed the door and went back to her room.

I remained still, staring at the door after she'd left. Her verbal assault swathed me in guilt.

'But someone *is* killing me,' I whispered, 'every time I shut my eyes.'

8

Intensity

'YOU SURVIVED,' MY MOTHER DECLARED with a laugh when I walked through the door.

'Um, hi,' I replied, surprised to see her. 'What was that supposed to mean?'

'Your first time ice skating with Sara,' she explained. 'How was it?'

'Cold,' I responded, shedding my layers before joining her in the living room. 'I wasn't expecting you to be home.'

She picked up the wine glass that was on the end table as I sat down next to her on the couch. My stomach churned as I watched her take a sip.

'And how was the concert?'

'Uh, it was amazing,' I responded, trying to conceal my discomfort. 'How was your date?'

'He's so incredible, I could die,' my mother gushed, instantly transformed into a giddy sixteen-year-old. 'He took me to this sushi restaurant, and then we went dancing. He makes me feel like I'm the only girl in the room.

And believe me, *every* girl in the room is looking at him. He's so . . .'

If she said *dreamy*, I was going to laugh.

'. . . intense.'

This description got a raise of an eyebrow out of me.

I knew she was talking about the same guy who had walked into the house last night. I could feel my cheeks heating up just thinking about how nonchalant he'd been about at seeing me in a towel, like it was the most common thing in the world. And of course, I couldn't have been any more awkward. I hadn't told anyone about it, not even Sara. It was not a moment I wanted to relive.

'He sounds great,' I replied, distracted again when she took another sip from the wine glass.

'I can't –' She stopped when she saw me staring at the glass. She set it down and adjusted herself uncomfortably. 'I really am sorry about what happened a few weeks ago. I wish more than anything you hadn't seen me like that.'

I nodded, unable to tell her how helpless it made me feel to watch her drown her pain in vodka.

'I'm okay though, I promise,' she reassured me with a hint of a smile. 'I don't drink like I used to, really. I know my limit.

'I was hurting that night,' she continued. 'And I needed to take the edge off. I wasn't ready –'

'For me,' I finished for her, knowing the only reason she'd searched for the pictures was because I reminded her of my father, and remembering him crushed her.

'No. That's not it at all.' She paused, averting her eyes, before explaining. 'I've made myself forget him, so I won't hurt so much. It's why you had to . . .' She couldn't finish the sentence, but I knew she was talking about why she'd left me with George and Carol. 'But I'm better. I just had a bad night, that's all. So you don't have to worry if you see me having a drink or two. I have it under control, I swear.'

'Okay.' I wasn't exactly convinced, but in the month that I'd lived here, I'd really only seen the one lapse. I guess I understood what triggered it, but I hoped more than anything that it wouldn't happen again.

'So, I told Jonathan about you,' she said, smiling brightly. 'I wasn't sure how he was going to react to knowing I have a teenage daughter. But he wants to meet you!'

She said it like it was the most exciting news ever.

'Really?' I was tempted to tell her I'd already met him – however briefly. 'Why?'

My mother drew her brows together, appearing offended that I didn't understand.

'Because he wants to date me,' she explained emphatically. 'So, he wants to make sure you're okay with us – you know, when he starts coming over.'

'Oh,' I responded with big eyes, finally understanding. 'Great.' I feigned excitement, but the thought of seeing this guy again made my stomach flip.

'What's wrong?' she demanded, her smile faltering.

'Nothing.' I forced the words through a frozen smile. 'That's really great.'

'You're such a horrible liar,' she stated. 'But I understand why you'd be nervous. Don't worry, he's so great. You'll love him.'

'So, when am I meeting him?'

'Monday night,' she exclaimed jubilantly, her eyes sparkling.

'Great,' I repeated as excitedly as I could fake. It seemed to be the only word my brain could form. 'Great,' I grumbled in dread under my breath when she left to top up her wine glass. 'Can't wait.'

Text me as soon as you get home. I want to hear all about him! Sara sent as I pulled into the parking lot.

I called my mother to make sure she was at the restaurant before I went inside. She picked up on the third ring.

'Hi, Emily,' she answered. 'Are you there?'

'There?' I questioned in alarm. 'You mean you're not here yet?'

'Um, no,' she faltered. 'I'm still at work.'

'What?' I demanded, panic beginning to take over. 'So what am I supposed to do?'

'Start without me,' she suggested. 'It will give you some time to talk without me there, you know, to get to know each other.'

I didn't respond. I sat in the car with my mouth open, shaking my head.

'Please,' she begged. 'You can do this.'

'Uh huh.' I stared at the large glass windows, wondering which one of the people in there was waiting for me. 'Does he know you're late?'

'I just talked to him. I won't be too much longer, I promise. Just take a deep breath; you can get through this.'

The fact that she understood my anxiety wasn't at all comforting. It only gave me another reason to panic.

'Please,' she begged.

I filled my lungs with air and blew out quickly. 'Okay.'

'Thank you, thank you, thank you!' she exclaimed joyously.

'Hurry.'

'As fast as I can,' she promised.

I walked into the steakhouse, trying to remember what this guy, Jonathan, looked like. I had been too stunned and embarrassed the other night to really get a good look at him. All I knew was that he had intense brown eyes.

'Can I help you?' the hostess asked as I looked past her into the dining room.

'Umm, I'm meeting someone.'

'Emma.' A man stood at a table in the middle of the room.

'Found him,' I told the hostess, who shot me a curious look. I glanced back a couple of times as I approached the table, finding her still following me with a stunned expression on her face.

'Hi,' Jonathan said, pulling out a chair for me.

'Hi,' I responded, draping my coat on the back of the chair before taking a seat.

That's when I looked at him – I mean really *looked* at him – and nearly slid off my chair as I pulled it forward. He was not the guy I remembered from the bottom of the stairs.

'I was afraid you wouldn't come in,' he said, sitting across from me.

Jonathan definitely looked young. But it was difficult to pin an age on him, except to say he was in his twenties. He was bigger than I remembered as well, but then again, he'd had a jacket on when I'd last seen him.

He had an All-American quarterback look. His dark wavy hair was stylishly unkempt on top, with the sides trimmed tight. But it was his eyes that kept me from speaking. *Intense* was absolutely the word for them. It felt like he could peer right into me, and that kept me a bit on edge.

'Emma?'

'Huh?' I looked up. I'd been fidgeting with my napkin to avoid making eye contact. My cheeks became hot when I found him and the server waiting for me to respond to whatever she'd asked. 'Sorry. What was that?'

'Do you want something to drink?'

'Um, water's fine.'

The tall blonde paused before leaving, looking me over with judgement. Then she turned towards Jonathan and smiled brightly. 'I'll be back with your drink.'

I raised my eyebrows at her odd behaviour and watched her walk away.

Jonathan laughed. 'What's wrong?'

I quickly turned back towards him, my entire face heating up again when I realized he'd read the look on my face.

'Wow, I thought Rachel had all the hues of red down,' he said playfully. 'But you have a few shades I've never seen before.' He chuckled before adding, 'Did she do something wrong?'

'No,' I answered quickly, my napkin falling off my lap as I adjusted myself in the chair. I bent down to pick it up.

While I was out of his sight, I closed my eyes and willed myself to pull it together.

'Everything okay?' he asked in amusement when I sat back up in the chair.

'Just my napkin,' I explained feebly.

Jonathan's phone beeped and he pulled it from his pocket, still grinning at my social ineptitude.

'Looks like she's running later than she thought. She wants us to order, and she'll be here for dessert.'

'Great,' I muttered without enthusiasm.

'Would you rather not do this?' Jonathan questioned, his bemused expression was replaced by one that was suddenly too serious.

'Sorry.' I grimaced. 'That sounded really bad. I'm just . . . nervous.'

'Because of me?' He sounded genuinely surprised.

I shrugged, reluctantly looking over at him. His brows creased apologetically. I wanted to slink under the table.

'I'm not very good at this,' I confessed in a rush. 'I guess you could say I'm not the most social person, so even if you looked like that guy –' I nodded towards the overweight, balding man at the next table – 'I would still be a fumbling idiot.'

His cheeks creased around his broad white smile as he examined me curiously. I closed my eyes and cringed, realizing I'd just inadvertently told him he was hot. This was going *great*.

'You're just like her,' he mused, studying me. 'I mean, you don't look like her at all, and she talks a lot more when she's nervous, but you're just like her. She spilled coffee on me the first time we met.'

'And probably apologized a hundred times while trying to clean you up,' I grinned, thankful that he'd skipped right over my comment.

'I don't think I've heard someone talk so fast before,' he laughed. 'At first, I thought she was speaking a different language.'

I laughed, easily picturing it. 'So you met in a coffee shop?'

'No,' he answered. 'We met at work. I work for an architectural firm which collaborates on projects with her engineering firm. We met about six months ago, but we didn't go out until just recently. She refused to go out with me for the longest time.'

'Really?' The shock in my tone was heavier than I intended.

'The age thing,' he explained with a shrug. 'She kept saying I was too young.'

'Right,' I nodded, remembering her dilemma when she first spoke of him.

'But it's not a big deal, right?'

'Nope.' I shook my head. 'Age shouldn't matter.'

He looked right into me and grinned. I could feel my cheeks changing colour again, and I wanted to dump the water over my head to cool them off. I felt like an idiot. I still couldn't hold his eye for more than a second when he spoke to me. I'd never had anyone focus on me so intently before, but I wasn't sure he intended to do it. My mother had said he made her feel like she was the only one in the room when he looked at her – and I guess I didn't want to feel that way.

'Have you decided what you'd like to have this evening?'

the server asked, setting Jonathan's drink down. She glanced at both of us, but her bright smile re-emerged when Jonathan looked up at her.

While he was deciding, I glanced around the room and realized she wasn't the only one who couldn't stop staring. I was amused by the women adjusting their chair positions ever so slightly to get a better look.

'And you?' she asked, barely making eye contact with me. Every other glance flipped back to Jonathan to see if he was looking at her, but he was obliviously watching me, waiting for me to decide.

'I'll have the rib eye, medium rare,' I ordered, closing my menu and handing it to her.

'Are you sure you're okay?' he asked, reading me so easily.

'You attract a lot of attention, huh?' I stated honestly.

Jonathan grinned abashedly.

'Sorry,' I floundered. 'That was internal dialogue that should have stayed *inside* my head.'

'You're funny.' He chuckled.

'Unfortunately,' I groaned.

'They recognize me from the ads,' he admitted, averting his gaze. He was visibly uncomfortable as he took a sip from his glass.

'Ads?'

'I did a shoot for jeans when I was in college, to earn some money for school.'

'Oh,' I reacted. 'You think the reason just about every girl in this restaurant is staring at you is because they saw you in a magazine ad, like what, five or six years ago?'

Jonathan looked up at me with an embarrassed grin.

'Wow, I did it again, didn't I? I can't seem to keep from saying the most –'

'Honest,' he interrupted. 'You're being honest. It's pretty funny, really.'

'I'm an idiot,' I admitted, sinking in my chair. 'How's that for honesty?'

Jonathan laughed again. I was definitely giving him plenty to laugh at.

'Okay,' he said, trying to sound serious. 'We're supposed to be getting to know each other. Tell me something about you.'

I stared at him blankly, like he'd just asked me to recite the capitals of every country in the world.

'Okay.' He contemplated while I remained mute. 'Play any sports?'

My shoulders eased up and I nodded. 'Yeah, I'm playing basketball right now.'

'Are you any good?'

I released a breathy laugh. 'I'm decent.'

'You're better than decent,' he stated, challenging my dismissive tone.

'Why would you say that?' I questioned, my cheeks peaking in colour.

'You laughed, so you're not comfortable talking about yourself, meaning you're probably really good.'

I shrugged, my cheeks igniting as I adjusted my position in the chair. His ability to read me like a book was a bit disarming.

'Okay, let's put it this way. What would the papers say about you?'

'Umm . . . I guess they'd say that I'm the co-captain and

point guard of the first place team in our division. That I average twenty points a game and was All-American last season.'

'That's impressive,' he said with a slow nod. I shrugged sheepishly.

'What about you? Did you play any sports?' I was pretty certain I already knew the answer.

The server arrived, placing our plates in front of us.

'Is there anything else I can get for you?' she asked Jonathan.

'Emma, do you need anything?' He purposely diverted her attention to me.

'No, I'm fine,' I answered, trying to keep from smiling. She walked away with her shoulders slumped.

'What were we talking about?'

'What sports you played,' I reminded him.

'I played football.'

I nodded, having pretty much predicted it, based on his thick neck and broad muscular build.

'Don't nod like that,' he shot back, 'like you knew I was going to say that.'

'Well, come on,' I retorted, 'look at you.' He rolled his eyes. 'Fine.' I continued, 'What would the papers say about *you*?'

'The papers wouldn't mention me at all; I spent most of my time on the bench.'

I laughed. 'Really?'

'You don't have to *laugh*,' he feigned offence. 'I was second string receiver. I just wasn't as good as the starter.' He paused before blurting out, 'Okay, fine, I sucked. I couldn't hold on to the ball to save my life.'

I laughed again.

'But I swam. Still do when I can.'

'Would the papers mention *that*?'

'I guess they would,' he admitted modestly. 'I swam on the team at Penn State. It helped pay for my tuition.'

'So you were really good, huh?' I noted, impressed.

He shrugged with one shoulder.

'Wait, I thought modelling helped with your tuition?' I grinned.

'Yeah, that was a one-time thing, and it really didn't pay that much.'

I nodded, taunting him with a smirk on my face.

'Shouldn't have told you that, huh?'

'Sorry,' I laughed. 'I just think it's funny that you're immune –'

'Hi,' my mother greeted us excitedly before I could finish. Jonathan stood up to greet her with a hug and kiss – which made me suddenly interested in the food on my plate. I was still trying to wrap my head around the fact that she was dating, and I wasn't quite ready to handle seeing it. I knew I needed to get over it . . . fast. Especially when she sat down with us and clutched his hand throughout dessert, dominating the conversation in her nervous rush.

I watched as Jonathan hung on to her every word, every so often calming her enough so she actually sounded coherent.

It was evident that she was enthralled with him and he really cared for her. By the time we were ready to leave, I was . . . okay. She was happy. And that was all that mattered.

I pulled out my phone to check the time. 'Um, I have to go,' I said, interrupting my mother's story about the time she accidentally uploaded a YouTube video of singing cats for a presentation. 'Thank you for dinner.'

'What do you mean?' she questioned, sounding slightly disappointed.

'Evan's supposed to be meeting me at the house in twenty minutes.'

'Do you want to come back to the house?' she asked Jonathan, completely taking me by surprise.

'Sure,' Jonathan responded, signing the check.

Hellooo?! What's he like? lit up my phone when I entered the car.

He's nice, was all I texted back to Sara before driving home.

Evan was waiting for me when I pulled into the driveway.

'Sorry,' I said, grimacing as I hurried up the walkway.

'I just got here,' Evan assured me.

I unlocked the door as my mother and Jonathan pulled in behind me.

'How was it?' Evan asked before they entered the house.

'Okay,' I responded with a shrug. Evan eyed me curiously, knowing how nervous I had been about the dinner. 'He's nice,' I said, providing him with my standard response.

'Evan,' my mother greeted him happily. 'How are you?'

'Great. Thanks,' Evan replied, hanging up his jacket. He paused for a moment with the hanger in his hand when Jonathan walked in. Then he took my jacket from me and hung it up as well.

My mother introduced them. 'Jonathan, this is Evan.' Jonathan held out his hand with a broad smile.

'Nice to meet you.' Evan shook his hand in return.

'You too,' Jonathan responded. There was a strange silence while we all just stood there in the foyer looking at each other.

'We're going upstairs to study,' I finally announced, taking Evan by the hand.

'That's him, huh?' Evan said, closing the door behind us.

'Yup,' I said, sitting down on the bed. 'That's him.'

'Not who I was expecting,' he stated.

'Who were you expecting?' I asked, surprised by the contemplative look in his eyes.

'I don't know,' he said dismissively, sitting next to me on the bed. He leaned down and was about to kiss me when we were interrupted by a knock at my door.

'Hi!' Sara burst in. Then she narrowed her eyes at our frozen posture and rolled them with an impatient breath. 'Did I interrupt something?'

'No,' I replied quickly, struck by her annoyed tone. I slid up the bed to sit against the wall, distancing myself from Evan. 'What are you doing here?'

'I had to see the guy. Your text was pathetic.' She shot me an accusing look. 'Holy hotness. He is beautiful. I mean truly beau-ti-ful. Like the kind of beautiful they build statues to worship.'

Evan looked at her in amusement. I shook my head with a roll of my eyes.

'How old is he, like twenty?'

'No,' I replied like she was insane. 'He's twenty-eight.'

'Well, nicely done, Rachel,' Sara stated enviously. 'And just think, you'll get to see him like every day.'

I widened my eyes, silently begging her to shut her mouth. Evan's troubled looked returned. Obviously he did not share Sara's enthusiasm.

9

Just Not Right

'I'M NOT SURE WHAT I'M DOING.' MY MOTHER stared out the window while leaning against the counter.

I waited, but she didn't continue. So I prodded. 'About what?'

'Jonathan.'

I waited again, but she wouldn't say anything else. So I prodded a little more. 'What about Jonathan?'

And that opened the floodgates. She spun around. 'I'm not sure I'm ready for this. I haven't really *dated* a guy in a *very* long time. What if he doesn't really like me? What if he's too perfect for me? Look at him. He's so gorgeous; I have no idea what he's doing with me. I notice how the girls look at him. They're probably wondering the same thing. I don't think I can do this. I can't do this. Forget it, I'm ending it.'

I stared at her, stunned, wondering if she'd taken a single breath during that whole explosive monologue.

'Wait,' I said, shaking my head to make sense of her

dizzying words. 'Did you just convince yourself to break things off with him in ten seconds flat?'

She sighed in defeat.

'First of all, do what feels right. If you're not ready, then you're not ready. But don't end things because you think he's too good for you,' I scoffed. 'Besides, he doesn't give another girl a second glance when he's with you. It was obvious last night. He's into you. So give him a chance if you want to, because you like him. And don't walk away because you're afraid to find out *how much* you may like him.'

She exhaled audibly. 'Thank you. I can't believe I'm getting relationship advice from my seventeen-year-old daughter.' She laughed. I couldn't believe I'd just given my mother a pep talk on dating – apparently I'd taken a page from Sara's book of straightforwardness.

'Okay, so I'm going to do this.' She was convincing herself more than me. 'Do you think it would be okay if he spent the night some time?'

'Uh, sure,' I mumbled, wondering how we'd gone from whether she should date him to when she was going to sleep with him.

'That wouldn't be too weird, right? I can make sure he leaves before you get up.'

'It's okay,' I answered slowly. Apparently she had no idea I'd already gone through this *weirdness* more than I cared to remember.

The next night, Jonathan was over watching a movie with my mother when I arrived home from Sara's. I didn't stop on my way up the stairs, not wanting to interrupt them.

'Hey, Emma,' Jonathan called, despite my best efforts to be invisible.

'Uh, hi,' I replied, not looking back.

I stayed in my room for the rest of the night, reading. Without consciously meaning to, I'd find myself listening for the front door, indicating that Jonathan had left. But I never heard it before I dozed off.

'Is she okay?'

I froze at the sound of Jonathan's voice. Clamping my hand over my mouth I stifled my breaths as I sat upright in my bed. I remained still. He sounded close, like he was right outside my door. My eyes flickered in the dark, waiting to see if he'd actually come in.

'She does that,' my mother explained apologetically. 'Just come back to bed, okay? She'll be all right.' There were a few seconds of silence, and then his footsteps trailed off towards her room. I heard the distinct click of her door, and collapsed back into my bed, feeling terrible that I'd woken them up. Which transitioned into an alarmed recognition that he'd stayed the night.

I stared at the ceiling, waiting for the sun to make its appearance, listening to the wind screech against my windows and finally succumbing to the realization that sleep had evaded me once again. I pulled the covers up to my chin, wishing I were in California, not stuck in this never-ending winter and this ice box called a house.

I finally threw the covers off, resigned to starting the day, despite the lack of sun. I slid on a pair of socks and rifled through my drawers, pulling out clothes for the day before dragging my feet towards the bathroom. I paused outside my door when I noticed the kitchen light was on, creating a soft glow in the dark foyer. The coffee maker gurgled, and the robust aroma drifted up the stairs.

Jonathan emerged from the kitchen with his hair wet and brushed back, creating smooth dark waves. He was dressed in a shirt and tie. His professional attire made him appear older. This mature look made me grin. He looked so . . . grown up in a GQ sort of way. Jonathan stopped abruptly when he spotted me, startled.

'Sorry,' I said. My cheeks flushed with colour at being caught watching him.

He held his finger to his mouth and pointed to my mother's door. 'She's still sleeping.' I nodded in understanding. 'Did I wake you?'

'No,' I whispered in reply.

He continued to the closet to remove his jacket and set the strap of his computer bag over his shoulder. He raised his hand in a wave before slipping out the front door. I watched him leave without a word, finding my hand still frozen in the air long after the front door had closed and his truck could be heard starting up. *Why am I still standing here?* I shook myself out of my daze and continued to the bathroom to shower and prepare for the day.

'Rachel's here,' Sara informed me as I was getting ready to run out on the court for our night game. 'Oh, and we're going to a party tonight after the game.'

I watched her walk into the gym, waving to somebody with an exaggerated smile, mouthing, 'Hi.' I stared after her in shock. What kind of bomb was that to drop right before a game with our school's rival?!

I could hear my mother screaming my name as I dribbled the ball down the court. I blocked her and the rest of the chanting crowd out as I called the plays to put my teammates in motion. I let the movement on the court keep me focused.

I passed the ball to Jill outside the key along the baseline. She dribbled in towards the net and popped it back to me. Another teammate set up a pick to allow me to dribble down the paint and lay it in. The bleachers erupted, but all I could hear was a buzz of voices.

Weslyn walked away with a three-point win, thanks to Jill's aggressive rebounding and unshakable accuracy on the free-throw line. I held my own, contributing double-digit points and multiple assists. I was relieved to walk away with the win.

I grabbed my things from the bench and heard someone shout, 'Emily!' among the crowd of faces. I turned to find my mother walking towards me, and nearly fell over when I spotted Jonathan a few steps behind her.

She greeted me with a smile. 'Hi! So glad we came to this game. It was intense.'

I smiled awkwardly, my face fiery as I looked everywhere but at him.

'Nice game,' Jonathan congratulated me, moving in closer to my mother.

'Thanks,' I replied, my pulse racing. I had no idea why I was so nervous to see him. It wasn't like I'd never met him before.

'I was hoping you were going to score more so Jonathan could see your outside shots, especially the three-pointers.'

'The defence was tough,' I replied with a shrug. 'But thanks for coming.'

'Are you coming home?'

'Umm, I guess Sara wants to go to a party or something.' I wiped the sweat off my chin using my shoulder, scanning the gym for Sara and Evan. But I knew they'd be in the lobby like they usually were after my games, nowhere around to rescue me from the awkwardness.

'Have fun,' she replied. 'See you later then?'

'Yeah.' I glanced up to catch Jonathan's eye as he nodded with a smile. My mother took his hand and blended in with the remaining fans exiting the gym.

'*Who* was that?'

I turned to discover Jill and Casey standing behind me, practically drooling.

'My mother,' I responded casually, knowing exactly who they meant. That's when it occurred to me why I'd been so uncomfortable. Every girl in the school was ogling him as he and my mother made their way out of the gym. It was kinda pathetic.

'And *he's* her boyfriend?' Jill asked, still gawking after his perfectly placed hair.

'I guess,' I mumbled, shaking my head as they practically melted in front of me. I grabbed my warm-ups and stranded them by the bench, staring.

'And why did you tell Evan he couldn't hang out with us at the party?' I asked when we pulled out of the school parking lot.

'I need girl time,' Sara explained briefly. 'And besides, does he always have to hang out with us?'

'We're going to *a party*,' I pointed out bluntly. 'If you want *girl time* then we should do something else. And *no*, he does not always have to hang out with us, and he doesn't. Did he do something wrong? What's going on with you? You've been acting kinda strange lately.'

'Nothing's wrong. I'm fine,' she sighed impatiently. Her perpetual bad mood was so very confusing, and far from resembling my best friend – it was freaking me out. And what, if anything, did it have to do with Evan?

We walked in the side door between the house and the garage. Bass boomed from the basement; laughter and hollering could be heard further down the hall. This house was modest compared to some of the monstrosities in Weslyn. We were considered on 'the other side of town', closer to where I used to live.

We ventured towards the laughter to find a group sitting around the kitchen table with cards in their hands and red cups in front of them, daring one another to drink for various absurd reasons. There were others crammed into the small kitchen, either leaning against the Formica counters or passing through to get to the keg.

Sara made her way to the back porch where the keg rested in a trash can filled with snow.

'Can you stay over tonight?' she asked before taking a cup from the stack.

'Sure,' I replied with a shrug, hugging myself with a shiver. I texted my mother as we walked back through the kitchen, then followed Sara down the shag-carpeted stairs to the basement. I stopped at the bottom when I saw Evan playing pool to the right and hesitated long enough to wave and apologize with a grimace as I continued after Sara in the other direction. We walked into a small, wood-panelled space with a beat-up couch covered in multicoloured afghans and a console television pushed into a hollowed-out fireplace.

Mandy Cochran smiled at the sight of us, shuffling through the bodies to get to where we stood, while Sara inspected the scene. I didn't really know Mandy; she played volleyball with Sara. But this was her house, so I knew we should at least make an effort to say hi.

Sara scanned the room, not thrilled with what she saw. 'Back upstairs,' she insisted, completely ignoring Mandy. My face twitched in confusion, but I followed after her anyway. I held up my hand to wave in apology when I saw Mandy's smile fade as she watched us disappear up the stairs.

By the time we were back in the kitchen, Sara needed a refill. Instead of following her out to the deck like a pathetic sidekick, I took a seat on a wooden stool next to the kitchen counter. I watched the card game, trying to figure out the rules and if there was a point to the absurdity. I quickly discovered there really wasn't a point – it was all about getting drunk and making people do stupid things in the process. I sighed and shook my head.

'Hey, I didn't know you were going to be here,' Jill exclaimed when she and Casey walked into the kitchen with pink bottles in their hands. 'Where's Evan?'

'I don't know,' I replied, making a face – finding it strange that was the first question they asked. 'I'm here with Sara.'

'Ooh, are you fighting?' Casey asked, leaning in like she was about to hear a secret.

'No,' I answered, drawing out the 'o' and looking at

them like they were crazy. 'I think he's downstairs playing pool.'

'So what do you know about your mother's hot boyfriend?' Jill drilled.

'Not much,' I replied shortly, annoyed with the question.

'I think he may be hotter than Evan,' Casey interjected.

'No,' Jill argued, then paused and said, 'Okay, maybe.'

'Seriously?' I finally interrupted, wanting to put an end to the conversation.

'I was just saying,' Jill retorted defensively.

'That's messed up,' I shot back. 'You don't compare my boyfriend with my mother's. That's so very twisted.'

'True,' Casey agreed, 'but he is –'

I walked away before she could finish. Unfortunately, this wasn't a big enough house to lose them, so I slipped into the bathroom when I saw the door open. This was the first party I'd been to in Weslyn since last May. Apparently, I hadn't missed much.

I looked around for Sara upon exiting the bathroom and found her in a corner talking to a tall blond with dark eyebrows. They were laughing and leaning towards each other, her hand occasionally brushing his arm – all the signature flirting moves.

'That's Neil's cousin,' Jill explained from beside me. She had apparently been waiting for me to get out of the bathroom. 'He's visiting for the weekend from New Hampshire.'

'Oh great,' I groaned. This was not going to go down well. And right on cue, Sara's smile faltered. She turned abruptly and stormed out on to the deck. The guy was left dumbstruck, looking around to see if anyone had noticed. The girls giggled next to me, indicating that not only did they witness the ditching, now everyone at the party would know about it as well.

I sighed and followed after Sara.

'Hey.'

She continued to pour the beer into her red cup, not looking up.

Before I could find the words to make her feel better, which wasn't something I was used to doing, I heard, 'I dare you to jump.'

I looked over and a guy with a dark green flannel shirt and a backwards baseball hat was standing on the top railing of the deck.

'Is he serious?' I asked Sara. She just let out an amused laugh.

Then he was gone. I rushed to the railing. All I could see was his baseball hat. The rest of him had disappeared into the mountainous snow bank below the deck. He thrust his arms out of the snow and tilted his head back, releasing a guttural holler of triumph. I was stunned to see him emerge in one piece.

That's when the insanity took over. More guys leapt into the snowdrift, yelling and whooping as they jumped off the railing.

I had no interest in watching these guys break their necks, so I went back inside, discovering Sara already there. I passed Evan as he and a few guys made their way to the deck to watch the recklessness. I caught his eye and he brushed his hand along mine. That subtle connection sent a current through my body with a warm shiver.

Sara slammed her red cup down, redirecting my attention. 'Let's get out of here.'

As we pulled down the street, two police cars drove past with their lights on. I wondered where they were going. Then it hit me that the neighbours must have called them. There weren't acres of land or trees separating the houses on this street, so the noise in the back yard had probably carried, disrupting the neighbourhood.

I glanced over at Sara to say something about the busted party, but she remained still, staring out the window. I wanted to cheer her up, but I had no idea *what* to say. Just as I was about to break the silence, she exclaimed, 'New Hampshire! He was from fucking New Hampshire!' She clenched her fists. 'Are you kidding me?! This is so not funny!'

My mouth dropped open. She continued to rant about how well they'd got along. He had even asked her to go out this weekend before he'd finally told her where he lived – indicating that they'd probably never see each other again.

'Sara, you have to tell me what's going on with you,' I demanded emphatically. 'And don't say "nothing", because I know there is. It can't just be this guy.'

'There's nothing wrong with me,' she snapped, practically biting my head off.

'Really?' I countered defensively. 'I think there is because you're acting like a bitch.'

And just like that the car was silent, and I was filled with remorse. 'I'm sorry. I didn't mean that,' I said as we pulled into the driveway. 'I'm just frustrated because I don't understand what's going on.'

'I'm fine,' she huffed, slamming the car door after her.

Snow started to fall when I stepped out of the car. Perfect. We'd just finished shovelling after the last storm. This winter was as miserable as Sara.

I walked up the stairs after Sara, who refused to even look at me. My phone beeped as she shut the bathroom door.

Meet me out front when Sara passes out.

I remained as patient as I could, staying in the bathroom, pacing, while I waited for her to groan herself to sleep. Fifteen minutes later, I slipped out and poked my head into the bedroom to hear the sound of deep breaths.

I crept down the stairs and out the front door. Evan was sitting on the front steps, snow coating his knit hat. He stood when I stepped out.

'Finally.' He pulled me towards him, my hand still on the doorknob, barely closing it behind me. I breathed him in as he pressed his firm lips against mine. I melted in relief, needing this connection more than he realized. 'That bad, huh?' Then again, maybe he did realize.

'You got out just in time,' Evan said, sitting next to me. 'The cops showed up and broke up the party.'

'Yeah, we saw them,' I muttered, still feeling guilty about what I'd said to Sara. I sat down on the top step, not caring that I was sitting on a sheet of snow.

Evan sat down next to me. 'Are you okay?' He nudged my shoulder with his and took my hand.

'I have no idea what's wrong with Sara. She's miserable.' Then I considered it and realized. 'She's been a little off for a while now, but it wasn't that bad until now. Something happened and she won't tell me what.'

Evan breathed in contemplation. 'I think I know what to do.'

I looked at him hopefully. He pulled out his phone and looked at the screen.

'What? What should we do?' I demanded desperately.

'Oh, sorry,' Evan replied, distracted as he texted. 'It's Jared.'

Then he put his phone back in his pocket and said, 'Maybe we can at least make her smile.'

'I'll try anything.'

Evan leapt down the stairs, sinking into the snow up to his shins.

'What are you doing?' I asked, like he was insane.

'How about we make a snowman?'

I laughed. 'You *are* crazy.'

'True,' he agreed with his infamous smile, 'but that's why you love me.'

'You're probably right.' I smiled wider and joined him in the snow, sinking up to my knees.

I fell over several times, losing my footing while rolling the large ball around the front yard. Evan kept chuckling at my inability to stay upright. Sara would have been laughing uncontrollably if she'd seen me. I hoped this ridiculous semblance of a snowperson would at least crack a smile.

As Evan was lifting the head to place it on the other two body parts, I slipped for the millionth time and slid down the small incline on my back. I let out a loud yelp and began laughing when I finally slid to a stop. Instead of helping me up, Evan opted to lie down next to me. From above our heads, light spread across the second-floor windows, and a curtain was pulled back.

Anna spread the curtains wider and opened the window.

We remained still, hoping she wouldn't notice us. She squinted. 'Emma? Is that you? And . . . Evan?'

'Good evening, Mrs McKinley,' Evan waved from our flattened position on the snow-covered lawn.

'What are you . . .' she stopped herself when she saw the snowman beneath her window. 'Come in soon, Emma. It's late. And try to keep it down please.'

'Sorry.' I cringed guiltily.

She shut the window as Carl asked, 'What are they doing . . .' A moment later, the windows darkened and all was still.

That's when I realized the snow had stopped. I looked up at the wisps of clouds quickly passing over us, weaving through the stars. Evan lay quietly beside me, our hands clasped between us.

'I'm not sure I can feel my legs,' I shivered as the cold from the ground seeped into me, but I still didn't make a motion to get up.

Evan sat up, and just when I thought he was going to pull me up too, he leaned down and found my lips, melting the crystals of snow that had landed on my face. His mouth moved gently along mine, warming my entire body.

'You make me forget how much I hate the cold,' I breathed with my eyes still closed.

'Let's finish the snowman,' Evan finally said, pulling me to my feet. I looked down at my snow-caked jeans and tried to brush them off without success.

While I packed snow between each layer, Evan rifled through his car and pulled a bag of candy out of his backpack.

'Sweet tooth?' I questioned when I saw the massive amounts of chocolate, liquorice and jelly beans in the white paper bag.

'You could say that,' he confessed with a grin.

We pulled red liquorice and jelly beans out of the bag to create a face and waves of hair.

I took off my scarf for the finishing touch after he'd inserted stick arms that looked like they were reaching for the stars. We stepped back to take in our creation. I couldn't stop laughing.

Evan admired it proudly. 'She has to at least smile.'

'I hope so,' I sighed.

Evan left to drive home as it started to flurry once again. I seriously had lost feeling in the majority of my body and desperately needed to thaw.

I took off most of my snow-caked clothes in the foyer, exposing pale legs that were now bright red. Sneaking up the stairs, I placed my crystallized items in the bath-tub, readied for bed and snuggled in under the blankets, shivering.

I looked across at Sara's bed. She looked so peaceful, like nothing in the world could possibly be wrong. I just wanted her back.

My phone beeped next to my head, and I picked it up to read, *Don't worry. We'll fix her.*

10

Distraction

WHEN I AWOKE, SARA'S BED WAS TOSSED and vacant. I found her in the rec room, scowling over a bowl of cereal, watching a syndicated reality television show. I left her to fester, assuming she hadn't seen the snowman yet.

I walked down the stairs and peeked out the window that overlooked the front lawn. As I was about to walk to the kitchen, what I had seen struck me. I opened the front door and stared at the sad image. Shutting the door with a grunt, I stormed up the stairs.

'What did you do to the snowman?' I demanded from atop the stairs.

'I kicked it in the face,' she answered, continuing to watch the television without a blink.

I went into the bedroom and got dressed, grabbed my things and left without a word. I couldn't look at the pathetic dilapidated head lolling on the ground as I backed out of the driveway. I clenched my teeth in aggravation and drove away.

I couldn't respond to Evan's *So what happened?* text. I just wanted to get away from the miserable girl who had over-taken Sara's body.

The front door was unlocked when I arrived home, but there didn't seem to be anyone there. My mother's car was still in the driveway covered with a dusting of snow, and the kitchen light was on, but the house was quiet as I kicked off my boots and shed my jacket.

I froze when I pushed my door open and found Jonathan at my desk. The squeak of the hinges made him spin around with a start.

'Emma, hi.' He greeted me with an inflated smile, like he'd just been caught doing something he shouldn't.

I was so shocked to find him in my room, I couldn't say anything.

'You scared me,' Jonathan laughed uncomfortably, attempting to recover, and then explained nonchalantly, 'Rachel said to use your computer to check my email. Sorry. I obviously freaked you out.'

His words shook me from my gaping expression. 'It's okay,' I assured him slowly, my cheeks warming at my overreaction.

'Are you sure?' he asked, clenching his teeth with a grimace. 'You don't look okay.'

'Really, it's fine,' I repeated, easing the tension in my shoulders.

'So, did you check it?' I finally asked.

'What?'

'Your *email*,' I emphasized with a laugh, recognizing how ridiculously we were both acting.

'Oh, yeah. I did,' he faltered, folding down the laptop

before standing up. 'I was about to leave but noticed the pictures. You play soccer too?'

'Yeah. I'm better at it than basketball,' I replied, setting my backpack on the floor at the foot of my bed.

'You were quite amazing last night,' he stated, making me shift uncomfortably. 'So if you're better at soccer, then I would definitely want to see that.'

'Well, it's paying for me to go to Stanford,' I admitted, embarrassed embers lighting up my cheeks.

'Do you always turn this red?' he asked, examining my face.

'Usually,' I admitted, my eyes drifting towards the floor.

'Sorry,' he chuckled. 'It's . . . cute.'

My breath faltered for a second.

'Thanks for letting me use your computer.'

'Any time,' I nodded, still unable to meet his gaze without my face flaming up.

He paused before continuing. 'I've been meaning to say something, but . . .'

'What?' I asked, suddenly nervous.

'I'm really sorry about the first time we met. Rachel said you were going out and to just come in. I really didn't mean to walk in on you like that. I don't want you to feel uncomfortable around me.'

And just like that, it was *even more* uncomfortable. I nodded, not sure what to say, wishing he'd never brought it up.

'I just made it awkward, didn't I?'

Of course, my glowing cheeks gave that away.

'Umm . . . a little,' I admitted with a half grin.

'Sorry,' he grimaced. 'That's not what I wanted to do. Wow, I'm usually not so bad at this.'

I couldn't help but smile at his faltering confidence. With that one sentence, he had just become a little more, well, like me.

'What?' he asked, his eyes searching mine. 'Did I say something wrong again?'

'No,' I answered, connecting with his dark brown eyes with a slight smile, making the corners of his mouth curve as well.

'Can you give me a hand?' my mother called from downstairs. When Jonathan and I emerged from my bedroom, she cocked her head to one side at the sight of us. 'Uh, hi. What are you guys up to?' Her words came out in a hesitant pattern, with a hint of unease.

'I was checking my email,' Jonathan explained casually. 'Remember, you said to use Emily's computer?' I looked over at him, surprised to hear my formal name. But then again, seeing my mother's questioning eyes, it was the right choice.

'Oh,' she stated, suddenly remembering. 'Thanks for letting him use your computer.' And instantly, all was right with the world.

I shut myself up in my room for the rest of the day; reading, studying and listening to music. I wasn't an expert at occupying my time. I actually preferred not to be alone for too long because that's when the thinking began.

And that's where I found myself late Saturday night, lying in my bed staring at the white above me. I ran my hand along my neck, and a cold chill ran through my body.

An image flashed through my head as fast as the snap of a picture, but the panic and fear wrapped in it forced me to sit up in bed. I shook off the remembrance that had forced its way to the surface – her frigid hands and my silent pleas for help. And then it was gone. I was alone in the house once again.

I searched the kitchen for something to eat, but there were scarce pickings. My mother and I kept missing each other for dinner, so I'd stocked up on microwavable anything to keep me nourished. But my supply was dwindling.

I called to order a pizza, and decided to pick up a movie along the way. As much as I wished I could hibernate for the winter to avoid the bone-chilling cold, I sucked it up and drove towards the commercial side of town, far away from the homes that paid for the silence, where the neon was allowed to glow.

I pulled into the gas station that had a movie rental machine. There were a few carloads of Weslyn students lingering inside, trying to decide where to go – whose party to crash. I didn't make eye contact as I waited behind an older man to pick out a movie.

'Hey, Emma.' One of the girls recognized me. I looked over at the soda cooler where she and two other girls were choosing forms of caffeine. I smiled politely, trying to place her. She may have been in my Art class, but I was pretty sure she was a junior.

'Great game last night,' one of the guys said.

'Thanks,' I returned in a low voice, stepping up to take my turn at the movie machine.

'Do you want to go to a party with us?' another girl asked.

'No, that's okay,' I replied, trying to make a hasty decision and selecting a movie. 'I'm staying in tonight.'

'See you around.'

I made my way out of the gas mart and waved with an awkward smile. It was strange being recognized outside school without Evan or Sara. But at the same time, it felt kinda good. It was like waking up to discover I was my own person and people actually wanted to hang out with me. I grinned as I started my car.

I returned to the house, prepared for my solo night, with a new found sense of confidence. I was somewhat disappointed to see Jonathan's truck had returned. It was barely nine o'clock.

I pushed open the front door and heard the buzz of the TV in the living room. After abandoning my shoes at the door, I brought the pizza into the room. Jonathan was sitting alone, and appeared surprised to see me.

'You're back early.' I set the pizza on the coffee table.

'Rachel's sick,' Jonathan explained. I nodded in understanding. 'I thought you'd be out.'

'Staying in,' I replied. 'Hungry?'

'Uh, sure.' Jonathan got up from the couch and crossed over to the kitchen. 'What do you want to drink?'

'Diet Coke, please,' I answered, looking around for my mother. I hung up my jacket and Jonathan came back over with drinks, paper plates and napkins. 'Is she in bed?'

'Yeah. She drank a little too much cough medicine,' Jonathan explained, sucking in air through his clenched teeth. He handed me the soda bottle. 'And then had a couple of glasses of wine on top of it. I wouldn't be surprised if she's out till Tuesday.'

'Great,' I said with a shake of my head.

'What movie did you get?' he asked, eyeing the plastic casing.

'You know what? I have no idea,' I admitted, pulling it open. 'I was in a rush and just picked a new release. Do you want to watch it with me?'

'Sure,' he responded.

I looked at the title and groaned, 'Oh great. It's a horror flick. Exactly what I don't need.'

Jonathan laughed. 'We'll keep the lights on while we watch it.'

'Did you think for a second I'd let you turn them off?'

He laughed again, taking the movie and inserting it into the DVD player while I doled out pizza on the paper plates.

There wasn't really a point to the plot, except maybe to sear my brain with lifelong nightmares – but then again, I already had those. I watched the entire movie with my knees pulled into me and a pillow clutched to my chest. I'd shove my face into the pillow whenever the music chimed in warning. Jonathan would talk me through what was happening and then let me know when it was safe to look again.

By the time the credits rolled, I wasn't sure if I was ever going to sleep again. Jonathan changed to the sports channel, where talk of the Super Bowl helped to dispel the disturbing images.

'What are you doing for the game tomorrow?' Jonathan asked, tucking in the lip of the pizza box and stacking the crust-laden plates on top of it.

'Oh, uh, nothing. I mean, I'm watching it, but I don't have plans.'

'I'm sure there's a few Super Bowl parties you could go to.'

'Maybe,' I admitted, not having given it a second thought. 'But, I think I'd rather *watch* the game. You know?'

'Yes,' he agreed. 'We're going to a party with some of Rachel's friends, and I have a feeling the game's going to be background. I'd actually like to watch it too.' He shrugged and carried the box into the kitchen.

It felt like I hadn't moved the entire movie. I stretched my legs and stood to go to bed.

'Are you sure you'll be able to sleep?' Jonathan asked when he saw me head for the stairs.

'Probably not,' I admitted, 'but that's not different from any other night.'

He gave me a questioning look, but didn't say anything.

'Goodnight.'

'Goodnight, Emma,' Jonathan replied, watching me enter my room.

'Emma,' the dark beckoned. A banging followed. I fought to hold on to the bed, but the sheets were slipping. The room continued to tilt, determined to dump me into the black hole at the end of my bed. Horrific screams cried out from the abyss.

'Emma,' the dark called out again.

I kicked my feet to work my way further up the mattress.

The banging grew louder, and I shot up in bed. My sheets were tangled around me, and I was breathing so fast, I was practically hyperventilating. I turned on the light next to my bed.

'Emma?' came from the other side of the door. 'Are you okay? Will you open the door?'

It was Jonathan. I inhaled deeply to calm my nerves. 'I'm fine,' I answered, sweeping strands of sweat-soaked hair from my face with a shaking hand.

'Please open the door?' he requested again.

'I'm okay, really,' I responded, unravelling the sheets around my legs.

'Please,' he pleaded. 'Just open the door, okay?'

I hesitated and stared at the door. 'Fine. Just a minute.'

I crawled out of the bed and flipped the blanket over the top to hide the mess beneath. I tied my hair back in an elastic and pulled on a hoodie before unlocking the door and slowly opening it.

'I'm okay, see.' I looked up at him, shoving my shaking hands in the front pocket of my sweatshirt. His eyes softened as he took me in. 'It was just a dream. Sorry I woke you.'

'You shouldn't go back to bed,' he advised calmly.

'Huh?'

'When you have a nightmare like that, you need to get out of your bed, to get away from it,' he explained. 'Get a glass of water, watch television, something to clear your head. That way, when you go back to sleep, the nightmare's not still there, waiting for you.'

I remained quiet, taking in his words. His eyes were soft and empathetic. 'Come on. Let's watch TV for a while, okay?'

'Sure,' I agreed, surrendering. 'But you don't have to stay up.'

'Don't worry about me,' he responded. 'Let's go see what they're selling at this hour.'

I followed him down the stairs and curled up on the couch under a blanket while he sat on the love seat, flipping through the channels. I glanced over at him as the soft light of the television lit the lines of his strong jaw.

I would never have predicted that he'd know anything about needing to escape nightmares. He seemed impervious to fear, so confident and assured.

'The infomercials can be addictive,' he noted, glancing over at me. I flipped my eyes to the TV, my cheeks peaking with colour, having been caught staring. He continued as if he hadn't noticed. 'You need to stay away from them because the next thing you know you're watching the sun come up, convinced that a six-inch cloth can wash your entire car, and still be clean enough to wipe the windows.'

I nodded, not completely paying attention; a part of me was still trapped in the dark.

'It gets better,' he promised, observing me intently. He sounded so sure of his words.

'How would you know?' I peered into his dark brown eyes, trying to look past them for answers, but he wouldn't let me in.

'Believe me, it does,' Jonathan whispered, looking away. In that quick moment, the confidence in his eyes faltered, giving way to something else. I wasn't quite sure what I'd seen, but I inadvertently shivered when I caught a glimpse of it.

11

All Better

'HOW ARE YOU FEELING?' I ASKED, WHEN MY mother slumped down the stairs the next morning. Her nose was raw and red around the edges; her eyes were watery and puffy. She looked miserable – I shouldn't have even asked.

'I think I'm dying,' she snuffled.

'You should go back to bed. Tell me what you need and I'll get it for you.'

'Tea,' she requested pitifully. 'And some flu medicine so my head doesn't feel like it's going to explode any more.'

'I'll get that,' Jonathan offered, appearing at the kitchen entrance, showered and dressed.

'Thanks,' she said in a nasally voice, before sneezing into the balled-up tissue in her hand. 'I wish you weren't seeing me like this.'

'Don't even go there,' Jonathan consoled her with a warm smile. 'You're sick, and even sick, you're beautiful.' He wrapped his arms around her as she flopped on to his chest. He held her and smoothed the damp strands of hair that were stuck to her feverish face. He was braver than I was. I was afraid of going within three feet of her. She was oozing from every orifice.

'I'll bring the tea up in a minute,' I told her as Jonathan escorted her back up the stairs.

'I'll be right back,' Jonathan announced a few minutes later on his way out the door.

I took the tea to her room and set it down on the night stand. She had her eyes closed and the blankets pulled up to her nose.

'Do you like him?' she asked as I was walking towards the door.

I turned back towards her. She propped herself up on her elbow and carefully sipped the hot tea.

'Jonathan?' I clarified, not expecting her question.

Before I could answer, she said, 'I *really* like him, and I hope you do too.'

'Um, yeah, sure. He's nice.'

'Thanks for the tea.' She nuzzled back into the blankets, closing her eyes with a grin on her face. Even in her sickness, she was still a love-struck teenager.

'Looks like you'll get to watch the game after all,' I noted after Jonathan returned from the pharmacy. 'Where are you going?'

Jonathan hesitated. 'Actually, I told Rachel I'd stay here with her.'

'I'm not going anywhere,' I offered. 'I can take care of her if you want to do something else.'

'I'd rather stay here, if that's okay.'

'Sure,' I answered in surprise.

'Where are Evan and Sara?'

'Evan's at Cornell with his brother, and . . . I don't know what Sara's up to.'

Jonathan looked over at me, hearing the change in my tone upon mentioning Sara. He didn't ask; he just nodded.

I offered to pick up football food while Jonathan tended to my mother. Especially since we were running low on . . . everything. I'd pretty much assumed the role of grocery shopper in the house. My mother would shop when she wanted to prepare a specific meal, but with our conflicting schedules, that wasn't very often.

I didn't mind too much. She'd leave me a twenty and a small list of things she needed. The list was usually more than twenty dollars, but whatever. I covered the rest with the money that was deposited into my account each month. Money I hadn't had access to for years, but was now in my total control.

I'd gotten to know the aisles well enough to get in and out of the store quickly. Except for today – it was insane.

'I think every person in three towns was at the grocery store today,' I complained to Jonathan, struggling with white plastic bags strung across both arms.

'Let me help you.' Jonathan rushed from the living room, relieving me of half the bags. 'Is that everything?'

'If it's not, then too bad. I'm not going back to that zoo.' I slipped off my shoes and followed him to the kitchen.

'I meant, is there anything else in the car?' He smiled at my dramatic response.

'No, this is everything,' I answered, embarrassed by my reaction. 'How's Rachel?'

'Passed out,' Jonathan responded, proceeding to empty the bags and put everything in its place. 'I have to go out for a while. Would you mind covering for me until I get back? I'll be here in time for kick-off. If she wakes up, just tell her I went to buy more tissues or something.'

'Sure,' I replied. 'You shouldn't need an excuse, you know.' I knew I shouldn't have said it as soon as I did. 'Sorry.'

'No, you're right,' he agreed. 'I just feel bad leaving when she's not feeling great. Although, I'm not sure I can do anything to make her feel better. But she keeps saying she wants me to stay.'

'She always wants you to stay,' I blurted – my filter apparently shut off.

'Wow,' he absorbed my candour with wide eyes. 'Am I here too much?'

'No,' I replied quickly. 'That's not what I meant. Sorry, I'm a complete idiot today.'

'You're doing that honesty thing again. Don't worry about it.' He paused and added, 'Don't ever feel like you can't say what you're thinking, okay?'

'Are you sure?' I questioned with a smirk. 'You'll probably end up hating me.'

'Unlikely,' he said with a bright smile, putting the milk in the refrigerator. My cheeks warmed with his comment. 'Oh, here's my phone number.' He scribbled on a piece of paper on the kitchen table. 'Just in case you do need something while I'm out.'

'Okay. Thanks.' I picked up the number as he walked out the door and decided to program it into my phone, *just in case*.

My mother didn't stir the entire time Jonathan was gone, thankfully. I hadn't been looking forward to telling her he wasn't there.

I texted back and forth with Evan most of the afternoon. He and Jared were at an all-day Super Bowl party off-campus. It sounded like quite the spectacle from the details Evan provided. I let him go right before kick-off, wanting him to enjoy the game with his brother and not worry about responding to me.

I kept checking my phone anyway, still not having heard from Sara. I wanted her to be the first to reach out after the way we'd left things, and it took everything I had not to text her as I grew more anxious.

Jonathan returned five minutes into the game.

'Ah,' he groaned, looking flushed and freshly changed. 'I missed kick-off.'

'Don't worry,' I consoled him. 'Nothing's happened really. You look . . . different.' It was hard not to notice.

'I had to tap back into my life for a while,' he explained, sitting down on the couch next to me with his eyes fixed on the game. 'Got a haircut, went to the gym, made sure my place hadn't burned down.'

I laughed, not expecting his sense of humour. 'Well the hair looks good.'

'Thanks.' He flashed me a blush-inducing grin. I reached for a handful of chips, to keep from saying something else outlandish about how good he looked. 'I bought beer. You don't mind, do you?'

'Uh, no,' I answered, surprised that he asked. 'It's football. Isn't that part of the guys' book of conduct? That a beer must be in your hand while watching?'

He laughed. 'Do you want one? I could overlook the fact that you're a girl for the night.'

'No,' I responded emphatically. 'Not legal, remember?'

'Oh, that's right,' he answered, feigning forgetfulness. 'I'm supposed to be the responsible adult, right?' He shook his head like the thought sounded ridiculous. He got up from the couch and went into the kitchen, coming back with a beer and a Mountain Dew.

'Perfect, thanks,' I said, taking the bottle from his hand.

We watched football and ate overly greasy food while making fun of the overpriced commercials that fell flat and laughing at those that were worth the millions. And we'd take turns checking on my mother whenever we heard her moan.

In the middle of the third quarter, the doorbell rang. Jonathan and I peered at each other quizzically, neither expecting a visitor. I shrugged and got up to answer the door.

'Hey,' Sara said, as soon as the door opened. She had a number nine written in gold on her cheek, with her red hair pulled back into a high ponytail. I let the door go so she could enter. She peered into the living room to find Jonathan.

'Hi, Jonathan.' She gave a small wave.

'Hey, Sara,' he responded. 'Nice look.'

'Thanks,' she smiled.

Sara looked back towards me nervously. 'I tried to call you,' she said, pulling on the corner of her shirt.

'You did? I'm sorry, I didn't hear my phone.' I groaned inwardly, frustrated that I'd missed it – most likely I'd been checking on my mother when she'd called.

'Can we talk?' she asked in a quiet voice, flipping her eyes from the floor up to me. 'I mean, if you guys are watching the game, I can come back.'

'Seriously?' I stared at her incredulously. She pressed her lips into a small smile. 'Let's go upstairs.'

I closed the door behind us and sat at the end of my bed, expecting her to sit next to me, but she began pacing.

'Sara, what's wrong with you?' I demanded. 'You know you don't have to worry about what to say to me. You never have before.'

'But I've never been such a bitch to you before either,' she blurted out. She stopped pacing, realizing what she'd just confessed. She looked at me and I started to laugh. I knew the honesty would find its way to the surface eventually. She smiled in return.

'What happened?' I asked. Sara sat down next to me. 'Did I do something wrong?'

Sara sighed. 'No. I just . . . I'm an idiot really.'

That didn't explain anything. 'You're going to need to be more specific.'

'I think I was a little jealous of you.' She kept her eyes on the floor.

'Of me?' I questioned in disbelief. 'That doesn't even make sense.'

Sara took in an audible breath. 'I know it's stupid. And it's going to sound even more pathetic when I say it, but I'm jealous of the way you and Evan are together. I mean, I want to find that – that guy who looks at me the way he looks at you. You don't have to even touch; he could seriously be at the other end of the house, but you have that connection – no matter where you are. It's crazy. And I want it.'

Wow, I mouthed, stunned.

'I know. It's so stupid, and selfish, and pathetic. And totally my issue. So I should never have taken it out on you. I'm sorry.'

I couldn't form words. I didn't even know what to say. It was unfathomable that Sara McKinley, the girl every guy wished would give him the time of day, the girl who had everything, wanted the one thing that I had. There had to be someone who made her feel . . .

'But you do,' I realized out loud.

'What?' She looked at me like I'd been having a conversation without her, because I pretty much had.

'Sara, you have to give Jared a chance,' I urged. 'He's the only guy who's ever made you feel truly amazing. I mean, you like him so much you wouldn't even have sex with him.'

'Hey.' She gave me an offended shove, but a smile emerged on her face. Then it disappeared in the next breath. 'Em, I can't. It doesn't make sense.'

'Yeah it does,' I countered. 'Why don't you just try? What do you have to lose?'

'My heart,' Sara answered without pause. She took a breath and rested her head on my shoulder. 'Do you forgive me?'

'Sara, I just want you to be okay. I'm not sure how to make you feel better, but I'll try.'

'I have an idea,' she grinned deviously. It was almost like I'd set her up to tell me, 'You can help me throw a party next weekend.'

'A what?' I questioned, afraid I'd just heard her ask me to help her with a *party*.

'It will be the best way to take out all my frustration,' she explained with a devilish gleam in her eye. 'It'll have a theme and everything.'

'I'm afraid to ask.'

'It'll be my *Love Stinks* party,' she boasted, like it was the best idea ever. 'And it can even have rules.'

'Rules?' I questioned in disbelief. 'Since when do parties have rules?'

'Mine will,' she stated proudly. 'Since it's a *Love Stinks* party, no one will be allowed to touch the opposite sex. So, no hook ups, kissing or hand holding.'

I stared at her with my mouth open. 'That's . . . cruel.'

'Are you going to help me with my party and enforce my rules or what?' Sara demanded with a tilt of her head. 'You said you wanted me to feel better. *This* will make me feel better.'

'Torturing everyone else on Valentine's Day?'

'Yes,' she smiled smugly.

'Fine.' I caved in, dreading this already. 'How are we going to enforce your *rules*?'

'I haven't decided yet.' She pondered, giving it serious consideration.

'Great. This is going to be ranked the best party of the year.'

'It better be,' Sara replied seriously. I shot her a sceptical look – she ignored me.

Sara stood up. 'Wanna watch the rest of the game?'

I'd almost forgotten we'd left Jonathan in the living room, watching the game by himself. I stood to join her.

Before opening the door she said, 'I'm sorry for kicking your snowman's face in.' She was trying to be sincere, but the apology sounded funny and we both couldn't help but laugh.

'And I'm sorry I called you a bitch,' I replied once we stopped laughing.

'Don't worry,' she assured me, 'I'll be fine. I'll snap out of it. This party will help.'

She was about to turn around, but then added, 'I hope you know how lucky you are to have Evan. He would give up everything for you. You have no idea. So if you ever do anything to screw it up, I'll never talk to you again, got it?'

'Uh, yes,' I responded, afraid if I answered differently she'd kick my ass. She smiled, her vibrant smile instantly mending us.

We joined Jonathan for the fourth quarter. Sara took him up on his beer offer. The volume of the cheering rose to a whole new level with Sara as a spectator, so much so that my mother made a point of shutting her door. We looked at each other guiltily, but were dragged right back into the game moments later.

My mother had to miss two days of work to get over her illness, and right around then Jonathan disappeared, having contracted the flu himself. He stayed at his place as he fought through it. My mother was a bit of a wreck the rest of the week, until that Friday when Jonathan finally emerged from the land of the dead – right around the time I was about to enter it.

I spent the weekend at Sara's to prepare for the party, and to give my mother and Jonathan time to make up for lost . . . I didn't really want to think about it. It was hard to be all romantic and sentimental when thinking about my mother and her boyfriend – and while hanging torn hearts and blood-dripping arrows.

I 2

F— Valentine's Day

'THIS IS A LITTLE GOTH, DON'T YOU THINK?'
I questioned as Sara heavily lined my lids in black.

'Exactly,' Sara smirked. 'Here, just put this on and you'll
be all set.'

'You want me to wear black lipstick? I didn't realize this
was a costume party.'

Sara rolled her eyes. 'Just put it on. I know you won't be
kissing Evan if your lips are black.' I scowled and grabbed
the lipstick from her hand.

I finished getting dressed while Sara was in the bathroom. She hadn't shown me what she was wearing, and I
just about fell off the bed when she emerged from the
bathroom.

'How are guys not going to want to grope you dressed
like that?' I gawked at Sara's skintight wet black leather
pants and black corset top that accentuated . . . everything.

'I didn't say I had to play fair, did I?' Sara grinned, her
lips glossed brightly in red. I shook my head, feeling like

a henchman to her goddess in my girly black outfit. She handed me a red plastic gun. 'Here.'

'And what am I supposed to do with this?' I asked, tilting it in my hand.

'Any contact between a guy and a girl, squirt them,' she instructed.

'Sara, I can't squirt people with water for touching!'

'Emma, come on – you promised!'

'I'm going to die,' I groaned, plodding down the stairs in my black knee-high go-go boots. Sara stayed upstairs to lock everything up, so people couldn't wander into bedrooms to defy the rules – and be inappropriate on her parents' bed.

'Is this night over yet?' I grunted upon entering the McKinleys' entertainment room where Evan was programming the music.

'Wow!' He gaped, eyeing me from head to toe, swallowing hard. 'How am I supposed to *not* touch you dressed like a Goth schoolgirl? Sara's sick.'

'What?' I baulked at the thought. 'You *like* this?'

'I'd have to be dead not to think you looked hot,' he grinned, 'and even then . . .'

'Omigod,' I groaned. 'Are you kidding me?'

Evan slid his hands around my exposed waist and ran his lips along my neck. My head swirled as I released a defenceless breath. I wanted nothing more than to kiss him back, but I was a prisoner to Sara's black lipstick. He ran his hand along my stomach and breathed in my ear, making my knees weak.

I needed to escape before I melted. 'I think I need to walk away or I'll throw *all* Sara's rules out the window.'

136

Evan grinned. 'Rules end at midnight,' he proclaimed as I entered the kitchen.

'Who says?' I yelled back.

'I do.'

I smiled.

Sara *was* sick! Unbeknown to me, she'd put the message out to the girls to dress as vixens, all in black – but had neglected to warn the guys. So not only was this a 'look but don't touch' party, but she was playing dirty.

Let's just say as soon as the guys saw what was waiting for them, there were a lot of refills at the keg. That was the other rule: if you drank, you had to spend the night and your car keys were collected.

The guest list was extensive but exclusive. Cameras and cell phones were banned and collected along with keys. Picture taking was strictly forbidden. Underclassmen were not allowed, although some tried to crash. Evan and Kyle, Jill's boyfriend from Syracuse, manned the door – filling the bouncer roles perfectly. They broke a lot of freshmen hearts, shutting the door in their faces after the pathetic creatures got a glimpse of what they *weren't* going to be a part of.

Jill, Sara, Karen and I were armed with water guns. Casey had one for a while, but Sara revoked her privileges when she found out she'd filled it with a mixed drink and was squirting it into her mouth.

Jill's was later handed to Mandy when she ran her hand along Kyle's back. Sara told her if she couldn't obey the rules, then she had no right defending them and pro- ceeded to give her a quick squirt to the gut. I couldn't help but laugh when Jill truly looked heartbroken at her demotion.

I patrolled as instructed, but everyone was well behaved. Then again, the party had only been going on for an hour. The first floor was open to the partygoers, decorated morbidly in dead flowers and crushed chocolate strawberries then set aglow in red – it had taken quite some time to change the light bulbs.

The entertainment room was set up as the dance floor since it was the largest, most open space. The television screen was retracted into the ceiling, and the couches that lined the back walls had the cushions removed to keep people from getting lost in the dark to make out. That room remained vacant for the most part, since no one was ready to dance – or they couldn't figure out how to dance without touching each other.

Besides, the music was pretty angry. It was a compilation of aggressive songs, featuring Five Finger Death Punch and Disturbed – not exactly grinding music.

Things started to get a little more interesting during the second and third hours – right around the time the alcohol took effect. Sara had to refill her water gun twice, being the most prominent enforcer of the rules. I thought it was going to piss people off, but she seemed to be aiming for the guys – and they didn't have a problem being sprayed with water by a girl dressed like Sara.

It was innocent enough. Talking a little too close, then a hand slipped to the hip. One of the girls sitting down on her boyfriend's lap while he was playing cards at the kitchen table. The first kiss happened around ten thirty, and Sara and Mandy went ballistic, drenching the guy who thought he was finally hitting it off with one of the girls from the basketball team. As horrified as he was, there were plenty of people laughing – I mean, it *was* pretty funny.

'Sara, there's someone at the door for you,' Evan hollered when the doorbell rang.

'You can answer it,' Sara returned, taking a sip of her red martini.

'No, this one's for you.' He walked towards me, careful not to touch as he leaned against the wall beside me. 'Things are about to get very interesting.'

Sara approached the door. I watched her lips form, 'Oh no,' when she finally opened it. At the same time, Jared's eyes just about fell out of his head. 'Hi,' he choked. 'That's quite the anti-Valentine's day attire.'

'What are you doing here?' she responded, her cheeks a brilliant shade of red.

'Fuck Valentine's Day,' Jared exclaimed, handing Sara a dozen dried black roses. 'These are for you.'

'Aren't you going to let him in?' Jill scolded her, pulling Jared in by the arm and closing the open door that was making most of the scantily dressed girls shiver.

'Thanks,' Sara responded blankly, taking the dead flowers – obviously in shock.

I looked to Evan, who wore a devious grin. 'You don't play fair either, do you?'

'It's Valentine's Day!' he stated defensively. 'I kinda want to kiss my girlfriend.'

I smiled brightly, admiring his strategy. Sara spotted Evan and shook her head, shooting him a tight-eyed glare. She knew that Jared's presence was his doing. Evan laughed.

Jared had a guitar case strapped to his back. 'What's

that for?' Sara enquired, leading him to the help-yourself bar on the sun porch.

'Later,' Jared replied, grabbing a beer from the galvanized tub.

Without Sara realizing it, Evan switched the music to more popular dance songs, and the room started filling with bodies. She slacked on her patrol and handed her water pistol to another enthusiastic enforcer who took to the dance floor with a vengeance.

About an hour later, we were running low on ice, and I didn't have the key to the basement where the freezer was stored. I searched among the flashing lights and teasing bodies in the entertainment room, but didn't find Sara. After lapping the first floor, I decided to try upstairs.

The door to Anna and Carl's sitting room was slightly ajar. The crack allowed me to see Sara sitting on the love seat, leaning forward and completely mesmerized. I was just about to push the door open when I picked up on the strums of the guitar. I barely touched the door to open it an inch further and found Jared sitting on the ottoman across from her strumming the guitar. He was singing. I was too stunned to move.

'Be my, be my valentine,' he sang as he strummed the upbeat chorus.

'I think I'm in love,' Jill crooned drunkenly beside me, throwing her arms around my neck and laying her head on my shoulder.

'Do they breed them to be like that?' Casey cooed on the other side.

I hadn't even noticed they'd followed me. I quickly

closed the door and knocked hard to warn Sara of our presence – but I think she may have heard us.

'Sara, you need to get out here,' Casey yelled obnoxiously, knocking harder. 'Jill's breaking the rules big time.'

Sara opened the door wide enough to be seen, but kept Jared concealed in the background.

'Shoot her,' Casey demanded in her intoxicated enthusiasm, pointing to Jill. 'She's breaking the rules. Shoot her right in the face.' When Sara only looked at her in confusion, Casey grabbed my gun and shot a stream right in the middle of Jill's forehead. Jill let me go and screamed.

'I'm going to kill you,' she bellowed, sending Casey down the stairs in a fit of laughter with Jill in pursuit.

Sara and I looked at each other, shaking our heads. 'Hey,' I finally said as casually as I could, 'we're out of ice. Do you have the key to the basement?'

To my surprise Sara replied, 'Yes. Let's go.' She shut the door behind her and led me down the stairs. I clenched my teeth in a grimace, glancing at the door and hoping Jared didn't think she was rejecting his Valentine's ballad.

We filled up the tubs with ice, and Sara noticed the music change. She pointed to Evan accusingly, ready to pounce. He held up his hands, feigning innocence with an adorable grin on his face.

'You were in charge of the music,' she spat.

'And look,' he pointed to the swaying bodies, 'they're dancing. Not a bad job if I do say so myself.'

Sara rolled her eyes and disappeared upstairs. Evan yelled, 'You're welcome,' after her, and she flipped him the finger – which made us both laugh.

'It's almost midnight,' I said, walking past him, wanting to touch him so bad it hurt.

'Don't worry,' he promised, 'it'll happen.' I grinned and kept walking into the crowd.

The rule that Sara was most adamant about enforcing was that no one was allowed onto the deck that over-looked the enclosed pool and hot tub. They were deemed instant aphrodisiacs, with the waterfall built into the rocks at the far end of the pool and the rolling bubbles of the hot tub. She kept the lights off, so as not to tempt the hormone-driven drunkards.

I caught a glimpse of lights coming from the forbidden space and groaned in frustration – not wanting to be the person to kick them out. I waved Evan over and con-tinued on to the deck as he cut through the dance floor to follow me.

The pool was surrounded by what resembled a green-house, panes of glass arching over a stone floor. In the summer, it retracted away from the house to become an outdoor pool. In the winter, it kept the pool in use, even though the glass was frosted over and there was snow piled up against the exterior.

I stepped out into the balmy air to find the potted trees around the pool lit with small lights, creating a romantic setting. By the pool's edge were Sara and Jared, kissing. I wanted to scream!

'No way,' I fumed at the sight of them. I stormed down the stairs. She was the one who made up these asinine rules, and within an hour of Jared's arrival *she* was going to break them?! Not on my watch!

Before Sara even realized I was there, I exclaimed, 'Rule

breaker!' and shoved her. Jared tried to recover their balance, but it was too late; they plummeted into the blue water. Sara came up for air, gasping.

'What the fuck?' She stared at me in shock, her hair slicked back and her red lips smeared.

Evan started laughing, which made Jared start. A smile crept on my face, and I joined in. The commotion brought spectators out on to the deck.

'You are so dead,' Sara threatened without sincerity. Before she could lift herself out of the pool, Evan swept me into the water alongside him. This set off a chain reaction, and bodies began plunging in after us.

When I surfaced, I found Evan in front of me, smiling proudly. He pulled me towards the rocks, away from the splashing and jumping. I held on to the side of the pool, my weighted boots threatening to pull me under as Evan wiped my lipstick off with the sleeve of his shirt.

'Told you I'd kiss you by midnight,' he grinned, pulling me towards him. His lips encased mine. I could taste the chlorine of the water and feel the warmth of his breath. I gripped his shirt and pulled him closer, feeling his hand glide along the skin of my back. He turned me so that my back was against the pool's wall, placing his hands on either side of me, pushing himself against me. I wrapped my legs around his waist, and his hand ran along my thigh. My heart raced and I couldn't breathe.

Before I knew what was happening, I was under the water again. The submergence separated us, and I resurfaced breathing heavily.

'Now who's breaking the rules?' Sara gloated while Jared trod water with a grin behind her.

'I hate your rules,' I declared, splashing her in the face. She hollered and splashed back. A water war ensued. Among the splashing and dunked bodies, I caught sight of Sara again, her arms around Jared's neck as he kissed her cheek – and she was smiling.

I blinked my eyes open, the chiming ringing in my ear. The room was dark, and I could feel the weight of Evan's arm around my waist. There was a beep, then silence. I started to close my eyes again, sleep pulling me under. The chiming started back up. My eyes shot open.

I rolled over and picked up my phone from the night-stand. Without looking to see who it was, I answered, 'Hello?'

'Where are you?' my mother demanded in a panic.

I sat up, jolted awake by her desperation. My sudden movement disturbed Evan, but he just rolled over and remained asleep.

'What?' I tried to register what was going on.

'Where the fuck are you? Why aren't you home?'

'I'm at Sara's,' I replied, my heart racing. She was so upset. I tried to remember if I'd told her – but knew I had. Doubt coursed through me anyway. 'Remember she had the party tonight?'

'You don't want to live with me any more, do you?' she cried. I knew she was drunk; her words weren't forming properly, but I was too shocked to make sense of why she was saying this.

I felt Evan move beside me but my back was towards him as I sat on the edge of the bed, tears forming in my eyes.

'You hate me. I know it.' She'd reached the point of hysterics. 'That's why you never sleep here. You're going to leave me too, aren't you?' I gasped at the agony in her voice, a tear escaping down my cheek.

'Rachel, what are you doing?' I heard in the background. 'Who are you talking to?'

'She doesn't love me any more,' she sobbed, the pain smothering her words.

'Who?' Jonathan asked, sounding groggy. 'It's three o'clock in the morning. Give me the phone.'

'Why doesn't she love me?' she bellowed, the phone moving further from her mouth.

'Emma?' he asked softly. My mother's drunken rant continued in the background. 'Are you there?'

'Yes,' I whispered, barely able to speak with the knot lodged in the back of my throat. It was silent. He must have left the room, closing the door to block her out.

'Are you okay?' he asked gently.

'No,' I breathed, a whimper escaping. I put my hand over my mouth to contain it. Tears streamed down my cheeks, cascading over my fingers. A warm hand pressed against my back, but I didn't turn to face him. I just listened.

'She had too much to drink tonight,' he tried to explain. 'And we got in kind of an argument, so it's not you. I'm so sorry.'

I breathed in deeply through my nose, removing my hand and wiping my cheeks before Evan could see. He scooted over to sit next to me.

'Emma? Are you still there?'

'Yes,' I replied. 'I'm okay.' I took another breath to calm

the twisting nerves strangling my chest, wiping my cheeks dry. 'I'm okay,' I repeated in a whisper, convincing myself.

'Go back to sleep,' he murmured. 'It'll be over in the morning.'

'Okay.' I hung up the phone and set it on the table.

Evan pulled my quivering body into him, wrapping me tightly.

'Is everything okay with your mother?'

'Yeah,' I breathed. 'She forgot I was staying over at Sara's, so she was upset. She thought something had happened to me.'

Evan didn't say anything. He held me tighter while gently rocking me and pressed his lips against my forehead. He moved back down on the bed, and I followed, lowering my head on to his chest. I pressed my ear against his heart to hear its rhythmic beats. Eventually, his breaths lengthened, and I knew he had fallen asleep. A tear ran over the bridge of my nose and dripped on to his smooth skin.

I listened to his calm, wanting it to capture me as well, but the storm inside me wouldn't rest.

13

Overreaction

I SNUCK OUT OF THE GUEST ROOM BEFORE Evan woke. I could hear whispers and movement further down the hall, although it was barely dawn. I suspected there was a need to escape before the sun shed too much light on faces that didn't want to be seen.

I found a few girls searching through the basket of clothes that had been pulled from the dryer, picking out items that belonged to them, stuffing them in their overnight bags.

'Emma,' a petite blonde beckoned. 'Could you get us our keys and phones so we can go?'

'Sure,' I answered. I took out the bag that we'd hidden in the back of the hall closet and started laying out the Ziploc bags labelled with each person's name. They took their possessions and left. Most of the girls and a few of the guys were gone by the time Sara dragged her feet down the stairs, looking like she was still in need of a few more hours of sleep.

'Whatcha doin'?' she asked, stretching her arms with her hair twisted in a pile on the top of her head.

I tied up a trash bag filled with cups, bottles and stale chips and set it next to another full bag. She looked around. The kitchen was beginning to resemble itself again since I'd already peeled back a layer of party leftovers.

'Thanks for picking up.' She sat down on a stool, rubbing her palms over her eyes. 'The cleaners are coming around noon, so we don't have to go crazy.'

'How are you feeling?' I sat down next to her.

She propped her head up on her hand and yawned wide. 'Tired. You?'

'Tired,' I concurred. 'Almost everyone's gone. I think there are a few guys sleeping on lawn chairs by the pool, a few more on the couches. Mandy, Casey and Jill are upstairs in the rec room.'

'Alone?' she stressed.

'Kyle may be up there too, but Jill was luggage last night, so I don't think you have anything to worry about.'

She groaned, 'I hope not,' then collapsed her head into her arms. 'I think my head is going to fall off.'

I smiled. 'Are you going to tell me what happened between you and Jared last night?'

'No,' she answered, her voice muffled from within her arms.

'What?' I shot back. 'You want me to tell *you* everything.'

'But you don't,' she retorted, lifting her head up. 'Honestly, we just passed out.'

'And now what?' I pushed.

The tiredness disappeared from her eyes with the emergence of a smile. She lifted her shoulders in a knowing shrug. I knew exactly what that meant.

'Looks like you'll be putting some miles on your car, huh?'

'Yup,' she beamed.

'So, just like that?' I asked curiously. 'He shows up at your party, and that's all he needed to do?'

'Not exactly,' she confessed guiltily.

I waited for her to continue.

'He wanted to keep seeing me after New Year's.' I raised my eyebrows at this revelation. 'I just couldn't see it working out. But he called and emailed a couple of times trying to convince me. Then he stopped, and that's pretty much when I became a stupid girl. So when he showed up last night . . .' She paused and grinned. 'I knew I couldn't say no again. You're right. I have to at least try.'

'Good morning,' Evan said from behind us. 'Wow, we have some work to do before we leave, huh? Sara, what time's your flight?'

'Three,' she answered, sliding off the stool to begin tearing the hearts off the wall. She was heading to Florida for February break, and Evan had skiing plans in Tahoe with the California guys – leaving me alone in Weslyn. They had both invited me to go, but I felt I should spend the week with my mother, since that had been the point of moving in with her in the first place.

'Do you want a ride? My flight's at three fifty.' He came up behind me to wrap his arms around my shoulders, kissing me on the top of my head.

'That'd be great,' she agreed. 'Except my parents aren't coming back until Sunday.'

'I thought you were too?' I questioned.

'Umm . . . no,' she responded with a smirk.

'I'll pick you up on Friday,' Jared's voice answered before he came into view on the stairs. Of course. It all made sense now.

'Perfect,' Sara replied, colour returning to her face and her hangover miraculously disappearing.

Jared and Evan woke the rest of the guys. A few helped put the pool furniture back in place, but the other pale, grumbling faces took their possessions and dragged themselves out the door.

The girls slunk down the steps once Sara turned on the music. If she was up then everyone else had to be too. Aspirin and sodas were passed around as we tackled the repercussions of throwing a party. I stepped in something wet on the carpet in the family room in my bare feet, and every inch of me shuddered. I wouldn't even let myself think about what it might be.

When the cleaning ladies showed up, the house was stripped of the anti-V-day decor, but the after-effects still lingered in the air, which was apparent when they scrunched up their noses upon entering. Sara left them a huge tip before we headed out for breakfast.

'I still owe you a Valentine's Day,' Evan stated in the car, after I'd stuffed my face with way too many blueberry pancakes.

'No you don't,' I replied honestly. 'I don't think anything will be able to top last night. It was pretty great.'

'It was,' he agreed, pulling down my street. 'But would you be interested in going on a normal date? You know, adventure-less? Dinner, movies or something?'

I grinned at the thought of the two of us in a restaurant and nodded. 'That would be nice.'

'After I get back,' Evan promised, turning into the driveway.

I only half heard him because I was staring at the cheerful yellow house, fearful of what awaited me after my mother's distraught phone call.

'Are you okay?' Evan asked from beside me.

'Huh?' I answered, pulling my eyes away to look at him.

'Is everything all right between you and Rachel? You were really upset last night.'

'I felt bad that I worried her, that's all. Just a miscommunication,' I explained lightly, not wanting him to hear the guilt beneath the sugar coating. 'We're fine.' When he didn't look convinced, I insisted with a smile, 'Really.'

'You'd tell me, right?' Evan looked into my eyes, trying to read the truth. I blinked away, turning my eyes to the floor.

'Of course,' I answered, opening the door. I leaned over and pressed my lips to his, begging him to believe me. 'Have fun in Tahoe with the guys. I'll see you on Sunday.'

He pulled me towards him and gave me a kiss that would be sure to tide us over for the entire week. Barely able to stand, I staggered towards the door – turning once to wave before he backed out of the driveway.

I took a deep breath, sobering instantly when I clasped the cold door handle. I pushed it open with my pulse racing, not sure what was about to happen. I quietly shut the door behind me, and froze when I heard laughter coming from the kitchen. Not at all what I was expecting.

'Emily,' Rachel exclaimed, still giggling from within the kitchen. 'How was the party?'

The radio playing in the background was suddenly cut off by the high-pitched sounds of a blender.

'Don't let it get too thin,' my mother instructed. I walked to the doorway to find the counters covered in food in different stages of preparation. Tomatoes were diced on a cutting board; garlic skins littered the table; lime slices lay squeezed and abandoned. The entire kitchen smelled like a Mexican restaurant.

'Hi,' I greeted them hesitantly.

'Hey,' Jonathan smiled, appearing completely relaxed. 'We're, umm . . .'

'Preparing for *Margarita Call Out of Work Day*,' my mother explained. That's when it struck me that they were supposed to be at work, it being Monday. 'We're going to Heidi's to play cards and pretend we're in Mexico.'

'Oh,' I responded, thrown by her exuberant disposition. 'Sounds fun.'

'Yes it does,' she answered excitedly. 'I figured Jonathan could handle making salsa.' She examined the contents of the blender. 'Maybe I was wrong. Sweetie, just go start packing the bag, and I'll fix this, okay?' She kissed him on the cheek when he grimaced apologetically.

'He can't cook either,' she explained with a comical shake of her head. 'So, how was the party?' she asked again once Jonathan had passed me to get a bag out of the coat closet.

'It was fun,' I answered, wondering if I'd dreamt the

phone call. 'But I didn't get a lot of sleep. I think I'm going to crash for a while.'

'That happens – means it was a great party.' She smirked knowingly. I hesitated, examining her. She looked perfectly fine, not at all devastated as she had been on the phone last night.

'What?' she questioned when I lingered too long.

'Have fun in Margaritaville,' I said with a smile.

She laughed at my reference and declared, 'Oh, we will.'

'Where are the mixers we bought?' Jonathan hollered from the living room, placing bottles and glasses into a reusable shopping bag.

'Upstairs in my room,' my mother responded. Jonathan was a few steps behind me as I dragged my body up the stairs.

'Hey,' he said quietly before I could enter my room. I turned to face him. 'How are you?' That one question, combined with the anticipatory look in his eyes, confirmed I hadn't imagined anything.

'Confused,' I answered honestly, opening my door.

'I don't think she remembers,' he explained. 'I kinda screwed up last night, so she took it out on you. My fault, and I'm sorry.'

'What do you mean?' I asked, the confusion still looming.

'I mentioned that I hadn't slept at my place in a while, and that I should probably stay there a few nights this week.' He hesitated before admitting, 'It wasn't the best thing to say on Valentine's Day.'

I pressed my lips together and shook my head. 'She thought you were breaking up with her, didn't she?'

Jonathan sighed and nodded. 'We talked it over this morning, and she understands. So I won't be over much this week. I just need to . . . breathe a little I guess.'

His choice of words alarmed me. I suddenly understood my mother's distress. 'Wait. *Are* you breaking up with her?'

'No.' He shook his head adamantly. 'She and I are having a lot of fun together, honestly.' He was about to say something else when my mother's voice interrupted, 'Did you find them?'

Jonathan looked at me and then down to the kitchen. 'I found them,' he lied, not making a move for her door. Then he returned to me and quickly said, 'I wanted to explain since you might not see me around for a bit. I'm still here; I just need to back off a little.' Then he went down the stairs and into the living room.

I backed into my bedroom when my mother came into sight carrying a sealed glass container of salsa. I realized he'd never intended to get anything from her room; he only wanted to check in on me, to explain things. He hadn't explained much, in all honesty. I knew that he hadn't told my mother half of what he'd just told me, or else she wouldn't have been smiling that way.

Someone had left a red heart-shaped box filled with chocolates on my bed. There was a heart drawn on top in marker with an 'R' scrawled underneath. I held the box in my hand and stared at it. I didn't want to be the person who made things harder for her.

I lay on my bed with my hand on the heart, considering if my being there was what was best for her. How was I supposed to decide that? She'd sounded so hurt last night, convinced that I didn't want her. The irony was that I'd been afraid she was going to say the same thing to me.

I eventually fell asleep on top of my covers. The house was dark when I woke a couple hours later, but it wasn't exactly quiet. This house never rested. I turned on music to mask the house's distress, so I wouldn't jump at every little noise.

I was searching for a shirt to wear when a loud bang suddenly drew my attention. I shut off the music, remaining perfectly still and holding my breath, convinced I'd heard a cabinet slam shut in the kitchen.

I crept to my door. The hinges creaked as I slowly opened it. I listened intently and jumped when the radiator rattled on. I took a breath and rolled my eyes at my overreaction, turning the music back on.

I gathered a pair of sweats and a long-sleeved shirt in preparation for a shower, so I could feel a part of the human race once again and rid my hair of the chlorine smell. I had texts waiting for me from Sara and Evan when I emerged, clean and revived.

I turned each light on as I walked through the house, making my way to the kitchen to microwave a frozen macaroni cheese dinner. I poured a glass of milk and brought the plastic tray into the living room. I wasn't sure I'd ever feel comfortable being alone, at least not in this house.

I got sucked into a pathetic reality television show with explosive drama and so many words bleeped, the sentences didn't even make sense. After wasting an hour of my life, I found a black and white movie I'd seen enough times to know just about every other line.

*

'Emma, you should go up to bed,' the voice whispered. 'Emma.'

'Yeah?' I answered, not sure if I was talking in my dream.

'It's late,' the voice responded.

I pulled the cover up under my chin, slowly realizing I wasn't in my bed. I pushed my eyes open to find the television playing highlights of a basketball game. I blinked heavily, waking in the dark with the lights extinguished except for the television.

'Sorry to wake you,' Jonathan said from his seat across from me. 'But I figured you'd be more comfortable in your bed.'

'What time is it?' I asked, trying to focus on the glowing clock of the cable box.

'After two,' he answered.

I pushed up to sit, slowly coming to the surface.

'You should go up to bed,' Jonathan encouraged again.

I took a breath. 'Okay.' But I didn't move. My brain started functioning, and I looked at him quizzically. 'What are you doing up?'

'Needed to step away from a dream,' he answered vaguely, but with words I could understand.

Then it struck me. 'Wait, I thought you weren't staying over this week.'

'I'm not,' he confirmed, then corrected with, 'I wasn't supposed to. I had to drive her home; then she asked me not to leave her. I just . . .' He pressed his lips together, not finding the words to support his decision.

'You know she's always going to ask you to stay.'

'And that's the reason I shouldn't.'

I was confused by what he said, and slightly alarmed. But I let him decide if he was going to explain what he meant, and he eventually said more than I expected to hear. 'I've sent out applications to graduate schools, and the closest one is in DC.'

'Oh,' I breathed, starting to understand, and not liking where this was headed.

'I like being with her. She's a lot of fun, and has the craziest perspective on the world. She doesn't ask questions about me or where I came from; she only cares about who I am now and just wants to be with me.'

'And that's good, right?' I asked, suddenly curious why keeping his past hidden was important to him. But then again, I was the last person to want to talk about mine.

'Yes, not talking about my past is a relief, honestly,' Jonathan replied. 'But, I don't want her to need me like she does. I just want . . .' He searched for the right words. 'I don't want any pressure.'

'She's always needed someone,' I blurted. I hadn't planned to say it, but as soon as I did, I knew it was true. I looked up at him, my honesty shrouding me with guilt. 'I didn't mean it like it sounded . . .'

'You're probably right,' he interrupted. 'I'm not sure it's *me* she needs, exactly.'

I started pulling at a thread on the blanket.

'I shouldn't really be talking about my relationship with you anyway,' he suddenly said. 'Sorry, I'm sure it's weird.'

'A little.' But my conclusion started to make sense, looking back over the years. She'd never been without a man in her life, even for short spurts of time. I'd always believed it was her desperate way of replacing my father.

I looked over at Jonathan and wondered what she'd seen in him that reminded her of my father. Maybe it was his smile. When it spread across his face, the edges of his eyes would crinkle into a smile too. My lips curled up just thinking about it.

'What?' he asked, catching me in my memories.

'Nothing,' I answered quickly, adjusting the blanket around me uncomfortably. 'I was just thinking. I can understand why she'd want you to stay.'

'Then does that make me a horrible person for needing some space?'

'No,' I answered. 'I'm just not sure how *she'll* do with the space. She really likes you.'

'I like her too,' he admitted with a sigh. 'But you'll be here with her.'

I let out a short laugh. 'It's not the same.'

Jonathan grinned, his eyes locked with mine. My smile faltered for a moment when I couldn't look away.

'I guess I should go to bed.' I blinked, pulling the blanket off me. Before I got to the stairs, I turned to him and said, 'Jonathan?'

'Yes, Emma.'

'Please don't hurt her,' I asked, my voice soft and edged with emotion. 'I don't want to see her hurt again.'

He paused for a moment, scanning my face thoughtfully. 'I don't want to hurt her either.' He offered a consoling smile before I turned away and walked up the stairs, not sure if he'd promised what I asked – fearful that he hadn't.

14

Under the Surface

JONATHAN WASN'T IN THE HOUSE IN THE morning. Neither was my mother, who was once again fulfilling her obligations as executive assistant at the engineering firm. We didn't see Jonathan for the rest of the week either, and she *appeared* to be adjusting to the separation.

I tried to keep her busy. I even suggested a cooking lesson one night, but after the smoke detectors went off and we had to open every window in the house for ventilation, we opted to eat out. She worked late a couple of nights, coming home after I'd eaten and joining me on the couch to watch television.

'I hope he doesn't leave me,' she said one night with a glass of wine in her hand. She'd kicked off her work shoes under the coffee table, and her blouse was untucked from her skirt. She was staring at the TV, but her thoughts were obviously with him.

'He cares about you.' I tried to sound encouraging, but it fell flat.

'When does Evan get back?' she asked, changing the subject. Her gaze readjusted to the present, and she looked over at me with bright eyes.

'Sunday,' I answered slowly, not prepared for the 'on' switch to her personality.

'Wouldn't it be nice to take off to wherever you wanted, just because you wanted to?' She said this with an equal measure of envy and possibility. 'We should have him over for dinner soon.'

'Uh, okay.'

'I'm going to bed,' she announced. I watched her climb the stairs and hoped that whatever Jonathan was doing, it wouldn't leave her devastated in the end. I didn't think I could handle watching her heart break.

I met up with Jill and Casey the next afternoon; we ended up going to a movie that night. After a half day of incessant giggling, combined with soda and candy, my teeth hurt from all the *sugar*. I could only take the two of them in small doses, and I'd OD'd today.

I had barely taken off my jacket when my phone rang. I pulled it from my pocket to see *Rachel* lit on the screen.

'Hi,' I answered.

'Is this Emily?' a deep voice asked. Not answering, I looked at the phone again to make sure I'd read it correctly. It had my mother's phone number as the caller. I put the phone back to my ear, my stomach clenched.

'Hello?' he bellowed over the voices and music clashing in the background.

'Yes,' I replied, my heart picking up its pace. 'This is Emily.'

My brain flashed through a thousand different images of what might've happened to her, inciting a panic.

'You need to come pick up Rachel. I can't let her drive home.'

'Um, okay,' I responded with a heavy heart. I should have been relieved that she was okay, but then again, she really wasn't. 'Where is she?'

'Mick's Place, on Route One Thirteen in Stenton.'

'All right. I'll be there soon.' I sank onto the steps with my phone in my hands, bowing my head in dread. I shouldn't have been surprised that she was drunk once again. It was what I'd become accustomed to as a child, but I'd hoped I wouldn't have to deal with it this time around.

My entire body hollowed with the acceptance of her condition, shutting off the emotion that threatened to take over. I just needed to focus on getting her home, and then I'd figure out the rest later.

I tried to locate the bar on the GPS on my phone, but nothing came up. I had no idea where she was. That left me with only one choice. I shook my head and groaned, 'Shit,' not liking what I was about to do, especially since he was probably the reason she was drinking.

I dialled the number and held my breath as it rang.

'Hello? Emma? Is everything okay?' The urgency in his voice made it clear that he was expecting the worst.

'Um . . . not really,' I replied softly. 'Can you help me?'

'Of course. What's going on?' he responded in a rush.

'I need to pick up Rachel, but I don't know where she is.'

'I'll be there in fifteen minutes, okay?'

'Okay,' I said, exhaling with relief.

Jonathan's truck pulled into the driveway, and I stepped on to the porch to lock the door behind me.

'Will you drive my car?' I asked before he'd said a word.

'Sure,' he responded, taking the keys with a questioning look.

'I think she's going to need to lie down,' I explained glumly.

He took in my drawn expression. 'It'll be okay. We'll pick her up and everything will be fine.'

'Yup,' I answered, not believing a word.

I told Jonathan where she was, and his brows pulled together in concern.

'What?' I demanded nervously.

'It's not the best place to hang out,' he noted with a heavy breath. 'You should stay in the car while I go in and get her, okay?' I closed my eyes and nodded, trying to hold it together.

When we arrived, I understood why he didn't want me to go in. The bar was a single-storey box with neon lights nailed to its roof. Several of the letters were dark, and the end of 'Place' was flickering red, fighting to stay lit. The small slots that were presumably windows were covered with glowing neon beer signs. The building was a dingy shade of white that the years and lack of care had rotted away. There were shingles missing in some spots or broken in others. It looked like a strong wind could bring the entire place down.

The dirt parking lot was poorly lit. A single spotlight

hung from the corner of the building, casting more shadows than light. The lot was covered in patches of ice. It was a hazard to walk on while sober, forget about after drinking until you could barely stand. A group of rough-looking men with dark, stubbly faces stood outside, smoking cigarettes and making comments to the patrons coming and going. I was convinced they hadn't showered in days. A line of motorcycles would undoubtedly be parked in front of them if it weren't the middle of winter. They blended with the dilapidated background perfectly – the sight of them made me squirm in disgust.

'Stay in the car. I'll be right out.' Jonathan instructed me, shutting the door behind him.

I sank into the seat with my arms crossed, watching one of the men in leather clasp the hand of another who approached from a Camaro. The guy from the Camaro had a shaved head and broad shoulders, and wore a pair of black sunglasses, even though it was nearly midnight. Creepy characters flocked to this place, making me wonder why my mother would ever stop here.

One of the smokers glanced in my direction, and my heart started racing. I quickly looked down, hoping he couldn't see inside the car.

'Keep your fucking hands off me, John,' a woman threatened, redirecting my attention.

The men were laughing as a woman with tight jeans and a cropped leather jacket thrust the door open to enter, glaring at them. The man with the leather trench coat and long, thick moustache was still watching me. I shuddered and tried to sink further into the seat. He nudged the tall guy with the straining waistband next to him, nodding towards me and saying something. The guy laughed and nodded his head.

'Jonathan, where are you?' I whispered, anxiously staring at the black door, begging him to come through it. I looked back and the moustached cretin grinned at me. My heart spasmed and my hands started shaking. I quickly flipped my eyes down, hoping he'd lose interest.

'Come on out of the car, sweet thing,' he called, beckoning, making the rest of the men take notice. 'Let me buy you a drink.' There were laughs and sinister grins in reaction to my panic-stricken face. I made sure the doors were locked and silently pleaded once again for Jonathan to appear with my mother.

The scruffy man made a move towards the car, and my breathing faltered. I was trying to decide what to do when the black door was thrust open, stopping him in his tracks. Jonathan emerged with my mother passed out in his arms. I exhaled in relief, unlocked the doors and jumped out of the car to open the back door for them.

Jonathan gently laid her across the back seat. I threw a sideways glance at the man standing at the front of the car. The grin on his face was abhorrent. I couldn't keep my hands from shaking while I waited for Jonathan to adjust my mother. I just wanted to get away from there as fast as possible.

'Hey, buddy,' the man hollered to Jonathan. I remained frozen by the door. Jonathan shut the back door and started to walk around the back of the car, not paying attention. 'Hey, you.' Jonathan stopped, recognizing that the burly man in the trench coat was talking to him. 'Why don't you let me take one of those girls off your hands? I could show this one a good time.' I cringed as he molested me with his eyes.

'Are you talking to me?' Jonathan demanded, his threatening tone making my eyes widen in alarm.

'Yes, I'm talking to you,' the man growled. 'I want a taste.' His moustache-covered mouth spread into a detestable smirk, and he started in my direction. I pressed against the car, blindly feeling for the door handle while keeping my eyes on him. I was fearful of provoking him with any sudden movement – *move slow and he won't attack*.

'I wouldn't do that if I were you,' Jonathan's deep voice warned through clenched teeth. I flipped my eyes towards Jonathan, shaken again by the edge in his voice. The rest of the men became quiet and squared off towards Jonathan, whose hands were slowly flexing into fists by his side.

The man crept towards me until he had me in his direct sight, not taking any notice of Jonathan.

'I think you'd taste good.' His cigarette and alcohol-laden breath coated my face. I closed my eyes and swallowed hard, paralysed. Fear held me hostage as he leaned in. The car rocked, and I opened my eyes to find Jonathan gripping the man's collar, pinning him against the car.

'Don't you fucking touch her,' Jonathan grunted. The guy was taller than Jonathan, but Jonathan was broader. Jonathan glowered inches from his face. The crowd shuffled forward, prepared to join in if necessary.

The two men stared at each other for a second before the cretin snarled, 'What are you going to do?'

Jonathan raised his fist.

'Jonathan, don't,' I begged, released from my paralysis when I realized what was about to happen. 'Please, let's just go.' The crowd was prepared to brawl. My entire body shook as the tension mounted.

Jonathan caught sight of me out of the corner of his eye. His face was hard and full of rage, but his expression flickered when he saw the fear on my face. His eyes softened and he slowly lowered his fist.

Jonathan was about to let him go when the man warned, 'Listen to the girl. Why don't you just get the fuck out of here before I have to mess up that pretty face of yours.' Jonathan narrowed his eyes at the threat, his jaw flexing. I inhaled sharply.

'Please, Jonathan,' I begged, reaching for his arm in desperation. His muscles eased up at my touch, and he slowly let the man go, backing away.

'Get in the car,' Jonathan ordered gruffly. He opened the passenger door and I crawled in. He slammed it behind me, not taking his eyes off the guy, who was smoothing the crinkles out of his jacket with a malevolent grin. I watched the silent showdown as Jonathan crept around the car, prepared to attack if the stubbly-faced man made a move for my door. My heart was pounding so hard, my chest was about to explode.

'If she weren't here . . .' Jonathan began as he opened the driver's door.

'Then we wouldn't even be talking, now would we?' the man interrupted. 'Don't come back unless you're willing to back that up.'

Jonathan slid in and shut the door. His eyes were hard coals, fixed on the man standing at the front of the car, who was focused on me. He moved his lips to form a kiss and then challenged Jonathan with a snarky grin. My whole body convulsed in disgust.

'Let's just go,' I repeated urgently. Jonathan gripped the steering wheel so tightly his tendons stood out along his forearms. He backed out of the space with such speed I had to grab the handle above the door with both hands. The tyres squealed when they made contact with the road. A cloud of dust blew up behind us as we tore out of the parking lot.

Except for my hands that were shaking on my lap, I couldn't move. A few miles down the road, Jonathan finally slowed and darted his eyes in my direction. His dark eyes were released from the rage that had possessed him. I let out a quivering breath and blinked away the tears clouding my vision.

'I'm sorry about that,' he said softly, darting sideways glances in my direction while he drove. I stared out the window, trying not to cry.

He veered to the shoulder of the road and stopped the car. 'Emma.'

I slowly faced him, swallowing against the tightness in the back of my throat.

'Are you okay?'

I could only nod. His eyes searched mine. I pulled away from his probing, too vulnerable to let him see how shaken I truly was.

My mother groaned, deflecting his attention to the back seat.

'What's going on?' she mumbled, blinking but unable to sit up.

'We're taking you home,' Jonathan answered, pulling the car back on to the road.

'Jonathan?' she rasped.

'Yes.'

'I called you,' she whimpered. 'I called you,' she repeated in a slur.

'I know,' he said to pacify her, while staring at the road.

I turned towards her, and she tried to focus on me.

'Emily?' she asked as if uncertain. 'Oh, you're not supposed to be here.' She sounded so sad, I had to turn away.

I followed Jonathan up the stairs when he carried my mother to bed. After removing her shoes and covering her with a blanket, I looked down at her calm face with a broken sigh. I left the room and collapsed on the couch in the dark living room, drained. My hands were still shaking, and my chest ached.

'You should get some sleep,' Jonathan said from the doorway. I looked up at him, dazed.

'I don't think I could if I tried.'

He came over and sat next to me on the couch. We listened to the silence, letting the stillness settle in around us. My mind searched for understanding, unable to find solace among my thoughts.

'I don't know what to do,' I said in defeat. 'I really wanted it to be different.'

'This is my fault. I should have called her back.'

I knew his need for space had triggered this catastrophe, but this was how my mother handled things when she was upset. Unfortunately, that hadn't changed as much as I'd hoped.

'It's not your fault,' I assured him. I thought of my

mother in her bed and wanted to believe this was just something she was going through, that she'd adjust and get over it. I wasn't certain how far *hoping* would get me.

'What are you thinking?' he asked when I was quiet for too long.

'What was she even doing there? That place was *awful.*'

'I don't know,' he replied, just as confused.

The night replayed itself in my head: the phone call, the sketchy bar, the confrontation with the creepiest guy on earth.

'Were you –' I began, just as Jonathan asked, 'What did –'

We both stopped and he encouraged me to speak. 'Go ahead.'

'Were you really going to hit that guy?'

Jonathan pressed his lips together, like he was considering his words carefully. 'You mean, if you hadn't stopped me?'

I nodded.

'Definitely.' He answered without hesitation. My eyes widened at his bluntness. He looked down and rubbed his hands together. 'It's a part of my past that I don't like to talk about.' He raised his head. 'But that's never happened before.'

'What?'

'No one's ever been able to stop me. I usually lose it, and there's no holding me back.'

'You're a fighter?' I asked, not expecting the confession. For the first time I noticed a thin scar under his chin, and another above his right eyebrow, both barely visible.

'Used to be,' he corrected. 'My past, remember. I haven't gotten that angry in a long time. It scared me.'

'It scared me too,' I admitted.

He stopped rubbing his hands together, troubled by my admission.

'The whole thing scared me,' I said, still feeling the after-effects trembling beneath my skin. 'Let's just say tonight sucked all around.'

'Yeah, it did,' he sighed. Jonathan leaned towards me to make certain he had my attention. His dark brown eyes focused on me, pulling me in when he said, 'I don't ever want to scare you again.' I couldn't say anything. The conviction of his words poured into me, and I could barely breathe.

He leaned back against the couch, releasing me from the connection. I took a deep breath to ease the pounding in my chest.

'What were you going to ask me?' I was finally able to get out.

'You said you thought it would be different. What did you mean?'

'I haven't lived with her for almost five years,' I explained evasively, staring out the window into the night. 'She's been hurt before, and I don't want her to go through that again. I just want it to be different for her, for us.'

'Where were you during those five years?'

'In hell,' I breathed, resting my head against the couch. He was quiet. I continued to stare into the dark, eventually breathing myself to sleep.

When I opened my eyes, the room was a warm gold as the sun filtered through the trees. My heavy lids closed again, and I pulled the blanket over me. I was about to drift off when I set my hand down and felt the hard lines of his thigh beneath it. My eyes stretched wide. My instinct was to jump up from the couch, freaked that I had fallen asleep with my head on his leg. But I didn't want to wake him, so I sat up slowly. Jonathan remained seated on the end of the couch, his head lolling to the side, breathing deeply.

I found my jacket draped over the arm of the rocking chair and my shoes placed beneath it – though I knew I'd had them on when I'd fallen asleep. I rubbed my eyes to ward off the remaining drowsiness and carefully rose from the couch. A floorboard creaked when I stood. His head rocked in response, and his eyes blinked open.

'Sorry,' I whispered, my heart beating quickly. I'd really wanted to be gone by the time he woke up.

'What time is it?' he asked, squinting as he read his watch. 'I should get going.' He yawned and stretched his arms over his head.

'You're not staying?'

'Um,' he stalled, not expecting the strain in my voice. I bit my lip, realizing how I sounded.

'I mean,' I fumbled, searching for a way to fix it. 'I thought that –'

'I can stay,' he interrupted. He sighed as his eyes climbed the stairs.

'You don't have to.' I could tell he was unsettled by his decision.

'I don't understand what happened last night,' he said, resting his head on the couch and searching the ceiling. 'I've seen her drunk, and I've seen her get emotional. But I've never seen her that bad before.'

I hesitated, taking in his troubled face – debating if I should just go up to my room. He was obviously concerned about her, and so was I.

I sat down on the couch, with one leg folded under me so I could face him. 'She was upset.' He rolled his head over to look at me. 'I'm sure it's been hard having me move back in, too. I remind her of my father, and that . . . hurts her. I want to fix us, but I don't know how if I'm the reason she's in pain.'

Jonathan studied my eyes, as the truth of my words swallowed me.

'You didn't do this to her,' he said soothingly. I averted my eyes. 'And as much as I feel guilty for not calling her back, I didn't do this to her either.'

We sat in silence for a minute. I tried to convince myself that what he said was true, and I *knew* it was. But I couldn't help feeling that if I hadn't forced myself back in, she wouldn't be forcing herself to forget.

'Can I ask you something?' Jonathan enquired hesitantly.

'Sure.' I turned back towards him, waiting.

'What happened to your ankle?' He eyed the scar on my right foot, which was curled under me. I pressed my lips together, not prepared for the question.

He opened his mouth to say something when I answered, 'A going-away present.'

He was quiet a moment. 'From hell?' I raised my brows in confirmation, not expecting him to get it. 'I have one of those.' Before I could react, he lifted the right side of his shirt to reveal a long, thin scar that ran under his ribs. 'Lived there once too.'

There were so many questions I wanted to ask him, but

shock stole them from my tongue. I eventually excused myself to go to my room.

Jonathan remained on the couch, not leaving as he'd promised – but not making any attempt to go to my mother's room.

Despite being exhausted, I couldn't fall back to sleep. I wondered if he was downstairs lying awake as well, trying to figure out what might have happened to me. I couldn't even imagine how to begin to ask someone to reveal their nightmares.

15

Another Chance

'JONATHAN, I'M SO SORRY. I PROMISE I'LL BE better.'

My eyes blinked open, only moments after they'd finally shut. I remained still, listening.

'Please, don't leave me,' her words were broken with emotion. Footsteps creaked down the stairs. Cries filtered through my door. I didn't dare move, fearing they'd know I could hear them.

'I won't leave,' he stated from the bottom of the stairs. His voice sounded consoling but defeated. 'I need to clear my head, okay? But I'll come back tonight and we'll talk about it.'

'You promise?' she asked in an elevated voice that sounded desperate. His answer wasn't verbal because the next thing I heard was the door shutting, followed by gasping sobs at the top of the stairs.

It was difficult to listen to her. My insides ached, wanting to take away the hurt – but I didn't. I curled into a ball and waited. Waited for her to find her breath and put herself back together. Her whimpers only quieted with the click of her door.

I crawled out of my bed and dressed in running pants and a long-sleeved running shirt, pulling a fleece over it. I needed to get out of the house, away from the consuming emotions. I tied my sneakers and slipped on gloves, hiding my hair under a baseball cap. The brisk air filled my lungs as I stepped out the door.

The sun was out, and the temperature was above freezing, melting away the icy edges along the shovelled sidewalk. I eased into a jog and breathed deep, releasing the tension in my shoulders as I followed the concrete squares beneath my feet. I'd forgotten my iPod, which would have been ideal to distract me from playing the previous night over and over in my head. Instead, the racing thoughts remained trapped.

I explored the intertwining neighbourhood, finding a park a few streets away. It was filled with kids in snowsuits jumping off whatever they could into the thick mounds of snow. Their laughter and squeals were a welcome sound in contrast to the cries that echoed in my head.

As I rounded the corner of the park, my jogging slowed at the sight of the blue pick-up truck. When I saw Jonathan sitting on a bench staring at nothing, I stopped. I considered turning around and running in a different direction, pretending I hadn't seen him. But then he spotted me, and I wasn't going anywhere.

I walked towards him, tucking my hands in my fleece pockets.

'Hey,' I said, standing in front of him. 'It's not bad out today. It's not California, but it's not bad.'

Jonathan nodded lightly. His eyes remained troubled. I sat down next to him on the wooden bench. Neither of us said anything for at least a minute.

I was contemplating getting up to continue my run when he spontaneously confessed, 'My father didn't like me very much. I wasn't submissive like my mother. I didn't worship him like my younger brother. I didn't let him control me, so he'd do anything he could to break me. My life's been complicated, and I can't . . .' The words trailed away and he stared into the distance.

'I can't do this. This . . . drama.' He took a breath and finally looked over at me. 'I need my life to be simple. I need to know what's coming, to be in control. I don't handle the unexpected very well.' He dropped his gaze.

'I understand. So does that mean you're done? That you're leaving?'

'Why? You think I should?' He waited for me to answer.

'I don't think I'm the person to tell you what to do. But I don't want her to hurt either.'

'Emma, I promise that I don't want to hurt you . . . I mean, her.' I turned towards him, confused by his stuttering sentence. His eyes flickered in apology. 'I don't want to hurt Rachel,' he emphasized. 'You believe me, right?' His dark brown eyes delved into me the way that they did, invading my thoughts and leaving me too vulnerable to resist. He held me captive until I was able to pull away with a shiver. 'Right?'

I nodded, staring down at my lap.

'My aunt didn't like me very much either,' I blurted out of nowhere, redirecting my gaze towards the house across the street. 'Actually, I'm pretty sure she hated me. I mean, you don't strangle a person if you like them even a little, do you?'

Jonathan's eyes widened in surprise. I guess he hadn't seen that coming.

'Wow, that was kind of a messed-up thing to say,' I admitted with a nervous laugh.

'Yeah, a little,' he said with a slight chuckle.

'I can't believe I just told you that.' I shook my head in embarrassment. 'You'd think that I'd be over it by now. I mean, she's in jail. But I can't seem to let it go.'

'Believe me, I understand. My father's been dead for years, and he still gets to me.'

Any remnants of a smile fell from my face. 'I'm sorry.'

'I'm not.' I was taken aback by the conviction in his voice. His face was emotionless and smooth. And in that moment, I was envious. I shifted uneasily, struck by guilt for wishing she were dead for even that one second.

Jonathan exhaled audibly. 'Wow, we're depressing as hell, aren't we?'

I laughed at the tension breaker. 'Pretty pathetic.'

'So, what are you up to today?' he asked, averting the heavy topic that threatened to overwhelm us.

'Well, I guess I'm going to finish this run,' I answered. 'Then . . . I don't know. And you?'

'Exercise sounds good,' he agreed. 'Maybe I'll go for a swim. Then, I guess I'll be back over.'

'What are you going to do?' I asked, fearing his motives for returning.

'Don't worry,' he assured me, 'no more drama. Despite what happened, I don't freak that easy. I'm not going to break it off.'

'Good.' I smiled lightly, finding myself hoping my mother wouldn't continue with her liquid therapy and end up pushing him away for good.

I left him on the bench with a promise of seeing him later and returned to my run. I had a hard time making sense of what was happening, connecting with someone through shared misery. I didn't get it, but I wasn't ready for him to leave either.

I returned to the house cleansed with sweat, and discovered that I'd missed a call from Casey. After stripping off the layers and guzzling a glass of water, I called her back.

'Will you go to a party with me tonight?' she asked, straight to the point.

'Uh,' I stumbled, not expecting the question. 'I don't know.'

'Please, Emma,' she begged. 'Jill and Sara are away, and this party is supposed to be amazing. I don't want to go by myself.'

I sighed, having a feeling I was going to regret saying, 'Fine, I'll go.'

'Yes!' she exclaimed loudly. 'I'll pick you up at nine, okay?'

'Sure,' I agreed. 'Where are we go—' She'd hung up. I supposed it didn't matter. They were basically all the same anyway.

'That's a cute sweater,' my mother noted as she watched me concentrate on brushing my lashes with mascara. It was the first time I'd seen her. She'd stayed in her room most of the day.

'Thanks,' I responded, twisting the tube back together. 'It's really warm though, so I hope I don't get too hot.'

'Cashmere does that. Wear a nice tank top underneath. I have a white one that would look great if you needed to take off the sweater.'

'Okay, thanks,' I replied, glancing at her reflection in the mirror.

She hesitated and said, 'I keep fucking up, huh?' I turned to face her as she let out a disheartened sigh. 'I'm sorry.'

Before I could respond, she went to her room and returned holding a ribbed tank top with a sweetheart neckline.

'Thank you,' I said, not sure how to recognize her apology. I pulled off the hooded green cashmere sweater and slipped on the tank.

'Fits perfectly,' she stated, then asked, 'Where's the party?'

'Not sure exactly,' I admitted. 'Do you want me to call you?'

'No,' she replied with an indifferent shrug. 'You're not the troublemaker kind, too much like your father.' She smiled gently and turned to walk away.

'Mom,' I said, 'I mean, Rachel.' She turned back towards me, her face worn and sad, even though she was trying to hold a semblance of a smile. 'Are you okay?'

My mother blinked away the tears that formed in her eyes. She cleared her throat and tried to laugh. 'I can't believe I'm acting like this.' She swiped a hand over her lids. 'I'm behaving like a sixteen-year-old.' Then she quickly added, 'No offence.'

I smiled.

'I knew he was younger. And I knew that I get attached easily,' she explained. 'I shouldn't be surprised that I freaked him out.' She appeared distraught as she confessed with a pained voice, 'I just like him so much, Emily.'

'I know.' I smiled in sympathy, absorbing the crushed look in her eyes. I wanted to tell her that it would be okay. That he wanted to be with her too, but I wasn't convinced that was the truth. So instead I told her, 'You're stronger than this.'

My words left her without any of her own. She appeared surprised, and a tear slid down her cheek.

We were interrupted by a honk.

'Oh, that's Casey,' I stated. Then I paused. 'Do you want me to stay?'

'No.' My mother smiled, smoothing her damp cheek with a shake of her head. 'Go. Have fun. Besides, he should be here any minute.'

Jonathan was on the walkway as I headed to Casey's car.

'Party?' he guessed.

'Yup.' I shrugged. 'See you later. Oh, and be good to her,' I said quietly as he passed me. I turned away before he could answer.

When I opened the door to Casey's Mini, electronic beats were released into the quiet neighbourhood.

'Hi,' she yelled, not making an effort to turn down the music that reverberated through my chest. I just nodded in return.

Casey wasn't a non-stop talker and messenger of all things gossip like Jill. She usually got the stories mixed up or completely wrong, so she'd listen and repeat what she didn't understand – which was most of it. She was genuinely a good person, but carrying on a conversation would take patience I didn't possess at the moment – so I just let the music do the talking.

We zipped through the winding dark roads of Weslyn, venturing into a neighbourhood lined with iron gates. The hidden houses were set within the hills, displaying all their grandeur while overlooking the rest of us below. I knew this was going to be quite the party.

Casey turned the music down as we entered a long drive. The electronic gates slid open when we pulled in front of them. She eyed me in expectation.

'Are you mad?' she asked, biting her lip – preparing for my reaction.

'Uh, no,' I replied, eyeing her suspiciously. 'Why would I be mad?'

'You've never been here?' she questioned in surprise.

I watched the stone castle emerge before us as we crept up the wide circular drive filled with cars. It even had a tower in the centre, with wings upon wings spread out on either side. The flawless structure had been built with large round stones. It was impressive, but had a cold facade.

'I would remember this place.' I gawked up at it. 'Who lives here?'

Casey stopped the car for the valet and put it in park. 'Drew.'

Before I could react, she was out of the car and taking a number from the guy in the black jacket.

Now I was mad.

'Why are we at Drew's? What made you think this was

a good idea? And why would you invite me to come with you?' I shoved my car door open.

'Geez,' Casey sulked. 'He never has parties, and I really wanted to see the inside of his place. We'll leave in an hour, okay?' She looked like a pathetic puppy who'd been scolded for chewing on the furniture, her blue eyes big and her brows tilted down. I released an annoyed sigh.

'Fine, an hour,' I grumbled. 'But don't lose me, okay?'

'I promise,' she chirped, all perked up again. I almost expected her to jump up in the air and clap.

I followed her through a large wooden door with a cast-iron knocker as large as my head. We entered the open-ceiling foyer, where a large table displaying an enormous floral arrangement was centred in the space.

There wasn't much of a crowd yet. The people we passed could have come from anywhere, since most were unrecognizable to me. Casey paraded through, handing her jacket to someone behind a closet door. I followed her loose bobbing curls, but she made a turn down one of two halls and disappeared.

I turned the corner, and the space opened into what must have been the family room. There were dark brown leather couches pushed against one wall. And a sleek, handcrafted twenty-foot bookcase climbed up another wall, displaying books and artefacts of various shapes and sizes. Large arching windows spread across two sides of the room, and at the far end, lights were suspended on poles, flashing on a dance floor. Tall, thin speakers framed a guy standing at a computer with large black headphones on his nodding head.

The room was scarcely populated – a few people sat on

the couches and a few more stood around the perimeter talking. But Casey was nowhere to be found.

'Where's the bar?' I asked the first random person who passed me.

'Down those stairs.' The girl pointed, then continued after her friends.

There was an arch in the wall, barely noticeable as the hall rounded a corner. I entered to find wide curving stairs – leading down to the dungeon, I presumed. I followed the polished wooden steps around the bend, into the largest rec room I'd ever seen. There were several pool tables, two bars, couches, televisions, foosball tables and a basketball shooting game. Soft lighting filtered through sconces around the perimeter of the stone walls.

There were more people down here than upstairs, but it still wasn't crowded – or maybe the space was so large it didn't feel like it was. I thought I spotted Casey at the bar at the far end of the room, and I passed several groups of people to get to her.

'Emma Thomas?' a girl asked behind me. I turned to find a group of girls in glittery tops holding martini glasses, gawking. 'I *never* would have expected to see you here. This is crazy.'

I looked from one to the other, not recognizing any of them.

'We graduated two years ago,' the petite brunette stated when it was evident I didn't know who they were.

'Oh, hi,' I said, not coming up with anything better to say.

'How've you been?' the girl with black curly hair and full red lips asked.

'Um,' I stumbled, not really believing that they cared, but deciding to answer with, 'Great, thanks. I'm actually looking for Casey Straus. Have you seen her?'

'No,' she replied apologetically. 'We should totally catch up later though, okay?'

'Definitely.' I forced a smile as they waved and walked away. What had I gotten myself into?

I turned towards the bar again, but the blonde curls had disappeared. I collapsed on to one of the stools, not wanting to chase her all night. I figured after the hour was up, I'd text her and meet her wherever she was.

'What can I get for you?' the guy in the white Oxford asked from behind the bar. I couldn't believe there was an actual bartender, but then again, there was valet parking.

'Something with caffeine,' I requested. As he reached for a liquor bottle, I specified, 'Non-alcoholic.' He nodded and handed me a Mountain Dew.

I looked past him to the screen suspended behind the bar and occupied myself with basketball highlights so I wouldn't have to make conversation with people I didn't know. Or people I did . . .

'I told him, "You're a douche and you're going to wish you were dead."'

I don't know why I turned around. Perhaps it was because he had one of those obnoxious voices that carried through a crowd, attracting attention. It was almost an instinct, like hearing a car horn and turning to see who was honking as the car's about to hit you.

Jay's mouth dropped open. 'Shit, Emma. I didn't know you were here. Sorry. I didn't mean anything by it.'

It took me a moment to understand what Drew's

annoying best friend was talking about. When it connected, I rolled my eyes with a groan and slid off the stool – walking past him and the awed eyes that surrounded him.

There was a steady stream of people flowing down the stairs, so I continued to the other side of the room, keeping my head down. I found a sliding door leading to a stone patio next to the other bar. I unlocked it and slipped out before anyone could say anything else to me.

I wasn't sure why I bothered to keep coming to these parties. I blew out a cloud of frustration into the frosty air and shoved my hands in my pockets, trying to decide my next move.

I pulled out my phone, recognizing that I still had an unbearable forty-five minutes to go. I searched the dark, trying to spot a path that led to the front. Maybe the valet would let me sit in Casey's car while I waited for her.

The patio connected to a stone walkway that was cleared of snow. It branched out; one way led to a pool covered in a snow-crusted blue sheet, and another to a long building with a dark wood finish. Light spilled from the small windows that lined the top of the tall walls.

I approached the door, just to peek in, but when I opened it I was drawn inside. The distinct scent of freshly waxed floors with a hint of rubber filled my senses. I wasn't exactly surprised to find an indoor basketball court in Drew's back yard, but I couldn't understand why he'd never told me about it.

The court was empty, creating the perfect haven in which to hide for the next half hour or so. I unzipped my jacket and dumped it on the bench. Perfectly painted black lines framed the court, and two benches for the competing teams bordered one side. A professional scoreboard hung high on the wall at one end of the court. There was even a door leading to a locker room in one of the corners. I laughed, shaking my head. This was unbelievable.

I took off my black-soled shoes and strode on to the court, eyeing the rack of balls along the baseline. I pulled one off and started dribbling towards the foul line. Squaring up to the basket, I released the ball, bouncing it off the back rim and through the orange hoop. I slid my feet along the floor for the rebound, then dribbled back for another shot.

I continued to work my way around the perimeter, watching the minutes tick away on the caged-in clock behind the basket. When the door banged shut I stopped with the ball poised in the palm of my hand. I spun around.

'I thought I'd find you in here,' Drew said with a soft smile, his dimples slightly creasing. 'Then again, I wasn't expecting you to be at the party at all.'

'Sorry,' I apologized, my entire body breaking out in a nervous sweat.

'No, it's okay,' he assured me, walking towards me. 'Just surprised when I heard you were here, not a big deal.'

Drew wore a light blue sweater that played off the colour of his eyes, making them look like reflective pools of water. His black hair was swept to the side, more tamed than the surfing style I remembered, but it could have easily been mussed to resemble it.

'Where's Sara?' he questioned.

'Cornell,' I responded.

'Then who are you here with? Because I know it's not Evan,' he mocked.

'Casey,' I shared, picking up on his teasing tone. He nodded.

I balanced the ball on my hip, trying to figure out the best way to leave without it being any more uncomfortable.

'Wanna shoot?' he asked, holding up his hands in expectation.

'Why not.' I tossed him the ball with a shrug. I thought I might as well since I had to leave in a few minutes anyway.

He dribbled in closer and pulled up for a shot, the ball sliding through the net with ease. I shuffled to collect the ball and tossed it back to him for another attempt. He took a few steps to the right and landed the shot.

'Congratulations on winning States for soccer again this year,' Drew said, accepting the ball again.

'Thanks,' I responded, focusing on the rebounds so my nerves wouldn't get the better of me.

'Heard the girls' basketball team is pretty decent too,' he continued, hitting every shot he took.

'Yeah, we have a good team.'

He tossed the ball back in my direction, allowing me to take some shots. I dribbled out to the three-point mark and let the ball go, nailing it.

'Nice.' He bounced the ball to me. I stepped up to receive it and set up for the shot; it bounced off the back-board and into the basket.

'Syracuse ball, huh?' I concentrated on the basket, not looking at him as I spoke. 'How come I never knew they picked you up? That's pretty huge.'

'No one really did,' he responded. His indifference caught me off guard. I hesitated, flashing him a quick glance, before taking the shot. 'I didn't want to make a big deal about it. My dad brags enough for the two of us. Besides, I'm redshirted this year, so I don't play much.'

'Right.' I nodded, still not understanding how the entire school hadn't known he was a prospect when they scouted him during his junior year. It made me wonder just how important basketball was to him, since it was obviously a huge deal to his father. I squared up to shoot. Drew moved in quickly, intending to tip the ball out of my hands. I pulled it down and when his hand sank, I popped back up to hit the shot.

'Nice try,' I taunted, rushing in to gather the rebound. Drew hurried after the ball, bumping alongside me. He was quicker, having the shoe advantage.

He grinned cockily and dribbled the ball back out. I took a defensive stance in front of him. He made a move on the inside, and I followed in tight, jumping when he released it. But it sailed over my fingers into the basket.

'Lucky,' I jeered.

My anxiety dissipated with each shot. Drew pulled off his sweater revealing a grey T-shirt with a surfing logo. I was beginning to sweat myself, so I took off my sweater too and tossed it next to his on the bench. As I turned back towards the court, Drew shifted his eyes down from the fitted white tank top. I ignored the slight grin on his face.

He checked the ball back out to me and I dribbled, deciding where to make my move.

'How come we never played before?' he asked, jabbing

his hand in to attempt a steal. I turned to block him with my shoulder, letting out a wicked laugh.

'I don't know,' I responded. I spun around to release a quick shot over him, slicing through the net. 'How come you never told me you had a basketball court in your back yard?'

'Graduation present,' he explained. I nodded my head in understanding, knowing we hadn't been exactly speaking, nor had I been in any condition to play ball, when he'd graduated last June.

'I can't play in socks,' I decided after sliding after the ball. 'Barefoot rule.'

'Fine,' Drew agreed, kicking off his shoes and stripping off his socks.

We continued with the one-on-one match, the game intensifying with each rebound and score. I shoved up against him to sneak in under the basket, and he elbowed me a few times to earn space to take a jumper. I couldn't say who was winning; we weren't exactly keeping score.

I went up for a jump shot inside the three-point line, and Drew came in late for the block, nudging me with his shoulder. I landed hard on my right foot, and my ankle gave way under the pressure. I stumbled to the floor.

I pulled my knee into my chest, grabbing my ankle and sucking in air through clenched teeth.

'I'm so sorry.' He bent down beside me. 'Are you okay?'

'Yeah,' I grunted, inspecting the damage. 'Just landed wrong.'

'It would suck if I took out the captain of the team right before play . . .' His sentence trailed when his eyes connected with the scar. 'Oh, Em. Are you okay? Really?'

'Yeah, I'm fine,' I tried to answer lightly, downplaying the strain in my voice. He held out his hand, slowly pulling me to my feet. I tested my weight and limped to the bench.

'I'll get an ice pack.' Before I could refuse, he was jogging to the locker room. He returned a minute later with a white plastic pack, twisting it to initiate the cooling process. I rested my leg on the bench, and he set the pack on top of my ankle.

'I'll be fine,' I stated adamantly, slightly embarrassed by his concern. 'Besides, aren't you throwing a party or something? You don't have to take care of me.'

He smiled. 'The party takes care of itself. And I wish I'd taken better care of you when I had you.'

His words stilled my chest as I remained silent.

'What I meant to say is that I'm sorry,' he said softly, sitting at the end of the bench near my foot, holding the ice pack in place. 'I was such an asshole at that party, and I wish I could take it back. So I just . . . I wanted you to know I'm sorry.'

I swallowed, since it seemed to be the only thing that I was capable of doing. I met his eyes, sincerity glistening in their tranquil hue. I didn't know what to say. But I believed him.

My view shifted past him to the clock on the wall. 'Shit. I'm late.'

'What?' Drew asked, my panic unexpected.

'I was supposed to meet Casey about an hour ago. I'm such an idiot.'

'She's probably still inside,' he assured me.

I pulled my foot out from under his hand and shoved on my socks and shoes. My ankle was tender, but I'd been through worse. I grabbed my jacket and headed for the door.

'Wait,' Drew called after me, grabbing his jacket and fumbling with his shoes.

I pulled my phone from my pocket to call her and noticed I had five missed calls, three of them from Casey, and a string of texts. I groaned.

The last text read, *Have no idea where you are, but I left. At another party across town. Call me if you're stuck.*

'Great,' I grumbled.

'What's wrong?' Drew asked, tying his shoes beside me.

'She left. Now what am I going to do?'

'Do you want to leave?' he asked, standing up and sliding his arms into his sweater before pulling it over his head.

'No offence, I'm sure it's a great party, but . . .'

'I get it,' he concluded. 'I'll drive you.'

'You can't leave your own party,' I objected.

'They haven't missed me yet,' he smiled sardonically. 'I haven't had more than one beer, and I can't say that for just about anyone else at this party besides you. Still don't drink, right?'

I shook my head.

'Then let me drive you home.'

I took a breath to give me a moment to decide. 'Fine.'

I followed Drew to the house so he could grab his keys. We shuffled through the crowd that had grown to raging proportions during our absence.

'Where've you been?' a girl with long, flowing blonde hair and a fitted strapless top asked Drew as we neared the stairs.

'I've been here,' he responded without really looking at her. 'I'll be back.' We passed by, and I avoided the daggers that followed me up the steps.

A man dressed all in black stood at the top of the stairs. He looked like he was about to stop us when he recognized Drew. 'Good evening, Mr Carson.'

'Hi, Frank,' Drew greeted him. 'Anyone giving you a hard time?'

'No one I can't handle,' the muscular figure responded. I noticed an ear piece in his ear, and he squeezed a small mic on his collar to talk, conversing with someone.

'You take partying to a whole other level,' I observed, continuing down the long, wide hallway.

'I know what can happen when it goes wrong,' Drew responded, stopping at a door. I remained still when he opened it. 'You can come in if you want.'

'No,' I answered quickly. 'I'll wait in the hall.'

Drew smirked and entered his bedroom. He re-emerged a few minutes later with a jacket on and keys in his hand. We retreated down another staircase at the far end of the hall, with another man dressed in black posted at the top.

'I'll be back in a while,' Drew told the guard.

'Don't worry. Everything's under control,' he promised in return.

The stairs led to a hallway near a side entrance, away from the crowd. We disappeared without anyone noticing. His SUV was parked on the side of the house, making for an easy escape.

'Thanks for driving me,' I said, securing the seat belt.

'No problem,' he responded, starting the vehicle.

We were quiet most of the ride. I was afraid to say

anything, not wanting to begin a conversation I wasn't prepared to have. As we continued, I looked around in a sudden panic.

'Where are we going?' I demanded in a rush.

'To your . . . oh shit.'

My heart was beating so fast, I couldn't catch my breath. Drew opened his mouth in aggrieved apology. He pulled the SUV into the parking lot of the closed coffee shop.

I closed my eyes, trying to pull some semblance of composure together.

'I can't believe I did that,' Drew said, shaking his head. He pulled away, putting distance between me and the house. 'Where do you live now?'

I gave Drew directions to my mother's house on Decatur Street, finding it easier to breathe the further away we drove.

Drew pulled into the driveway behind Jonathan's truck. He put the SUV in park and turned towards me.

'It was good to see you,' he said.

'Yeah,' I replied, unbuckling the belt.

'Hey,' he said, stopping me from reaching for the handle. 'I wish I had known.' I faced him, letting him continue but knowing I shouldn't. 'You know, about what you were going through,' he explained softly.

A twinge of nerves spiked through me. I closed myself off, determined not to let his words in.

'I know I was a dick at times, but I really did care about you.'

Those words snuck in unexpectedly, and I felt a warmth rush through me. 'I know.'

'I tried to visit you,' he confided, 'when you were in the

hospital. But the police wouldn't let me in. I really am sorry, Emma – for everything.'

I smiled slightly. 'Thanks, Drew. No one knew, so it wasn't just you.'

'Do you think I could call you some time?' he asked slowly. 'You know, to keep in touch?'

'It was good to see you too, Drew,' I said, without answering. 'Thanks again for the ride.' I opened the door and got out. He waited in the driveway until I opened the door. I didn't look back, shutting it behind me.

16

Ready?

I PULLED THE EARBUDS FROM MY EARS AND
set the magazine next to me on the bed when I heard the
knock on my door.

'Hi.' My mother smiled, easing the door open. 'Can I
come in?'

'Sure,' I answered, not sure why she was acting so nervous. Then I noticed the frame in her hand.

'I wanted you to have this,' she said, propping the frame
on the top of my bureau, next to Leyla and Jack's framed
Christmas card. I slid off the bed to get a better look. 'I
figured you should have it, since it's the only one that
escaped my clumsiness.'

It was a picture of my father balancing me on his shoulder, smiling proudly. I was laughing, wearing a soccer
uniform and holding up a trophy. My mouth turned up at
the sight of it.

'Thank you.'

'He loved watching you play soccer,' she recalled.
I examined the picture, but couldn't place the moment.

I appeared to be around five or six. Perhaps I was too young to remember. 'You understand why I don't have pictures of him out, right?' she asked tentatively. I nodded. 'Well, it doesn't mean you can't.'

I wasn't sure what to say. It was obvious it had taken a lot for her to share this with me. And I wanted to tell her how much it meant to me. I probably should have hugged her. But we just stood there awkwardly, having difficulty even meeting each other's eyes, forget about touching.

'So how was the party?' she finally asked, breaking the emotional tension.

'It was a party,' I sighed indifferently.

'Did anyone say anything about the sweater?' she pushed.

'Oh no!' I exclaimed, shaking my head.

'What?' she questioned in alarm.

'I forgot my sweater,' I explained, upset with myself. 'I can't believe I forgot it.'

'Can't you just go there and get it?' she asked, not understanding my dilemma.

'Well . . . it was at my ex-boyfriend's house, so I'm not so sure that would be a great idea,' I groaned.

'Ex-boyfriend's?' my mother mused with raised eyebrows. 'Does Evan know you went?'

I pressed my lips together guiltily. 'No. And I'm not looking forward to telling him.'

'Good luck with that,' she scoffed lightly with a shake of her head.

'Oh, thanks,' I retorted, my stomach twisting at the thought of having to tell Evan I went to Drew's *and* that he drove me home. 'That makes me feel better.'

'Sorry,' she chuckled.

'Ready?' Jonathan hollered from the hallway.

'For what?' my mother questioned in confusion, just as red and purple squirt guns thumped on my bed.

Jonathan appeared in the doorway, armed with a blue one. 'For this,' he smiled wickedly and released a stream of water.

I ducked towards the bed when he shot at us again. My mother yelped in laughter.

'Oh, you are so going to get it,' she squealed, snatching the red gun and chasing after him down the stairs, spraying the entire way.

I grabbed the other gun and pursued them, losing sight of Jonathan as my mother ran into the kitchen for cover. I led with the gun, pointing it into the living room, but he wasn't there.

I turned and crept back towards the foyer. My mother stuck her head out and nodded towards the dark hallway that led to the basement door. Before I could react, Jonathan emerged from the shadows and grabbed me by the arm, pulling me in front of him just as my mother popped out of the kitchen, aimed to squirt.

Jonathan pressed his arm across me, taunting my mother to shoot.

'You're using me as a shield?' I accused him, as he waved the gun, flashing it from my mother to me – ready to squirt whoever made a move first.

'She's not going to shoot *you*,' he explained, steering me further out into the foyer as my mother attempted to circle around to get a clear shot.

'Sorry, honey,' my mother said, aiming the gun at my head.

'Mom?' My eyes spread wide in disbelief. Then I noticed her eyes flip towards the floor, and in that second, I dropped out of Jonathan's arm and onto the floor while she squirted him. I spun around and began streaming water at him as well.

Jonathan held up his hand to protect himself while he shot back at us. None of us attempted to retreat, allowing the water to fall on us as we laughed, until there wasn't anything left in our guns.

'Time to refill,' Jonathan proclaimed with his hands raised in surrender.

My mother took my gun as I sat on the stairs, wiping my face, still smiling.

'Okay, we get a head start,' my mother instructed me a few minutes later, handing back the filled water guns.

'Jonathan, you have to stay in the kitchen for twenty seconds before you can come out. Ready, Emily?'

I nodded. Jonathan eyed us suspiciously before retreating to the kitchen.

'Quick,' she whispered, 'up the stairs.'

I scampered up the stairs with her right behind me. Ducking into the bathroom, I hid behind the door, as she lay on the floor of the hallway, ready to ambush him when he came up the stairs.

'Ready?' she asked, glancing back at me. I thought I heard a knock at the door, but I couldn't be sure from where I was.

'Wait, you can't go outside,' my mother hollered when the door squeaked open. She popped up and started shooting in that direction before she was even on her feet. I stepped out of the bathroom to follow her. But she'd stopped. She stood frozen at the top of the stairs with her hand covering her mouth.

'I am so sorry,' she gasped. I followed her horrified gaze to find Evan at the bottom of the stairs with water running down his forehead and over his nose, stunned and confused.

I opened my mouth in shock and then burst out laughing.

'What did you do?' Jonathan asked from beside the door. 'That's not the best way to greet someone.'

'Evan, I thought you were Jonathan trying to escape,' my mother explained in a rush, her face bright red. I shook my head, still laughing as I went down the stairs.

Evan ran his hand over his face. 'It's okay. It's only water.' He eyed me with his amused grin. 'You're laughing? You think this is funny, right?' I recognized that look.

Before I could turn back up the stairs to get away, he had his arms wrapped around my waist and I was off the ground.

'Oh no, Evan. Don't,' I begged. I had no idea what he planned to do, but I knew I was in for it. Jonathan appeared entertained, but my mother scrambled after us.

'What are you going to do?' she asked, watching as he wrestled me into the kitchen.

'Mom, help –' My pleas were broken with laughter. I tried to squirm away when one of his hands released me to turn on the faucet. 'Evan!'

He squeezed the sprayer and doused me over the head as I broke free. My mother and Jonathan hid behind either side of the doorway to get out of the way. By the time I was out of range, I was dripping wet.

'Now *that's* funny.' Evan's laughter was echoed by Jonathan and my mother.

'Thanks for your help,' I sulked, looking down at my drenched T-shirt.

'What? And be soaked like you?' my mother chuckled.

'Nice, Evan,' Jonathan admired. 'Next time, you're on my team.' I shook my head and dripped up the stairs.

I returned a few minutes later with a dry T-shirt and my wet hair pulled back. Evan was helping wipe up the water in the kitchen.

'You missed a spot,' I teased.

He turned towards me and grinned, taking in my wet hair. 'No I didn't.'

'Oh, you're so funny,' I smirked. 'Ready to go?'

'Where are you going?' my mother asked, taking the wet towel from Evan.

'To Evan's.'

'Really?' Evan queried, obviously not aware of the plan. I nodded. 'Okay, to my house then.'

'I'll be back later,' I announced, pulling my jacket out of the closet.

'Good luck,' my mother said, making me hesitate before leaving, suddenly understanding what she meant. Maybe we should've stayed after all.

'Are you okay?' Evan asked when he saw my face drop.

'Yeah,' I muttered. 'I just thought I forgot something.' I grumbled under my breath, walking out onto the porch, 'But unfortunately I didn't.'

'You didn't want to stay?' Evan asked when we entered the car. 'Looked like you guys were having a good time.'

'Yeah,' I said, distracted. 'But I haven't seen you all week, so I wanted to be alone with you.' *Or I did*, I thought.

By the time we arrived at Evan's, my stomach had twisted to the point of nausea.

'Are you okay?' he asked again, examining me intently when we entered the rec room. I could only imagine how pale I was.

'No,' I blurted out before I'd even taken my jacket off. I released a deep breath and confessed what I'd rehearsed a thousand times in my head on our way over. 'You're going to hear this tomorrow, so I'm just going to say it.' I twisted my hands as he leaned against the back of the couch, waiting. 'I went to a party at Drew's. I didn't know we were going there, and I never would have gone if I'd known where we were going. I'm sorry.'

I let the shock of it settle in, but his mouth curved up and the concern in his eyes disappeared.

'Why are you looking like that?'

'That's it?' he questioned, unfazed.

'Yes, I mean no,' I answered guiltily, not understanding his comical expression. 'He ended up driving me home because Casey took off, but nothing happened – I swear.'

'I know,' he answered casually, taking off his jacket and flinging it on the back of the couch.

I studied him, not understanding why he appeared so calm while the nerves in my stomach were about to devour me.

'You know?'

He stood in front of me with his hands on my waist. 'Emma, I trust you. I'm not worried about what party you go to at whoever's house, even Drew's. Was he a dick to you?'

'No,' I answered, still in shock.

'Good,' he said, giving me a kiss on the top of my head. He continued to the pool table and began pulling out the balls from the pockets.

I shook my head and uttered, 'Where did you come from?'

'What?' he laughed.

'How did I end up with you? I mean, my life's so messed up and then . . .' I kept shaking my head in wonderment. 'And then there's . . . you. I couldn't have made you up if I'd tried.'

'I don't understand what you're talking about,' he replied, racking the pool balls with a sparkling smile. While I was still gawking at him, he walked over and wrapped his arms around me. 'Most of your life wasn't your decision. You didn't get to decide who your parents were, that your dad was going to pass when you were young, or that you'd end up with . . .' His jaw tightened slightly, and he couldn't finish. 'Those weren't your choices.

'The things you do get to choose, you put everything you have into them – school, sports, protecting the people you care about. And you chose me.'

Warmth fluttered through my chest. I had a hard time meeting his eyes.

'So your life *is not* messed up . . .' Evan paused, placing his forehead on mine, demanding my attention. 'You've actually done a pretty amazing job at living it.' He kissed me gently and pulled me into him.

'I love you,' I murmured into his chest, holding him tighter. I tilted my head back and met his steel-blue eyes.

'That I know too,' he smirked, causing my mouth to drop open.

'Nice,' I shot back, pushing him away. He grabbed my hand and pulled me back against him.

'I love you too,' he whispered, before tilting his head towards me.

I closed my eyes and felt the warmth of his breath on my lips just before they pressed into mine. I inhaled deeply at the touch of them, flutters instantly rushing through my chest. He ran his hand along the back of my neck, his mouth slipping across my parted lips.

My heart raced and my breath quickened as I pulled him into me. He unzipped my jacket and slid it off, dropping it on the table. The tease of his lips along my neck captured my breath as I hopped up on to the side of the pool table and wrapped my legs around him.

He slid his hands under me and picked me up, balancing me while walking towards the couch, our mouths frantically kissing. My entire body was pulsing. He laid me on the couch and eased himself over me.

I ran my hands under his sweater and he pulled back to remove it. I sat up to run my lips along the hard lines of his chest, before pulling my T-shirt over my head. Evan grabbed the blanket at the end of the couch to cover us as I reached for his waistband.

My quickened pulse stirred a heat that crept through my entire body. We eased across boundaries, unfastening bindings, slipping beneath fabric. Our lips brushed in a breathless exchange.

Our mouths pressed harder; our breath grew faster as our hands slid along curves. He inhaled quickly at my caress, his heart beating against my bare skin. His breathing quickened, and his muscles flexed along his back, the tension rippling through his entire body as he groaned in my ear. I gasped when he found me, closing my eyes. A flush swept across my skin at his gentle touch. I writhed under the growing sensation until I was released with an exhilarated breath.

Evan pulled the blanket tighter around us, exhaling deeply. 'Wow.'

'Yeah,' I breathed, still unable to focus clearly. I tucked myself into his arm and rested my head on his chest, draping my leg over his. 'Can I ask you something?'

'Anything,' he said, running his warm hand along my back.

'When are we going to have sex?'

'Umm . . .' Evan laughed. 'I wasn't expecting *that* question.'

I popped my head up to look at him. 'I'm not saying that I don't like what we just did, it's just –'

'I know,' he smiled. 'We will. It's a big deal, and I don't want to do it on the couch in the garage, or in the back seat of a car. I want it to be what it should be.'

'What if it's horrible?' I sulked, resting my chin on his chest. 'I have no idea what I'm doing. You want it to be this epic moment, and I'm afraid I'm going to fail miserably.'

'You're ridiculous,' Evan said with a small laugh. 'I'm not worried.' He released a calming breath and repeated,

'Believe me, I'm not worried.' He put his hand under my chin to pull me in for a kiss.

Despite his lack of concern regarding my sexual prowess, I *was* worried. No matter how much I tried not to let it consume me, it was all I could think about. I'd only been waiting for it to happen, since well . . . forever.

My phone rang as I lay on my bed later that night, waiting for Sara to respond to my text. I quickly pressed *Answer*.

'What's going on?' Sara demanded before I could say hi.

'How was Cornell?' I asked, suddenly regretting sending the text.

'Shut up, Em,' Sara shot back. 'Your text said you needed my help. What's going on?'

After gathering myself, I finally stated bluntly, 'Sara, I want to have sex.'

'Well, of course you do,' she responded like I'd said the most obvious thing in the world.

'But what if I'm terrible at it?'

Sara started laughing hysterically. I hung up the phone. She called back ten seconds later.

'Sorry,' she said calmly. 'You're serious. I thought you were having one of your delusional episodes.'

I didn't say anything.

'Emma, you and Evan love each other, so there isn't a wrong way of doing this. But I'll give you some pointers if you want.'

I let out a short nervous laugh, the anxiety making my stomach squirm. 'Maybe.'

'Don't worry. I won't draw diagrams or anything. Oh, or maybe I should.'

'Sara!'

'Emma, don't you dare act all embarrassed to talk about it,' she scolded. '*I'm* not the one to be telling anyone to have or not to have sex, but if you can't even talk about it with me, then maybe you're not ready. I know this is huge for you, and you of all people need to be emotionally prepared for it.'

'I know,' I replied. 'I mean, I'm ready – I think. What do you mean by *emotionally prepared*?'

'Well, you don't trust . . . anyone, really. You barely trust me and Evan. And having sex is all trust. You can't take it back once you do it, and it leaves you completely emotionally vulnerable. You trust him totally and completely, right?'

'Of course,' I answered automatically. How could I not trust Evan? Especially after everything we'd been through.

'Emma,' Sara scolded, 'do you? No matter what's happening in your life, however complicated and personal, you'd trust him with it?'

I wasn't sure why I hesitated, but a streak of panic flicked through me at the thought of being completely open with *anyone*, even Evan.

'Yes,' I answered, without as much conviction.

'That's what I thought,' she said honing in on the waver in my voice. 'I'm not saying don't have sex. I want you to. It's amazing. I just want you to go into this completely aware of what happens to you after you put your clothes back on.'

'Thanks,' I sighed, feeling a little deflated. 'See you in the morning?'

'Yes,' she replied enthusiastically. 'I have so much to tell you!'

We said our goodbyes and hung up.

I stared at the ceiling, contemplating trust. Evan was the most trustworthy person I knew. I believed in him, knowing he would never not be there for me. But when Sara asked if I trusted him enough to tell him my most personal secrets, I'd choked.

The vulnerability of letting someone, *anyone*, into the dark places I couldn't face myself was unfathomable. It wasn't because I didn't trust him. I didn't want to reveal them to anyone, not even me. After all, they were secrets for a reason.

17

Freaked

SARA LOOKED LIKE SHE WAS READY TO
burst with whatever it was she needed to tell me when I
saw her the next morning. She was seriously glowing. But
the first thing she did was swat me across the shoulder.

'Hey,' I hollered. 'What was that for?'

'For going to Drew's party and starting up the gossip
chain when you let him drive you home.'

'Oh.' I shrank guiltily. 'It wasn't a big deal. Nothing
happened.'

'I know that, but people in this school are stupid. If
you don't want them talking about you, don't do something that will make them talk.'

'It doesn't matter,' I said with a shrug. 'They'll talk
about me even if I stand still all day.'

Sara laughed. 'You're probably right.'

'Are we done with this?' I questioned, slightly annoyed.
'Are you going to tell me about your week, or what?'

Sara didn't hold back. What she couldn't fit in before
our first class she continued with at lunch. I don't think

Evan was all that thrilled to hear her talking about his brother. He finally said something about needing to talk to his coach before the next period. I was pretty sure he just needed to escape.

'I'll see you in Art.' He departed with a kiss on my cheek.

'What's with him?' Sara asked, noting his sudden need to leave.

'Sara, you're dating his *brother*. Don't you think it's kind of weird for him?'

She shrugged as if she hadn't considered it before. 'I guess. I don't know.' When she'd exhausted all things Jared, she blurted, 'So what do you want to know about sex?'

My eyes widened, not braced for the question in the middle of the cafeteria.

'Tell me what you've done so far,' she enquired with all the seriousness of a therapist.

'Do we really need to talk about this now? You're the one who warned against giving ammunition to circulating rumours. This is definitely not something I want anyone overhearing.'

'Fine,' she replied. 'Come over after practice tonight.'

I hesitated. I wasn't embarrassed to talk about sex, I was just . . . okay maybe I was a little. It wasn't like I'd ever had *the talk*. What I knew, I'd learned in health class, so I wasn't exactly well versed on the subject. Sara would share stories, but she'd never go into explicit detail, like auditory porn or anything.

'If you get any more red I think you may catch fire,' Sara observed with a shake of her head. 'Just come over later, okay?'

209

'Okay.'

When we returned to our lockers after lunch, Sara pulled a textbook from her messenger bag. 'This will help.'

I took the book and my eyes spread wide at the title, *Our Sexuality*. 'Omigod, are you serious?' I flipped through the pages and shut it quickly when I saw way more skin than I was anticipating.

'It's a college textbook,' Sara explained casually. 'Thought you might appreciate the technical explanations versus the *Cosmo* version – you know, the science behind it.'

'Uh, thanks.' I went to shove it in my locker and it fell to the floor, spreading open with the spine up.

'Here,' Evan said, bending down to pick up the splayed textbook. I scooped it up before he could touch it, my pulse racing so fast I couldn't talk.

'What was that?' he questioned, when I stuffed it in my backpack.

'Just pointers on how to pleasure you,' Sara whispered with a smirk before walking away. I about fell over. I looked up at Evan with my mouth dropped open. He arched a brow curiously.

'Really?'

'We're going to be late for class,' I said, slamming my locker door shut. My heart was pounding so hard I was beginning to sweat. He let out an amused laugh and followed after me.

'You don't need the textbook,' Evan murmured in my ear from his stool beside me.

'Evan!' I whispered, with wide eyes.

'Sara has no idea, does she?' he continued with a sly grin.

'We are not talking about this,' I stated adamantly, burying my fiery face in my hands. He chuckled.

'Good afternoon,' Ms Mier greeted us from the front of the class, setting a large piece of wood on an easel. 'Today we are going to create visual art using nails.' On the board was a profile of a woman created with various oxidized nails pounded into the wood at different depths and angles to create a three-dimensional work of art. I was fascinated by the technique – the way the nails created the slope of her cheekbone and tilt of her nose.

'I've laid out boxes of nails for you to work with. You can each select a plank of wood and a hammer to get started.'

'I can guarantee I'll have a purple thumb by the end of this assignment,' I commented, turning towards Evan. He nodded, not looking at me.

We retrieved the supplies from the front of the classroom. I was considering what I wanted to create while filling my bowl with nails.

When I got back to the stool, Evan had the hammer balanced in his hand – examining it like he'd never seen one before. He ran his eyes over it, appearing a million miles away.

'Evan?' I sat down and tilted my head towards him to look up at his face. 'Evan, are you okay?'

He was pale and wouldn't focus on me. 'Evan, what's wrong?'

Without a word, he set down the hammer and left the room. It took me a moment to realize that he'd just walked out. I rushed to the door to go after him, but he wasn't in the hall. I stood in the middle of the corridor, at a complete loss.

I returned to the Art room and slowly lowered myself onto my stool.

'Is everything okay with Evan?' Ms Mier questioned when she came around and found Evan's spot vacant.

'I don't know,' I answered honestly. I didn't make much progress with the assignment because I kept watching the door, waiting for him to return. He never came back.

Evan wasn't at my locker after class either. I took my phone out of my backpack and texted, *Where are you? Are you okay?*

I set the phone to vibrate and stuffed it in the front pocket of my jeans, pulling my sweater over it so my Calculus teacher wouldn't see it.

Halfway through class, my phone vibrated. I slipped it out and held it under my desk to read, *Not feeling great – went home.*

I read it again, baffled.

Want me to come by after practice?

Evan responded, *No. See you tomorrow OK?*

Nothing about this felt right. He hadn't seemed sick all day. I was obviously missing something, but I didn't know what else to think so I typed, *Okay.*

'I'm going to go home after practice tonight,' I told Sara as we gathered our things at the end of the day.

'Everything okay?' she asked, taking in my sombre mood.

'I hope so,' I answered before shutting my locker door. 'I'll call you later.'

'All right,' she answered, studying me as I skulked away.

*

I called Evan as soon as I got into my car after practice. He didn't answer. I was wrecked with worry by the time I got home, my stomach twisted into knots.

'Maybe he's really sick,' Sara consoled me when I called.

'Maybe,' I agreed, but I didn't really believe it.

'Don't start overthinking like you do.'

'I won't,' I assured her, but I'd already gone there – replaying everything he and I had said throughout the entire day. I still couldn't figure out what would've caused him to leave school so suddenly. Something must have happened in those few minutes I was away from him in the Art room. Maybe he got a text that I didn't see? Whatever it was, it was sudden, and he wasn't sharing.

'We'll see if he's in school tomorrow. Text me if your brain hijacks you and you need to vent.'

After I'd hung up, I pulled my books from my bag. I needed to distract myself, and I was hoping homework would help.

I was interrupted from the miserable depths of Political Theory by a knock at my door. Before I could respond, my mother stuck her head in.

'Hi,' she said, opening the door wider upon seeing me on my bed. 'I wanted to see if Evan would like to come to dinner tomorrow night. I thought he might be up here with you.'

I'd opened my mouth to answer when she picked up the textbook Sara had given to me that was peeking out of my backpack. I scrunched my face when she read the title out loud.

'What's this?' she asked, then started flipping through

the book. 'Wow, they're really teaching you everything in high school these days. I could have used this when I went to school.'

Without thinking, I blurted, 'It's not for school.' My mother's eyes widened and her mouth rounded in sudden realization. I wanted to close my head in the book.

'This is for *you*?' she asked, the shock still on her face.

'You're still a virgin,' she slowly concluded, like she wasn't expecting that to be the truth. The mortified look on my face made it obvious that it was. 'I would have thought that you and Evan . . .' I dropped my head face first on my bed. This day could not get any worse. 'Do you want to talk about it? I never thought I'd have to give *the talk* before, but I can if you want.' My head shot up at her offer, and that's when I found Jonathan paused in the hallway – yup, it had just gotten worse.

'No . . . um, that's okay,' I stammered, cringing inwardly.

'Really, you can ask me anything,' she continued. I think she would have sat down on my bed to keep talking about it if Jonathan hadn't knocked on the open door, letting her know he was there.

'Are you ready?' he asked. I couldn't look at him. I wanted more than anything to disappear.

'Oh, yeah,' my mother responded, brought back to what she was supposed to be doing before she crossed all mother–daughter boundaries. 'Well, ask Evan about dinner, okay?'

I could only nod, my explanation of his illness lost in the back of my throat. When she set down the book, I quickly shoved it deep inside my backpack.

Jonathan held the door open to let my mother pass, then said, 'Goodnight.' I looked up, and he grinned widely.

'Goodnight,' I returned, my entire body on fire.

A few minutes later, I heard the closing of the front door. I tried to turn my focus back to my assignment, but kept finding myself checking my phone – begging it to light up with a message from Evan.

About an hour later, it did. *Sorry I missed your call. I'm okay. Pick you up in the morning?*

Yes, I texted back. I knew I wouldn't find the relief that his text was supposed to provide until I actually saw him.

Falling asleep in the restless house was never easy. Staying asleep was virtually impossible. I flipped on the light next to my bed with my heart thumping. I stared at the door. A moment ago I could have sworn there had been a hammer driving through it, trying to shatter it to pieces so she could get to me. In the light, the black door was intact and still.

I got out of bed and pulled on a sweatshirt before quietly tiptoeing downstairs to escape the panic that still shot around inside me. Exhausted, but knowing sleep was probably a good hour away, I settled on the couch with a blanket covering me. I found a movie that had more dialogue than action, the perfect plot to drone me to sleep.

About a half hour later, the creak of a step drew my attention. Jonathan cringed at the sound and paused before continuing down the stairs.

'Hey,' he greeted me wearily, pulling the blanket off the back of the love seat and sitting next to me on the couch. 'What did you find?' He motioned towards the television.

'Not sure,' I whispered, not completely surprised to see him up. 'I have no idea what's going on.'

After watching the underwhelming drama on the screen for a few minutes, he asked without looking over, 'Do you always have the same nightmare or is it different each time?'

'It's different each time,' I answered, with my head pressed against the pillow. 'But they usually end right when I'm about to die.'

Jonathan was quiet.

I turned my head to find him appraising me, his mouth bowed in sympathy. 'I take it yours aren't like that, huh?'

He shook his head, redirecting his gaze towards the TV. 'Mine are always the same,' he answered in a low voice, his jaw tightening as he stared straight ahead. His eyes hardened as he muttered, barely audible, 'They won't let me forget.' The features of his face looked carved from stone as he pressed his lips together in a tight line. The dim light glinted off his dark eyes; I couldn't see his pupils. A chill ran through me.

I almost asked what it was that kept him up most nights, but then again, I wasn't sure I wanted to know what made him suddenly so . . . hateful. He looked like a different person – a person I didn't want to know. I pulled my legs in tighter to ward off the frigidness.

Jonathan faced me, his lips turned up and his eyes creased around the edges – instantly returned to being the guy who'd started a squirt gun fight. I wanted to shake my head, wondering if I'd just imagined the transformation.

Maybe it was the lighting, and my lack of sleep, messing with me.

I pulled the blanket further up under my nose. 'I just want to sleep,' I murmured, my eyes burning with fatigue.

'I know,' Jonathan yawned.

We returned our attention to the movie. My lids were getting heavy, harder to blink open. I was thinking about going back to bed when he asked, 'So, do you need any guy advice?'

Exhaustion vanished instantly and colour rushed to my cheeks. 'Don't even start,' I threatened, sitting up and hitting him with the pillow. He held up his hands to ward off the blow and started laughing.

'You should have seen your face when your mother offered to give you *the talk*,' he chuckled. 'I was trying so hard not to laugh.' His chest spasmed with laughter.

'Oh, yeah, that was *hilarious*,' I shot back. 'Can we please not talk about one of the more humiliating moments of my life?'

Jonathan smiled widely, his perfectly straight teeth gleaming in the low light. 'Sorry.'

'Are those real?' I blurted out without thinking.

'What?' he asked, completely perplexed.

'Your teeth.' I continued to stare. They seemed too white in this low light, and too straight. I couldn't stop looking at them. A true indication that I needed to go to bed.

'That was a rather bizarre change of subject,' he noted in amusement. 'And yes, they're real. After years of braces, of course, but they're mine.' He shook his head, still grinning.

'What?' I demanded, not sure why I wanted to know what kept the grin on his face. But I asked anyway.

'Forget it,' he said playfully, 'you don't want to talk about it.'

I rolled my eyes. 'My personal life is not up for conversation.'

'Not your *personal* life,' he corrected, 'your *sex* life.'

'I don't have a *sex* life,' I retorted quickly, my face flushing as soon as I said it.

Jonathan laughed again. 'I know.'

I buried my head under the pillow and groaned.

'Why is everyone making such a big deal about it?' I murmured from beneath the pillow.

'Because it is *a big deal*,' Jonathan responded bluntly. His tone lost its humour when he confirmed, 'But you're serious, right? You and Evan?'

I peeked out from under the pillow and found him waiting for me to answer. I nodded.

'And what's going to happen when you go to Stanford?'

'Hopefully he's coming with me,' I answered, sitting up and smoothing the hair that was floating around my head.

Jonathan nodded. 'He's as smart as you?'

'Pretty much. He also has some influence that I don't.'

'Money,' Jonathan concluded with a smirk.

I shrugged. 'Part of it.'

'And powerful parents,' he added. He didn't even wait for me to answer. 'Do they want him going to Stanford with you?'

I looked down, not wanting to think about Stuart's harsh words on New Year's Eve.

'Aahh,' Jonathan surmised. 'Not so much.'

'It's his dad,' I explained quietly. 'He doesn't exactly approve of me.'

'Not approve of you?' he laughed like that was completely ridiculous. 'It's probably the money. I know *that* dad. But I went to college with her anyway.'

His words caught my attention. He nodded guiltily. 'I did it too. Fell in love with the rich girl. Her parents approved of me enough, until they realized how serious we were. But we went to Penn State together anyway, even though I really wanted to get as far away from this area as possible – and Pennsylvania was still too close.' He took a deep breath. 'I shouldn't have stayed.'

'You broke up?' I asked, even though the answer was obvious since he was now dating my mother.

'Something like that,' he grinned, the smile not reaching his eyes. I could tell by his uneasiness that the emotion was still raw, even after all these years. 'College is . . . different.'

I waited, not sure if I should ask him to continue – but wanting to know the story.

Jonathan gripped the blanket and looked towards the dark foyer. I could tell he was thinking about it, what had happened between them.

'People change. I mean you barely know who you are when you enter, and you spend that time figuring out what you want from life, and who you want in it. The next thing you know, the people you always thought would be there, aren't. And the person you thought you could trust with everything, isn't the person you knew at all.'

His shoulders sank. 'And then six years later, you have a fraction of the life you thought you would.'

I was quiet. I wanted to say something to distract him from going back there, to the place that bowed his head and caved his chest. But he did it himself.

'I got into University of Southern California,' he declared with a proud smile, dispersing the emotion with ease.

'You did?! Jonathan, that's so great. Congratulations.' I was genuinely happy for him, but then it hit me. 'Wait. You haven't told her yet, have you?' I closed my eyes in dread.

'I will,' he sighed.

All of a sudden, I felt the air go out of me, like someone just punched me in the stomach.

'Emma, what's wrong?' His voice was heavy with concern.

'He was supposed to know by now,' I gasped, unable to catch my breath – consumed by panic. 'If he'd got in . . . he was supposed to know.'

'Evan?' he confirmed. I nodded, my chest squeezing. The entire day was starting to unravel. His needing to leave at lunch. And then right after in Art, the look on his face. He couldn't look at me or even answer my call.

'He didn't get in.' I couldn't breathe.

'Emma, don't do this,' Jonathan said soothingly. 'Don't start freaking out before you know for sure.'

'Easy for you to say,' I squeaked, feeling like my world was tipping upside down.

'What if he doesn't get in?' he challenged. I stared at him with huge eyes, like he'd just told me I'd lost everything. I shook my head, denying that it was possible. I couldn't imagine being in California without Evan. I didn't want to even think about it.

'Wow,' Jonathan observed, 'this is everything to you, isn't it?'

I sank back into the couch, trying to ease the pain in my chest.

'Ask him. Don't go crazy thinking about it until you've asked him.'

I nodded. 'Just like you have to tell her that you're leaving.' I watched Jonathan's face fall.

'Just not sure how to do it,' he admitted glumly. 'Her birthday's in a few weeks, and I was hoping to be around for it. Is that bad?'

'So you'd rather break up with her after her birthday?' I questioned, not sure which scenario I preferred.

'It's just that . . . I'm not ready to go yet.' He paused and concluded, 'It *is* bad.'

'It's not my call,' I told him. 'But she should know.'

'I know.'

'Wait.' I narrowed my eyes, suddenly recalling his reference to how different his life was *six* years later. 'How old are you?'

Jonathan cringed guiltily. 'How old am I, or how old does Rachel think I am?'

'Oh.' My mouth dropped open. 'You lied to her about your age.'

'She has a problem with the age difference as it is,' he explained with a guilt-ridden smirk. 'I wasn't about to tell her I'm twenty-four.'

'You *are* bad,' I said, shaking my head, but unable to keep a scornful face.

'You have no idea,' he replied with a wry smile, making us burst out laughing.

'Jonathan?' my mother called from the top of the stairs. Guilt quieted our laughter.

She turned on the hall light and came down a few steps, enough to see into the living room. When she saw us on the couch, her face dropped and something flashed across her eyes. I wasn't certain if it was shock or anger, but it was so brief I could've convinced myself I didn't see it at all.

'Couldn't sleep?' she asked with a sympathetic smile. I wasn't sure who she was talking to. I shook my head.

'I'll be up in a minute,' Jonathan told her. She nodded and went back to her room, shutting off the light before closing her door.

'I should go to bed,' I said, standing up and folding the blanket.

'I like this,' Jonathan said suddenly, before I could walk away, 'talking to you. I feel like I can tell you things . . . things that I usually keep to myself. Most people don't understand.'

'I know.' I hesitated before turning from him.

It was true. Until that moment I hadn't realized what was happening. I was able to share the demons that wrestled with me in the night, and Jonathan understood in a way that no one else did. He was fighting with them himself, and that had drawn us together.

The corner of his mouth turned up softly. For a moment I couldn't look away. I was trapped in the darkness of his eyes. They sifted through me, searching for what haunted me. I pulled away with a blink. 'Are you staying up?'

'I'm not quite ready to sleep,' he admitted, picking up the remote.

'Be careful of the infomercials,' I advised, borrowing his words from the first time he'd rescued me from my nightmare. He smiled. 'The next thing you know, the sun will be up.'

I left him on the couch and slipped back to my room. I didn't sleep much, but it didn't have anything to do with the nightmare. I kept thinking about what I expected from my future, and hoping more than anything that Evan would be in it.

Jonathan was still on the couch, asleep, when I got up before dawn to use the bathroom. I thought about waking him to send him to bed, but he was sleeping. And that was, after all, a good thing.

18

Story Time

A SOFT KNOCK DREW MY ATTENTION TO the front door while I was rinsing my oatmeal bowl in the sink. Without allowing me a chance to answer, the door crept open and Evan stepped in.

'Hi.' He seemed tentative, not his usual confident self.

'Hi,' I replied, checking his face for any signs of illness. He looked tired and sullen, which only heightened my concern.

He smiled slightly, but the trouble that flickered in his eyes remained. I approached slowly, preparing myself for the news that he wasn't going to Stanford.

'Are you okay?' he asked, examining the stress lines on my face.

I couldn't mask the signs of sleeplessness that hovered under my eyes or the worry that weighed down the corners of my lips.

'Are you?' I asked in return, continuing closer until I was less than a foot in front of him.

'I worry about you,' Evan stated, tracing every inch of my face. 'Are you really okay?' He ran his hand along my cheek. I closed my eyes, soaking in its warmth.

'I'm okay.' That's all I could offer, because on the inside I was a mess. I needed to understand why he was acting so strangely.

Evan leaned in and softly pressed his lips to mine, loosening the knot of worried tension that had held me captive since the moment he'd stepped out of the Art room.

'That's a little better,' I murmured when he pulled away. 'Are you going to tell me what happened yesterday? Is it Stanford? Did you not get in?'

He looked at me in surprise. Then a smile eased on to his face. 'You think yesterday was about Stanford?'

'I don't know what it was about,' I continued, not at all relieved by the amused look. 'You were supposed to know by now.'

'I did get the letter,' he admitted.

I stopped breathing, anticipating the next sentence.

'But I don't know if I got in.'

'What?' I asked, my shoulders sinking. 'What does that mean?'

'Oh, Em,' he shook his head. 'I'm sorry I didn't tell you. My parents won't tell me which college I'm attending until all the acceptance letters come in. We're still waiting on Yale.'

'Does that mean they get to decide for you?' I asked in horror, realizing that if Stuart had his say Evan wouldn't be going to any school in California.

'No,' Evan chuckled, wrapping his arms around me

and holding me against him. 'I write down my first three choices, and then my mother reveals which school I'm going to. She makes a big production out of it. We go to a nice restaurant, and then she hands me an envelope with the name of the college inside. Don't panic. You're not losing me, no matter what.' He kissed the top of my head.

'Why does she do that?' I asked, completely baffled.

'It's something she came up with for Jared. Jared didn't get his first choice. He picked Dartmouth. So she conjured this *celebratory reveal* to soften the blow. She thinks it's only right she does the same for me. You'll come to the dinner, right?'

'Of course,' I replied. But I quickly reconsidered. I didn't know if I could fake excitement if he wasn't accepted by Stanford.

'Better?' he asked, inspecting me again. I nodded. He leaned down and kissed me gently. 'Ready to go?'

'Just need to get my jacket,' I answered. He released me so I could go to the closet.

I followed him out the door, and he took my hand after I'd locked the house behind us.

It occurred to me during our drive to school that he'd never explained what had happened to him yesterday. I couldn't keep from trying to read his thoughts as he drove. His eyes lacked the light that usually shone within them. I knew something was still troubling him.

'What's wrong?' I finally asked. 'Because I know something is.' He exhaled deeply, as if he'd been preparing himself for my question.

'Will you come over tonight?' he asked in return. 'There's something you should know, and I want to explain it when we're alone.' I stopped breathing *again*. His tone was too serious for it to be anything good.

I nodded slightly, my chest burning in a storm of panic.

Evan pulled into a parking spot and glanced at me, then did a double take. I knew the panic was evident – I wasn't even trying to hide it. 'Em, I'm sorry.' He tried to console me, 'That sounded much worse than I meant it to. You don't have to worry, I swear.'

I nodded.

He met me on my side of the car and pulled me towards him. 'I love you,' he said softly, his blue eyes filled with sincerity. 'Know that before you spend the whole day freaking out. Okay?'

'Okay,' I whispered.

Before he could lean down to kiss me, I heard, 'And that's Evan and Emma, one of Weslyn High's power couples. Evan's gorge but don't even bother looking – he won't see you.'

I poked my head around Evan, astounded. Jill walked by with a petite blonde with big doe-brown eyes and pouty red lips. The girl's eyes darted away when they connected with mine, realizing I'd overheard them.

Evan took my hand and turned towards them, shaking his head in amusement. When he spotted the new girl, he spoke warmly, 'Hi, Analise.'

She quickly replied, 'Hi, Evan,' with an abashed smile, her cheeks turning rosy.

Jill dragged her off quickly, most likely to get the inside story on how they knew each other.

'How do you know the new girl?' Sara asked from behind us. I turned quickly, unaware of her approach.

'Good morning, Sara,' I greeted her.

'Good morning,' she replied before turning towards Evan and demanding, 'So?'

'My mother hired Analise's mom to work for her new consulting firm,' he explained. 'They moved here from New York.'

'I'm sure my parents will be taking hers out for dinner soon enough to welcome them to Weslyn,' Sara sighed.

'It's just her mom,' Evan noted. 'I think we're supposed to have them over for dinner on Friday. In fact, I'm pretty certain your parents are coming too.'

'That's not surprising,' Sara returned with a roll of her eyes. 'Is she a junior?'

'I think so.'

As we walked past her and Jill in the hallway, I took a closer look at the new transfer who was receiving so much attention. She was very pretty in a pure and innocent sort of way. Her fair skin made her red lips and blushed cheeks that much more pronounced, reminiscent of a porcelain doll. Her blonde hair tossed in waves, barely touching her shoulders; she nervously twisted a strand around her finger. She seemed shy, barely able to make eye contact with anyone, but she'd certainly found the best person to tell her the ins and outs of the social hierarchy at Weslyn High.

And for no reason I could explain, other than pure territorial insecurity, I didn't want to picture her having dinner at the Mathews' dining room table. I was ashamed of myself for even thinking it, but the guilt didn't make me change my mind.

'My mother's hoping you'll come over for dinner tonight,' I told Evan before he departed for his locker.

'Are you feeling okay, Evan?' Sara asked, interrupting us. 'You look tired.'

'I'm trying to get over something,' Evan admitted. I was instantly struck by his meaning, wanting to know more than ever what he was planning to tell me.

Then he responded to my invitation with, 'Sure. We'll go to your house after practice.' He kissed my cheek and walked away.

'And *you* seriously need to start wearing concealer.' Sara shook her head as she looked me over. 'You could probably count the number of times you've slept through the night on one hand, and it's doing a number on the circles under your eyes.'

'Thanks, Sara,' I huffed, stopping in front of our lockers. 'It doesn't help that I live in the creepiest house in Weslyn. And as much as your black wall looks chic during the day, at night I swear it breathes.'

'Maybe you should try the medication your doctor prescribed,' Sara advised. When I didn't respond, she changed the subject. 'How's Rachel? Or better yet, how's Jonathan?'

I smirked sardonically at the eagerness in her voice. 'Fine. Although she did see your textbook last night and was ready to give me step-by-step instructions before Jonathan walked in and overheard. I wanted to die.'

Sara laughed. 'Did you read it?'

'No!' I shot back quickly, making her laugh harder. 'I don't think I'm going to. You can have it back.'

'Just thought it would help.' Sara shrugged, giving me a sly grin.

'I'll falter through it on my own, I guess,' I murmured,

shutting my locker door with my first period books resting in my arm.

The rest of the day was filled with a buzz of oohs and ahhs over Analise. Since she was a junior, I didn't have any classes with her. I could avoid most of the gawking that stalked her. But as luck would have it, I found her sitting on the stool at my table in the Art room, exactly where Evan should have been.

'Hi,' Analise said tentatively as I sat down next to her.

'Uh, that's Evan's seat,' I responded coolly.

'He won't be a part of this assignment,' Ms Meir said from behind us, causing us both to spin around. 'So, Analise, you are more than welcome to sit there for the duration of this project. Emma, will you explain what we're working on?'

'Sure,' I answered slowly, not getting past the sentence in which she'd explained that Evan wouldn't be part of this assignment.

I must have come over as the most horrible person in Weslyn High to this girl. I provided an abbreviated explanation of what we were working on, and basically ignored her for the rest of class. I was too busy trying to figure out what Evan needed to tell me and why he wasn't in class, convinced the two were connected. I didn't give her the slightest bit of attention.

'It was nice meeting you,' Analise said as we put our things away. I felt wretched.

'I'm sorry I wasn't very talkative,' I responded guiltily. 'It's been a weird day.'

'I've heard you keep to yourself,' Analise stated. 'I understand.'

'I'll see you tomorrow.' I tried to recover with a soft smile.

'Sure,' she smiled back kindly before we parted ways.

Evan was waiting for me at my locker.

'Did you drop Art class?' I questioned before he could say hi.

He hesitated with his lips pressed together. 'No. I just asked to work on something else for a while, so Ms Meir gave me a photography assignment.'

'Oh,' I responded, embarrassed by the paranoid thoughts that had raced through my head the entire class. This wasn't the first time he'd opted for a photography project. My shoulders eased down. 'Yeah, that makes sense.'

I opened my locker and started stuffing my books in my backpack.

'We're sharing the court today for practice,' Evan told me, watching me gather my things. 'So we should be able to leave together to go back to your house.'

'Sounds great,' I replied. He gave me a quick kiss and disappeared down the stairs to the locker room.

I lifted my eyes from my Physics book when his thumb ran across my scar. Evan gently grasped my ankle in his hand as we sat facing each other on the couch, attempting to study before dinner. He absently smoothed the marred skin while remaining focused on his History book. A strange tingling spread up my ankle with each stroke.

He lifted his head and found me watching his hand, but he didn't remove it.

'Sorry we weren't able to talk,' I said, resting the open book on my stomach.

'We still can.' He paused, and I watched nervously as he gathered his thoughts, searching for the right words. 'When I heard –'

'Do you like broccoli?' my mother yelled from the kitchen, the sound of water filling a pan in the background.

Evan pressed his lips into a smile. 'Yes,' he hollered in return.

I raised my eyebrows when he looked at me. 'So . . . you were saying?'

He flipped his eyes towards the kitchen where my mother was moving her hips to the classic rock station coming from the small radio in the window. 'It can wait.'

'Are you sure?' I tried to read his expression, afraid that waiting was only going to continue to torture him – and me.

'Yes, it can,' he assured me, leaning over and kissing me. I put my hands around his neck, not wanting him to move away. He pressed in closer.

'Umm . . .' my mother cleared her throat. Evan pulled back, and my cheeks caught fire instantly. My mother's face was as red as mine felt. She darted her eyes towards at the floor and announced, 'Dinner's ready.'

Just then, the smoke detector went off in the kitchen. I waved my hand and coughed as we entered. My mother went to force the window above the sink open, while I grabbed a towel and fanned the screeching alarm. This had practically become routine for us. The alarm had gone off almost every time I'd attempted to cook.

'Stupid oven,' she grunted, pushing the wooden window up a half inch at a time. 'It must have fifty years of burnt food in there.'

'Do you need help?' Evan asked, moving towards her.

'No, I've got it,' she grunted, pushing it up a bit more. She hopped down from the sink and smiled. 'You can sit.' The detector was silenced and I sighed in annoyance.

I sat down at the small table in the spindly chair facing the wall. The legs shifted slightly as my weight settled on it. Evan sat to my right in the sturdiest of the three chairs.

My mother placed bowls of broccoli and mashed sweet potatoes in front of us, then proceeded to fork a chicken breast on to each of our plates.

'What do you want to drink?' I asked Evan, pushing my chair back, the legs slanting with the movement.

'Water's fine, thank you,' Evan responded, fanning the smoke in front of him in amusement, while my mother and I acted like it was part of the dining experience. Well . . . it usually was.

As I poured us two glasses of water from the gallon in the refrigerator, my mother settled on the chair across from Evan with a large glass of red wine. I spotted the bottle on the counter, already two thirds depleted, and eyed her nervously. She still seemed to be okay, although she was busying herself inserting utensils in the bowls.

'Help yourself,' she said, encouraging us by placing a few stalks of broccoli on her plate.

I sat back down as Evan scooped a spoonful of sweet potatoes.

'How's basketball?' my mother asked, ignoring her food to take a sip from her glass. Then she continued in a rush, 'I love basketball. It took forever for me to convince Emily to play since she was so obsessed with soccer because of her father. But she's actually pretty good at it.

233

I never played, but I love watching it. Soccer seems so all over the place, and I can never keep up with where the ball is and why they're blowing the whistle.'

She stopped, noticing we were staring at her. I had had no idea she was nervous until this moment.

'Sorry,' she grimaced.

'It's okay.' Evan consoled her with a smile, giving me quick a glance out of the corner of his eye. I pressed my lips together in apology. He reached for my hand under the table and squeezed it. 'Basketball's great.'

'Did you make the playoffs?' I could tell she was trying to concentrate on one sentence at a time, taking a sip after the question. Her cheeks glowed red.

'Barely,' Evan admitted, setting his fork down to answer her. 'We have an away game Thursday, and if we survive that, we'll play at Weslyn on Saturday night.'

'I have to see you play!' my mother exclaimed excitedly. 'If you make it till Saturday, I'm there.'

'Great,' Evan replied politely, flashing me another glance as I remained still – trying not to show how disturbed I was to have my mother attend my boyfriend's basketball game.

'Emma's playing Friday,' Evan revealed.

'That's if we win Wednesday,' I stated.

'You will. Your team's favoured for the championship.'

'That would be so amazing,' my mother burst out. 'We'd definitely have to have a party.' My eyes widened at the thought, making Evan laugh.

'What?' my mother asked, not understanding the impact of her suggestion.

'Emma and parties don't coexist well,' Evan explained with a smirk.

'Come on, Emily,' my mother begged. 'It would be so much fun.'

'Yeah, no.' I shook my head adamantly.

'Well, I'm having a party for my birthday in a few weeks,' she announced. 'You'll be here for that, right?' She looked at both of us eagerly.

'Of course,' I answered, not sure what I was agreeing to.

'Evan, did Emily ever tell you about the time she fell out of a tree?' She laughed lightly as I rose with my plate in my hand. My mother pushed her plate away, having barely touched it.

Evan began to stand. 'I've got it. You can sit,' I said to him, taking his plate. He looked to me for assurance. I smiled with a nod and took the plates to the sink.

'No, I haven't heard that one,' he answered, lowering himself back in the chair.

I listened intently while I loaded the dishwasher, not sure if *I* even knew the story she was about to tell.

'Emily was always running around, climbing trees and covered in dirt. That's why we got her involved in sports, so she wouldn't kill herself jumping off rocks.'

Evan chuckled at the image. I rinsed the dishes absentmindedly, trying to remember.

'We lived in the woods, surrounded by trees, bugs and whatever other creatures slithered out there – it was pretty awful.' I turned to catch her shudder. 'Sorry, I'm not a bug person.'

Evan laughed.

'Anyway, one time, she climbed too far up this tree, and the branch broke under her. She fell, banging into branches the whole way. I heard her crying and found her hanging about twenty feet up. She'd managed to grab the last branch before she would've hit the ground.'

I leaned back against the sink, absorbing a story that I couldn't connect with. Although there was something about it that opened a hole in the bottom of my stomach.

'Derek had to use a ladder to get her down,' she laughed, like the sight of me dangling from the tree, needing to be rescued by my father, had been humorous. 'She didn't break anything but was covered with bruises from head to toe. And she never climbed a tree again.'

Then she directed her attention towards me. 'Are you still afraid of heights?'

I stared at her, recognizing that the void in the bottom of my stomach was triggered by fear. I swallowed and replied, 'I don't love them.'

'I didn't know you had a problem with heights,' Evan noted, examining my pale face. 'You did okay when we went rappelling last year.'

'I was pretty convinced I was going to fall to my death,' I admitted. 'I wasn't about to tell you that. Besides, I didn't really have to look *down*, just for the next step. But we never did it again, right?'

'No, we didn't,' Evan agreed. 'I had no idea.'

I could only shrug, since I hadn't known why I was afraid of heights until I'd been blindsided by the memory. I couldn't recall a single second of it – but the emotions were there. The fear and desperation. I knew her story was true.

My mother continued with childhood stories. I should've been embarrassed, but it didn't feel like she was talking about me. It became apparent that I didn't have a single recollection of my childhood, and it was unsettling. That time had completely escaped me, leaving me in the present without a past.

When the cleaning up was done, so was my mother's bottle of wine – she was a giggly mess.

'Want to go for a walk?' I asked Evan. He stood from the table, smiling at another unrecollectable moment about some haircut I'd insisted on when I was eight that made people think I was a boy.

'Sure,' Evan responded. 'Thank you for dinner.'

'My pleasure,' she grinned fondly.

After wrapping a scarf around my neck and pulling on my gloves, Evan and I escaped into the cool crisp air of the lingering winter. It hadn't snowed in a while, but what was left wasn't going anywhere fast.

I stared silently at the ground with my hands in my pockets.

'That bothered you.' His voice drew my attention. 'It wasn't that bad from where I was sitting.'

I shrugged. 'No, it was fine.' And it was partly true. I wasn't really bothered by my mother's nervous chattering, even after a bottle of wine. Evan waited, but I didn't continue.

'Are you going to tell me what you're thinking?'

I breathed in deeply, sifting through what I wanted to say. 'I don't remember our house the way she does.'

I paused in thought before continuing. 'I remember loving it, but I don't remember anything about it at the same time. All I can picture is lots of sun and trees. I felt safe there, so it couldn't have been as horrible as she's making it out to be.'

I directed us towards the park, and we followed a worn path to the playground. I sat on the chilly seat of a swing. The black plastic hugged my hips. 'I didn't realize how blank that time was for me until she was talking about it.'

'You were young,' Evan responded.

'Not *that* young,' I countered. 'You'd think I'd remember something as traumatic as falling out of a tree.'

Evan sat next to me, watching as I rocked the swing gently with my feet on the ground. I stared at the flattened snow, still troubled. I'd locked everything up, blocking out the good with the bad, leaving myself with not much of anything to hold on to.

'I do remember one thing,' I said, gazing at him with a soft smile on my face.

'What's that?'

'My dad made me this swing out of a piece of wood that he hung from one of the trees. I would pump so high my toes would touch the branch above. I'd tilt my head back and close my eyes; it was the most amazing rush. I was convinced that's what flying must feel like. I spent hours on that swing.'

Evan smiled affectionately. I allowed the warmth of the memory to fill the emptiness.

'Sometimes, I wish I were back there, when everything was perfect and I was happy, swinging my life away.'

19

Waiting for Friday

'DID I TOTALLY SCREW UP LAST NIGHT?' MY mother asked as she poured her coffee. 'I did. I completely embarrassed you. I was nervous, and I drank too much wine, then told too many stories. I am so sorry, Emily. Tell Evan –'

'Mom, I mean, Rachel.' She looked up at me with her lips pressed together. 'It was fine. I promise.'

'You didn't look fine,' she recalled, eyeing me nervously. 'You looked mortified.'

'I wasn't.' I smiled in an attempt to make her feel better.

Her nervous guilt got the better of her, so she questioned me further, 'Are you sure?'

I didn't know how else to convince her, so I just nodded.

'I'm sorry I can't make it to your game this afternoon.'

'I understand. You have to work.'

'Do you mind that I invited myself to Evan's game?

Was that a bad idea? I really want to see him play. I was honest about that.'

'It's okay,' I laughed, wanting her to take a breath before she fell over. 'You were great. Really. And I don't mind if you go to his game on Saturday. You can bring Jonathan too, if you want.'

Her eyes shifted away from me and fell to her coffee cup.

'What?' I pushed, noticing the pinch between her brows.

'I'm not sure what's going on with him,' she murmured. 'I think he's keeping something from me.' I felt a pang at seeing her so distraught. 'Does he say anything to you, you know, when you're up at night?'

I shook my head, not confident that I could answer her. After all, I would be lying.

'What do you talk about?' She asked it like she was being left out of a secret club or something.

'Not much really,' I answered. 'Sports, commercials, how we wish we could sleep.'

'Do you know why he can't sleep?' She watched me closely. I shrugged and looked away. 'He doesn't tell me anything. We don't really talk about our pasts. It's good, you know, because it hurts me to think about it, but I wish he could trust me enough to tell me *something*.'

I nodded, my voice paralysed with guilt. I felt like the worst daughter in the world. I should have told her that he was moving to California. That he had a painful past too that was hard for him to share. I should have let her know that it had nothing to do with her and that he really cared about her. But she'd probably wonder why he was telling me all this and not her. And then I wouldn't know what to say – especially since I wasn't sure how to explain why I'd talked with him about things I'd been avoiding with everyone else in my life. So I stayed silent, watching her face twist with uncertainty and doubt.

'When do you see him again?'

'Friday,' she answered with a sigh. 'I'll ask him about the game then.'

'I'm sure it's nothing,' I finally said, feeling even more horrible for trying to comfort her with a lie.

'Well, I should go,' she said, looking at the microwave clock. 'Text me the score, okay?'

I nodded, and as I watched her walk out of the kitchen, I could feel the heat turning in my gut. I was angry with Jonathan. Angry that he'd put me in this situation. Angry that my mother was being tormented by his inability to just tell her the truth.

I pulled out my phone and texted him, *You have to tell her!*

I received a response when I arrived at school, *In NYC til Friday – I will, promise!*

Friday couldn't come fast enough.

'Hey!' I heard when I opened the door that night. 'So happy you won!' I found my mother on the couch, curled up with a wine glass in her hand, still in her work clothes.

'Hi,' I responded solemnly, dropping my things by the stairs.

'That's an excited face,' she noted sarcastically, leaning forward to pick up the wine bottle and empty it into her glass. 'Everything okay?'

'Yeah,' I replied unconvincingly. I wasn't up for talking

about seeing Analise by Evan's side after the game tonight, and how miserable I was that he'd offered to drive her home when I was hoping to spend some time with him. I didn't want to feel this way . . . jealous. And there wasn't any reason I should. But the rationale didn't relieve the slithering in my stomach every time she looked up at him with her big Bambi eyes. So, I deflected her attention. 'How are you doing?'

My mother laughed humourlessly. 'I'm fucking great.'

She couldn't see my face as I closed my eyes and ground my teeth, picking up the intonation in her voice. She was drunk.

Instead of going to my room to work on my English paper as I had intended, I joined her on the couch, hoping to comfort her enough so she wouldn't keep drinking.

'It was my highest scoring game,' I told her, trying to assess just how far over the edge she was. Her head swivelled towards me, rocking slightly. She smiled lazily, the effort pushing her eyes into slits. She was pretty far gone.

'That's awesome, Emily,' she praised me in her drunken drawl. 'I wish I could have seen it.' She took a long sip of her wine, keeping her eyes closed for a moment after she'd removed the glass.

'Sorry about this,' she gestured to herself. 'I didn't have dinner, so it got to me.'

I nodded, wanting to take the wine glass out of her hand. Instead, she drained it in two large gulps. I widened my eyes as she tipped her head back, determined to get every last drop.

'I'll take that for you,' I offered, holding out my hand.

'Thanks,' she smiled, her teeth tinged purple. She

handed me the glass and I took it into the kitchen, finding a second empty bottle on the counter. I sighed with a shake of my head and set the glass in the sink.

My phone beeped. *Can I come over?*

I hesitated, not sure how to tell Evan 'no' without it coming across wrong. *Trying to get this paper done. See you tomorrow, okay?* I looked at the bottle again and pressed *Send*. I didn't want him to see this. To see her.

Okay, he texted back. I returned the phone to my pocket as I walked back into the living room.

'You must think I'm pathetic,' she said, her heavy tongue making her words jumbled. She ran her hand across her face, clumsily pushing her hair behind her ear. 'That I'm like this over a guy.'

'I don't think that,' I said calmly. I watched as she breathed in deeply through her nose with her eyes closed, having a hard time forcing them open. 'Why don't I help you upstairs to bed?'

'Yeah,' she breathed, 'getting tired. Should've eaten.'

I offered her my hand to help her from the couch. She grabbed on to it and hoisted herself up, swaying slightly. 'Whoa, head rush.'

I shut everything off – the disappointment, the frustration, the anger – and just focused on getting her up the stairs before she passed out. She crawled into the bed, and I removed her shoes before covering her. She pulled the blankets under her chin and looked up at me guiltily.

'It's not because I like him so much,' she explained. 'That's not it. I mean I do like him a lot.' She took a deep breath, her eyes watering. I swallowed hard, stung by the sadness surfacing in her eyes.

'I don't want to be alone.' Her lower lip quivered, and she rolled away from me.

Her words punched me in the chest. Her back shook as she began to cry. I bit my lip and hesitated, tempted to touch her, to try to console her. But I quietly walked out the door, shutting it behind me.

My mother's sobs could be heard through the door. Still incapacitated by her words, I slid down the door frame and hugged my knees into my chest. The anger and disappointment were replaced with heartache. Tears slid down my cheeks as I listened to her cry.

I'd done this before. *We'd* done this before. I'd spent most of my childhood listening to her cry. Her cries haunted me, still echoing through my head when I tried to sleep that night.

'Are you okay?'

'Huh?' I shook myself out of my stupor to find my locker door wide open and Sara watching me carefully.

'You've been staring into your locker for forever and haven't touched anything. What's going on?'

'Didn't sleep much,' I replied. My mother's cries were still ringing in my head. Half-forgotten memories pulled at me, the nights of tantrums, full of rage and pain – I used to hide under my covers, shaking. I blinked to force myself back into the bustling halls.

'What else is new?' she grinned, bumping me with her shoulder. 'Want to sleep over tonight?'

I opened my mouth to say yes, but I didn't. Jonathan wouldn't be back until tomorrow, and I wasn't so sure it was a good idea to leave my mother home alone.

'How about Saturday?' I suggested instead.

'Okay.' Sara closed her locker and headed to class. I grabbed my books and went to the computer lab, skipping Political Theory to get my English assignment done. The assignment I never touched last night.

I fought through the rest of the day and faked pleasantries with Analise in Art class, wishing the nail assignment was done already so Evan could take back his place next to me.

'Are you staying for Evan's game tonight?' she asked, bright and eager.

I nodded. I didn't bother to ask if she was staying, because I already knew that answer.

'Maybe we can sit together,' she chirped happily.

'Maybe,' I forced myself to say pleasantly, not looking up from aggressively hammering the nail into place.

Her sunshine and rainbows smile was too bright for my emotional hangover. I was afraid I'd have to squint to look at her, so I kept my head down – making it look like I was concentrating on my work. She let me be for the rest of class.

Evan was waiting for me at my locker with his backpack over his shoulder.

'Hi,' he said with a smile that shook me from my funk.

'I'm so happy to see your face right now,' I sighed, throwing my arms around his ribs and burying my head into his chest. I inhaled and let his clean scent release the tension in my shoulders.

'Uh, okay.' He laughed and squeezed me back. 'Bad day?'

'Something like that.' My face was still pressed into him, muffling my words.

'What are you doing after my game?'

I looked up, my arms still wrapped around him. 'I have practice.'

'That's right,' he remembered. 'We're getting something to eat after, and I was hoping you would come.'

'Sorry,' I replied with a grimace, finally releasing him. 'But I'll see you tomorrow night after my game, right?'

'Of course,' he smiled. 'It's our date. Are you going home first to change, or are you doing that here?'

'I was hoping to shower at home. Is that okay? Or will that make us late?'

'No, that's not a problem. I need to do the same thing anyway. That should give you enough time, don't you think?'

'Yes,' I responded, finally finding a reason to smile for the first time all day. 'That sounds perfect.' It was still all about waiting for Friday – for my date with Evan, and for Jonathan to come home to . . . tell my mother he was moving to California. But I refused to think about that part. I would deal with the repercussions of his talk with her *after* my date with Evan.

I kept Jill and Sara in between Analise and me during Evan's game. But it was hard to ignore her gleeful yelps whenever he blocked a shot or rebounded the ball. Sara cocked her head towards Analise after a particularly enthusiastic round of cheering. She looked to me, about to say something, but I shook my head with a roll of my eyes. Sara laughed, reading my thoughts without a word.

'Are you coming with us for pizza?' Analise asked me as we made our way down the bleachers.

'I have practice,' I told her, not thrilled that she was a part of the 'we' Evan had mentioned.

'Don't worry, I'll be there,' Sara gushed, her smile a little too forced.

'Oh,' Analise replied, her joy faltering slightly, 'great.'

Sara turned to me behind Analise's back with a wide mimicking smile. 'Great.'

I laughed and swatted her arm. 'Don't be mean.'

'Yeah, you're right.' She groaned like it was difficult. 'I'll be nice, I promise.'

Sara was the easiest person in the world to get along with, and most people loved her instantly. But if she didn't like you . . . she could be vicious. She and I both knew that there was nothing particularly unlikable about Analise, but for some reason, we both found ourselves not exactly fond of her. I was actually kind of relieved that I wasn't the only one to harbour these inexplicable feelings towards the spritely girl who was eternally smiling.

'Evan, you were amazing,' Analise praised him merrily.

'Thanks,' he responded. Finding me behind her, his eyes locked with mine. I squeezed past her and kissed him on the lips, despite the sweat that pressed against my cheeks. He exhaled slowly when I pulled away. 'Thanks,' he grinned, squeezing my hand.

'I should get ready for practice,' I told him. 'See you tomorrow?'

'I'll wait for you in the lobby,' Analise told him, interrupting us.

'Okay, sure,' Evan responded, glancing at her quickly. 'I'll be a few minutes, but I'll find you.'

I looked from Analise's blonde curls to Evan.

'I drove her,' Evan explained, noticing the confusion on my face. I could only nod, afraid of what might spew out of my mouth if I opened it. He leaned down and kissed me again. 'I'll see you tomorrow.'

When I walked towards the locker room, my phone beeped.

Pathetic me going out with the girls after work. So so sorry about last night. Jonathan's back tomorrow – yay! Promise to be good tonight!

Yup. Friday couldn't come fast enough.

20

No Such Thing as 'Normal'

NOTHING WAS GOING TO KEEP ME FROM enjoying every second of our date – nothing. Not Analise and her adorableness, or the fact that she'd *had* to sit next to Evan throughout my entire game – yes, I'd noticed. Not the fact that I hadn't slept last night because I'd stayed up listening for my mother to come home. And when she finally did, she was staggering and giddy. And not even the fact that I was running late because I'd left my lights on in the parking lot and Jill had to jump start my car. I was *determined* to have an amazing night.

I jiggled my key free from the front door and slammed it behind me, barely noticing as I raced up that my mother had left the lights on at the top of the stairs. I flipped off my sneakers and flung them across my room, peeled off my socks and left them on the floor, then threw my sweaty game jersey in the hamper. I was struck with déjà vu – recognizing how similar this felt to the night Evan took me to the concert. All that was missing was Jonathan walking through the door unexpectedly.

I ran to the bathroom in my shorts and a sports bra, pushing open the door and shutting it behind me in one swift motion. And then I stopped in my tracks. Irony punching me in the face . . .

'Hey?' Jonathan stood in front of me gripping the waistband of his running pants, his dark brown eyes staring at me in shock.

'Uh, sorry.' I gaped, instinctively crossing my arms over my chest as I stood immobilized in front of the door. Sweat ran down the side of his face, along the tendons of his thick neck and over the grooves of his broad shoulders and sculpted chest. His face was still flushed and his sweaty T-shirt was crumpled on the bathroom floor. I clamped my mouth shut – it had inadvertently flopped open. 'I didn't know you were here.'

I quickly turned around and gripped the handle of the door. I had started to open it when Evan called out, 'Em? I'm here.'

I clicked the door shut. 'Shit,' I said through clenched teeth, banging my forehead against the frame. 'Uh, I'm running late,' I hollered through the door. 'I'll be down in a little bit.'

'Okay,' he responded.

I breathed with my head still pressed against the wood, trying to figure out what to do.

'Wow,' Jonathan breathed behind me, 'this is awkward.'

I spun around and glared at him. 'You think?'

'So . . . you have a date?' he asked casually like we weren't standing in front of each other half naked and sweaty.

'Jonathan!' I scolded him with wide eyes. 'What am I supposed to do? How do I explain you coming out of the bathroom while I'm supposed to be taking a shower?' I was on the verge of hyperventilating.

'It's okay,' Jonathan said soothingly. But his comical expression lingered. 'Just take a shower.'

'What?' I snapped, a little too loudly, then covered my mouth with my hand and listened, praying my voice hadn't carried downstairs. I heard the squeak of the front door and the rattling of the glass when it closed.

'Evan!' my mother acknowledged. 'How are you? Where's Emily?'

My eyes couldn't stretch any wider without popping out of my head. Jonathan let out a small laugh, and my mouth dropped open in disbelief.

'She's taking a shower,' he told her. 'I guess she got held up after the game and she's running late.'

'Emily!' my mother bellowed, the creaks of the stairs drawing closer. 'Are you almost done?'

The handle jiggled, and the door started to open. I thrust my back against it, slamming it in her face.

'Hey!' she cried out.

'Sorry,' I grimaced, latching the door so she couldn't open it. 'I'm about to get in the shower. Do you need to get in here?'

'I can wait,' she told me. 'Have you seen Jonathan? He was supposed to be here by now.'

I stared across at him as he pressed his mouth into a smile to keep from laughing. I was so annoyed I wanted to throw something at him.

'Uh, no,' I replied, 'but I didn't really look for him either.'

Jonathan couldn't hold back and let out a constrained, breathy laugh.

'Stop!' I uttered, my brows pulled together in warning. He only smiled wider.

'Okay, well, Evan's waiting for you.'

'I know. I'll hurry.' I closed my eyes and shook my head, knowing I had no choice. When I heard her walk away, I whispered, 'Fine. I'll take a shower, but you have to stand by the door.'

'Don't worry,' he smirked, 'I won't peek.'

'Funny,' I snapped sarcastically. 'We have to switch spots so I can get to the shower. Please don't make this any more awkward than it already is.'

In order to exchange places in this closet of a bathroom, I had to shimmy past him, pressed between the bathtub and the sink.

I turned my head to the side, inching past him with my stomach sucked in to avoid touching him. I could feel his hot breath on my neck and inhaled the mix of sweat and a crisp cologne that reminded me of the ocean. His slick skin slid across mine, despite my efforts to be as small as possible.

Jonathan chuckled from above me. I tilted my head up, our faces inches apart. 'We have to stop meeting like this,' he teased. I pulled past him quickly, my heart racing.

I picked up his damp T-shirt and threw it at him, making him laugh even more. I shook my head in exasperation and stepped into the tub just as Jonathan turned towards the door. I secured the shower curtain and stripped off the rest of my clothes, my heart beating so fast I was still sweating.

I cracked the curtain open enough to drop my damp clothes in front of the toilet before turning on the water. It was the fastest shower of my life – and I'd been forced to take some pretty quick showers. I somehow managed to wash my hair and body at the same time.

When I'd turned off the water, I peeked out from behind the curtain, but Jonathan was gone. The door was closed but the latch was undone. I took a deep breath and grabbed the towel.

'Jonathan?' my mother's confused voice floated up the stairs. 'You've been here this whole time?'

Realizing I hadn't brought any clothes into the bathroom with me, I took my mother's bathrobe off the hook on the closet door and secured it around me.

'I was using Emily's computer,' he explained calmly. He was a very convincing liar; I almost believed him. 'I was on a video chat with the office, so I couldn't get off when you came in. Sorry.'

Without listening to whether or not my mother bought his story, I opened the door and scurried to my room, catching a quick glimpse of Jonathan watching me out of the corner of my eye. I thought I noticed him grin. My face continued to radiate heat.

'I'm out of the bathroom,' I called behind me, shutting my door.

'I'm going to take a shower, okay? I didn't get to after my run,' I heard Jonathan tell her from outside my room.

I plugged in my hairdryer and let the hum block everything out – the lying, the hint of suspicion in my mother's tone, the racing beat of my heart that hadn't quite recovered from being stuck in the bathroom with Jonathan.

I could hear music playing downstairs when I turned off the hairdryer, and the water was running in the bathroom. I gathered my hair and pinned it into a bun at the nape of my neck – the only style of Sara's I was able to replicate fairly well. I retrieved the dress from the back of my closet and removed the plastic cover with a smile. I knew this was going to be perfect for our *normal* date.

I took a deep breath, inspecting myself once more in the full length mirror, swishing the hemline of the red empire dress as I turned from side to side. I tried to find the calm that would return the shade of my skin to its natural tone. As long as I didn't see Jonathan before we left, I thought I should be okay.

I finally emerged from my room, somewhat composed. I could hear Evan and my mother talking in the living room where the music was playing. From the sounds of it, she was recounting animated tales of the bands she'd seen and the insanity that had ensued.

The skirt of the dress brushed against my thighs as my hand slid along the railing. Hearing my footsteps, Evan stepped into the foyer. His eyes lit up, calming me instantly. Then I heard the sound of the door opening behind me. I refused to turn back, fearful of being enveloped in flames.

'You look so beautiful, Emily,' my mother sang with a smile on her face.

'Yeah.' The comment wafted through the air, barely audible. I'd expected it to come from Evan, but the word drifted down the stairs, and I almost faltered on a step.

Evan reached out, prepared to catch me, but I steadied myself again and offered an embarrassed smile. 'Still not the best in heels.'

'I won't let you fall,' Evan promised, taking my hand when I reached the bottom. I smiled, knowing he wouldn't.

'Hello, you,' my mother said excitedly as she scrambled up the stairs towards Jonathan. My cue to get my jacket.

Evan helped me put it on, and when I turned to say goodbye, my mother had both arms around Jonathan, holding him tightly like he might float away. He stood watching us, with his arm casually draped over her shoulders.

'Bye,' we both called. I turned and was out the door before they could respond. I heard my mother say, 'Have fun,' before Evan shut the door.

'That's one of my favourite things,' Evan said out of nowhere, backing out of the driveway.

'What's that?' I questioned, my thoughts replaying my mother's giddy excitement and Jonathan's ambivalence. I couldn't help but be worried for her. I pushed thoughts of them away, turning my attention to Evan.

'Watching you come down the stairs.' He rested his hand on mine, bringing my heart to life in a whirling flutter.

We drove to a restaurant a few towns over along the waterfront. I practically floated in, tethered by the warmth of Evan's hand. We were seated at a corner table overlooking the water. I was beginning to like 'normal' dates.

'What happened after the game?' Evan asked when we'd placed our drink orders.

'Oh, I left my lights on and my battery was dead. Jill

had to jump start my car. I should have called you to tell you I was late, but I was too focused on getting home to change. Sorry about that.'

'It's not a problem,' Evan assured me warmly. 'I learned a lot about your mother's concert-going experiences while I waited.' He let out a quick laugh, but I could only nod – not finding her adventurous life all that amusing, especially when it had taken place after she'd abandoned me.

The server returned with our drinks and we placed our order. The harmonious notes of a quartet swirled through the air, enveloping the hum of conversation. I could've easily been convinced that we were the only two in the restaurant. The candles' glow softened the angles of Evan's face and reflected in his eyes. He reached over the table and took my hand, giving it a small squeeze that I felt in my chest.

'You know, I don't know that much about the guys in California,' I said, after I was able to form sentences again. 'Will you tell me about them?'

Evan smiled at the request. 'Sure.' He paused for a moment then started with, 'Well, there's Brent. He's very . . . easy to get along with. He thinks he's better with the girls than he is, and always wants the best outcome in every situation.

'Ren is the most laid back guy I've ever met. He lives and breathes surfing, and I'm convinced he'd sleep on the beach on top of his board if he could. He would do any-thing for anyone, doesn't matter if he knows them or not – if he can help out, he will. I'm lucky to know him.

'Then there's TJ.' Evan paused with a smirk, deliberating how to describe him. 'He's a lot to take, but he's always entertaining, and some of the things he gets away with make us laugh for days. But he's still a good friend, regardless of how many times we'd like to throw him in the ocean.

'And that leaves Nate. Nate's my best friend. I trust him with . . . well, everything. I'd trust him with you if I ever needed to.' His eyes connected with mine, and a pang shot through my chest, suddenly realizing what he meant. 'That's where we were going to go. Where we should have gone. His family has a summer place in Santa Barbara that they hardly ever go to, even in the summer. The guys basically take it over after school's out. I'm hoping we can spend at least a week there before you need to be on campus for soccer.'

'I'd like that,' I replied just as the server set the entrees in front of us. 'I wish –'

My words were cut off by, 'I will not lower my voice.'

We located the source of the outburst across the room where a man in a dark suit was arguing with the maître d', who was bent over and speaking in a low voice to him. The woman across from him darted her eyes around the room in embarrassed apology. She handed the server the bill and gathered her purse.

'Come, Roger. It's time to take me home,' she implored him. All movement and conversation ceased to watch the spectacle.

I turned my back to the couple, empathizing with the woman, who looked like she wanted to crawl under the table. 'I guess I'll never understand it,' I mused under my breath with a shake of my head.

'What's that?' Evan asked.

I lifted my eyes, realizing he'd heard me. 'Why people

drink, I guess. It just seems to make them stupid. They end up saying something they regret or acting like an idiot. I just don't get it.'

'Well, there is such a thing as moderation,' Evan said.

I nodded, recalling seeing Evan drink without acting out of control. 'Have you ever been drunk?'

Evan laughed. 'Yes. I have. And it's not pretty either. I'm sure I've qualified as the idiot a few too many times.'

'Really?' I was surprised by his answer. I couldn't even imagine it.

'It doesn't happen very often. I actually haven't been drunk in a while. I don't really like how it makes me feel, especially the next day. Have you ever had a drink?'

I shook my head. I didn't want to recount the sips I'd taken at the parties my mother threw. I'd been too young to know better, so as far as I was concerned, they didn't count. 'Don't think I ever will. Besides I have no desire to have my face splattered across Facebook doing something humiliating. I already get too much attention.'

Evan let out a short laugh.

'What do you want to do on Sunday?' I asked, changing the subject.

'Want to go hiking?' he suggested. 'It's not supposed to be cold, and it's better to go now while there's still snow, before it gets muddy.'

'Sure,' I responded. Fresh air and the calm of the woods were the perfect escape from everything and everyone in Weslyn. I just needed to survive the next night's basketball game, alongside my mother, before I could get there. 'I'd like that.'

*

When we returned to Evan's car after dinner, I said, 'Do you want to go back to my house to watch a movie? I'm pretty sure my mother and Jonathan will be out.'

'That sounds perfect,' Evan replied.

We stopped at a movie rental machine on our way, and arrived to a dark house as I'd anticipated. Not bothering to change, I just took off my shoes and settled in under Evan's arm. We kept the lights off. The action movie cast a flickering light in the dark room.

Halfway through, we heard a car door shut in the driveway. I glanced at Evan in surprise. 'They're back early.'

That's when we heard the yelling. I tensed at the sound of my mother's elevated voice, not wanting Evan to see her like this. I could hear Jonathan calling after her.

She rushed through the door. 'Then explain it. Go ahead, I want to hear it.' She held something in her hand. Evan pulled me closer as my entire body went rigid. 'How the fuck did her sweater get in your truck?'

Jonathan stepped in and looked from my mother to us sitting on the couch. That's when it hit me. She was holding the sweater I was certain I'd left at Drew's. 'I thought it was yours,' he said in a low voice, shifting his eyes between me and my mother.

My mother turned towards us, realizing we were watching the entire scene. Her jaw was tight and her eyes enlarged, symptomatic of a full-out fit. I had a split second to evaluate her. If she was drunk, everything was about to explode.

She shook the green sweater at me. 'I thought you said you left it at your fucking ex-boyfriend's.' It wasn't a question. It was an accusation.

I couldn't move. I had no idea what to say. I could feel Evan looking at me, waiting for me to answer. Jonathan kept his eyes on me as well, attempting to silently apologize. I was still trying to make sense of what was happening, and how he could possibly have my sweater.

'I know there's something going on,' my mother glared at us accusingly. 'I'm not stupid.' When we could only stare at her speechlessly, she screamed, 'You can all go to hell!' stomping up the stairs and slamming her door so hard I don't doubt it cracked.

'I'm really sorry,' Jonathan said. 'We had . . . we had a bad night, so she's not thinking clearly.'

My chest caved. He'd told her. He had to have told her he was leaving, and that was why she was so upset. It didn't explain the sweater, but it explained enough. Jonathan disappeared into the kitchen.

'Do you want to go?' Evan asked in my ear. I nodded. We stood and I slipped on my shoes while Evan retrieved our jackets. He held my hand as we walked out the front door.

My chest hurt, and I was having a hard time forming thoughts. As we neared his car, I started to worry. I couldn't tell exactly how drunk my mother was in her tirade, but I knew she was hurt. And when she was hurt . . .

I stopped. 'I can't go.'

'What do you mean?' Evan was completely confounded.

'I have to stay,' I told him with a grimace. 'She's upset, and I need to be here for her.'

'She needs to calm down,' Evan explained, not following my logic.

'Yeah, you're right. But I need to be here for her when she does.'

Evan studied me for a moment. 'I don't really know what just went on in there, but it wasn't good. Are you sure you don't just want to give them time to sort it out?'

She needs me, was all I could think, and I couldn't leave knowing she might get worse in my absence.

'I'll stay with you,' he said, squeezing my hand.

'No,' I countered, causing him to cock his head. 'It's complicated. Besides, you don't need to see this. I'll see you tomorrow, okay?'

Evan didn't say anything. It was obvious he was completely disturbed by the entire scenario, and I knew he didn't want to leave me.

'It'll be fine, I promise,' I assured him with a faint smile, then attempted to downplay it. 'It's a girl thing. She's having boy trouble, so . . . that's it. She's going to need a girl to talk to, okay?'

Evan took a breath and nodded reluctantly. 'All right. Call me if you need me for anything, okay? Even if it's in the middle of the night and you just need to talk.'

I leaned up and kissed him. 'I will.' I was about to walk away when he pulled me back towards him and kissed me again, gripping me tightly like he was afraid to let me go. 'I'll call you, okay?' I whispered, out of breath. He nodded and I walked back towards the house.

I pressed my back against the door when I'd shut it behind me, staring up at her room in deliberation.

'She's drunk,' Jonathan stated from the dark of the living room. 'She's probably passed out already.'

'Great,' I grumbled, wanting to slide down to the floor – emotionally drained from my mother's tirade. I pulled off my shoes. 'I'm going to bed.' I had a thousand questions for him about what had happened tonight, but I was too deflated to talk about it. Whatever had happened, it had brought out a side of her that was angry and spiteful. A side that made my insides shudder. All I wanted was to shut it out with the blanket pulled up over my head.

'She told me she loved me,' Jonathan's voice broke through the stillness. I turned towards him. 'She told me she loved me, and I told her I was leaving.'

I sank onto the bottom step, absorbing what he'd just said. He walked over and sat next to me. I continued to stare at the floor.

'She was upset at first. She wanted to know how long I'd kept it from her, if I was just using her. She started drinking . . . a lot. Then she started to cry.' He paused. 'When she calmed down, we talked and decided that we still wanted to see each other, and would try it until I had to leave.'

I turned towards him. 'Why did you do that?' My voice was sharp and angry.

'What do you mean?' His face twisted in confusion.

'You're only making it worse by leading her on,' I accused him harshly.

'I'm not.'

'Yes, you are,' I insisted in agitation. 'Can't you see how messed up she is? You can't give her something and then tell her she can't really have it.'

'That's not what's going on,' he said defensively, his voice growing stronger.

I shook my head, then dropped it to my chest.

'I'm sorry, Emma,' Jonathan murmured softly.

I was too angry to hear him. I stood up and climbed the stairs to my room without looking back. I turned on the light, and my stomach clenched at the sight of my green sweater lying on my bed, cut up into shreds.

21

Drama

JONATHAN WASN'T AROUND IN THE MORNING. Neither was my mother. I was still too upset to face either of them.

My mother returned around noon with a shopping bag in her hand.

'I'm really sorry,' she said, unable to meet my eyes as she set the shopping bag on the couch next to me. She hesitated a moment, fidgeting with her hands and shifting uncomfortably. Without saying anything more, she turned and went up to her room.

I watched her until she disappeared, then opened the bag and pulled out a green sweater. It wasn't the same one. But that wasn't the point.

'Thanks,' I said from the entrance of her bedroom as she folded clothes from the laundry basket and stuffed them into her drawers.

'Are you mad at me?' She sounded small and fragile.

'No,' I replied with a small smile.

'Can I still come to the game?' Her blue eyes were big

and sorrowful; her lower lip stuck out in an exaggerated pout.

'Yes.' I laughed lightly at her comical expression – reminiscent of a child getting caught colouring on the walls.

'Great! What are you doing later?' my mother asked, her voice suddenly peppy and excited.

'Uh, I'm not sure,' I fumbled, still not used to the quick flip of her moods. 'Jill and Casey were talking about going to a party; Sarah's at Cornell again visiting Jared. But Evan and I haven't made any commitments.'

I leaned against the door frame.

'You can come in,' my mother encouraged me, hanging up her clothes in the closet.

I hadn't really seen my mother's room before. It had always been dark when I'd entered to help her to bed. It was simply decorated with white curtains hanging on the windows. The leaf-patterned bedspread was still rumpled, as if she'd made it by pulling the comforter over the creased sheets.

A dresser with a mirror sat across from the bed with necklaces dangling from the mirror's edges. Perfume bottles and rings were scattered on its scratched surface. A framed picture caught my eye.

'I'm not sure what to wear tonight,' she sighed.

'It's just a basketball game, so jeans work,' I advised her, picking up the frame to examine it more closely. It wasn't a picture at all, but a drawing done in pencil. The shading and detailing were phenomenal. I brought it closer to inspect the strokes of the artist's work.

'Yeah, but I'm hoping –' She stopped to watch me.

I quickly set the portrait down, afraid that I'd upset her by touching her things.

'You can look at it,' she told me.

I picked up the frame again and looked from the drawing to her, realizing it was my mother captured in a laugh, done before the stress lines around her eyes and mouth had formed. Her happiness was evident. I couldn't help but smile looking at it.

'You don't remember that drawing, do you?' she asked, studying me. My eyes twitched, puzzled by her question. 'Your father drew that, back before you were born. You used to stare at that picture all the time when you were little.'

'I did?'

'Derek drew pictures for you too. You'd sit at the kitchen table and he'd ask what your favourite part of the day had been, and then he'd draw it for you. You had his drawings plastered all over your room. Don't you remember?'

I scanned the floor, searching my memory, wanting to recall the moments she spoke of. I could hear laughter, and catch a glimpse of his face, but the memories refused to form. I shook my head, knitting my brows together in frustration.

'Do you remember *anything*?' my mother enquired, her tone careful. She examined my confused face like she was just as confounded. 'You mean you don't ... remember ... What I went through when ... Why you had to go ...'

I was unable to follow her cryptic sentences. She shook her head slowly and stared into the distance, or perhaps the past. She closed her eyes and swallowed, then composed herself easily, not a trace of distress left upon her face.

'Want to go out to dinner before the game? It's at seven, right?'

I couldn't answer for a moment, completely confused by what I'd just witnessed. 'Yes it is. And sure, why not.' I tried to smile but faltered, still disturbed by the sheen in her eyes that she was trying to smile away. I decided not to ask what I should be remembering. Not today.

'I should get some homework done since Evan and I are going hiking tomorrow. Let me know when you're ready to leave.'

'Okay,' she replied, going back to her closet.

I closed my door and sat on my bed, replaying the stunned look on her face when she realized I couldn't remember anything. I'd never been aware of how little I could recall from my childhood. I was always so determined to focus on my future and getting out of Weslyn. I'd held on to the feelings of being safe and happy for so long. That had always been enough for me. But now, I wanted to remember. Somehow it was important that I figure out what had happened in the blank spaces of my life.

I opened my closet and reached for the stack of pictures under my sweatshirts on the shelf. I laid them on my bed and returned to my door to slide the lock in place, concerned about how my mother would react if she saw I'd kept the pictures she'd smashed at the bottom of the stairs.

I sat on my bed and slowly flipped through the images.

There was a photo of my father holding me right after I was born; another of me on his lap while sitting on the rocking chair, holding a book. I ran my finger along his cheering face, as we kicked a soccer ball back and forth. He looked so happy. *We* looked so happy. My mother wasn't in a single picture. I could only assume she was the one taking them.

There were others of the two of them, laughing and obviously in love. I'd expected to see a wedding picture, but there wasn't one. I figured she'd kept those safe somewhere, or I hoped so anyway.

After examining every detail of each photo, I lay back on my bed and shut my eyes. I tried to conjure up an image, begging for the vault to open. But nothing came – not a single moment. I sighed in frustration and slid the photos back under the sweatshirts.

I went downstairs and turned on the television, but my focus kept drifting towards the rocking chair. I *did* remember the chair – that was something. I thought of the picture of my father reading to me in it, and tried to picture the actual moment. Nothing.

'Ready?'

I jumped, suddenly pulled out of my head. My mother slid her arms into her coat, studying me oddly.

'What are you thinking about?' she asked, trying to read my face.

'Nothing.' I shook my head. Maybe it was better not to remember.

I noted my mother's choice of a tight denim miniskirt with leggings. She *had* taken my advice to wear jeans, but not quite in the way I'd hoped. Considering her daring attire, I hoped I could convince her to sit in the parents' section, although that wasn't exactly a gossip-free zone either.

For dinner, we ended up at a small crowded pub, where college basketball games on the screens incited spontaneous hollers from the patrons.

'I don't know if Jonathan's coming tonight,' she told me after ordering a beer from the overly friendly server. Her face was drawn as she stared at the menu. 'I was so awful last night.'

'He told me about going to USC in the fall,' I consoled. 'I'm sure that was hard for you. I know how much you like him.'

'I thought I'd fallen for him,' she admitted, setting down her menu with a sigh. 'I don't know. I'm so confused. A part of me wants to end it and move on since it's going to end anyway. But the other part knows how much I'll miss him, and if I can still be with him for five more months, then why not?' She looked to me in expectation. 'What do you think I should do?'

I hesitated, not sure what to say. 'Whatever will make you happiest,' I finally suggested.

'That sounds easier than it is,' she sighed. 'It's going to hurt either way. I hope he comes tonight. I apologized to him like a million times today. He said he'd try, but he has a project due at work, so he wasn't sure if he could make it.

'And I'm sorry about accusing you of . . . you know.'

I took a sip of my water, hoping we were going to avoid that part of last night.

'It's just that I know you two get along. I hear you

talking and laughing in the middle of the night. Some-times I think he waits to hear you get up before he goes downstairs – like he doesn't even try to sleep. I know that sounds paranoid and crazy. I mean, you're my daughter, and . . .'

'He wouldn't do that,' I consoled her, freaked by her jealous thoughts. 'Besides, we really don't talk about anything interesting, I swear. Maybe you should ask him . . . you know, about his nightmare.'

'I've tried.' She paused to let the server set our burgers in front of us. 'Does he tell you what it's about?'

I shook my head.

'He's been distant lately. I think I screwed up and he's not going to want to be with me, not even for the short time before he leaves. I mean, we haven't had sex in over a week.'

I just about choked on the bite of cheeseburger I'd just taken.

'Sorry,' she grimaced. 'That was probably too much information.'

'A little,' I admitted with a cough.

When we arrived at the school Jonathan wasn't there, as my mother had anticipated. I couldn't bring myself to ask her to sit away from the students' section after watching her face drop when she received Jonathan's text.

'He's running late,' she muttered, dropping her phone into her purse. 'I know he's not coming.'

'Maybe he hasn't finished what he needed to do for work yet,' I suggested, trying to cheer her up. My words bounced right off as if they were never said.

We bought sodas at the concession stand and made our way to the bleachers.

'Hey, Rachel!' a few voices hollered.

'Hi, Mark! Hi, James!' she yelled back with a bright smile, her sullen mood masked instantly.

'You know people?' I questioned in disbelief.

'Where do you think I sit during your games?'

Oh, I mouthed, never having considered it before. I was shocked when more faces recognized her. She knew more people in my school than I did.

'Hi, Rachel,' Casey burst out, cutting across the bleachers to get to us, with Jill right behind her. 'What are you doing here?'

'Watching Evan,' my mother explained. Casey nodded like it made sense.

'Hey, Emma,' Jill greeted me, sitting next to Casey, who opted to sit next to my mother. I was starting to feel like a stranger even among my friends – who evidently preferred my mother over me.

'Where's Jonathan?' Jill asked, making my eyes widen.

My mother shrugged evasively, not looking away from the court as they were about to tip the ball. The cheering erupted around us as the ball flew into the air.

She chanted along with the rest of the school, like she was just another student. I was a spectator, not only to the game, but to my mother's popularity – it was beyond strange.

As the half progressed, she became more boisterous and made remarks that sent those around her into fits of laughter. I grew suspicious as she became more animated. Something was off. Her popularity grew the more vocal she became. The boys scooted in around her. I would have been nudged out of my position next to her if I hadn't been her daughter.

During half-time, my mother disappeared into the bathroom with Casey and Jill. I followed a few minutes later to find her dumping the contents of her flask into their fountain sodas. Her flagrant behaviour suddenly made sense – I should've known better.

'Casey, you were supposed to lock the door,' Jill scolded her with a huff.

'Sorry,' Casey responded guiltily. 'But it's just Emma.'

My mother watched for my reaction. 'You're not mad, right?'

I looked from one face to the other as they waited for me to say something. I shook my head and stepped into the first stall without a word. I leaned against the wall and listened as they giggled and Casey gushed about some cute boy sitting behind them.

'Do you want us to wait for you?' my mother called out.

'No, it's okay,' I responded, trying to keep my voice steady. My insides were a slithering mess. I couldn't believe I'd caught my mother feeding my friends alcohol so they could get drunk together. I took a breath and tried to clear my head, to think of how to keep this from escalating out of control.

I pulled out my phone and sent Jonathan a text, *Are you still coming?*

If Jonathan didn't show up, then I knew my mother would just keep drinking, and the more she drank, the more unpredictable she'd become. This was going to be horrible.

My phone beeped. *On my way. There in 15.*

I contemplated waiting for him so I wouldn't have to return to the bleachers alone. In the end, I trudged back to my seat beside my inebriated mother and her giggling clique. I kept glancing over at them, watching as they laughed and gossiped.

Finally, I saw Jonathan along the sideline, scanning the bleachers to find us. My mother stood and waved frantically, making her easy to spot. He climbed the steps closest to me and excused himself across the row. I scooted over so he could sit between me and my mother.

Before he could say anything, she leaned over and kissed him. He pulled back in surprise.

'What?' she snapped as he pulled his brows together.

'Are you drunk?'

She shrugged with a smirk.

'At a high-school basketball game? Really, Rachel!' Jonathan didn't even try to sugarcoat his disapproval.

My mother huffed with a roll of her eyes. 'What happened to you? You used to be fun.' She turned her back to him and started cheering along with the girls.

Jonathan turned towards me. 'So, what happened?'

I shrugged. 'She's afraid you don't care about her any more.'

'Why?' he questioned emphatically. 'Because I had to work?'

I didn't answer, and sank further into the bleachers – not sure how to make this whole thing go away.

My mother reached into her purse and took out her mini Altoids tin.

'Are you serious?' Jonathan accused her as she popped a pill in her mouth.

'Well, if you're not going to be any fun, then I need something to make me happy.'

'What was that?' I asked, having seen her pop the little white pills too many times to count, without really knowing what they were. Jonathan only shook his head in disgust.

He observed her silently as she grew more and more enthusiastic, drawing more attention. His jaw set and the tendons in his neck tightened.

About five minutes later he muttered angrily, 'I'm sorry, Emma, but I can't – I can't do this.' Jonathan stood up and passed by me towards the steps.

'Where are you going?' my mother yelled after him. He didn't look back. I could only watch after him in shock as he paced down the sideline and out the gym doors.

'Where is he going?' she demanded in a panic.

'I don't know,' I replied uneasily.

'Make him stop,' she pleaded, about to cry. 'Please, Emily, you have to stop him from leaving.'

She sniffled and her eyes flickered, overflowing with tears.

'Okay, okay,' I said desperately. 'I'll stop him.'

Jill turned towards my mother and her smile changed to a look of concern. 'Rachel, what's wrong?'

'Please help her calm down,' I begged Jill before I rushed down the steps and out of the gym. Jonathan was nearing the exit when I caught up with him.

'Jonathan!' I called after him. He turned at the sound of my voice. 'Where are you going?'

He waited until I was near before he said, 'Emma, I can't do this any more. I don't want to be responsible for her every time she gets paranoid and emotional.' He sounded defeated, releasing a heavy breath.

'Please don't leave,' I begged him. 'If you do, I am so afraid she's going to make a huge scene, and I don't know how to handle that.'

Jonathan hesitated, deciding what to do. My stomach was a mess just thinking about the potential breakdown my mother was on the verge of having in front of the entire school.

'Are you leaving me?' my mother asked from behind us. 'I knew you were.'

'Rachel, stop,' Jonathan stated firmly. 'Not here.'

'Then where? What does it matter where it happens? I know you don't want to be with me any more, no matter what you said last night.'

'Mom, let me drive you home,' I urged her. 'I'll get our jackets.'

'Don't call me that,' she snapped, stumbling slightly as she took a few steps towards Jonathan. I remained still, frozen by her harsh tone. Her eyes watered as she took another step in Jonathan's direction. 'Please don't leave me. I can't lose you too.'

'Let Emma drive you home,' he suggested sombrely, glancing towards me to make sure I was still okay with driving her. I nodded slightly. 'I'll meet you there and we'll talk. Okay?'

'Why can't I leave with you?' she sulked, starting to sniffle.

'I know you'll want to talk as soon as we get in the truck, and I can't. I'll meet you at the house where we can sit down and talk.' Before she could say another word, he left. Tears started seeping from my mother's eyes. I sighed and tried to remain composed, despite the crushing feeling in my chest.

I texted Jill to ask her to hold on to our jackets. I'd get them from her later.

'Come on,' I encouraged my mother softly, not sure if I should touch her or not. 'Let's go.'

She trailed after me to the car. Her legs lazily crossed in front of each other as her balance wavered.

My mother stared out the window the entire ride to the house. I kept my eyes on the road, not wanting to watch her suffer beside me. Jonathan's truck awaited us in the driveway when I pulled in. I hesitated to get out of the car, watching her stumble up the steps.

I really wanted to leave, to not witness what was about to happen. But I couldn't. I had to be here for her, no matter what happened. I pulled out my phone to text Evan, *Had to drive my mother home. Sorry I missed you – call me when you can.*

The cold started setting in around me, so I took a deep breath and headed into the house. As soon as I'd opened the door, I wished I hadn't.

'This isn't going to work,' Jonathan told her. 'How do you expect me to talk to you if you're going to continue to drink?'

'Fine,' my mother yelled, throwing the wine glass on the floor, shattering it and spraying red wine all over. 'I won't drink.'

The shattering glass paralysed me with the door handle still in my grasp.

'Rachel!' Jonathan hollered. 'What the hell is wrong with you?'

I quietly shut the door behind me. But I wasn't quiet enough.

'*She's* what's wrong with me.' My mother pointed at me. My eyes widened as I looked from my mother's finger to Jonathan's disgusted stance, his hands on his hips. I opened my mouth in confusion, not understanding what I'd done to warrant the spiteful look on her face.

'This has nothing to do with Emma, so don't even start.'

'Why do you keep calling her that?' she snapped. 'Her name is *Emily*. And she's going to take you away too, just like him.' Her words cut into me like barbs. I had no idea where the hostility was coming from, but it was incapacitating. I remained frozen, unable to find the words to soothe her or defend myself.

'You're not making any sense,' Jonathan argued. 'I'm not staying here to listen to this.' Jonathan walked towards the door.

I had nearly made it to the top step when more glass shattered in the kitchen.

'What the fuck, Rachel?!' Jonathan turned quickly at the sound. 'Don't throw a fit every time you don't get your way.'

'Don't leave,' she whimpered, followed by the sound of glass crunching.

'Don't move,' he urged her. 'You're stepping on glass.'

Jonathan disappeared into the kitchen and emerged carrying my mother in his arms, her head resting on his chest and her face slick with tears.

'Will you stay?' she slurred. Jonathan didn't answer, but continued up the stairs and into her room.

I exhaled, my chest tight from the tension that consumed the house. I considered following after him to help her into bed, but I couldn't bring myself to face her. Instead I crept down the stairs to investigate the mess. I stopped in the doorway, scanning the kitchen with a shake of my head. Trying to avoid the wine that covered most of the floor, I carefully stepped over the shards of broken glass and pieces of the wine bottle. As I reached for the broom, my phone rang.

I pulled it out to see Evan's name displayed. I took a deep breath before answering, 'Hi.'

'Hey. Got your text. Is everything okay?'

'Oh, yeah,' I replied, trying to sound as casual as possible. 'My mother and Jonathan got into another fight, so I had to drive her home. She was overly dramatic as usual, so I had to listen to her go off for a while. Sorry I didn't get to see you after the game.'

'Are you sure you're okay?'

'Yeah, I'm fine. She's about to go to bed now anyway, all talked out.' My stomach turned at my lie. 'Can I meet you at your place in a little bit? I'd really love to see you.' I wanted nothing more than to be released from the consuming emotions, and being in Evan's arms was exactly what I needed.

'Ah, I um,' Evan stumbled; a few voices hollered in the background as he stalled.

'Are you ready?' I heard a girl ask, sounding closer.

'Just a second,' he answered her. My heart skipped a beat, knowing exactly who she was. 'I just, uh, promised

278

Analise that I'd take her to Jeff's party. It's her first one and she doesn't know many people yet. But I can see if she can go with someone else or something. Let me –'

'It's okay.' I tried to sound unaffected, despite the pain twisting in my chest. 'You go. I'm pretty tired anyway.'

'Em, are you sure?'

'Yeah, I'm fine,' I said, swallowing against the tightness in my throat, forcing the emotion out of my voice. 'It's been a stupid night, and I'm really exhausted. I'll see you tomorrow?' My voice shook despite my efforts. I closed my eyes to fend off the tears.

'Okay,' he answered, and before he could say anything else, I hung up the phone. I stood in the middle of the kitchen with the broom in my hand, trying to breathe against the swelling in my chest.

I took a deep breath before opening my eyes, turning everything off until I felt nothing. Then I began sweeping up the aftermath of my mother's fit.

'Let me help you.'

I turned to find Jonathan in the doorway. I didn't answer as he filled the mop bucket with soap and water and began wiping the wine that had run down the cabinets. We remained silent while we cleaned.

After bringing the bag of broken glass outside to the trash, I collapsed on the second step in the foyer, covering my face in my hands with my elbows propped on my legs, emotionally drained. Jonathan shut off the kitchen light and sat next to me.

'What's going to happen now?' I asked without looking up. 'Did you end things with her?'

'I wasn't about to do that in her condition,' he explained

quietly. 'I'm sorry you had to see any of that. It really wasn't about you.'

I lifted my head. 'I have no idea what happened tonight, but she was so . . . angry. I think she does blame me, but I don't know what I did.'

Jonathan shook his head in contradiction. 'This is between me and Rachel. It has nothing to do with you.'

'But you are going to leave her now, aren't you?' I concluded dryly.

Jonathan was quiet for a moment. 'Do you want me to stay?'

My eyes tightened; I was not sure how to answer. I didn't know exactly what he was asking.

'If I left right now, would it be worse for you . . . to live here?'

'Don't worry about me,' I assured him without much conviction. 'That wouldn't be the right reason to stay anyway. It would only be worse in the end, for everyone. She'll just have to get over you.'

'I'm sorry, Emma,' he said in a hushed tone.

'Me too,' I breathed. He peered at me with sympathetic eyes, pulling me in. It took me a moment before I was able to break away. 'I think I've had enough drama tonight, so I'm going to bed.'

'And I should go,' he responded, standing with me. I paused in my ascent when he opened the door.

'Goodbye, Jonathan.'

'I'm not leaving *you*, Emma,' he assured me. 'If you ever need me, I'm here.'

'Thanks,' I answered, exhaustion heavy in my voice.

I watched him disappear behind the closed door and continued to my room.

As I pulled the blankets over me, my phone beeped. *I'm coming over* appeared on the screen.

I'm in bed. I'll see you in the morning, I typed back.

10 a.m., my house?

OK.

I sank under the blankets, not looking forward to seeing anyone in the morning – not even Evan.

22

Inside Out

I DIDN'T REMEMBER SLEEPING. BUT THE NEXT thing I knew, it was morning. It seemed unlikely that I'd made it through the night without a nightmare, especially since I was still exhausted when I pulled the covers back – but I couldn't remember that either.

It was eerily quiet while I got ready, other than the house's occasional groans. There still wasn't any movement when I shut the front door behind me. I sat in my car for a minute before starting it, gripping the steering wheel with my eyes fixed on the house like I was expecting it to tell me what to do – how to make everything better. It just remained still, staring back at me.

'Sure,' I whispered, 'now you're silent.' I drew in a long breath and started the car.

I pulled into the Mathews' driveway to find more cars than usual. Along with Vivian and Evan's BMWs and Stuart's Mercedes were a black Lexus and a blue Prius.

I parked in the middle of the long driveway, blocking them all in – figuring we'd be leaving as soon as Evan put on his jacket.

I knocked. No one answered. I knocked again and waited longer – still no one came to the door. I turned the knob and slowly let myself in, cautiously scanning the kitchen.

'Hello?' I called out, creeping further into the large kitchen. That's when I heard laughter. I stopped to listen and then moved towards the voices down the hall.

One of the doors along the long hallway, a door that was always shut when I visited, was cracked open. I could hear the voices coming from inside. I recognized Evan's.

'You are far from awkward,' he said.

'Believe me, he knows awkward,' Stuart teased with a light laugh.

'Dad!' Evan said scornfully, but with a playfulness in his voice. 'She's not awkward either.'

'She's something else entirely,' Stuart chuckled.

'What do you mean?' she asked. Analise – of course.

I knocked. All conversation ceased as I became visible at the entrance.

'Hi.' I scanned each surprised face and noted the stacks of envelopes piled on the large conference table where they were sitting.

'Hi.' Evan acknowledged me with a dazzling smile. 'It's ten?' I nodded. 'Sorry. Lost track of time. Do you want to help? I promised my mother we'd stuff all these envelopes before we left. We're almost done.'

'Oh.' I glanced from Analise's bright eyes to Stuart,

who wouldn't look at me at all. 'Um, I need to get my things together for the hike. I just kinda threw them in my car so I could get here. I'll meet you outside, if that's okay.'

'Okay, sure,' Evan replied hesitantly. 'I won't be long.' I nodded and slowly walked away.

I'd obviously interrupted something, and I wasn't about to ruin it with my *awkwardness*. I couldn't believe I'd heard Stuart *laugh*. I'd never even seen him smile. I closed the kitchen door behind me, shutting out the voices and laughter with it.

I walked towards the garage instead of my car, leaving my expertly-packed backpack resting on the back seat. I made my way up the stairs to the rec room, plopping down on the couch.

I lay there, staring at the beamed ceiling.

My phone beeped. *How are you this morning?* lit up the screen.

Tired. And you?

Same, he answered. *I'm really sorry about last night. How is she today?*

Didn't see her.

I'm going to talk to her. Going to be honest.

I stared at the last text, not sure what part he planned to be honest about. Before I could respond, I heard, 'Here you are.' Sara stood at the top of the stairs.

'Hi,' I sat up in surprise. 'What are you doing back?'

'We're going hiking with you,' she revealed in excitement.

'Great,' I responded, but my voice fell flat.

Sara eyed me suspiciously. 'Do you not want us to? Did you want to be alone with Evan?'

284

'No, it's great.' I smiled weakly, truly not concerned with the added company.

'You're not right,' Sara observed, coming around to sit next to me on the couch. 'Spill it.'

'It's nothing really. Just tired. My mother and Jonathan had a fight last night, and I thought they broke up . . .'

'I heard,' Sara exclaimed. 'I thought Jill was exaggerating.'

I groaned. Of course. Jill had had a front-row seat for most of the debacle. 'Did Jill say anything else?' I asked, suddenly concerned that the drinking part had been leaked as well.

'No,' Sara returned. 'Why? Is there something else?'

'No,' I lied. 'That was enough drama for one night.'

'That's why today is exactly what you need,' Sara beamed, before jumping up and pulling me to my feet. 'Fresh air with your best friend and your boyfriend. And, of course, my boyfriend too. I've missed you. We all need this.'

'True,' I agreed, a smile eventually taking shape without effort.

I followed Sara down the stairs. Anna's SUV was parked behind my car, and Jared was tossing two backpacks into it. I added my backpack to the pile and eyed the bags, coming up with one too many.

'She's what?!'

Sara stood on the bottom step, eyeing Analise, who was standing next to Evan on the porch, all bubbly and excited. At Sara's reaction, Analise's smile deflated. I walked closer to hear what was going on.

'Come on, Sara,' Evan countered. 'What's one more person?'

I realized what they were discussing, and my shoulders sank. Evan looked to me for support. I forced my cheeks up and cheerily called, 'Analise, you're coming with us, right?'

'Is that okay?' she questioned, looking from me to Sara. Sara tightened her eyes in my direction, not appreciating my betrayal. Then she turned back towards Analise with a sugary smile.

'Sure,' Sara exclaimed with forced excitement. 'It'll be great.' I couldn't help but smile wider at her exaggerated reaction. 'Jared, why don't you drive? That way Emma and I can get to know Analise.' She tossed him the keys.

After moving my car on to the street, I jumped into the back seat of the SUV and we headed north along the Connecticut-New York border into the mountains.

For ninety minutes, Sara interrogated Analise. Of course she did it in her own Sara way, laughing and getting excited when they liked the same things. But every so often, she'd shoot me an *are you kidding me* glance that kept a smirk on my face.

We headed out along the trail, adorned with backpacks. Analise kept up alongside Evan and Jared, allowing Sara and me to follow behind – evidently she'd had enough *girl time*.

'What's with her?' Sara asked, watching as Analise giggled and swatted at Evan's arm. 'She seems nice enough, but I just . . . I just don't like her.'

I laughed – probably louder and harder than I should have, making the trio turn back towards us.

'Emma!' Sara scolded, chuckling. 'Stop. She's going to think we're talking about her.'

I continued to smile, keeping enough distance between the two groups so we wouldn't be overheard. 'I'm sure she *knows* we're talking about her.'

'She's way too excited for my taste. Like a pathetic puppy dog.'

'If she's too excited for *you*, then that's an issue.'

'A *huge* issue,' Sara laughed. 'And if she touches Evan one more time, I think I may have to take her out for you. Why aren't you bothered by it?'

'Oh, I am,' I told her. 'I just thought I was being a stupid, jealous girlfriend.'

'You're not,' she assured me, but that only made me feel worse. 'She needs to take those big brown eyes of hers and back the fuck off.'

'Sara! Omigod!' I laughed. Sara joined me.

'What's so funny?' Evan asked, stopping to wait for us to catch up.

'Sara,' I stated with a smile, like that was the only explanation needed.

Evan grabbed my hand, and Sara quickened her pace to catch up with Jared, sliding her arm through his. Analise, being the odd person out, continued along the trail, feigning interest in the tops of the trees to avoid looking at us.

Evan slowed down as we neared a bend, allowing the rest to disappear before stopping completely. 'Hi,' he smiled, vanquishing the jealousy that seethed under my skin. He leaned down and sent my heart into convulsions with the touch of his lips. 'I've wanted to do that for way too long.'

'I've *needed* you to do that for way too long,' I breathed.

'How are you after last night? I heard about the argument at the game.' He studied me intently.

'It's hard to watch,' I admitted. 'I have a feeling they're on the verge of breaking up, and I don't want her to get hurt.'

'I know,' he said, kissing me softly. 'Well, it's good to get away from the tension then.' I nodded. Evan squeezed my hand and we continued along the trail. This *was* exactly what I needed, despite Analise's presence.

'Can I ask you something?' Evan climbed up next to me on a rock after handing me our lunch.

'Sure,' I answered, unwrapping the sandwich.

'What was that sweater thing all about the other night?'

I stopped mid-bite, not having considered how it may have looked to Evan. I pulled the sandwich away and said, 'It was a misunderstanding.' I took a bite, and Evan waited for me to continue. Before I'd even thought about what I was saying, I added, 'It wasn't my sweater.'

'Oh,' Evan replied, dismissing the subject as he unwrapped his sandwich and began talking about how we both had one more game next week before the championships.

I forced myself to take another bite out of the sandwich, having lost my appetite. Lying made my stomach volatile. I didn't know why Jonathan had had my sweater. But for some reason, I couldn't bring myself to tell Evan that.

We returned to the car just as the sun was hiding behind the trees. Evan and I sat in the back with Analise. I made certain to sit in the middle. She really was nice, truly. But it was so very evident that she had a thing for Evan, and I wasn't going to pretend to be oblivious.

I nestled in under Evan's arm, resting my head on his chest. I breathed in his clean scent swirled with the mustiness of the outdoors and closed my eyes. He kissed the top of my head and played with my fingers, running his through mine and lightly drawing circles on my palm. I let the tingling of his touch lull me to sleep.

I looked at his face as he held my hand, walking with me along the beach. He hadn't shaved for a few days, making him look like he should be camping, not collecting seashells with his daughter. The ocean air ruffled his dark brown hair but his smile was permanent, making the lines along his eyes crease, like they were smiling too.

I held the pail in my hand, swinging it lightly. My eyes flitted everywhere except the ground – the birds darting along the shoreline pecking at the sand, the dark rolling water crashing into the rocks, then back to my father's face that looked so relaxed and peaceful.

'There's a good one,' he said, stopping to bend down and pluck a white pearly shell from the sand. 'What do you think of this one, Emma?' He held it up for me to inspect.

I took the shell in my hand and ran my fingers over its smooth surface.

'It's perfect . . .' I looked up, but he wasn't there. I turned around, searching, but I was alone.

'Emma?' the smooth voice whispered in my ear. 'Emma, we're home.'

I blinked my eyes open in a panic. I was still wrapped in Evan's arm, but the empty car was quiet and dark. I inhaled deeply, and stretched to sit up.

'I wish I could've let you sleep,' Evan said softly, still holding my hand in his. 'You looked so peaceful. You haven't been sleeping much, huh?'

'Not really,' I admitted. 'I can't believe I slept the entire car ride. Did everyone leave?'

'Sara and Jared are inside.'

He opened the car door and held it open until I stepped out.

'Wanna sleep over tonight?' Sara asked when Evan and I entered the kitchen door.

'Of course,' I answered, deciding I'd already witnessed way too much strife between my mother and Jonathan, and I didn't want to be there for whatever was about to happen tonight.

After saying our goodbyes, Sara followed me to my house. Seeing Jonathan's truck in the driveway, I parked along the street since I planned to leave my car at the house. I just needed to run in to grab my books and clothes for the next day. For a moment, I considered jumping in the SUV with Sara and forgetting about my things – having no idea what I was about to walk in on – but I had assignments due that I couldn't leave behind.

'I'll be right out,' I told Sara before jogging up the walkway. I stopped at the front door and hesitated. I couldn't hear voices; I could only hear music. I assumed they were in her room since the downstairs was dark.

I took a deep breath and slowly opened the door, planning to slip in and out so they didn't even have to know I was there. I closed the door and concentrated on the stairs. *I just need to get my things and I'll be gone*, I kept thinking over and over.

I clenched my teeth as the loose board squeaked beneath my foot halfway up the stairs. I froze, listening. A caressing voice came from the speakers, filling the entire house, but then I heard . . . a moan? I held my breath as I slowly turned on the stairs.

The breathing became louder. There was movement on the couch. I focused in the dark and my mouth dropped as intertwined legs came into view. I remained frozen, unable to look away, scanning the length of his body. His muscles rippled as she gripped his back. Her eyes were closed as her mouth rounded.

A moan escaped him, releasing me from my paralysis. I practically flew down the stairs and out the front door. I ran to Sara's SUV and slammed the door behind me, panting.

'What's wrong? Where's your stuff?' Sara asked in a panic.

'I couldn't . . .' I panted, trying to catch my breath, the image seared into my brain. I tried to shake it away, but I couldn't.

'Are they fighting?' Sara asked, her tone anxious.

'No,' I replied adamantly. 'They are *not* fighting.'

'Omigod,' Sara gasped. 'No way. You didn't just walk in on . . .' She started laughing in amazed disbelief.

I flopped my head against the headrest. 'Yup,' I breathed, 'I guess they didn't break up.' Sara laughed even harder.

I looked back at the house as we drove away – an uneasiness washing over me.

23

Boundaries

'FEELING ANY BETTER?' SARA ASKED AT breakfast the next morning. Her parents had already left for work, so it was just the two of us.

I shook my head, still haunted by the compromising position I'd caught my mother and Jonathan in the night before.

'I don't know how I'm ever going to look at either of them again,' I groaned. Sara laughed, overly amused by my trauma. 'Sara, I saw his *ass*, his *naked* ass – on top of my mother! I may seriously need to go back to therapy after seeing that.' I flopped my head onto my folded arms.

'I bet he has an amazing ass,' Sara mused dreamily, the smile consuming her entire face.

I peered up at her, appalled, with my cheeks scarlet. My reaction only made her laugh harder.

'I don't think I've laughed this hard since you tripped in front of those college guys in California.' Sara held her stomach.

'You love seeing me tortured and humiliated,' I sulked. 'Great friend you are!'

'Stop,' Sara chuckled, unable to hide her smile. 'It is funny, really.'

'Walking in on my mother and her boyfriend, sure, it may be horrifyingly hysterical. But he was supposed to break up with her. This is so not good.'

'They made up,' Sara offered with a shrug. 'Couples fight and make up all the time. What's the big deal?'

'He's leaving to go to grad school at USC,' I explained. 'My mother's in love with him.'

'Does she know?'

'Yes,' I told her, 'but she wants to be with him until he leaves.'

'Why is that so bad?' It was obvious she didn't understand my concern.

'I'll be gone when he leaves,' I continued.

'And you're worried about her being alone?'

I nodded, biting my lip to keep the tears from forming. Fear ate at the pit of my stomach, as I wondered what my mother would do in her isolated misery. I didn't want her to have to go through it without me.

Sara and I stopped by the house first thing in the morning to pick up my books. Thankfully, the house was empty. I avoided my mother and Jonathan that entire day, staying in my room, out of their sight.

And I thought I'd timed it perfectly when I left for school the next morning, emerging from my room right after my mother had pulled out of the driveway. But as

I headed down the stairs, I heard the refrigerator door close and realized Jonathan was still home. I paused in frustration – he was never home when I left for school.

I kept walking down the stairs and straight out the door, shutting it behind me just as I heard him call, 'Emma!'

I picked up my pace, not wanting to see him, forget about talk to him. Jonathan stepped out the front door with a coffee in his hand and a laptop bag hanging from his shoulder. He glanced in my direction as I unlocked my car, hesitating slightly. When I avoided eye contact and slipped into my car, he continued to his truck.

I turned the key in the ignition and . . . nothing happened.

'No way,' I grunted, pumping the gas and turning the key again. The car didn't even make an attempt to start. I collapsed in my seat, banging my hands on the steering wheel.

Jonathan braked at the end of the driveway. I remained in my car, ignoring him, grumbling profanities under my breath. This was the last thing I needed this morning.

He tapped on my window, forcing me to roll it down. 'You okay?'

'No,' I huffed, still unable to look at him. 'My car won't start.'

'I'll give you a ride,' he responded. 'Then I'll take a look at it later.'

I hesitated, glancing at my watch. I knew Sara and Evan were already on their way to school, and it didn't make sense to have them come all the way out here to get me.

'Please, just let me drive you to school,' Jonathan repeated when I didn't answer.

'Fine,' I grumbled. I opened my car door and slammed

it in frustration. I tossed my book bag on the floor of his passenger side before pulling myself up onto the seat. I shut the door and fastened my seat belt, determined to ignore him.

We drove down the street and out of the neighbourhood without a word.

'Can we talk about it?' Jonathan finally pleaded, turning down the radio when the tense silence became too much.

'No,' I snapped. 'I definitely *do not* want to talk about it.'

But after only ten seconds, I turned towards him and practically yelled, 'Why are you doing this to her, Jonathan? I don't understand!'

'I . . . I know,' he stuttered. 'I couldn't end it. I knew it would make things worse.'

'So you'd rather torture her by making her fall more in love with you so you can dump her right before you leave. That's real great!' I shot back, my anger rising with each word.

'Emma, please don't be mad at me,' he begged. 'That's not what I want, really. I just . . . wasn't ready.'

'Prolonging the inevitable isn't helping her,' I lectured sternly. 'It's torturing her. You can't protect her forever. You're coddling her.'

'And you aren't?' he rebutted, glancing at me out of the corner of his eye. I opened my mouth to defend myself, but nothing came out. In truth, I didn't really know what he meant. He continued, his voice growing stronger, 'Emma, you clean up after her when she throws a fit; you comfort her when she's irresponsible, and the other night she basically accused you of ruining her life. You're protecting her as much as I am.'

I continued to stare.

'I'm sorry,' he said, his tone softening. 'I shouldn't have said that.'

I let his words sink in. He pulled into the parking lot of the school, stopping alongside the walkway that wrapped around the building. Putting the truck in park, he turned towards me. His brown eyes were heavy with apology.

'So how do we fix this?' I questioned glumly. 'Besides having *sex* with her.' The words flew out of my mouth before I could catch them, delivered with a bite that I didn't anticipate.

'Uh,' Jonathan stammered, shock flashing across his eyes. 'You should never have seen that. I'm so sorry.'

I clenched my teeth and stared at the floor, more disturbed by his actions than I could rationalize as heat rushed through my chest. 'So now what?'

'You're right,' he answered firmly. 'I have to end things with her.'

I flipped my eyes towards him, not convinced he meant it.

'Should I still wait until after her birthday?'

I groaned. I hadn't thought of that. 'I don't know.'

Our eyes connected in deliberation until I realized I was lingering too long and blinked away.

'Thanks for the ride.' I reached down to pick up my backpack and it struck me. 'My sweater.'

'Huh?' Jonathan didn't follow.

'What were you doing with my sweater?' I demanded.

Jonathan took in my expression. 'I found it on the chair on the front porch when I was leaving for work a while ago. I thought it was Rachel's. I'd honestly forgotten I had it.'

'Oh,' I replied, my cheeks reddening at my accusatory tone. What was I really insinuating anyway? Maybe all this drama was making me overreact. I reached for the door handle, spotting Evan a few rows away, shutting his car door. I smiled at the sight of him. Then Analise appeared, shutting the passenger door. My heart froze and my smile disappeared.

'Are you okay?' Jonathan asked, noticing the change. I remained motionless, at a loss for words. 'Emma?'

'Yeah, I'm fine,' I choked, gripping the strap of my backpack. I opened the door.

'Emma.' Jonathan stopped me before I could hop down. His eyes held me captive long enough to confess, 'She's not the reason I decided to stay.'

'Emma?' Evan hollered as I was about to ask what he meant. I hesitated for a second, but knew I had to leave.

'Thanks,' I choked, barely able to form words. I hopped down from the truck and shut the door behind me.

As Jonathan drove off, Evan emerged from behind the truck.

His eyes tightened. 'Was that Jonathan?' He found my hand and securely laced his fingers through mine.

'My car wouldn't start,' I explained, trying to ignore Analise on the other side of him.

'Want me to take a look at it later?'

'That's okay,' I replied. 'Jonathan said he would, but thanks.' Evan nodded slightly, his eyes following Jonathan's truck as it pulled on to the street.

'Hi, Emma,' Analise chirped, poking her head around to flash me her blinding smile.

'Hi, Analise,' I replied, acknowledging her impassively. 'Where's *your* car?'

'Evan and I are doing some work for Vivian after school, so we thought it made sense for him to drive me,' she announced. As I listened, my feet faltered. Evan clearly saw the stunned expression on my face.

'That's great,' I replied flatly. Analise went her separate way towards the junior lockers as Evan continued towards mine.

'You're upset,' Evan noted as soon as Analise was out of earshot.

'No,' I mumbled, not looking at him. 'I'm just flustered because of my car.'

'Good morning,' Sara interrupted. 'How are you . . .' Her eyes flipped from me to Evan and she pressed her lips together. 'Um . . . I see that you're not into mornings. I'll talk to you later.' She nodded knowingly and took off to class.

I pulled my books from my locker, unable to face Evan without giving away just how much his time with Analise bothered me.

'Em, you don't have to –'

'I have to go to class,' I muttered, brushing past him quickly. This morning sucked. I just wanted this day to be over, and it had barely begun.

Sara was waiting for me around the corner. 'I'm coming over tonight. We're talking about this whole Analise situation.'

'Okay,' I sighed, knowing I needed it.

The day didn't get any better when Analise plopped her fluffy ass down at our table for lunch. Sara eyed her in

298

disbelief, like she'd trampled over all sorts of boundaries. Sara opened her mouth to say something but I shot her a pleading look and begged in a whisper, 'Don't.'

'You sure?' she questioned incredulously. I nodded just as Evan sat down between me and Analise.

The awkward silence lingered until Analise broke it with, 'This food looks better than Mrs Timmins' dinner last night, huh?' She let out a light laugh. 'That was the strangest version of chicken I've ever seen. You should have seen it, Emma. I think it was grey. Right, Evan?'

I couldn't move. I knew Evan was watching me, but I remained still.

'What dinner?' Sara demanded, staring at me, silently begging me to speak up.

'Oh one of those business dinner thingys,' Analise gushed with a nervous laugh, realizing she must have said something wrong.

'What did you think of it?' I asked, feigning curiosity with a strained smile.

Analise hesitated. Probably trying to decide if I was sincere or about to rip her head off. 'It was actually pretty nice. Stuart and Vivian are sweet, so they made it easy. And Evan can talk to anyone and he introduced me to a lot of people, so it wasn't as bad as I feared it would be. We ended up having a really great time.'

I stood from the table and stormed out of the cafeteria. I'd barely made it to the hall when Evan caught up with me.

'It was just a stupid dinner for my father's firm,' Evan explained in a rush.

'Yup.' I responded flatly and kept walking, not caring if he was next to me or not. I remained stoic on the outside, but my insides were squirming – I thought I was about to be sick.

'Em, stop,' he begged. 'Please, just listen.'

I turned abruptly and gave him my full and cold attention. He drew back when he saw the disconnect in my eyes.

'My mother wanted Laura to meet some potential clients affiliated with my father's firm,' he explained calmly. 'Analise just came along with her mother. It's not as bad as it sounds.'

I turned and started walking again, choking on the fumes of anger that cut off all logic and rational thought to my head. I could only feel, not think – and I was afraid if I opened my mouth, I would regret anything I said.

'Besides, you hate those dinners,' Evan hollered after me.

I spun around. 'So did *you*,' I bit back and rushed off, leaving him behind.

'Hey, Emma,' Jill said from beside my locker as I forcefully pulled the books from the top shelf, grumbling to myself about how I couldn't believe Evan had taken Analise to a firm dinner. 'How's Rachel?'

I whipped my head to the side. It took every ounce of willpower I had not to snap at her. To tell her to mind her own business. But I swallowed the anger and said, 'Fine.'

'We never told anyone about the drinking,' she assured me. Her voice was low; she was careful not to be overheard. Her words struck me as odd. My eyes twitched, questioning. Her face filled with sympathy.

Then it hit me, *Omigod. She thinks my mother's an alcoholic.*

'Thanks,' I replied quickly, needing to look away as the heat crept across my face.

'We shouldn't have done what we did,' she continued. 'Casey and me. I'm sorry about that.'

'Yeah sure,' I muttered, my stomach twisting in knots.

'If you ever need to talk,' she said consolingly, making me want to turn from her and run as fast as I could.

'Yup,' I answered shortly. 'See you in practice. I have to get to class.'

'Oh yeah, sure,' she replied uncomfortably, her cheeks slightly pink. I walked away with my head down, so people wouldn't notice how red I was.

I couldn't live in denial any longer, and it took Jill's words of solace to snap me out of it. Despite my mother's assurances that she was fine, she wasn't, and it was time I faced the truth. I had wanted to believe her so much that I'd convinced myself that she only drank to excess when she was upset or sad – and that was okay. That was *okay*?! What was wrong with me?

'Hi, girls,' my mother greeted us cheerily from the kitchen when Sara and I arrived after practice.

'Hi, Rachel,' Sara replied, setting her bag near the bottom of the stairs and walking into the kitchen. I followed her, suddenly afraid to face my mother. It was like I was seeing her for the first time – noticing the wine glass next to her on the counter as she cut vegetables. The sight of it made my chest hurt.

She picked up the glass and took a sip. 'Are you staying for dinner?'

'I'm not staying long,' Sara told her. 'I gave Emma a ride home, and we're just going to talk for a while before I go.'

'Oh, okay,' my mother responded. 'Jonathan went to pick up a new battery for your car.'

'Great,' I answered in a flat tone. 'Well, we'll be upstairs.'

'Um, Sara,' my mother called as we were about to leave the kitchen. 'It's my birthday on Saturday, and I'm having a few friends over. I thought it would be nice if you came over too, you know, for Emily. I think we're just going to play poker and listen to music.'

'Sure, that sounds great,' Sara agreed.

'Really?' My mother's eyes lit up. 'I'm happy you'll be there. I really want it to be fun.'

'It will be,' Sara assured her. 'If you want me to bring anything, or do anything to help, let me know.'

'I will,' my mother beamed. It became evident to me just how important this party was to her, and with everything that had gone on the last few days, we hadn't really talked much about it. Despite everything, all I really wanted was for her to be happy.

'I think Evan has a poker table we could borrow,' I added.

'That would be amazing,' she said, glowing. 'Thanks.'

'Sure,' I replied with a small smile before following Sara up the stairs. As I entered my room, I texted, *Wait til after her birthday. And dont worry about me.*

I unzipped my jacket and tossed it on the chair at my desk while Sara shut the door and settled on my bed. My phone beeped, and Jonathan responded with, *Okay. But I do, cant help it.* My cheeks flushed with heat, and I stuffed the phone in my jacket pocket.

'Okay. So, you have to say something to him,' Sara

began before I could even sit down. 'You have to tell him that he can't hang out with her any more.'

I started to worry about what potential disasters awaited us at my mother's party. How Sara and Evan would react at the sight of it. Maybe she'd just get giddy drunk, like she sometimes did, and talk too loudly, spewing semi-embarrassing comments. I could live with that.

'Emma!'

'Uh, what?' I redirected my focus.

'The invasion of Analise,' Sara stressed. 'What's going on with you? Have you heard a single word I've said?'

'Yes,' I replied. 'I need to set boundaries.'

'No,' she corrected me sternly, '*Evan* needs to set boundaries. He can't have an obsessed girl doting on him all over the place and expect you to be the loving girl-friend who's pretending nothing's happening.'

'Right,' I agreed without the gusto Sara was looking for. She gawked at me disapprovingly.

'But what if I'm overreacting?' I asked quietly, lying on my bed next to her.

'Overreacting? Um . . . the whole school is talking about *them*. They went to a party together last Friday. She's over at his house all the time, and he drives her to school. They look more like a –'

'Okay,' I interrupted, not needing the detail. 'I get it. I'll talk to him.'

'Why do I feel like I'm talking you into this?' she questioned me in concern. 'Do you not remember being blindsided at lunch today? I saw the look on your face when she brought up the dinner.'

Just the mention of it made me clench my teeth. 'Yes. I'll talk to him.'

'Okay. I have to go. My mom's waiting on me for dinner. I'll see you tomorrow,' Sara said, grabbing her things and opening the door.

Evan appeared at the top of the stairs. Sara stopped short. 'Uh, hi, Evan.'

'Hi, Sara,' he replied. She scooted past him and flashed me a teeth bared, *good luck* look as she disappeared down the stairs.

Evan remained outside my room, hesitating at the sight of me.

'Hi,' he said quietly, shutting the door behind him.

'Hi,' I replied, barely audible. I sat against the headboard, pulling a pillow on to my lap.

Evan sat down on the end of my bed – the strain between us suffocated me.

'I should have invited you to the dinner,' Evan began. 'I guess I know how much you hate them . . . but I should have given you the choice.'

'It's not just the dinner,' I returned, letting out a distraught breath. 'You've been spending a lot of time with her, and I . . . I don't like it. It's that simple.'

'Em, I don't see her like that, I swear. She's like a little sister to me.' He silently pleaded for me to believe him.

'You may feel that way about *her*, but Evan, she has a thing for *you*. You have to know that.'

'I know,' he sighed. 'It's not what I meant to happen. I just wanted to make her feel welcome, being new and everything. I know how hard it can be.'

His words drifted through me and swelled my heart.

I knew he meant it, because that's exactly who he was. 'Evan, you're the most thoughtful person I've ever known, and I love you for that. But you need to set boundaries with her.'

'I will,' he agreed, moving closer. 'So, did you just say that you still love me?' He teased, continuing to scoot along the bed until he was next to me.

'Yes,' I battled to hide my grin. 'Some sunshiny sprite is not –'

'Emma!' Evan baulked in surprise.

'Sorry,' I smirked. 'She's nice. I just . . .'

I was interrupted by the warmth of his mouth pressed against mine. And suddenly she wasn't important any more. I wrapped my arms around his neck and pulled him towards me, sinking down along my headboard so that I was lying on my back as he pulled the pillow off my lap.

Evan continued from my lips, trailing his mouth along my neck and sliding his hand across my stomach to the small of my back, positioning himself over me. I relaxed my knees as he lowered himself on to me, my legs wrapping around him.

Our breathing quickened as our kisses became more frantic. I ran my hands along the tight, lean muscles of his back, gripping the end of his shirt, sliding it up.

My door squeaked open. 'Your car's . . .'

Evan rolled over quickly to sit up. I pushed myself up, smoothing the back of my hair, staring at Jonathan's wide eyes and open mouth.

'Sorry, should've knocked,' he said in a single breath and shut the door.

'Uh, boundaries?' Evan stressed from beside me.

'Yeah,' I breathed, staring at the door.

24

Happy Birthday

'SHOULD I BE WORRIED?' I ASKED UNDER MY breath as my mother danced around the kitchen, putting bowls on to the counter – dumping bags of chips and spooning containers of dip into them.

'Honestly?' Jonathan asked from beside me, watching the same spectacle.

'Of course,' I replied, feeling stressed.

'Probably.' His honesty made my stomach churn.

'That's what I thought,' I exhaled in defeat.

'Hi,' Sara greeted me joyfully as she opened the front door. I turned towards her, covering the worry with a smile.

'Hi,' I responded.

'Sara!' my mother exclaimed, brushing past me to give Sara a hug.

'Happy birthday, Rachel,' Sara said, hugging her in return while eyeing me in shock over her shoulder. I shrugged in response.

'I brought you something,' Sara told her upon being released. She opened her bag and pulled out a neatly wrapped package about the size of a deck of cards.

'You're so sweet.' My mother opened it without hesitation and removed a necklace from the box. She held the delicate silver chain in front of her. 'It's beautiful. Thank you.'

'You're welcome,' Sara replied, taking off her jacket.

'Sara, you must know how to cook,' my mother insisted, fastening the chain around her neck.

'Not really,' Sara confessed. 'My mother's tried to encourage it, but it hasn't taken yet.'

'What's with you guys?' My mother shook her head. She returned to the kitchen where she proceeded to pull ingredients out of the refrigerator. 'I'm going to have to give Anna a hard time about this. What are you going to do when you go to college?'

There was a knock at the door. Jonathan went to open it as Sara and I took the bowls of chips into the living room. Jared entered carrying a bottle of wine with a bow around it. I stopped short at the sight of it.

'Well, hello,' my mother greeted him with a smile.

'Rachel, this is Jared,' Sara said, introducing him and slipping her arm through his.

'Happy birthday,' he said, presenting the bottle to my mother.

'My favourite,' she gushed, taking the bottle from him. 'Thank you.'

'Where's Evan?' I asked, scanning the driveway. When I didn't see any sign of him, I shut the door.

'He drove separately,' Jared explained, following after my mother and Sara towards the kitchen. 'He should be here any second.'

I remained in the foyer, hoping Evan would arrive soon – and not wanting to go anywhere near the kitchen in fear that I'd be recruited to cook something.

'Are you friends with Evan?' my mother asked, laying tortillas on a griddle.

'He's my brother,' Jared explained, standing in the kitchen doorway.

'I would have never guessed that,' my mother replied, eyeing his broader frame and blond hair, flipped out around his ears. 'You look as much alike as Emily and me.' She let out a laugh, making Jared smile. 'So *you* must know how to cook.'

'Not at all,' Jared confessed, glancing at Sara – obviously not sure what to make of my mother. 'My brother and I are pretty opposite in just about everything. Is there anything else I can do to help?'

'Do you know how to make margaritas?'

'*That* I can help with,' Jared replied, continuing into the kitchen.

'Great,' I muttered under my breath.

The door opened with a knock, and Evan entered with the poker table.

'Let me help you with that,' Jonathan offered, appearing from the living room to take the table. Evan followed him with folding chairs in each hand.

'Finally!' my mother exclaimed. 'Evan, please come help me cook these quesadillas. You and I appear to be to be the only ones who have any talent in the kitchen.'

'Jared has talent,' Sara said defensively. 'It's just not in the kitchen, that's all.'

'Oh, so what room are we talking about?' my mother smirked. 'The bedroom?'

'We did not just go there,' Jared blurted in disbelief, looking from my mother to Sara. Sara started laughing, and I stared, wide-eyed, in shock at my mother's inappropriate candour – wondering if she'd already started drinking.

Evan returned to the kitchen after hanging up his jacket. 'Uh, okay. So, what do you want me to do?' he asked, having no idea what he'd just walked in on.

'Flip them when they're ready,' she instructed, handing Evan the spatula. 'Want a drink?'

'I think *I* might need one,' Jared interjected. My mother pulled two glasses from the cabinet, filled them with ice and held them out for Jared to fill with the margarita blend he'd created.

She handed one glass over and held up hers with a smirk. 'To being talented.'

Jared raised his eyebrows in shock and clinked her glass.

'Hey, I want in on this,' Sara insisted, filling another glass to tap with theirs. I tried to keep from having heart failure as I watched my mother quickly drain half of her glass. I realized I had to prepare myself. This was about to happen.

'You okay?' Jonathan asked, passing me as he carried in more folding chairs from the porch and set them around the poker table.

'Not until tomorrow morning,' I muttered, deciding to follow him to help set up the chairs.

'Emily, would you put on some music?' my mother

hollered from the kitchen, although there was no need to yell since I could hear every word they were saying.

'Sure,' I replied. I flipped through the CD collection, not finding anything I would deem party-worthy.

'Here,' Jonathan offered, handing me his iPod. 'There's a playlist on there for Rachel's party.'

'Thanks,' I said, accepting the iPod and plugging it into the wire attached to the stereo. I scrolled to the *Rachel's Party* playlist. My mother hollered in excitement from the kitchen when the first song came on.

'Perfect, Emily,' she praised.

I was about to explain that it wasn't my selection, when Jonathan stopped me. 'Just let her think it was you.'

'Okay.' I shrugged, not understanding why it mattered.

About half an hour later, the door opened and six people let themselves in, carrying brown bags filled with alcohol and snacks.

'Is this where the party is?' a guy with a tightly trimmed beard asked, peeking into the kitchen. He opened his arms when my mother squealed in excitement and rushed towards him, wrapping her arms around his neck while kissing him on the cheek. 'Happy birthday, Rach,' he said, kissing her cheek in return. She hugged each person, directing them to hang up their coats and instructing them to place their beers in the cooler on the porch. She was so excited. I tried to let the worry go and be happy for her. This was her birthday after all.

'We brought the other poker table and chairs,' one of the guys announced, popping open a can of beer after returning from the porch.

We had to introduce ourselves since my mother was

too preoccupied pouring margaritas for the two women she'd dragged into the kitchen.

'Wow, Emily,' a woman named Sharon noted upon meeting me. 'I can't believe how much you've grown up.'

'Thanks,' I responded, studying the woman who obviously knew me. Her voice was crackly from too many years of smoking, and her face was etched with lines from a life that had not been kind to her. She wore her curly black hair long over her shoulders. Her dark eyes were heavily lined in black and layered with mascara.

'You still look just like your dad,' she continued.

'Right?' my mother chimed in from behind Sharon, holding out a glass for her to take. 'I swear she's not mine.' She laughed playfully.

Sharon cackled. 'You've been trying to get away with that one for years. But I was the one who drove you to the hospital when you went into labour, remember?'

'I couldn't exactly drive myself,' my mother huffed.

'The bottle of wine may have had something to do with that,' Sharon added, her laugh turning into a cough. I narrowed my eyes and looked from her to my mother.

'Relax, Emily,' my mother chuckled. 'She's only joking.' I nodded with an awkward smile. Sharon clamped her mouth shut to keep from laughing, causing her to convulse in a coughing fit.

'Can I smoke?' Sharon asked in a rasp, pulling a pack from her pocket.

'Porch,' my mother instructed. 'I'll come out with you.'

My mother and Sharon disappeared out the front door. Evan finally emerged from the kitchen with several platters of quesadillas. Jared and Jonathan were helping

311

two of the new arrivals move furniture to make room for the additional poker table. Sara and I brought in pitchers of margaritas and set them on the coffee table.

'I know, right?' my mother said to Sharon as they entered from the porch, the smell of cigarette smoke swirling around them.

'Evan, you can have a beer,' my mother insisted. 'It's my birthday. Besides, you're staying over, so you don't have to worry about driving.' She smiled and handed him a freshly opened bottle.

'Thanks.' He accepted it and placed his hand on my back, probably sensing my uneven breaths. I watched as my mother poured herself another drink. Closing my eyes, I exhaled quickly, trying to remain calm.

'You okay?' Evan bent down to ask in my ear.

I played down my worried expression. 'I'm not so sure I know what I'm doing with poker.'

'I'll help you,' he assured me. 'I'll give you a cheat sheet so you know what hand beats what.'

'Okay,' I replied, trying to appear relaxed. I met Jonathan's eyes across the room. He looked from my mother to me and shook his head. He was expecting something to happen, and my gut twisted in a knot, knowing it too. I looked away and tried to shake it off.

'Let's play,' my mother announced, herding everyone into the living room.

As she drank more and more, my mother played less and less. She finally declared that whatever Jonathan earned would be her winnings. She hopped from table to table, initiating conversations; then she'd jump up to select songs on the iPod and dance around with whoever she could pull away from the game.

And I played poker, or at least tried to. I had no idea what I was doing. I kept glancing at Evan's cheat sheet to decide if my hand was good enough to place a bet. We had to buy chips, so the betting was real – at the birthday girl's insistence. This kept a few of the guys a little too serious, considering it was supposed to be fun.

A few margarita pitchers later, my mother was a giggly mess, sitting on Jonathan's lap with her arms draped around his neck.

'Come on, baby. You need to bet big on this hand,' my mother urged, kissing him on the cheek. With that statement, one of the guys folded.

'Thanks, Rachel,' Jonathan replied, placing his bet.

'No, you should bet more than *that*,' she garbled, pushing a few more chips in. 'We're winning this hand.' She stuck her tongue out at Sara and the other guy who hadn't folded. Sara laughed at her, taking a sip of her margarita.

'Sara, I like you,' she spontaneously confessed, the effects of the tequila showing.

'Thanks, Rachel,' Sara replied with a smile. 'Happy birthday.' She raised her glass for my mother to clumsily tap.

'Come dance with me,' my mother insisted, popping up from Jonathan's lap and grabbing Sara's hand.

'But I'm still playing,' Sara argued feebly. My mother grabbed her hand and pulled her from her chair, making Sara abandon her cards on the table.

My mother twirled herself under Sara's arm as she held her hand above her head.

I watched from the other table as Jared shuffled the deck.

'You don't say much, huh?' the woman with bleach blonde hair noted. I thought her name was Sally, but maybe it was Ally.

'Not really,' I replied, keeping my eyes on the cards as Jared placed them on the table in front of me.

'Don't drink either, huh?' she slurred, holding her head up on her hand.

'No, I don't,' I answered.

'You used to make us drinks when you were little,' she told me, making me pause before picking up my cards. 'You were so cute, getting us beers. Rachel always had the best parties.'

I studied my cards intently, knowing Evan and Jared were watching me.

'I'll take two cards,' I requested, pretending not to be fazed by the glimpse of my previous life with my mother.

In truth, it was appearing to be not too much different than it was now – except I didn't take sips from the beer cans any more. Our life was full of emotional waves, and had been even more so when I was young – laughing one minute, crying and screaming the next. There was always music playing, and there seemed to be a constant flow of people in the house. But despite the bodies, I was very much on my own. That's when my focus became school and sports. Despite my mother's lack of interest in my academic achievements, she'd always made certain I had soccer and basketball – even if she was incapable of driving me to the practices and games herself.

My mother and Sara's laughter drew our attention. My mother bumped into the side table, knocking over a few pictures. Sharon joined them from her post on the porch, trailing cigarette fumes in with her.

'What do you do, Ally?' Evan asked, taking a sip from his beer bottle.

'I'm a bartender,' she replied, directing her attention towards Evan and lingering a little too long. 'Can't believe you're still in high school. And wait . . .' She looked from me to Evan. 'You two are dating, right?'

Evan nodded, before requesting two cards from Jared.

'I miss high school,' she sighed, taking a gulp from her glass.

'No you don't,' my mother countered, plopping down in the vacant seat next to Ally. 'You hated high school.'

Ally started laughing. 'That's true. But we sure did get away with a lot of shit.'

'Definitely,' my mother recollected with giggle.

'Do you remember when you convinced Mr Hall to let you skip that test because you told him you had wicked bad cramps, and then we went into the woods to get high?'

My mother laughed hard in remembrance, causing her eyes to water.

In between hysterics, Ally added, 'And the time you gave Emily that whisky and Coke and we videoed her bumping into the wall for like an hour.'

My mother held her stomach as she rolled around in laughter. The guy next to Ally chuckled, 'I remember that. You were hysterical.'

I forced a chuckle, like I remembered it fondly, then folded and made an excuse about needing to go to the bathroom. But when I opened the bathroom door to leave, my mother was waiting to get in.

'Emily!' she declared happily. 'Are you having fun?'

'Yeah, it's great,' I told her, trying to smile. 'Are you having fun?'

'I'm trying,' she said, passing me to go into the bathroom. 'It would be better if he would stop staring at you.' And with that, she shut the bathroom door, leaving me outside, stunned. Who was she talking about?

I turned towards the stairs as Jonathan was reaching the top.

'Hey,' he greeted. 'Are you in line?'

'No,' I replied, heading towards the stairs, still shocked by what my mother had said before shutting the door.

'What's going on?'

I shrugged, completely mystified.

'What?' The door opened behind us and my mother emerged. We both whipped around.

'Aahh,' she said, as if she'd caught us. 'And there you two are. You know I know. I mean it's so obvious. But can't you wait at least until you're in California? I mean it's my birthday. You don't have to shove it in my face.'

'Rachel, what are you talking about?' Jonathan laughed uncomfortably.

'Whatever,' she said, dismissing him. 'I'm over it.'

I continued to gawk at her. 'You can't think there's anything going on between us,' I insisted.

'Maybe,' she shrugged and went down the stairs, leaving us staring after her. I took a deep breath and followed her as Jonathan went into the bathroom.

The rest of the night, we didn't even look at each other.

Or at least I didn't look at him. I refused to fuel my mother's drunken delusions, and I really didn't want her saying anything in front of Evan.

As the money dwindled, so did the participants. Jared and Sara were the first to leave.

'I think I got a little drunk,' Sara laughed in my ear as she clumsily hugged me goodbye.

'It's okay,' I told her, patting her awkwardly on the back as Jared waited to help her put her jacket on. 'I'll talk to you tomorrow.'

Not long after, the other poker table and chairs were folded up as one of the carloads decided to head out as well.

'But you can't leave,' my mother begged them, hugging Ally.

'Happy birthday, Rach.'

My mother walked out to the porch to see them off.

'Who wants a shot?' she asked upon closing the door. It was a question that she didn't expect to be answered as she lined up the shot glasses on the coffee table, filled them with tequila, and began handing them to everyone, including me.

When she set the gold liquid in front of me, I cringed and glanced across the table at Jonathan.

'To being forever young,' she declared, holding her shot glass in the air. 'Come on, Evan, pick it up.'

Evan raised his shot along with everyone else, slinging it back with a grimace. I didn't touch mine. Jonathan slid it surreptitiously across the table and drank it down before sliding the glass back in front of me.

'Thatta girl, Emily,' my mother praised me, collecting the glasses.

While she was in the kitchen, Evan leaned over and asked, 'Want to stay or go?'

I bit my lip in consternation. Before I could make a decision, the bearded guy folded his hand and declared, 'Well, I think I'm broke enough. Sharon, we're going.'

'No,' she mumbled from her slouched position on the couch.

'Yeah, you're about ready to pass out,' he noted, standing up from the table.

'Not you too,' my mother sulked when she found him retrieving their coats from the closet.

'Your guy took all my money,' he told her, 'so happy birthday. Don't spend it all at once.' She gave him a hug and a brief peck on the lips.

With it just being the three of us, and my poker chips down to a handful, Jonathan suggested, 'Cash out?'

'Sure,' I answered standing up from the table. Evan remained to help Jonathan put the chips back in their silver case. I headed into the kitchen to begin picking up.

My mother came in from the porch shivering. 'It's just us, huh?' She observed the guys in the living room and me in the kitchen.

'I *did* have fun,' she said from behind me.

'Good,' I answered, dumping the half full glasses in the sink.

'I'm sorry about upstairs, you know, with Jonathan. I can be pretty stupid sometimes.'

I could only nod, not knowing how to respond.

Then out of nowhere she asked, 'So you don't remember, right?'

I turned around and tightened my eyes in confusion.

'What? About your parties when I lived with you? I remember.'

'I was just thinking,' she said, ignoring my answer. She settled down on the kitchen chair – probably because she was having a hard time standing. 'I've had to relive that day for all these years, and you don't remember it.' Her face was smooth and emotionless as her eyes lazily flipped up at me.

I opened my mouth to ask her what she was talking about, but then I realized – she was talking about the day my father died. I closed my mouth and averted my gaze.

'You always had to wear pink,' she remembered, lost in the past as her eyes glazed over. 'He bought you a new pink dress every year.'

I was held hostage by her words, unable to tell her to stop. My heart started to beat faster.

'You were waiting for him by the window, wanting to know why he was late. You kept asking where he was every five minutes.' Sorrow flooded her face. 'It's not fair that you don't remember the day I can never forget. When was the last time you celebrated your birthday, Emily?' Her question sliced through me.

My chest froze, and I had to force air into my lungs. All of a sudden, I wasn't in the room any more. I was in my pink frilly dress, staring out the window.

'He would drive home early from work to hang those stupid coloured lanterns in the back yard,' she recalled impassively.

For a second I saw them. They were different shapes and colours, hung in crisscrossing lines across the back yard. My stomach was swallowed by coldness, and I couldn't move.

'He'd bring home your cake, made by that ridiculously expensive bakery in the city. It always had to be chocolate with raspberry filling.'

'When's Daddy going to be home?' I asked, the curtains spread so I could keep watch.

'He shouldn't be long,' was what I was told each time. It wasn't my mother who answered me, but another woman. I looked over my shoulder to see her pulling a pan out of the oven.

'But it's getting dark, and he never comes home in the dark,' I argued, continuing to stare out the window.

'Anything yet?' she asked, concern resonating in her voice as a man entered the room with a phone in his hand.

'No,' he answered. 'They said he left the office hours ago.' The man looked familiar, but I couldn't place him.

'Rachel!' he hollered.

'What?' she called back from upstairs.

'I think we need to make the call.'

Before she could answer, the phone rang. She rushed down the stairs as the man answered. 'Who is it?' she demanded before he'd even said hello.

The anxiety in her eyes made me nervous. I kept watching her, unable to look away from her distressed face. It changed from worry to despair when the words spilled from his mouth after he hung up the phone. 'There's been an accident.'

'You took him from me,' she murmured, not removing her eyes from mine.

'Rachel? What did you do?' Jonathan's voice sounded like he was talking through a tunnel.

My vision blurred with tears. Her eyes widened in recognition. 'Oh,' she breathed, 'You remember.'

Pain eased through my body like venom. I opened my mouth to cry out, but nothing happened.

'What did you do?' Jonathan demanded again more urgently. 'Emma, are you okay?'

'Emma, what's wrong?' Evan's muted voice was etched with concern.

I looked into her eyes again, and swore I saw loathing. I winced.

I couldn't be there any longer. I needed to get out. But I couldn't move. My legs refused to cooperate. I choked on the sobs that were suffocating me. My body was on fire, searing in pain. I had to get away from her.

Before I knew what I'd done, I was out the front door – the legs that had failed me moments before were now carrying me in a run down the street. But no matter how hard I ran, I couldn't escape the ache that was crushing my chest. I breathed in, but I couldn't get enough air.

I ran down random street after street before collapsing on the damp, muddy ground, gripping my chest. It felt like it was about to burst open. I screamed in pain.

It all came back to me in a rush. The call. My mother yelling out in denial. I watched as if I were a spectator at a play. I didn't understand, but at the same time, I understood too well. He wasn't coming home. He was never coming home again.

I don't know how long I lay on the cold, wet ground, consumed in grief. I was pulled back to the surface when a warm hand brushed across my cheek. He gently propped my head on his lap as he soothed me with comforting words I couldn't quite make out.

'It's okay,' he whispered.

'It hurts so bad,' I gasped, my body tense. '*Please* make it stop.' The tears continued down my cheeks.

Evan pulled me off the ground and carried me to the car. He gently set me down on the passenger seat, bending to kiss my forehead. I curled up in a ball, still clutching my chest – afraid that if I let go, I would fall apart.

I began to shiver, the cold earth having seeped into my bones. The warmth of the car did little to ease the shaking. Evan draped his jacket over me, and I burrowed my nose into the collar, breathing in his scent.

I fought for each breath, my jaw quivering. I was consumed by the pain, unable to escape it. It was crushing me.

I was trapped in my grief, barely aware of where we were when the car stopped. I think he may have tried to talk to me, but I couldn't hear what he was saying. His voice was muffled and distant. I closed my eyes and pressed my face against his chest when he lifted me from the car.

I remained still as he rested me on his bed. I felt my shoes slide off my feet and my jeans glide over my legs. I couldn't focus, but my eyes were open. I could only feel, and I didn't know how to shut it off. I couldn't push it back down to the hidden depths of darkness where I'd been protected from it for so many years. I was losing him all over again.

Warmth pressed against my back and his arms pulled me into him. I gripped his hand, holding it tightly, keeping myself tethered to the present just enough so that I could regain perspective of where I was, lying on Evan's bed.

'I'm here, Emma. I'll never let you go,' he whispered in my ear, holding me tighter.

My frame shook as I cried, releasing the torment that had been trapped since that day ten years ago. I found reprieve some time in the early hours of the next day when exhaustion shrouded the pain and I drifted into a sleep filled with vivid images of my father.

25

All Over Again

Before I opened my eyes, I heard music playing softly in the background. I couldn't quite figure out who was singing, but his voice was calming. I breathed in, letting the melody float over me before deciding to open my eyes. They didn't open very wide.

My eyes were swollen and puffy, and my entire body ached, especially my chest. I eased myself out of the curled position I'd locked myself in throughout the night. Though he wasn't in the room, Evan had left behind the comforting lyrics flowing through the speakers.

I sat on the edge of the bed and breathed in deeply. I felt empty, like everything inside me had spilled out and there was nothing left. I rose from the bed and went into the bathroom, not bothering to look at myself as I passed the mirror, having seen the vacant look one too many times.

I stripped off and climbed into the shower, allowing the hot water to beat against my skin. The exhaustion held tight, even after the long shower. A pair of sweatpants and a T-shirt were set on the floor in front of the door when I got out. Evidently Evan knew I was awake.

I dressed in the T-shirt that hung past my hips, and folded the waistband of the pants over so I wouldn't trip on them. I braided my wet hair before stepping back into the room. He was waiting for me, sitting up against the headboard, flipping through the channels with the television on mute.

Evan clicked off the TV when I slid on to the bed and curled up on his chest.

'How are you doing?' he asked gently, wrapping his arms around me.

'Okay,' I rasped, my throat raw from the strain of emotion.

He squeezed me against him before asking, 'Can you tell me what happened last night?'

I swallowed hard. Tears filled my eyes at the thought of saying it out loud.

'If you can't –'

'It's okay,' I choked. Sitting up, I took another cleansing breath, and met Evan's smoky blue eyes. Worry forged a line between them. I knew I had to try to explain.

'My mother blames me for my father's death.' Just hearing those words coming out of my mouth hurt me.

His back stiffened. 'How?'

'He died on my birthday,' I explained. 'On his way home from buying the cake.'

'How is that your fault?'

I shrugged. 'Logically, it's not. But . . . she hurts, and I give her a reason for her pain. I ruined her life.'

'Emma, you *didn't*. She's an adult. She should realize that accidents happen. *You* can't believe that it's your fault.'

'I . . .' I couldn't find the words to say what he wanted me to – that I knew I wasn't at fault. Guilt captured the words off my tongue before I could say them. I understood what was true, but I couldn't deny how devastating it was to be the reason he had been on that road, at that moment.

Logic didn't matter when the person I loved most had been taken from me. I finally understood why my mother needed me to feel her suffering. It hurt her too much to keep it inside. For her to be the only one to miss him like she did.

'I couldn't remember him,' I told Evan, running my eyes along the lines of the duvet, allowing the images of my father to run freely through my head. 'Remembering him would mean that I knew I'd lost him, and the grief that went along with it. So, I didn't. I didn't remember, any of it – until last night. And it hurt . . .' I choked out the last word as tears flooded my eyes.

Evan pulled me against him and held me tight.

'It hurt so bad I couldn't breathe.' Warm tears streamed down my face. 'I felt it, all of it, as if it had just happened and . . .' I swallowed back a sob.

'It's okay,' Evan said soothingly, kissing the top of my head. 'I understand.' I stayed in the comfort of his arms until I could move again.

I sat up and wiped my wet cheeks.

'Can we just lie here?' I asked, sniffling. Evan handed me a much needed tissue.

'Of course.'

I rested back down on Evan's chest, listening to the beating of his heart. He pulled the blanket over us and embraced me as if the strength of his arms could ward off the sorrow.

The music faded and the television came on. Evan selected a movie for us to watch, but I didn't last long, still drained from the emotional beating I'd taken.

When I opened my eyes again, the room was darkening. Evan was on his side with his arms locked around me, breathing heavily in a restful sleep. I inhaled his scent with my face pressed against his shirt and leaned up to kiss his neck.

He stirred and hugged me closer. I ran my mouth along his neck, feeling the warmth of his pulse under my lips. A smile formed on his face while his eyes remained closed. I found the spot under his ear and kissed him again.

'Hi,' he murmured with a wide smile, slowly opening his eyes and inhaling deeply.

'Hi,' I whispered in his ear, tracing his carved jaw with my lips, making my way to his mouth. He parted his firm lips to receive me. I breathed him in and pulled myself against him, kissing him harder as his hands moved under my shirt, along my back.

Our bodies moved together, easing over each other. His warm hands pressed against my bare skin, inciting a flutter throughout my body that made my heart beat convulse. Our breathing quickened, and his touch trailed down to the waistband of the sweatpants, teasing along the elastic. I lifted his shirt and he pulled back to allow it over his head, revealing the smooth lines of muscle beneath.

I ran my hands over the definition of his chest and grooves of his stomach, kissing along his shoulder to his neck.

I went to remove my shirt, but he propped himself up and pulled back, his eyes scanning mine.

'What?' I asked in confusion, not sure if I'd done something wrong.

'Not yet,' Evan explained. 'Not like this.'

I collapsed against him, my body pulsing. 'Okay,' I breathed in disappointment.

'You understand, right?' He tucked my hair behind my ear.

'I do,' I answered, unable to look at him. Of course I understood. Our first time shouldn't happen after I'd spent the day mourning the loss of my father. But I wanted to feel him, *needed* to feel him, to be close to him – to mend the fissure that had split open overnight.

'Do you want to stay over again tonight?' he asked, breathing in my hair as he pressed his lips against my temple.

'I should go home.'

'To Rachel's?' he questioned in surprise. 'I didn't think –'

'Yeah, I should,' I interrupted. 'It's okay. I want to talk to her. I understand now, and I didn't before. Maybe . . . maybe we can really fix us.'

'Em.' Evan waited for me to look up at him. I tilted my head and absorbed his troubled expression. 'It's not your fault. No matter what she says, or believes, *you* have to know that, okay?'

'Okay,' I answered in a whisper, kissing him gently.

The house was dark when we pulled into the driveway, and my mother's car was parked at the end. I hesitated before opening the car door, staring at the black windows.

'Want me to come in with you?' Evan asked, putting the car in park.

'No,' I replied without taking my eyes off the house. 'I'll be okay.'

'Call me later, all right?'

'I will,' I answered, slipping out of the car and shutting the door behind me. I inhaled through my nose, preparing for whatever awaited me in the dark. Evan didn't move out of the driveway; he kept watch until I disappeared through the front door.

I flipped on the foyer light and listened. The house remained uncharacteristically still. I walked into the living room and watched through the window as Evan slowly backed out of the driveway. I turned on the lights and found the poker table still in place with half-eaten bowls of chips and empty shot glasses scattered about. I began collecting the remnants of the party and carried them into the kitchen.

Once I'd cleaned up and put everything back in its place, I climbed the stairs, having spent the past hour summoning the courage to do this. As I neared her door, I could hear her crying.

I froze, my insides squirming. Before I could back away, I tapped lightly on the door. The sobs ceased.

'Yes?' she answered, barely audible.

With my heart beating frantically, I slowly opened the door and stepped in.

'Hi,' I said lightly.

My mother was lying on her bed, her eye make-up

smeared with tears, her hair tangled and sprawled on the pillow. The red face and swollen eyes were all too familiar. She still wore the same clothes from the night before.

I sat down on the side of her bed furthest from her.

'I thought you'd left me too,' she rasped, pulling a tissue from the box next to her bed.

'No,' I explained. 'I just needed some time.'

'So, you're . . . you're staying?' She took short breaths, recovering.

'I'm staying,' I confirmed faintly.

My mother rolled away from me. I could make out small gasps as she continued to cry. My hand hovered over her, shaking slightly, hesitant to touch her. I let down the wall, the one that protected me from everything that hurt. I opened myself up and felt her pain, my pain, and became her daughter, resting my hand on her back.

I felt her chest expand as she inhaled a sobbing breath. I waited for her to surface, sitting beside her, letting her know I hadn't abandoned her.

After some time she became quiet. I took my hand away when she shifted on to her back to face me with reddened eyes.

'Do you want to watch a movie and eat a pint of ice cream with me?' I asked gently.

She attempted to smile. 'Sure.'

My mother slowly sat up, wiping the make-up and tears from under her eyes. 'I'm going to take a shower.' Before she left the room, she turned to me and said, 'I'm glad you didn't leave me.'

My mouth twitched into a fragile smile.

On her way to the bathroom, my mother yelled back,

'Nothing romantic and sappy – I may throw something at the TV.'

I laughed as she shut the door behind her. I went to my room to retrieve my wallet and keys. The red light was blinking on my phone, so I grabbed it on my way out the door.

After flipping through Jonathan's and Evan's missed calls and texts from the night before, wondering where I was and if I was okay, I deleted them all.

I got up the nerve to call Jonathan when I pulled into the grocery store's parking lot, not exactly sure what I should say.

'Hi,' Jonathan answered after only a couple of rings. 'How are you?'

'I'm okay.'

'Are you sure? You didn't look okay last night.'

'I will be,' I assured him, running my fingers along the steering wheel.

'I can't believe she did that. I wanted to go after you, but Evan was already out the door and she started scream-ing at me. Sorry. I should have gone anyway.'

'No,' I stressed, confused by his words. 'I understand.'

'Where are you now? At Sara's?'

'No, I'm back home,' I answered quietly.

'You are?' He sounded surprised. 'Why?'

'Umm . . .' I began, flustered by his disapproval. 'Because she's my mother, and I don't think she should have to go through this alone any more.'

'Emma, what she did was horrible. How –' he stopped. I could hear him exhale, as if to calm himself. 'I don't understand how you can let it go like it wasn't a big deal.'

'I'm not . . . exactly,' I replied weakly. 'I just think I understand better now, that's all.'

Jonathan was silent for a moment before he added, 'I couldn't let her treat you like that. I had to end it. You understand, right?'

'I knew it was coming.' I answered. He remained quiet. 'I should get going,' I finally said when the silence became too uncomfortable.

'Call me,' he said in a rush before I could hang up. 'If you need *anything*, even just to say hi, okay? Just call me.' His voice was heavy with worry and made me pause.

'I will,' I promised, not truly certain if I would, or *should*.

When I returned home, my mother was showered and on the couch with a blanket over her lap. She didn't have any make-up on to conceal the lines etched around her mouth and the creases at the corners of her eyes. She looked . . . worn. Defeated.

She tried to smile when I walked in carrying the movie and two pints of ice cream, but her eyes remained dull and unaffected.

I put the movie in and sat next to her on the couch. We ate our ice cream and watched the movie in silence, until her voice broke the stillness with, 'I can be such a bitch, can't I?'

I didn't know what to say. I was actually afraid to look over at her, hoping she wasn't really expecting an answer. So I scraped my spoon along the top of the ice cream and waited.

'I don't know what happens,' she finally continued. I glanced over at her out of the corner of my eye. She wasn't looking at me, but staring down at the floor, consumed by her thoughts. 'It's when I drink too much. I get . . . I say things I shouldn't. I'm a terrible person.'

'No you're not,' I said automatically. She peered up at me, her blue eyes heavy with guilt. My mouth softened into a small smile. 'I didn't understand what you were going through. I didn't know.'

'It takes the edge off,' she continued. My brow twitched, uncertain what she meant. 'The alcohol,' she clarified, 'makes the pain bearable. I'm not as strong as you. You can shut it off and block everything out. You were able to do that even as a little girl. You didn't even cry at . . . at his funeral.' Her voice broke.

My mother's eyes welled up and her lower lip quivered. 'I miss him.' Tears slid down her cheeks, as she gasped, 'I miss him so much, and I don't know how not to.' Her shoulders slumped forward as she gave in to the pain.

I set down my ice cream and scooted closer, putting my arm around her shoulders to comfort her. She collapsed against me, and I gripped her tighter as she cried.

I couldn't exactly say why, but I didn't cry. Maybe I had hurt enough and I just needed to shut everything off – like she'd said I would. I continued to console her without allowing her sadness to seep in. I couldn't recollect a time we'd ever shared an affectionate embrace. But in that moment, I could barely feel her against me. So detached and outside myself, I was anything but *strong*.

I remained by her side and ran my hand over her dark hair, soothing her with comforting words, assuring her that it was okay to miss him. That *she* would be okay.

My mother finally raised her head, wiping the tears

from her face. 'Thank you.' She tried to smile, but it was as if her cheeks were too tired and weak. She took a deep breath and sat up on her own. 'Birthdays suck in this house, huh?'

I raised my eyebrows, not knowing how to react.

She followed with, 'I think I'm going to bed. I didn't sleep much last night, so I'm exhausted. See you in the morning?'

'Of course,' I answered, watching her stand. I continued to watch her as she walked up the stairs to her room. I lay down on the couch and pulled the blanket over me, not ready to sleep yet.

A loud banging caused me to bolt upright with a start. It was silent in the dark. Perhaps I'd imagined it. Then the banging erupted at my door, making me jump. My heart beat in panic.

My room was so black, I couldn't even see the door. I blinked but still couldn't focus on a thing. I remained frozen in my bed.

A frantic voice yelled from the other side. It sounded like a child, a little girl. I fumbled with my blankets at the sound of her panicked voice. I stepped into the dark and felt the cool boards beneath my feet.

I couldn't make out what she was saying. Her pounding blocked out her words. I thought she was saying, 'Get me out.' She sounded so desperate. I needed to get to her.

I blindly searched for the door, my hands reaching out in front of me. I felt the hard surface with my fingertips. The wood shook violently beneath my hands as her small fists slammed against it. That's when I heard her scream, 'Get out!'

I gasped. My eyes shot open. The television was on, and I was lying on the couch. My heart pounded in my chest. The fear in her voice still reverberated in my head. I sat up with my hands shaking.

I eyed the stairs, considering going to bed, but knew I wouldn't be able to sleep. I picked up the remote and started flipping through the channels, though her plea still echoed through my head, sending a chill throughout my body. I wrapped the blanket around me tighter.

I picked up my phone, not really thinking about what I was doing, but needing another voice in my head other than the little girl's.

Almost instantly I heard, 'Hi. Can't sleep?'

My lips curled into a half smile at the sound of his voice. 'No. You either?'

'Nope. What are you watching?' Jonathan asked.

26

Disappointment

'So, how's Rachel?'

'She's okay,' I said, sitting on my bed, running my fingers along the patterns of my bedspread. 'She's been lying low the past couple of weeks. She's focused all her energy on teaching me how to cook – which is ... disastrous. And I've been trying to teach her how to play basketball – which is even *more* disastrous.'

He laughed. Just thinking of her chasing after the ball every time she'd lift her head and lose control made me smile.

'It sounds like the two of you are figuring things out.'

'We're trying,' I admitted. 'It's not always easy. There are still tears every so often, but nothing ice cream can't fix.' I paused and then added, 'She misses you.'

'I'm not so sure she misses *me*,' Jonathan replied. 'I think she misses being with someone.'

'Whatever,' I said, 'I'm not going to argue with you. But I'm pretty convinced it's you.'

He let out a breathy laugh, knowing I'd argued with him anyway.

'Sorry you didn't win the championship. It was a close game.'

'Yup,' I sighed, having replayed the last two minutes of the game in my head repeatedly over the last week and a half.

'That foul was a bad call.'

'Wait. You were there?'

'Uh, yeah,' he confessed slowly. 'I had to know how it would end.'

'Well, it ended, that's for sure. I wish you'd said something to me.'

'I thought it would be awkward, you know, with Rachel.'

'Yeah, maybe,' I admitted reluctantly. 'It's just been a while since I've seen you.'

'Maybe we should do something about that.'

'Maybe.'

'We should hang out sometime. Just . . . do something.'

'Oh, yeah, *something* sounds fun,' I teased. 'I do that a lot, and I always have a blast.'

'You're hilarious. But really, I'll pick a day and you'll just have to come along, to do whatever *something* I choose.'

'Bring it on,' I taunted, making him laugh.

'So, tonight's the *big night*,' he said with exaggerated excitement.

'Don't make fun,' I threatened lightly. 'It *is* a big night.'

'Only because you're making it that way. Emma, let whatever's supposed to happen, happen.'

'Great pep talk, thanks,' I snapped sarcastically. 'I don't

want to talk about it; I might throw up on my phone, and I like this phone. I would hate to have to replace it.'

Jonathan laughed again. 'Fine. We won't talk about it. But don't let his dad get to you, no matter what.'

'I won't,' I sighed, knowing that Stuart Mathews was the most intimidating man on the planet – there was no way I was *not* going to let him get to me. He scared the crap out of me!

'Tell me what happens. The suspense is already killing me,' he said, sounding overly dramatic.

'Ha ha,' I jeered. 'I gotta go. Don't be surprised if I call you at three a.m. with a nightmare about being stepped on by a giant men's dress shoe. I'd name a brand, but I have no idea what men wear.'

'I'll be waiting,' Jonathan chuckled. 'Bye, Emma.'

I watched as *Call Ended* flashed across my screen, trying to summon the courage to prepare for dinner with Evan and his parents. It would've been better if Jared could have helped deflect the tension – he always seemed to know what to say to make the most serious situations seem light and uncomplicated. But he couldn't drive up from Cornell in the middle of the week.

'What are you wearing?' my mother asked from my open door. I looked up in surprise, wondering how long she'd been standing there.

'Uh, I was thinking the grey pants with the white blouse,' I answered, motioning towards the two items hanging on the back of my closet. The pants were serious, like I was going to a serious interview with a law firm. But the short-sleeved blouse with the puffy capped sleeves was light and airy, keeping it a little more fun.

'Pants?' my mother questioned.

'I'm going to be so nervous. I'll be sweating like crazy. Do you know how uncomfortable it is to sweat behind your knees with a skirt on? It's pretty disgusting actually.'

My mother laughed. 'Don't be nervous. I'm positive everything will work out for you both.'

'You've never met his father,' I groaned.

'Well, he can't be any worse than your grandmother,' my mother countered with a roll of her eyes. I stopped and looked at her. I had no idea I had a grandmother. Carol and George had never mentioned anyone, nor had my mother until this second. I had always been under the impression that my grandparents had passed away before I was born. Maybe that's what she'd meant – past tense.

She didn't notice my stunned face. Or perhaps she chose to ignore it.

'Are you going to take a shower? It's getting late.'

'Oh, yeah,' I answered, jumping up from my bed, abandoning the phone that I still grasped in my hand on the bedspread. I gathered what I needed for the bathroom and moved past my mother down the hall.

After styling my hair in soft curls and dressing in my serious, but not too serious, attire, I was ready. Or at least, I *looked* ready. Sara would've been proud.

My phone beeped. I turned towards my bed, but it wasn't where I'd left it. Scanning the room, I found it on my dresser. I cocked my head curiously and picked it up to see, *On your way?*

Leaving now, I texted back before rushing down the stairs.

'Good luck,' my mother said from the top of the stairs, dressed in a short skirt and camisole.

'Going out?' I deduced.

'I'm overdue,' she replied. 'No reason to stay in on a Thursday night.' Her voice sounded off, a little strained. She smirked and added, 'Besides, it's April Fool's Day. What could possibly go wrong?'

Everything, I said to myself before saying, 'Well, have fun,' out loud. She turned and went back in her room. I paused in front of the coat closet, wondering if I should be concerned that she was going out. I took a breath and decided to focus on one nerve-racking situation at a time. I grabbed my coat and headed out the door.

When I arrived at the Mathews', Vivian was stepping onto the porch wearing a long white coat and holding a small black clutch.

'Perfect timing, Emily,' Vivian said in greeting, taking a key out of her purse. 'Evan, we're ready.'

Evan appeared, looking very polished, his overcoat covering what I assumed was a suit. I smiled at his shiny dress shoes, recollecting my nightmare prediction.

Dinners with the Mathews' always made me nervous – fearing I'd say the wrong thing or embarrass Evan with my lack of social skills. But tonight I was a wreck. I was convinced I wouldn't be able to eat at all.

'Evan, would you mind driving?' Vivian requested, handing him the key to her BMW.

'Sure,' Evan replied. Before heading to the car, he walked over and wrapped his arms around me. 'You look amazing. A little pale, but still amazing. You can breathe you know.'

'Not yet,' I murmured from within his coat. He kissed the top of my head before opening the car door for me.

'This is such an exciting night,' Vivian stated from the

passenger seat as we drove to the restaurant. 'I hope we don't have to wait too long for your father to arrive.'

'It doesn't matter if he's there,' Evan told her. 'He's not going to like where I'm going unless it's Yale.'

'Evan,' Vivian warned, 'don't be that way. He only wants what's best for you, and he will come around to accepting your decision. He may need more time, that's all.'

'Yeah, four years,' Evan mumbled loud enough for us to hear.

'Wait. You already know where you're going?'

'I already know where I *want* to go,' Evan corrected. 'I just need my mother to tell us if I'm going there or not. She's really great at keeping secrets, even from my father.'

'Well, if he knew where you were going, then this wouldn't be nearly as exciting,' Vivian smiled. 'I'm the only one who knows for a reason.'

I didn't understand her tactics, keeping his acceptance letters from him until tonight. Why did she need to let the suspense build? I thought I was about to pass out; I wanted to scream, 'Just tell us already!' But of course I didn't. I remained still in the back seat, barely breathing.

When we arrived at the restaurant, we were escorted to a table in the corner with a little more privacy. Evan assisted in removing my jacket before taking off his own. My mouth crept into a big smile when he revealed what he was wearing.

Beneath his tailored suit jacket, he wore the Stanford T-shirt I'd given him for Christmas.

'I didn't want there to be any misunderstandings about my choice,' Evan explained with a smirk when he saw me beaming.

'Very clever,' Vivian stated in admiration, with a shine in her eyes. 'I'm not sure your father will appreciate your sense of style, but I adore it.'

'Me too,' I added, feeling a little more confident at the sight of him wearing the T-shirt, like he already belonged at Stanford.

Vivian insisted we order while we waited for Stuart. I selected the dish she recommended, knowing I wouldn't be eating much of it. I had a feeling that regardless of where Evan wanted to go and which college accepted him, his father was going to have the final say. After all, it was his money that was putting Evan through college.

And then we waited.

Vivian drove the conversation without pause, but she couldn't keep Evan from checking his watch every few minutes. I remained quiet, listening and nodding – glancing over as Evan's face became tighter with each minute that passed. By the time our entrées were cleared, with more left on the plates than eaten, Evan was straining every muscle in his body to remain composed.

Vivian excused herself from the table, taking her cell phone with her.

'He's not coming,' Evan concluded dryly under his breath. 'He wants to make it perfectly clear he doesn't approve and won't support my decision.'

I wanted to say the right thing to make him feel better, but I didn't. His father had deserted him on one of the most important nights of his life. What was there to say? Instead, I held his hand as he gripped it firmly, allowing me just to be there for him.

Vivian returned and smiled tensely. 'Well, it doesn't

appear that your father will be able to make it. I apologize. So there's no use in delaying the suspense.

'Evan, you chose Stanford, and they also chose you. Congratulations.' She tried to appear happy for him, but Stuart's refusal to attend cursed the entire evening.

'Thank you,' Evan said graciously, but his face still looked as though he'd bitten into something sour. I kept a worried eye upon him, feeling his hand tighten around mine.

I tried to smile as well, looking towards Vivian for reassurance – but I couldn't find any in her troubled eyes. Evan's choice to attend Stanford had divided their family, and that wasn't worthy of celebration.

I returned home that night deflated and confused. The one thing I wanted more than anything suddenly felt so selfish and wrong. And I wasn't sure how to make it right.

The house was dark when I entered. I flipped on the hall lights and searched for signs that my mother had returned. Her car wasn't in the driveway. Her jacket wasn't in the closet.

I glanced at the clock and realized it was still early, so there wasn't any need to worry . . . yet. I went upstairs to change and brush my teeth before returning to the living room and curling up on the couch to wait for her.

My eyes blinked open, and I pulled my head off the pillow, listening. I squinted to make out the glowing time on the cable box. It was after three in the morning. I quickly swept the blankets off to peer out the window, finding my car the only occupant of the driveway. I ran up the stairs and opened her door. Her bed sheets were still crumpled after her half-hearted attempt to make her bed. She wasn't home.

I was trying not to panic, but I kept thinking of the night when Jonathan and I had had to pick her up at the bar. What if something had happened to her? What if she'd tried to drive home? My heart pounded with each racing thought, flashing through all the horrific possibilities.

I paced the foyer, trying to decide what to do, then instinctively picked up my phone.

'Was it a shoe?' Jonathan teased on the other end.

'She's not home,' I burst out. 'It's after three in the morning, and she's not home yet. What if something happened to her? What if –'

'Emma!' Jonathan raised his voice to get my attention. 'What are you talking about?'

'My mother,' I explained, my voice edged with panic. 'She's still not home and I don't know what to do.'

'Did you call her?'

It seemed so obvious a question. I closed my eyes and shook my head in embarrassment. 'No.'

'Call her and then call me back, okay?' he instructed calmly.

'Okay.' I hung up and immediately called my mother's phone. I didn't know why I hadn't thought to do that originally. I guess the image of her in a ditch, bleeding to death on the side of the road, distracted me from thinking clearly.

The phone rang three times before someone picked it up. 'Hello?'

'Hi, this is Emily,' I answered not recognizing the woman's voice. 'I'm looking for Rachel.'

'Oh,' the woman croaked; obviously my call had woken her. 'She's here, passed out.'

'Um,' I faltered, 'where's *here*?'

'This is Sharon.'

'Sorry,' I blundered.

'Do you need to talk to her?'

'No, I'll see her in the morning.' I hung up the phone and plopped down on the couch. I wanted to be relieved, and I was . . . mostly.

I called Jonathan back. 'She's at Sharon's. Sorry that I freaked out like that. I should have called her first. I wasn't thinking straight.'

'Don't worry about it,' he assured me. 'Are you going to be okay? Do you want me to come over or anything?'

I paused, not expecting the offer. 'Uh, no. I'm just going to bed. I have school in the morning.'

I did go to bed. But I didn't sleep.

27

Lines Blurred

'DID YOU REMEMBER YOUR BATHING SUIT?'

'Huh?' I turned towards Sara, who was awaiting my answer with her shoulder against her locker. She'd caught me staring at nothing again. Thinking about my mother and wondering why I hadn't seen her this morning. I'd expected her to come home to get ready for work. Maybe she'd borrowed something from Sharon. From what I knew of Sharon, the choices must have been limited.

'You brought your bathing suit, right?' Sara repeated with her brows scrunched. 'For Jill's party tonight.'

'Yeah,' I answered. 'Are we staying at her place or going back to yours?'

'Not sure yet,' she replied, walking next to me until we had to go our separate ways. 'See you at lunch.' I nodded and headed downstairs.

I felt like I was sleepwalking the entire day. The voices were murmurs of incoherent noise. I jotted down notes without really understanding what the teacher was talking about. Everything around me went by in a blur, but I was moving in slow motion.

I expected Sara and Evan to say something, but they didn't. It struck me that perhaps they weren't surprised by my glazed stare and lack of contribution to their conversations. They always looked at me like they were worried, so today was apparently just like every other day. But it felt . . . off.

I wasn't sure I could explain it, but there was something that didn't feel right. I knew I was exhausted, not having slept more than a couple of hours, but it was more than that. There was a queasiness in the bottom of my stomach, like I had forgotten to turn off the iron or something – but much worse.

I drove to the soccer field after school. The rest of the team hadn't arrived yet, since practice didn't start for forty-five minutes. I usually did homework and changed at school, but today I'd driven straight here. I reclined my seat and stared up at the clouds, waiting. I figured I'd change as the rest of the girls started to arrive.

My lids became heavier the longer I stared. I closed them, convinced I'd wake when the cars began pulling in.

'Do you have your shoes?'

'Yup,' I answered, picking them up by their laces.

'Do you have your shin guards?'

'Yup.' I stuffed them under an arm.

'Do you have your coach?'

'Daaad,' I laughed. 'Stop being silly.'

'I just wanted to make sure you had everything,' he teased. 'Guess I'll be in charge of the soccer star.' He scooped me up in his arms *and tickled my belly, making me squirm and squeal in delight. Then he pulled me in to kiss me on the cheek.*

'We're going to win today,' I told him, my voice proud and confident.

'We're going to have fun *today,' he corrected, rubbing the top of my head as he carried me to the car.*

When we arrived at the soccer field, I raced ahead to join my friends while my dad unloaded the soccer balls out of the trunk.

But as I got closer, the kids' laughter grew quiet, and the wind picked up. I squinted against the bright sun, spinning in a circle. Everyone was gone.

'Dad?' I called out, searching for him. My hair whipped in my face. I clumsily pushed it out of my face, trying to see. 'Dad!' I yelled, becoming more and more frightened. I spun around again, but I was alone. 'Dad!' I screamed.

'Emma!' I opened my eyes and shot up in the seat, blinking around in surprise, disoriented by the sun setting behind the trees. There was a knock on my window.

'Emma, have you been in your car the entire time?' Casey asked from outside. She was sweaty and her face was flushed. I opened my door and swung my feet onto the dirt parking lot, trying to catch my breath. 'You missed the entire practice.'

'I did?' I shook my head, trying to pull away from the dream completely. 'I can't believe I did that.'

'I hope coach will let you play in the game on Sunday.'

'Is he still here?' I asked, searching the almost empty lot.

'No,' Casey replied. 'I was about to leave when I saw your car. Are you okay? Are you sick or something?'

'No,' I shook my head. 'I got here early, and guess I dozed off. I still can't believe I slept that long. Wow.'

'Are you going to Jill's tonight?'

'Yeah. I should get to Sara's. I'll see you there I guess.'

'Okay,' she replied with an unsure smile. 'You'll be at practice tomorrow, right?'

'I will,' I promised, hoping that missing practice hadn't jeopardized my starting position for Sunday.

The team was part of a travelling spring soccer league. It wasn't affiliated with the school district, and there were strict rules about missing practice – especially since we only practised a few days a week. Coach wanted to make certain every player was serious about being there. He was more than willing to replace anyone who slacked. I needed this league to get into shape for Stanford and didn't want to jeopardize it by falling asleep in my car.

When I arrived at Sara's, I found her and Anna laughing in the kitchen. Sara was taking bites from a slice of red pepper that she'd plucked from a board where Anna was cutting up ingredients for a salad. I felt like I was intruding, and it struck me that I hadn't knocked. Maybe I was supposed to now that I didn't live here.

'Emma,' Sara exclaimed when she saw me. 'Perfect timing. You can tell my mother that she is wrong about Kyle, and that he's not going to bring his college friends to this party tonight.'

'Um,' I began, trying to catch up. 'No, Kyle's not like that.'

'Oh, because he likes hanging out with high schoolers, even though he graduated last year,' Anna replied with a smirk. 'I'm sure he's going to bring some friends from Syracuse.'

I shook my head when she said it, realizing who that could mean. 'I hope not.'

Sara started laughing, sensing my dread. 'That could mean Drew. Em, that would suck so bad. I have to call Jill.' She disappeared upstairs before I could say anything, even though her phone was in the front pocket of her jeans.

'It's great to see you, Emma,' Anna said, mixing the contents of the salad in a bowl. 'I feel like it's been a while since you've been over. How is everything going with your mother? I just had lunch with her the other day. She seems so happy.'

'Really?' I tried not to sound so surprised. 'Everything's really . . . good.'

'I'm glad to hear that. She and I talk a few times a week, so I get the updates on your busy schedule. But we've missed having you around.'

Before I could react to her comment, the front door opened and Carl bellowed hello.

'Hi, Dad,' Sara said as she came down the stairs. They appeared around the corner together.

'Emma, I'm glad you're here,' Carl told me, setting down his briefcase. 'How've you been?'

'Great,' I replied automatically.

'I spoke with your Stanford coach today, and I have your housing information. I think we should look into booking a flight soon.'

'Uh, yeah, sure,' I replied, hit with the realization that graduation was only two months away. 'I'm staying the night, so maybe we can do it tomorrow.'

'Sounds good,' he agreed. 'I'm going to change before dinner.' He kissed Anna on the cheek. 'Do you need me to do anything?'

'No. Dinner's ready whenever you come down.'

When Carl was out of earshot, Sara told us, 'Jill said Kyle was bringing a few friends, but she wasn't sure who they were. But it's not going to be a crazy college party or anything, Mom.'

'I just want you to be smart,' Anna warned. 'Call me if you need a ride home, okay?'

Sara smiled, her eyes twinkling, 'Of course.' I knew what she was thinking, that this party was just like any other – including the one we'd had here in their house, the one they still had no clue about.

We arrived early at Jill's, as promised. Jill needed our approval of her outfit – or I should say, *Sara's* approval. Casey was already there as well, along with . . . Analise.

I tried to keep smiling when I saw her, but I knew I'd failed when Sara elbowed me in the ribs. 'I forgot she was coming,' she whispered beside me. 'I'd better not drink too much. I might get too honest.'

I smirked, actually curious what Sara would say to Analise if she wasn't filtered.

'But if she mentions Evan *once* tonight, I may not be able to hold back, sober or not.'

'Sara,' I laughed, 'he talked to her. It's been a little better the last couple of weeks.'

'I suppose,' she admitted with a sigh. 'When's Evan getting here anyway? Who's he coming with?'

I pulled out my phone to check if he'd texted me. There was a missed call from an unfamiliar number along with a new voice message. My stomach flipped. 'I can't remember,' I admitted, suddenly distracted.

'You're more out of it than usual today,' she noted.

'I know,' I sighed. I was about to make an excuse to go to the bathroom, so I could listen to the message, when I was interrupted by a scream.

Sara and I rushed into the room, where the scream was now followed by yelling. 'You fuck!' Jill screamed. 'I can't believe you spilled a drink on Dad's leather couch. The party hasn't even started yet and you're already making a mess. Get out of here! Get out!'

The young guy with the bright red face and curly dark hair was trying to wipe up the mess with a piece of paper from the printer, which wasn't doing anything except spreading it around.

'Stop it,' Jill scolded him, 'you're making it worse. I'm pissed off that you even have to be here at all.'

Casey squeezed past us with a roll of paper towels.

Sara pursed her lips to keep from laughing. 'Glad I'm an only child.'

That's when I recognized the guy from a family picture hanging on the wall in the dining room. He was Jill's younger brother.

'How old is he?' I asked, walking away from the drama and into the kitchen.

'He's a freshman,' Sara told me. 'I guess he threatened to tell Jill's parents about the party unless he and a few of his friends could stay. She was so pissed off. Don't you remember her telling us this at lunch?'

'Uh, no. Another blackout moment, sorry.'

Sara scrunched her eyes. I knew she wanted to ask me if I was okay, but then she knew what my answer would be.

I looked at the clock and wondered what my mother was doing tonight. I'd texted her to say that I was staying over at Sara's, but she'd never responded. I still couldn't shake the feeling that something was wrong.

'I'll be right back,' I told Sara. 'I'm going to use the bathroom while I still can.' She nodded, and I walked down the hall and into the floral inspired bathroom.

I locked the door and pressed the code on my phone to listen to my message. It wasn't what I expected at all. 'Hello, Emily. This is Vivian. I was hoping you were available for brunch on Sunday morning at eleven. I have someone I would very much like you to meet. You are welcome to call me back at this number. I look forward to hearing from you.'

I removed the phone from my ear, completely taken by surprise.

Within an hour, the house was starting to fill with juniors and seniors, and the hand-picked five or so freshmen who were friends with Jill's brother. Evan arrived with a couple of guys from the baseball team. When I saw their faces, I vaguely remembered him mentioning that he was coming with them.

I smiled at the sight of him cutting through the crowd. He was easy to spot since he was taller than just about everyone, and I'm certain we were easy to locate with Sara's fiery red hair standing out in the crowd.

'Hi,' I said, glowing. He bent down and kissed me.

'So how's the party so far?' he asked, resting his hand on my back.

'It's actually pretty great,' Sara intercepted before

I could shrug it away as any other party. 'Did you bring your swimsuit? Jill has a huge hot tub on her parents' deck that she's only allowing a few of us to use later.'

'I didn't,' Evan replied. 'I may have shorts in my car though.'

'That's great,' a chipper voice said from beside us. I hadn't noticed Analise hovering until now. How long had she been standing there?

Sara squeezed my arm at the sight of her. I was beginning to get the impression that Analise got to Sara more than she got to me – if that was possible.

'Do you mean she told you about it, too?' Sara asked Analise, not hiding her detestation.

'Yeah,' Analise replied unaffected. 'She said it fits like twenty people or something. I guess Jill's parents have parties all the time.'

'That's what I heard,' Sara nodded. Then she mumbled, 'Let's hope they put extra chlorine in it.'

I eyed her in confusion as Evan chuckled and said, 'Nice, Sara. That's pretty gross.'

I scrunched my face in disgust. Sara rolled her eyes at me for taking so long to understand what she was insinuating.

'Don't you dare try to get out of it,' Sara threatened. 'If I'm going in, so are you.'

'Great,' I groaned, completely disturbed by the thought of what had potentially gone on in the hot tub.

Kyle arrived with a keg and some guys from college. I moved away from the crowd of people rushing towards the free beer, so I had no idea who came in with him. I was pretty certain that if Drew was one of them, I'd know soon enough.

I tried to be sociable, truly I did. But I kept looking at my phone to see if my mother had called or texted me. I wanted to ask where she was or even *how* she was, but I was afraid it would seem like I was checking up on her. Well, I *was* checking up on her.

'Let's get our suits,' Sara suggested, returning from refilling her glass with some red drink Jill had concocted.

'Where's Evan?' Sara asked as we made our way to Jill's room.

'Not sure,' I answered. 'He went to get a drink and then to look for his shorts, I think. I guess he'll find us.'

Sara knocked on the door. 'Who is it?'

'Jill, open the door. It's Sara and Emma.'

The door opened cautiously with a pair of eyes peeking through the crack. Sara rolled her eyes and pushed the door open, making the girl behind it stumble backwards. There were several girls in the room, adjusting their bathing suits and double checking their appearance in the mirror. Sara grabbed her suit and began changing, not caring who saw her. I waited my turn for the bathroom. I had never been comfortable changing in front of anyone – even after years of being on sports teams and having girls change in front of me without a care. I usually had too much to think about, like where my bruises were and who would see them. Now, I supposed it was just a habit that I couldn't quite break.

Before I left the bathroom, I examined my back one final time to make sure the scarred striations were barely visible. There were only a few of them where the belt had cut deep enough to leave a scar, but they were still there – even after a year. I convinced myself it would be too dark to see them, and besides, I'd be in the water.

I emerged wearing a white bikini top with orange polka dots and shorts covering the striped bottoms. I secured my hair high on my head to keep it from getting wet and folded a towel over my arm.

I wanted to ask Sara if the marks were noticeable, but I didn't want to draw attention to them. Instead, I pulled a tank top on until we were in the dark. I followed as we were led out of a sliding door on to a private deck. The deck wrapped around the back of the house where the hot tub was letting off billows of steam into the cool April night. It had rained most of the day so the wood was wet and cold under my feet. I didn't have the numbing power of alcohol to make me oblivious to the cold like most of the girls.

There were already four or five people in the hot tub. I noticed Evan was one of them, and next to him was Analise. The predictability of that was nauseating. Worse than that, sitting next to her was Drew. I stopped abruptly. One of the giggling girls behind me bumped against my shoulder.

'Sorry,' she said as she passed.

'Oh, shit,' Sara breathed from beside me. 'Where did he come from?'

Evan caught my eye and smiled, then saw my face and shrugged dismissively. If he could get over it, especially after having gotten into a fight with Drew last year, then I could too. The tightness in my stomach indicated otherwise.

I stripped off the shorts and tank top and slipped into the water. The heat of the water instantly warded off the goosebumps that had erupted while walking across the cold deck in my bikini.

I waded across to the other side and slid next to Evan.

He draped his arm behind me. The water foamed and bubbled up over my chest as I sank into it, relaxed by its warmth.

'I like the suit,' Evan leaned over and said into my ear. I grinned.

'That's right,' I noted, 'you've never seen me in a bathing suit before. This is actually the first time I've worn it.' We'd gone to the beach a couple of times last summer, but I'd still been in a cast. I'd ended up wearing shorts and a tank top since I couldn't go in the water.

'We'll definitely be going to the beach this summer,' Evan smiled. I couldn't help but look past him at Analise who was watching us, her eyes darting away quickly when I caught her. And I knew Drew was watching as well, with his elbows out over the sides and a beer in one hand.

'Hey, Emma,' he said, raising his bottle in the air. I nodded with a small smile before looking away.

Sara was across from us, talking to Jill and Natalie. She called Analise over to join them. Analise couldn't refuse, and I knew Sara had done it on purpose. Thankfully a few more people entered and sat between Evan and Drew. This could not get any more awkward.

'I think I need to convince my parents to get a hot tub,' Evan said, running his hand over the top of my thigh, causing me to inhale quickly, though no one noticed. They couldn't see under the water. 'They can put it out by the pool that we never use.'

'That's right, I've never actually seen your pool uncovered,' I replied, taking hold of his hand that was teasing the inside of my thigh. My face couldn't have been any redder, but that wasn't noticeable either in these conditions.

'Evan,' I scolded under my breath, squeezing his hand.

'Sorry, it's the bikini.' He defended himself with an amused grin. 'It's too tempting.' He leaned over and gave me a soft kiss, his wet lips sliding over mine. It was brief, but enough to incite a stutter in my chest. I almost forgot we weren't alone for that one second. Then I opened my eyes and saw Drew over Evan's shoulder and sat up a little straighter.

'Analise isn't watching you any more after that,' Sara said quietly. I hadn't noticed that she'd moved next to me. 'You're making it steamy in here.' She laughed and nudged my knee with hers.

'Did everyone see that?' I asked her, suddenly very aware of the number of people around us.

'No, just those who shouldn't have been watching.'

I let Evan keep his hand on my knee, and I refrained from kissing him, despite how tempting it was as the moisture clung to the smooth, sharp lines of his face, down his straight nose and over his slightly parted lips. I had to keep reminding myself that we had an audience, even though the steam made it difficult to see across to the other side.

His thigh brushed against mine, and my breath faltered. He squeezed my knee and I looked up at him. 'This is torture,' he said, leaning in closer. 'Maybe we should get out of here. My parents aren't home.'

My heart fluttered, and I smiled. 'Really?'

'Really,' he said, his breath tickling my lips. 'Let's go.'

'Okay,' I said, biting my lip, wanting to lean in a little closer to taste the water running over his mouth.

'You go first. I'll meet you by the door.' He leaned back,

and I had to gather myself for a moment before turning towards Sara, who was talking to a girl on the other side of her.

'I'm going to leave with Evan,' I informed her. 'I'll text if I'm coming to your house, okay?'

'*If*,' she stressed with a knowing look. 'Water too hot for you?'

'Something like that,' I grinned widely, standing up and moving towards the steps. I couldn't look back because I knew my thoughts were transparent, and no one needed to see what I was thinking.

'Leaving?' Drew asked from behind me as I wrapped the towel around my chest, the heat from the hot tub evaporating into the cold, damp night.

'It's getting kind of crowded,' I answered, barely giving him a glance.

'Did you get your sweater? I left it on your porch.'

'Uh, yeah, thanks.' I said vaguely, catching sight of Evan approaching behind him and hoping he hadn't overheard Drew.

Drew noticed Evan as well and said, 'It was good seeing you again,' before walking through the sliding glass door that led into Jill's parents' bedroom.

'See you in a little bit,' I told Evan over my shoulder before heading towards Jill's room. I gathered my clothes and entered the bathroom, my heart beating so fast I was light-headed. I tried to take calming breaths, but I was too nervously excited.

My phone fell out of my pocket when I picked up my jeans. The red light was flashing to indicate I had a message. I picked it up from the floor and slid my finger over the screen. The excitement drained away instantly when I saw the missed call and voice message from my mother.

I entered the code and listened to the recording. 'Emily? Emily, you there?' Her words were slow and barely audible. 'You with him? Fuckin' . . . You are.' Then there was silence. She was a mess. My stomach flipped and my jaw tightened. I wasn't sure if I wanted to scream or cry. Instead, I took a breath and shut it off.

After I'd dressed, I went back out onto the deck to find Sara. 'Are you going to stay here tonight?'

'I think so,' Sara replied. 'Why?'

'I was going to take my car,' I explained. I had driven so that Sara could drink.

'No problem,' she shrugged and then smiled, 'Details.'

I forced a smile, knowing there wouldn't be any details to share tonight.

I found Evan at the front door holding our jackets.

'Change of plans,' I told him, more crushed than I could stand.

'What's wrong?' Evan questioned in concern.

'Umm, I'm not feeling all that great,' I explained, my pulse quickening with my fabrication. 'I think I'm going to head home instead.'

Evan's eyes tightened in uncertainty. 'What?'

'Uh,' I faltered, recognizing he wasn't buying my illness. 'I think I need to go to bed. Maybe the lack of sleep is getting to me.'

'You were fine a couple minutes ago,' he countered sceptically. 'I don't understand. Did something happen?'

'No,' I said a little too adamantly. Evan arched his eyebrows. 'I'm sorry. I'm tired. Okay?'

'No, it's not okay,' Evan replied. 'I know there's something going on. But if you're not going to tell me –'

'Evan, I swear, I just really need to go home,' I explained softly, my eyes large and pleading.

Evan nodded with his lips pressed in a straight line.

'Talk to you tomorrow?' My stomach clenched as the disappointment showed on his face.

'Text me before you go to sleep?' he requested, leaning down to barely brush my lips.

He stood at the door, watching me rush to my car. My stomach was nauseous with the lies I'd spewed, especially since I knew he'd seen right through them. I'd have to deal with that tomorrow.

I gripped the steering wheel tightly, now focused on finding my mother. I tried calling her, but it went to voicemail. I decided to start at home and then go from there. I didn't have Sharon's number, but maybe I could find it in my mother's room. I wasn't sure where else to look after that. Maybe Jonathan would know.

I didn't call him. It was eleven o'clock; it wasn't late. But I didn't want to involve him if I didn't have to. If I could fix this myself, then I would.

My thoughts continued to race, and my stomach churned with worry all the way to my house. When I saw her car in the driveway, I released an anxious breath. I pulled in behind her and noticed the driver's door was still open and the front tyre was on the lawn. When I got out of the car, I could hear chiming, indicating the key was still in the ignition. That's when I realized the engine was still running.

I looked around the car, confused. My heart pounded.

I shut off the engine and closed the door. Then I spotted her, sprawled motionless on the top of the steps with her head and arms splayed on the porch. I rushed to help her.

She didn't have any shoes on, or a jacket for that matter. I knelt down beside her to see if she was hurt. Her knees were scraped and bloody from the fall, and there was a bump on the top of her forehead where it was pressed against the porch. I collided with her alcohol saturated breath wafting in the breeze within three feet of her.

'Mom.' I sat on the top step and lifted her head up. 'Mom, you need to get up.' I tried to roll her so I could prop her up to sit. She groaned, but otherwise she wasn't moving. I leaned her into me in a seated position. 'Mom. Rachel.' I raised my voice to sound more commanding. 'Wake up. Let's go. You need to go inside, then you can sleep all you want.' I shook her shoulder, but nothing.

I tilted her head towards me. And she threw up. Before I could turn her away, the warm liquid was running down the front of me and soaking into my jeans.

'Shit!' I exclaimed, leaning her towards the side of the stairs as she heaved again. She didn't wake up, even after vomiting all over me, herself and the stairs. I looked down at the sour, potent mess. My throat tightened in disgust and my stomach rolled.

There was no way I was going to be able to carry her. She was a dead weight. I could've dragged her in, but then what? I couldn't leave her covered in puke in the foyer. It appeared I needed to turn to my last resort.

28

To the Extreme

I SAT ON THE STEPS AND WAITED FOR HIM TO arrive. I was tempted to unroll the hose to spray us and the stairs down before he got there, but I had no idea where it was. I was afraid to leave her alone long enough to change and get cleaned up, so I just waited.

I was trying so hard not to cry when he pulled into the driveway. I was frustrated, sad, even a little angry that I was in this predicament. Oh, yeah, and extremely humiliated – especially when I saw him emerge from his truck in a suit.

'Oh shit,' I murmured when he neared. 'You were out. You had plans. Jonathan, I am so sorry. I shouldn't have called you.'

'Yes, you should have,' he countered without hesitating. He took us in with his hands on his hips. My mother's tight dress was pushed up, revealing her underwear. Her knees were bloody, and her hair was matted with the vomit that was smeared across her cheeks and oozing down her chest. She was collapsed to the side, completely unmoving. At first sight, she appeared not to be even breathing, but I knew that she was because her breath reeked of alcohol and puke.

And then there was me. Slumped and broken, covered in dark red vomit, like someone had just heaved their innards all over me. I couldn't move. The cold, slimy, vile substance made me cringe in disgust, sliding across my skin with the slightest movement.

'Bad night?' he observed with a shake of his head.

'Whatever gave you that idea?' I groaned sarcastically.

He took a deep breath and asked, 'Is the door unlocked?'

'We didn't make it that far,' I told him, handing him the house key. He crept carefully past us and placed his shiny dress shoes on the unscathed sections of wood. Opening the front door and flipping on the foyer lights, he disappeared into the house and re-emerged a moment later wearing a fitted T-shirt and the dress pants.

'Go ahead upstairs and get the shower ready for her.' He looked me over and added, 'And you.'

I shuddered when I stood up, my wet jeans sliding along my thighs.

'Don't think about it,' Jonathan instructed when I cringed.

I laid down a towel to kneel on and pulled the shower curtain out of the tub. Jonathan was a minute behind me, carrying my mother in his arms while trying to keep a distance between her and him. He wasn't successful. The dark red vomit from her cheek smeared across his T-shirt as he laid her in the tub.

I grabbed a garbage bag for her clothes as we slid them off her. I should have been uncomfortable seeing my mother in her underwear with Jonathan beside me, but I'd moved beyond that embarrassment. All I cared about was getting her cleaned up and into bed, so that I could do the same. We sprayed her down with the hand-held shower, doing our best to wash her and rid her of the putrid smell.

Jonathan removed his shirt before he carried her to bed, not wanting to get the puke on her clean skin. I helped him rest her on her side, placing the bathroom's empty trash bucket below her. It wasn't like she would aim for it. She hadn't moved a muscle the entire time. She just breathed heavily and groaned every so often.

'Go ahead and clean yourself up,' Jonathan said. 'I'll stay with her in case she gets sick again.'

Nodding silently, I went to my room to get clean clothes. I numbly removed my soiled items and dumped them in the garbage bag, tying it tightly to contain the sour odour. Then I lingered under the hot water, scouring the stench from my body. I didn't realize I was crying until I'd turned off the water and the hot tears kept streaming down my face.

I sat down in the tub, pulled my legs into me and continued to cry into my folded arms.

'Emma?' Jonathan's voice called to me from outside the door, interrupting my tears. 'Are you okay?'

'I'll be out in a minute,' I replied, trying to sound as normal as possible. But I know I didn't.

After dressing and rinsing my face with cold water, I grabbed the trash bag and opened the door. Jonathan was sitting on the floor outside my mother's room, his back pressed against the wooden spindles that lined the top of the stairs. He wore the white dress shirt untucked over his dress pants.

I tried to smile, but it was no use. 'Thank you,' I said quietly, setting the trash bag on the top step to throw out – deeming its contents unsalvageable. 'I'm really sorry for interrupting your night. Please don't tell me you were at a business dinner or –' even worse – 'on a date.'

Jonathan smiled warmly. 'I told you to call me any time you need me. And I meant it.'

I sat down against the frame of her door so I could see her and face Jonathan at the same time.

'What was this about?' he asked, motioning towards my mother with his thumb.

'I have no idea,' I sighed. 'She left me this weird message after she was already drunk, but I don't know what happened. Everything's been so great lately. We were talking more. I haven't seen her drink in a while, not even a glass of wine after work. She hasn't gone out, well . . . until last night.

'I just knew something was wrong today. I just knew it.' I rubbed the palms of my hands over my eyes. 'I don't know what to do any more.'

'You have to talk to her tomorrow. Find out what's going on. She can't keep doing this to you.'

I nodded, not having the energy to think about what I was going to say. I'd hit a wall, and I was exhausted.

He observed my worn face. 'You should get some sleep.'

'I don't want her throwing up and choking in her sleep.' I peered in at my mother, her mouth hanging open, the pillow damp under her wet, dark hair.

'I'll stay with her in her room,' he stated. 'I'll lie on her floor and keep an eye on her. I'm a light sleeper.'

'You don't have to. I can do that.'

'You look like you're about to fall over. I have a feeling that when you fall asleep, you wouldn't wake up for a tornado.'

I knew he was right. I was so tired, I could barely stand up.

'Thank you again,' I told him before shuffling to my room. I didn't bother closing my door, hoping I could help him if needed. I collapsed in my bed and fell asleep instantly.

'Emma.' I could hear his voice. 'Emma.' The side of my bed caved in next to me. 'Emma.' He ran his cool finger along my cheek, brushing the hair from my face. 'Emma, open your eyes.'

I pushed them open and Jonathan was above me, sitting on the edge of my bed. 'I'm going to leave.' I glanced at the clock. It read a little past seven. 'I don't think I should be here when she wakes up. She's going to have a pretty miserable day already. Call me later?'

'Okay,' I grumbled into my pillow, my eyes barely open. I heard the stairs creak and the glass rattle when he closed the front door behind him. I shut my eyes and fell back to sleep.

I opened them again, what felt like a minute later, to the buzzing of my phone rattling on the table next to my bed. I put it to my ear.

'Where are you?' Casey demanded from the other end. I bolted upright and looked at the clock that now read after ten. I was supposed to be at soccer practice. Panic flashed through me, and I whipped back the covers, prepared to rush to the fields, but they were a good half hour away.

'I'm sick,' I lied, flopping back down on my pillow. 'Sorry.'

'That's why you left the party last night, right? That's what Evan said.'

'Yeah,' I replied, thankful that my lying to Evan was paying off, sort of. 'I should have called, but I'm in bed.' Which was technically true.

'I'll tell Coach,' Casey said. 'He's going to yell at me for being on the phone. I should go.' Then she added quickly, 'If you feel better, you should still come to the game tomorrow. He may still play you.'

I knew that was wishful thinking. Missing two practices in a row – I'd be lucky if I started next week, forget about playing tomorrow. I blew out the frustration with a heavy breath and stared at the ceiling. I'd never missed a commitment before, and the thought of making my coach or teammates disappointed in me caused guilt to slither through me. I would go to the game tomorrow, supported by the lie that I'd been sick, and hope they wouldn't see right through me.

I might as well get up now, I thought and rolled out of bed.

My mother's door was open. She was still asleep when I peeked in on her. The bucket next to her remained empty – which made me think of the porch. I cringed at the thought of what it was going to look like in the daylight.

I shoved my feet into a pair of old sneakers and went downstairs, noticing that the garbage bag was gone. I'd been prepared to toss it in the trash when I went outside. I dug around in the kitchen and found the acrylic pitchers used for the margaritas and filled them with hot soapy water. Then I braced myself and opened the front door – but there was nothing there.

I stepped out onto the porch to investigate further. There was no trace of the putrid mess other than wet stained boards. I noticed the hose on the side of the garage – of course I'd found it now. Jonathan must have sprayed off the stairs before he left.

I didn't bother to return to bed, but curled up on the couch, pulling a blanket over me. My phone had a text from Evan and a missed call from Sara. I replied to both of them with a text promising to call them later. I wasn't sure I'd be a very convincing liar at that moment, and I needed time to decide what to tell them. But I wasn't ready to tell them the truth.

I returned Vivian's phone call, since it was time sensitive, and left her a voice message saying that I'd be happy to meet her for brunch in the morning. I could pull myself back together and be presentable by then . . . I hoped.

I closed my eyes and fell asleep. I was still so tired. I felt like I could sleep for three days straight.

The creaking stairs woke me. The room was bright, with the afternoon sun pouring in the windows. I squinted, trying to focus.

My mother had emerged dressed in sweatpants and a T-shirt, stumbling down the stairs, her eyes slits and her hand holding her head. I sat up. She looked at me and held up her hand.

'Don't want to talk about it right now,' she groaned, the anticipation evident on my face.

'Want me to get you something?'

'Aspirin, coffee and please cut my head off,' she croaked.

I followed her into the kitchen and found the aspirin in the cabinet above the sink. I set two tablets in front of her with a glass of water while I started brewing the coffee. She rested her head on her folded arms on top of the kitchen table. She made careful movements to take the aspirin, grimacing when she swallowed them down.

I set a cup of coffee in front of her and sat across from her, waiting. She took a sip of the coffee and reluctantly looked my way.

'You want to talk about it, don't you?'

'I think we should,' I replied, anxiously picking at my thumb. 'Before you say anything though, I have to ask you one thing.'

'What's that?' The pain from her hangover was evident in her glassy, bloodshot eyes. She could barely open them.

'Don't ever drive again if you've been drinking,' I told her. I meant it to be a request, but it came out harsher than I'd intended. She picked her head up at my tone. 'If something had happened to you . . . or someone else . . .' I shook my head, unable to say it. My jaw tensed just thinking it.

'I won't,' she whispered. 'That was stupid. I shouldn't have driven home.'

'You can always call me.'

My mother let out a laugh that sounded more like a cough. 'Not last night. I was so mad at you. There was no way I was going to ask you for anything.'

I sat back in my chair, stunned by her words. 'Why?'

'Don't pretend you're innocent,' she accused, her eyes

boring into me. 'I hear you talking to him in the middle of the night. I saw the texts on your phone. Why are you still talking to Jonathan, like every day?'

She was *still* angry with me. It was evident in her glare. But the crack in her voice made it obvious that she was hurt too. I lowered my eyes, wringing my fingers under the table.

'I didn't mean to hurt you,' I told her, not sure how to explain my friendship with Jonathan. 'We just talk ... that's all.'

She shook her head. 'Didn't you even think for one second how much that would hurt me? Emily, I was in love with him. I thought I'd finally found the person that would help me move on.

'I knew he was leaving, and all I wanted was the summer. I'd hoped by the end he'd consider asking me to go to California with him. Why wouldn't I want to move? He'd be there, and so would you. But . . .' She paused and pressed her fingers across her eyes.

'He was more concerned about *you* the night of my birthday,' she continued in a low shaky voice. 'He didn't even care that I was upset too. You forgave me. I don't understand why he can't. So, don't you realize how much you hurt me by still talking to him? It's like you don't care about me.' She sniffled and closed her eyes. My mouth hung open in silence. I felt like I'd been punched in the stomach and all the air forced out of me.

She stood with her coffee cup in her hand and walked out of the kitchen.

I'd never really thought about how my friendship with Jonathan would affect anyone around me. It wasn't like I was intentionally keeping that relationship a secret.

I sat in the empty kitchen, staring at the chair across from me, finally admitting that I *had* kept him a secret. And I'd refused to consider how it would make her feel if she found out. He was the only one who understood that dark part of me, and I could tell him things I couldn't tell anyone else – selfishly, I didn't want to give him up.

I covered my face with my hands and breathed in. Guilt devoured my insides like acid. I felt like I was going to be sick.

'Are you kidding me?' she screamed from the top of the stairs. I rushed into the foyer to find her clutching his white T-shirt. 'He was here last night? What the fuck, Emily?'

'I couldn't carry you,' I choked, my lower lip quivering. 'I didn't know what else to do. I'm sorry.'

'I can't believe you,' she seethed, shaking her head, infuriated. 'I can't believe you.'

She turned her back to me. My heart beat erratically with the suffocating fear that I had finally made her not want me. I ran up the stairs and blurted out desperately, 'I won't talk to him any more, I promise. But please don't be mad at me. I never meant to hurt you, I swear. I won't ever talk to him again, just don't be mad.' I bit my lower lip and my vision blurred with tears.

She stopped before entering the bathroom, absorbing my frantic pleas.

'It kills me to see you like you were last night. I don't want to do that to you. Please, don't be mad any more, please?' My throat ached from holding back the tears. I swallowed hard and waited as she turned around.

Her eyes softened as she took in my tortured face. 'Tell him you don't ever want to talk to him again, okay?'

'Okay,' I sobbed, a tear rolling down my cheek as the pressure in my chest released. She walked in the bathroom and closed the door. I shut my eyes and took a deep breath, dreading what I was forced to do next.

29

Fatherly Advice

THERE WAS NO MOVEMENT IN THE HOUSE when I left to meet Vivian on Sunday morning. My mother had pretty much been avoiding me, so I let her.

The guard at the gate checked me off the list, and I continued to drive further down the road that split the golf course in half. I followed the signs to the club house and parked in the lot outside a dark stone building with a wall of windows.

Vivian was in the lobby talking to a group of women dressed for brunch. I was relieved I'd asked Evan what to wear when I spoke with him yesterday afternoon, because I would never have thought to wear a dress to brunch.

'Emily,' Vivian smiled brightly, reaching out with her arms to embrace me and kiss me on the cheek. 'You look lovely as always.'

'Thank you,' I replied, draping my jacket over my arm.

She addressed the women who lingered before her, 'Ladies, this is Emily Thomas, Evan's girlfriend.'

'Of course,' one said with a smile. They each carefully

looked me over, forming their own opinions of the girl from the headlines.

'Shall we?' Vivian prompted me. 'It was so nice to see you all again.' We walked past the ladies and into the dining room.

'Perfect timing,' she whispered, 'I was having difficulty continuing to be polite to that group of shallow human beings.' I widened my eyes at her remark and she smirked. It was the first time I'd recognized Evan in her face. I smiled and followed her to a table by the large windows that overlooked the rolling green course.

'The woman I want to introduce you to is running a bit late,' Vivian began after ordering a mimosa for herself and an orange juice for me. 'So I thought this would give us time to talk about the other night.'

My heart skipped a beat, fearing she was going to tell me that Evan wasn't going to Stanford.

'Stuart is very strong-willed. Evan shares the same spirit. So when they have opposing opinions, they will never reach a resolution. That's usually when Jared or I intervene, since we tend to be more open-minded and willing to compromise.

'Unfortunately, I'm not certain how to find common ground regarding this matter. Stanford is a marvellous school, and I am so proud of Evan for being accepted. However, Stuart has wanted one of his sons to attend Yale since they were born. Jared didn't quite have the grades to be accepted, despite Stuart's efforts. But Evan does.

'Evan is convinced that he didn't get accepted to Yale on his own merit, and Stuart won't admit if he had any influence over the decision. But I do know that I've never seen Stuart so upset, and I'm trying to understand why.'

'It's me.' I said it so quietly that Vivian had to ask me to repeat myself. 'Mr Mathews doesn't approve of me, and Evan choosing Stanford is him choosing me over his father.' I looked out the window, trying to calm the spasm in my chest.

'Why would you ever think that?' Vivian questioned in complete bemusement.

'I overheard him telling Evan that I wasn't his future, the night of the New Year's Eve party,' I admitted softly, the words still stinging.

Vivian was quiet. Her face was smooth but her sharp blue eyes moved in contemplation.

'This is not about you,' she said firmly. 'This is between my husband and my son, and I'm so sorry that you were made to feel you had anything to do with it. Emily, I adore you, and I couldn't think of anything that would make me happier than for you to be my son's future.

'The only reason I was telling you this was to apologize for the tension the other night. I wish you hadn't had to witness my husband's silent defiance.' She cupped my hands that were clasped so tightly, my knuckles were white. 'Please do not worry about this matter. I am quite certain it will work itself out.'

'I want to promise you that I will never do anything to hurt Evan, and I will not come between him and his family. I love him, but I would walk away before I'd ever let anything jeopardize his happiness,' I vowed passionately.

Vivian smiled adoringly. 'I know, dear. That's why I wouldn't want him with anyone else.' My heart swelled with her words, and I blinked away my feelings with a smile. She laughed lightly at our emotional state, dabbing the corners of her eyes with a tissue.

'Oh, there she is,' Vivian stood to greet her other guest.

A tall, slender woman with dark skin and big brown eyes approached us. She seemed so refined, in a light blue dress with pearls strung around her neck. I stood with Vivian to be introduced.

'Emily Thomas, I am pleased for you to meet Dr Michelle Vassar. She is an alumnus of Stanford University, and was on their women's basketball team.'

Dr Vassar offered her hand. 'Nice to meet you, Emily.' I smiled and shook it firmly.

When we sat down, Vivian beamed and proceeded to gush about my acceptance by Stanford and my scholarship to play soccer for the university. I'd never had anyone so openly proud of me before, and at that moment I wouldn't have wanted it to be anyone other than Vivian Mathews.

After spending hours talking about Stanford, medical school and Dr Vassar's professional experiences, I drove to the soccer field feeling lighter and more excited about my future than I had in months, replaying the entire conversation in my head.

I emerged from the bathroom dressed in my soccer gear and spotted Evan standing along the sidelines.

'Hi,' I said, coming up behind him.

He spun around at the sound of my voice and his face lit up, making my heart falter. 'Hi. How are you feeling?' I was relieved that he was over his scepticism regarding my feigned illness.

'Great! I had a really nice brunch with your mom.'

'Good,' he replied, pulling me towards him. I wrapped my arms around his chest and held him tight. He gave me a kiss and said, 'Good luck in the game.'

I grimaced. 'Sorry, but I'm probably not playing today. You don't have to stay if you don't want to.'

'I'll stay.' His arms squeezed tighter around my waist. 'Then we can do something after.'

After benching me the first half of the game, Coach started me in the second half. I had a feeling it had more to do with us being down by one, and he preferred winning to upholding his policies. He announced that since I wasn't sick any longer, I could play. He conveniently didn't mention the two missed practices.

We came back in the second half and won by two. It was a good thing Evan had stayed after all.

'Do you want to follow me back to my house?' Evan asked. 'Jared and Sara are there. They want to go bowling with us tonight.'

'Bowling?' I questioned dubiously.

'Yeah,' Evan chuckled in amusement. 'You've never played before, have you?'

I shook my head, making him smile wider. 'Yes, I'll follow you,' I sighed.

'Emma,' Sara laughed, 'you've already let go of the ball. You can't steer it down the lane like *that*.'

I continued to lean to the right, hoping the ball would redirect itself and not veer so far left. My body movements didn't help. I only knocked down two pins.

'Sorry,' I frowned. 'I suck.'

'It's your first time,' Jared consoled me, trying to keep me positive. 'We'll come back. Just try to keep your wrist straight so you don't spin the ball so much. Don't worry. Sara's not all that great either.' He ducked away when Sara swatted at him.

It felt good to laugh. I hadn't done very much laughing lately.

After Evan had rolled a spare, Jared stood up and said, 'I'll try to take it easy on you, Evan.' Evan gave him a mocking smile. 'Oh, are you coming to New York this weekend before you take off to Hawaii for April break?'

'I'm not sure,' Evan told him, sitting next to me and draping his arm over the back of my orange plastic seat.

'You really can't come with me?' Evan asked me again while Jared selected the perfect ball.

'To Hawaii?' I laughed like he'd just asked me to fly with him to the moon. 'No way. I couldn't afford a trip like that. Besides I have to stay for soccer. It's the same reason I'm not going with Sara to the Keys.'

'First of all, I told you, you wouldn't be paying for it. And secondly, you've already got into Stanford to play soccer. You can miss a week.' He begged one more time, 'Please, come with me.'

I smiled, and before I could allow myself to even consider it, I said, 'Sorry, I can't.'

'I've tried, Evan,' Sara interjected. 'Believe me, I've tried. I think she's trying to soak in as much time in Weslyn as she can before you're off to Stanford.'

'Yeah, right,' I shot back with a horrified face that made her laugh. 'I can't get out of Weslyn fast enough.'

'Speaking of which,' Jared chimed in after he'd

motioned for us to admire his strike that was flashing on the screen above our heads. 'When are we going to officially celebrate your admission into Stanford? Both of you, actually.'

'Graduation?' I suggested. I wouldn't be convinced I was going until I walked down the aisle with the diploma in my hand.

Evan considered this. 'That's actually a great idea. We can have a huge graduation party in my back yard.'

'Yes!' Sara exclaimed in excitement before rolling the ball down the lane.

'And your dad will go for that?' I questioned sceptically, knowing that he and Evan weren't exactly on speaking terms – kind of like me and my mother, but for extremely different reasons.

'Who cares,' Evan shrugged. 'What's he going to do?'

Jared laughed. He widened his eyes, like he knew exactly what their father was capable of. Evan didn't seem fazed. But I couldn't help but shrink a few inches in my chair.

'Should I be worried about Evan and his father?' I asked Sara when I was driving her back to her house.

'Are you looking for insider information because Evan's making it seem like it's not a big deal?'

'Well, yeah,' I answered uncomfortably. 'Has Jared said anything?'

Sara was quiet, deliberating on what to say. She always got fidgety whenever she had to tell me something I didn't want to hear.

'Just say it, Sara,' I demanded flatly.

'I promised Jared I wouldn't, so you have to swear that

you won't mention it to Evan, no matter what.' I just stared at her impatiently. 'Fine. Mr Mathews has threatened to cut Evan off if he goes to Stanford. He said he could freeze his accounts, take away his passport and even his car.'

'Over choosing Stanford?' I struggled to get the words out.

'You know it has nothing to do with Stanford.'

'Yeah,' I breathed. 'I do. I can't let this happen.'

'It's not your decision to make, Emma,' Sara warned. 'It's Evan's.'

30

Unexpected Future

My MOTHER COULDN'T STAY SILENT FOR long. It was against her nature. So whether she'd truly forgiven me or not, she was talking to me like she had.

'I may be a little late tonight,' she informed me, rushing around as she tended to do most mornings before work. 'Do you have practice today?'

'No, not today,' I told her from my spectator position, on the couch with a bowl of cereal.

'Do you think you could cook dinner?' She paused and looked to me. 'Or . . . maybe order out? I don't think I'll be out of the meeting in time.'

I smiled and said, 'I may go to Evan's for dinner.'

'Great. I'll feel better knowing you're eating something that's not microwaved. But I won't be late, okay?'

'Okay.' She'd been letting me know her schedule for the past couple of days. I was pretty sure it was her indirect way of apologizing for making me worry about her last Thursday night when she'd passed out at Sharon's without calling me.

She rushed out the door with a lightweight jacket over her arm.

This week had seen a pleasant rise in temperature. They were forecasting near eighty by Friday, which was unheard of in early April in Connecticut. I wasn't complaining.

With the increase in temperature and only eight weeks to go until permanent freedom, the seniors were having a hard time concentrating. Class was more chatty and the halls were bouncing with energy.

'Want to skip last class?' Sara proposed during lunch.

'I can't,' I moped, 'I have a paper due.'

'What are you doing after school? You should come over.'

'I don't think I'll have time. I have to get some laundry done before I have nothing to wear, and then I'm going to Evan's for dinner.'

'This weekend then. I'm not leaving for Florida until Monday, so you can spend the weekend with me. Do you have a game?'

'On Saturday,' I told her. 'Yeah, I think we need some girl time.'

Sara smiled. 'Yes we do! I'm feeling a little disconnected from you lately, so we have some catching up to do.'

'Agreed.'

I'd decided even before this conversation that I needed to fill Sara in on everything that was happening with my mother. I didn't have Jonathan to talk to any longer, and Sara was my best friend. She was *supposed* to know these things. Now that we had actual time set aside for us, I somehow felt ... better. Sara would know what I should do. Or at least have a very candid opinion on the situation.

With a promise of seeing Evan at his house after baseball practice, I drove home with my windows down. Spring was starting to stretch its arms, and I welcomed it after a frigid and snowy winter. The early spring flowers were in bloom, and the trees were in varied stages of budding or flowering, which meant in a few weeks they'd be filled with green leaves.

I knew this warm and sunny weather was a fluke in early April – they were already predicting cooler temperatures and rain by the end of the weekend. But today the heat from the sun felt good blowing against my face as I drove home.

There was a man standing on my doorstep when I pulled into the driveway. First impression – from his dark suit and briefcase – was that he was a salesman. He even wore a fedora on his head. But when I stepped out of the car, I realized his tailored suit was much too nice to belong to a door-to-door salesman. Besides, I didn't think anyone did that any more.

'Can I help you?' I questioned as I approached him.

'Are you Emily Thomas?' the tall man asked, removing his hat to reveal thick white hair, brushed back to expose a receding hairline.

'Yes,' I answered cautiously, still standing on the walkway, hesitant to get closer.

'My name is Charles Stanley,' he explained. He stood erect on the porch, his perfect posture making him appear to tower a mile above me. 'I'm the lawyer for the Thomas family. I am your father's executor.'

'My father?' I questioned, unable to move.

'Yes, Derek Thomas,' he answered patiently. 'Is there

somewhere private we can talk? Do you expect Rachel home any time soon?'

'No, she's working late today,' I told him, ungluing my feet and tentatively walking towards the door. 'Do you have a card or something?'

'Of course,' he replied, pulling out a silver cardholder from his pocket. He opened it and extended a card to me, confirming who he was. I didn't have any real reason to doubt him.

I unlocked the door and held the screen open for him. 'We can sit in the kitchen.'

'Wonderful.' He followed me into the kitchen and set his hat on the table. I kept my eyes on him, fearing that if I blinked he was going to disappear.

'Can I get you something to drink?'

'No, I'm fine. Thank you,' he replied, sitting in the chair and unbuckling his briefcase to remove a file. I lowered myself into the chair across from him, my hands shaking slightly. 'I'm sure you're wondering who I am and what I'm doing here, so let's begin. As I said, my name is Charles Stanley. I have represented the Thomas family most of my career, focusing mainly on estate matters and preparing their trusts and other financial concerns.'

'I'm sorry,' I interrupted, already confused. 'You keep saying the *family*. I don't understand. Who does that include?'

Charles nodded and began again. 'Your father gave me permission for full disclosure, so I may reveal to you everything I know that pertains to him. Derek Anders Thomas was born to Laura and Nicolas Thomas. They lived in Lincoln, Massachusetts, most of his life. His brother George Samuel Thomas was born three years later.

'Derek attended private schools through high school and went on to Cornell where he studied Architectural Engineering and eventually graduated with a master's.'

'Cornell?' I questioned in surprise, wondering why I'd never known this.

'Yes,' Charles replied calmly, his smooth deep voice devoid of emotion. Then he continued, 'He decided to return to Massachusetts to be near his family, and took a position with the top engineering firm in Boston. This was where he met Rachel Walace.' He paused. I swore I saw sympathy flash across his dark blue eyes for a moment before he returned to his emotionless report.

'She was a temporary replacement for their reception-ist who was on leave for a short time. From this point forward, the facts that can easily be researched are com-bined with your father's first-hand account and his own opinions. So, unfortunately, I cannot substantiate much of what I'm about to tell you.

'Derek was under the impression that Rachel was older than she was when they first met. She indicated that she was twenty-six, and he at that time was thirty-two. They went out on several occasions, and he really enjoyed her company. She was different from most of the women in his social circle, and he described her as a "breath of fresh air". '

My insides were already chilled, because I knew how old my mother had been when I was born.

'In time, he discovered her true age to be twenty and broke off the relationship immediately. Your father believed in integrity and trust above all else, and she'd lied to him. She was distraught over the break-up, and made multiple attempts to regain his favour. Just when he thought she'd given up, she appeared by his car after work with the news that she was pregnant.'

I exhaled and closed my eyes, my stomach turning to ice. I hadn't been planned. They weren't married. They weren't even technically *dating*.

'Are you okay, Emma?' Charles asked. 'Can I get you a glass of water?'

'I'll get it,' I said in a rush, pushing myself out of the seat. I needed a break from the story, from the truth of how I'd come into this world. It was so different than I'd ever imagined. I returned with a glass of water, and after taking a small sip I said, 'Go ahead. I'm ready.'

'Derek agreed to restart their relationship, and to be there for you when you were born. Months later, he bought a house in Lincoln where you were raised for seven years. Rachel chose not to live there after Derek's death; the house was not rightfully hers and became a part of his estate. Which brings me to why I am here today.'

'Wait,' I interrupted frantically. 'Did they ever get married? Did he love her? What about his parents? Are they still in Lincoln?'

'I'm sorry. I am certain you have more questions than I am capable of answering. No, Rachel and Derek never married. He did care for her, and he was convinced that she loved him. But he admitted to me that he did not trust her. She was young and irresponsible, tending to be a bit excessive in her social habits.'

I smirked with a disgruntled shake of my head, knowing

he was politely saying that she'd been a drunk even back then. This was how she'd always been. It wasn't a symptom of grief, a way for her to cope. It was as much a part of her as the lies she'd led me to believe all these years. The lies that included a fairy-tale romance, a marriage that didn't exist and a love destroyed by a senseless accident. And where did I fit into her delusions?

My throat was tight. My insides were hollow. I thought my head might explode from all the conflicting emotions coursing through me.

'Your grandparents moved to Florida before you were born. They, your grandmother in particular, did not approve of having a child out of wedlock, so they disconnected themselves from Derek and Rachel, and, therefore, from you. Apparently your grandfather did not feel as strongly, and when he passed fifteen years ago he left a sizable inheritance to each of his sons – despite Laura's wishes.

'That inheritance is the foundation of your father's estate.' He opened the folder and began displaying sheets with numbers and charts in front of me. I was too overwhelmed to understand them. They became a blur of ink before my eyes.

'What is this?' I choked, my hands trembling in my lap.

'This, Emma, is your future,' he explained smoothly. 'Your father invested wisely, and with his earnings at the firm, the sale of the house in Lincoln and his life insurance policy, on top of what he had inherited from your grandfather, his estate is quite impressive. All these assets become legally yours when you turn eighteen in June.

'I decided not to wait until then to speak to you since

you have financial obligations with Stanford that need to be addressed more immediately. Congratulations on your acceptance.'

'Uh, thank you,' I replied automatically, staring at the figure at the bottom of the page – several commas floating before my eyes. 'So this is mine? I can afford to go to college?'

'My dear girl, you can afford college, medical school and you'd still be able to open a clinic in Africa if you wanted.' I looked up at his wrinkled face and for the first time his lips gave a hint of a smile.

'I still don't understand,' I said. 'George never claimed to have money. I mean, I lived with them for years.'

'George.' Charles said it as if the name itself was an enigma. 'George's choices were never made clear to me. All I know is that he was provided with an inheritance similar to your father's. What he chose to do with it or to divulge to his wife, is not something I know anything about.' He paused. His grave expression pierced me. 'I can never express to you how sorry I am for what happened to you while you were in their house.' My eyes stung with tears. I blinked hard to ward them off. 'No one should ever have to go through what you were subjected to.

'But your father would be proud of the person you have become, Emma. You are strong and intelligent, and the fact that you are here trying to make amends with Rachel means you have a good heart. He would be *very* proud.'

I nodded, swallowing against my closing throat. I averted my gaze, not wanting to cry in front of this man.

'You will continue to receive your monthly allowances,

and they will increase once you turn eighteen. You will not have full control of your funds until after you graduate from college, or when you turn twenty-one. However, if you need anything, you may contact me at any time, and I will make the proper arrangements for you, whether it is a computer, or a car or an emergency situation. Your father has entrusted me to use my best judgement in assisting you.'

'Thank you,' I whispered, still not processing half of what he'd just said.

'Emma,' he beckoned. I looked up at the aged face that remained impassive despite the intensity flickering in his eyes. 'You may call me *any time*, for *any* reason. Please understand that. I know you do not know me now. But I hope to gain the same trust and respect that I earned from your father. In the meantime, I wouldn't advise alerting Rachel of this visit, or your inheritance.'

'He never trusted her, did he?'

'No,' Charles answered flatly. 'He loved you more than anything, and wanted you to have both parents in your life. But he did not trust her with his finances, or with you.'

'What?' I questioned with raised brows. 'What do you mean *with me*?'

'He hired a woman to care for you when he was at work. Concerned about Rachel's impulsiveness, he didn't want you left alone with her. Unfortunately, we weren't able to secure an alternative custody agreement, in case of his death, before the accident. He was trying to find a way around the legal rights of a birth mother so that you could be raised by someone who was better suited to care for and love you.

'In the meantime, we set up a portion of his estate to go to Rachel, along with the monthly allowances to care for you, which then became accessible to George and Carol when they took custody of you.

'This was never supposed to be your life, Emma. He wanted so much more for you, and I believe he would be happy to know that you will finally get it.'

'But I'd trade it all, every penny, to have him back,' I wanted to say. I had a hard time raising my eyes to meet his, still too vulnerable with emotion.

We sat in silence for a moment before Charles picked up each paper and placed it in the folder. He handed it to me. I shook my head. 'I think you should keep it. I don't want her to find it.'

Charles nodded in agreement and inserted the folder into his case. 'Then you should program my number into your phone and not keep my card.'

I took out my phone and saved his number under the initials 'CS'.

'It was a pleasure to finally meet you, Emma,' Charles said, standing and pushing the kitchen chair back into the table. 'Do you have any other questions before I leave?'

'No,' I answered quietly, my mind spinning with more thoughts than I could process.

'Please call me if you do.'

I walked him to the door. He turned to me and placed his hat on his head. 'Take care of yourself.' He walked out the door before I could respond. I watched him as he continued down the walkway to the large shiny black car awaiting him on the street. I shouldn't have been surprised when a driver stepped out and opened the back door for him.

I was still staring at the empty space when my phone vibrated in my pocket. I pulled it out and answered it.

'We're getting out of practice early,' Evan announced excitedly. The lightness in his voice was a shock to my ears. I felt as if I'd just sailed through a hurricane. 'Do you want to meet me at my house in an hour?'

I realized I hadn't even started the laundry. 'An hour. Um . . . sure.'

I hung up the phone and mindlessly went into the basement, sorting through the clothes to make sure I washed something to wear the next day.

Then I went to my room and sat on my bed, still in a daze. I eyed the drawing on my dresser that Leyla and Jack had sent me, and went to pick it up. As much as I missed them, I kept thoughts of them at bay so I wouldn't be tortured by my choices.

I inspected the woman in the picture. The one with the grey hair. My grandmother.

This family would never be mine.

And then it hit me.

I buckled over like I'd been punched in the stomach and slumped to the floor. I still couldn't comprehend everything that had just happened, but one truth slammed into me with such force I couldn't catch my breath.

I was never supposed to exist.

31

What If

I STILL HADN'T COMPLETELY PULLED MYSELF back together by the time I arrived at Evan's. He was sitting on the front porch swing reading a textbook when I pulled in.

'Hi,' I said, sitting next to him, intoxicated by him immediately. It was obvious from his wet hair that he'd just taken a shower. 'What are you reading?'

'Nothing interesting,' Evan replied, closing the book and setting it on the porch below the swing. He lifted his arm and I nuzzled in under it, resting my head on his chest, breathing him in. 'I like this week.'

I knew he was talking about the weather, and the fact that we were sitting outside in short sleeves in April, but my thoughts were somewhere else when I inadvertently laughed in contradiction.

'What, you don't?' he questioned, peering down at me.

'Oh, sorry.' I shook my head, realizing he'd heard me. 'Yeah, it's nice out.'

'What were you thinking about?' Evan asked, knowing me too well.

I sat up to face him. My head was spinning, and I wasn't sure if I could verbalize what I was still trying to grasp myself, but I thought I'd give it a try. It took me a minute to open my mouth, but he waited patiently, watching my eyes flicker in thought.

'Not to sound too deep, but I've been considering how just one little thing can drastically affect so many different things. Cause and effect. Choices and consequences. Is there a reason behind it, or is it just chance? Randomness. Like one person bumping into another person. They date, have sex and the next thing you know – a baby's born. Whether that baby was supposed to be or not. Whether they loved each other or not. It happened. But . . . what if it was never *supposed* to happen?'

Evan was silent for a moment. 'Where is this coming from?'

'I found something out this afternoon, and I'm not sure I'm ready to talk about it just yet.'

'Do you want to go for a walk as we contemplate the meaning of life? Or we don't have to talk at all. We can just walk. But I have to insist on holding your hand, that's not an option.'

'Okay,' I answered, trying to smile so I wouldn't come across as so depressingly serious. 'I'd like it if you held my hand too.'

Evan led me around the back of the house, and we followed the cut section of the field that was his back yard towards the woods. We walked in silence for a while, letting the birds and the rustling of the breeze through the evergreens be the only sound. But my mind was not quiet, and it refused to remain calm.

'Will you do something with me?' I asked, mesmerized by our feet as they moved in unison.

'Uh . . . sure,' he responded hesitantly.

'Let's consider *what if*. But don't read too much into it; it's just hypothetical.'

'I can do *what if*,' Evan agreed, taking my request seriously.

'What if . . . what if I didn't exist,' I presented. 'As in, I had never been born.'

'Em,' Evan stopped me, pulling his brows together.

'It's hypothetical, remember? I'm not suicidal or anything, I promise,' I assured him in a rush.

'Okay, fine,' he conceded with a breath. '*What if* you had never existed? I think you've already considered this, so why don't you tell me.'

'If I'd never existed, then my father would still be alive.' I kept my eyes on the ground, because just saying that one statement out loud sent a shiver through my body and made my eyes tear up.

'If I'd never existed, then Leyla and Jack would have both of their parents.' I struggled to keep my voice even.

'If I'd never existed, then my mother might actually be happy.'

Evan stopped. We had reached the end of the path right before it opened up into the meadow.

'And what about me?' he asked, his eyes steady and focused, trying to read my thoughts.

'Well, you and your father would be talking,' I answered with false playfulness, trying to return it to the hypothetical game that I'd initially suggested.

Evan chuckled. 'That is probably unlikely. We'd find some reason to argue . . . or not talk.'

We were quiet as we walked through the meadow. It was starting to transition into the spring green that made it breathtaking. The brook was brimming from the recent rain. It rushed with force over the stones.

Evan sat down and I nestled next to him, facing the water.

'My turn?' Evan requested. 'I'd like to challenge your *what ifs*.'

'Go for it.'

'You don't know what would have happened to your father if he was still alive. I have a feeling he wouldn't have been half as happy as he was when he was with you. I saw the way he looked in that picture you have on your dresser; his whole face was completely alive just looking at you. You made him happy, and I would hate to have been the one to take that away from him, even if he couldn't have it forever.' I smiled affectionately with my eyes glistening and leaned my head against Evan's shoulder as he held my hand.

'And unfortunately for Leyla and Jack, Carol would still have been the same whether you were there or not. You certainly didn't make her the way she is, and I can't talk about her more than that.' I glanced up and noticed his neck was tense just thinking about her. I squeezed his hand in understanding.

'As far as your mother's concerned, I'm not sure I

understand enough about her misery to be able to rebut your *what if.* If you mean that your father would still be alive, and that would be what made her happy – perhaps. But she's harbouring a lot more than just sadness. That was evident the night of her birthday. As I said, I don't understand what's wrong with her, but I'm very doubtful that it has anything to do with you.' I didn't have the strength to convince him otherwise – but I knew I was critical to her misery.

'And I would absolutely not be the same person if you had never existed.' I lifted my head and remained still with anticipation. 'We can contemplate the meaning of your life all you want, but know that you're my meaning . . . the reason behind just about everything I do – and I would never want to change that.' A smile stretched across my face and a warm current rushed through my body. My chest swelled with love. I leaned up and kissed him gently.

'What about your father?' I prompted when I pulled away.

Evan produced a wry smile and said, 'You don't have to worry about me and my father. My mother will never let him take Stanford, or *you*, away from me. He raised me to be the person I am today, so now he just has to let go and allow me be that person. This decision is mine, and he will have to learn to live with it.' Evan's voice was strong but calm, not filled with the resentment or frustration I imagined he'd express when speaking of his father. I admired his maturity and restraint.

'So,' he asked with a grin, 'do you feel better about existing?'

'Yes.' I answered emphatically with a coy roll of my eyes. 'You have a way of making a girl feel . . . significant.'

'Good.' Evan smiled and leaned over to kiss me. His words calmed me, and lulled the storm in my head to a hum. I was still troubled by everything I'd learned earlier in the day, but I knew here with Evan was where I belonged.

I spread out on my back, resting my head on his leg and closing my eyes to absorb the sun. 'I like it here.'

'Me too,' Evan replied, playing with my hair. 'The sun looks good on you.'

I continued to lie on his lap, listening to the rush of the water beside us. The sun's warmth brushing against my face and his gentle touch made my skin hum with a delicate shiver. I wish I could've captured that moment and kept it safe in my pocket to experience whenever I wanted.

'I was told once that a girl needs time to prepare. So, Emma Thomas, would you like to go to prom with me?'

I sat up and gawked at him, my mouth open in a shocked smile. 'It's . . . omigod, it's next month, isn't it?' He nodded. 'Yes, Evan Mathews. I would *love* to go to prom with you.' Then I muttered in dread, 'Oh, no. That means I have to get a dress, doesn't it?'

'Or you could go nude. I hear that's the new pink,' Evan smirked. I laughed.

'You would love that, wouldn't you?' I teased. 'Oh, wait. Promise we won't have sex on prom night.' Evan's eyes widened. 'We can't be the couple who has sex on prom night.' The thought of it made me cringe. That was absolutely *not* how I wanted to remember our first time. It was a bad movie in the making.

'We won't have sex on prom night,' Evan promised, pursing his lips to keep from smiling. 'How about the night before?'

'What? Really?' I studied his face, and he raised his eyebrows to indicate he was actually proposing the idea. 'Are you serious about *planning* it?'

'Why not? The spontaneous thing isn't working out too well for us. We might as well set a date.'

'Then, yes, I will have sex with you the night before prom,' I vowed, sounding comically serious. 'It's a sex date.'

Evan laughed. 'Can't wait.' He leaned in and captured my breath with the touch of his lips.

When I arrived home, Rachel was just getting out of her car. It felt strange to call her that, *Rachel*. I let the word repeat in my head. That's what she'd wanted me to call her all along. And that's how Charles had referred to her. When he spoke of my parents, he said *your father* and *Rachel*. He never once called her my mother. I don't think that was an accident.

'How was dinner?' she asked, waiting for me before entering the house.

'It was nice,' I replied. 'Exactly what I needed.'

'Good,' she responded, looking a little confused by my answer.

'Did you eat?' We flipped on the lights in the foyer and the living room.

'We ordered take-out at the office.'

She kicked off her heels and pulled her blouse out of her dress pants. I watched to see if she'd get a glass of wine from the kitchen like she usually did, but she didn't. Instead, she sat next to me on the couch and flipped on the television.

The whirlwind of thoughts in my head overtook me, and the next thing I knew I was asking, 'Where are you from?' I kept my eyes on the channels as they flashed before me.

'What?' she asked, still continuing through the programmes, obviously not expecting my question.

I had the opportunity to take it back, to not pry any further. But I decided I wanted to know. 'Where did you grow up?'

She stopped, landing on a fishing programme. I knew she hadn't meant to do that, so she must have heard me this time. I turned towards her and she was looking at me like she didn't know me. I was prepared for her not to respond.

'Um, in a small farm town in Pennsylvania,' she said slowly. 'Why'd you want to know?'

'I guess because I never did,' I explained bluntly. 'Do your parents still live there?'

She was quiet. She looked from me to the television and back again – like she was trying to decide if she wanted to have this conversation. She obviously wasn't prepared for the questions, and maybe the shock of them was why she *did* answer. 'My mother may, but I don't really know. I moved away with some friends when I was seventeen and never looked back. Never knew my father. He was a drunk and took off before I could remember him.'

'How come I don't know any of this?' I questioned curiously. I wasn't completely surprised by the knowledge of her broken home life. It couldn't have been that happy if she'd never wanted to talk about it, or visit.

'I don't like living in the past. What's the point?' She redirected her gaze and began changing the channels again.

I found her words ironic, especially since she hadn't figured out how to move past my father's death. Or maybe she had, and his death was an excuse to be miserable. She didn't seem to be making any effort to be happy, except maybe with Jonathan – but even then, she had sabotaged it with her drunken tantrums. Perhaps she preferred wallowing in eternal sadness. I didn't understand why she wanted to live like that.

'Why don't you ever try to talk to me about what happened when I was with Carol and George?'

Rachel's shoulders pulled back; she was struck hard by my question. I realized I'd reached my limit, but I didn't hold back.

'Why was I there to begin with? Why did you leave me with them?' For years, this question had destroyed me; I always thought it was me – that I had been too much for her to handle. It's what had motivated me to be perfect, never to be a burden again. Perfection still left scars.

So now, I just wanted to know the truth.

'I didn't leave you,' she whispered. Her answer left me speechless. Before I could utter a sound, she stood up and walked out of the room. I watched as she went into the kitchen and gripped the refrigerator handle. She stayed like that for a moment, battling with the decision to open it or not.

I waited. She let the handle go with a shake of her head, appearing distraught and frazzled.

'I don't know why you want to talk about this,' she said from the doorway, her voice shaky. 'Why would you want to bring up things that have already happened? We can't change them, so let's just let them go, okay?'

I inspected her light blue eyes as they darted around the room nervously, and I nodded.

'I'm going to take a bath.' She disappeared up the stairs.

I had always been too afraid to question her. I wasn't sure where the courage had come from, but I was pretty certain Charles Stanley's visit had a lot to do with it.

I was prepared for her to be angry with me, and even yell. But that hadn't happened. Instead, she seemed nervous and uncomfortable. And maybe even a little . . . guilty.

32

In the Woods

I DIDN'T SLEEP THAT NIGHT, NOR WAS I expecting to. I kept flipping my phone over in my hand, wanting to call Jonathan. I needed him to distract me with absurd conversations about a botched sci-fi movie, or the pillow that cured athlete's foot. It was hard not to call, to hear his voice waiting for me on the other end. But I had promised I wouldn't, so I didn't.

I heard Rachel's door open, followed by the pipes thumping into action for the shower. I viewed the clock and recognized that she was up early, which probably meant she wanted to be out of the house before I woke up. She was avoiding me again. Maybe I hadn't been the only one who couldn't sleep last night.

I waited to hear the front door close before getting out of bed. While in the shower, I considered apologizing to Rachel just so that she'd stop evading me. Or perhaps it would blow over by the time I returned from practice tonight, or maybe time away at Sara's would help. Or maybe I didn't care.

That last thought was unexpected.

I didn't know where it had come from. It didn't feel like me. But at the same time, it felt more honest than I'd been with myself for a long time.

I dressed in a fitted grey T-shirt and jeans, and opted for the pink checked Converses that I'd only dared to wear a few times. They drew attention, and I didn't usually want that. It was supposed to be nearly eighty degrees today, which was unheard of in Connecticut in April. I decided to grab my zipped sweatshirt just in case the morning air was still cool.

I hated the weather teasing with summer-like conditions, knowing it would only return to the rainy and cool norms within a day or two. It was torture to think summer and graduation were *that* close, yet still two months away.

I grabbed my backpack and soccer bag before heading out the door. As I walked towards my car, a black motorcycle came into view. I stood by my car as the bike pulled into the driveway and coasted to a stop beside me.

The rider had on a black T-shirt and jeans with a pair of black leather boots. His head was covered with a helmet reminiscent of a combat helmet – not much protection if you asked me. The mirrored glasses covering his eyes reflected my dumbfounded stare. Then he smiled, and the creases around his mouth rocked me back slightly.

'Jonathan?'

'Good morning,' he replied after shutting off the engine. 'How are you?'

'Uh, fine,' I answered, flustered. 'What are you doing

here? I thought we weren't talking to each other; that we decided it was the best thing to do.'

'Not really,' he countered, taking off his glasses. '*Rachel* decided we shouldn't talk, and she's not here right now. I don't think it's the best thing at all, do you?'

I was stunned by his defiance and continued to stare at him, not knowing what to think, forget about what to say.

'Let's do something,' Jonathan demanded boldly, not at all a request.

I laughed. 'I have to go to school, and shouldn't you be at work?'

'This is not the kind of day when you should be at school. And no, *I* should be right here,' he stated. 'Come on, Emma. You've already been accepted by Stanford. One skipped day of school isn't going to change that.'

'I don't know,' I hesitated, inspecting the shiny black Harley with chrome detailing – determining if I was willing to even get on the bike, forget about ditching school.

'You agreed we would do *something,* so let's do it. Stop thinking so much and get on the bike, Emma.' His directive was bold; he wasn't willing to hear another excuse. He slid on his glasses and jumped on the starter, revving the motorcycle to life. The deep guttural engine roared, calling for the road with a twist of his wrist.

I took a deep breath . . . and stopped thinking. I opened my car door and tossed my bags inside, grabbing my sunglasses and sliding on my sweatshirt. When I turned around, Jonathan was holding out a black helmet with a crooked smile.

I fastened the straps under my chin, then slid my

sunglasses into place. He kicked up the stand, and I flipped my leg over the back. The leather seat slid us close together; the front of my thighs pressed against the back of his. I grabbed hold of his waist and closed my eyes in anticipation.

My brain might have been turned off, but my heart raced with adrenaline. I knew it would've been overloaded with panic if I'd taken a moment to think about the many ways this was not a good idea – particularly the gruesome death that was a possibility if he took one wrong turn. Maybe there was a benefit to not thinking.

Jonathan slowly backed the motorcycle up and then walked it forward to turn us around before accelerating down the driveway and out of the neighbourhood. That's when the thoughts broke through, and I wondered what the hell I was doing. Skipping school to hop on the back of a motorcycle with my mother's ex-boyfriend and taking off to who knows where *definitely* was not a good idea. But before I could allow the voice of reason to penetrate too deep, I shut it off again. Instead I watched Weslyn slip away and closed my eyes to feel the wind whip against my face as the engine roared between my legs. I let the adrenaline rush through me and decided just to go with it, regardless of the consequences.

I had no idea where Jonathan was taking us. I never even considered what his *something* could be before the impulsiveness had hijacked me. We ended up on the highway at some point and continued west, deeper into Connecticut, until we entered New York.

We exited the highway and followed winding roads lined with woods. The houses were set deep within forested driveways, each marked with a mailbox on the road. We slowed enough for me to attempt to talk, or holler, 'Where are we going?'

'There's something I want to share with you,' he turned his head to the side to yell in return.

A few more twisting roads later, we slowed practically to a crawl. Jonathan veered down a road that barely resembled one. The tyre-worn dirt tracks were filled in with weeds and splotches of grass. He weaved along the drive and pulled up in front of the skeletal remains of a house.

I took in the plot curiously, unfastening the helmet as Jonathan shut off the engine and kicked the stand into place. I dismounted, and my legs shook slightly from the long ride.

A fire had devoured the entire structure, leaving only remnants behind. A tall stone chimney remained erect among leaning beams and ash. On the far side of the house, a section of crossbeams stood defiantly, despite its black, scarred outer skin. It connected to what appeared to have been a porch. The stone foundation outlined the modest home, but the interior was unrecognizable since it had been completely incinerated.

'Jonathan, why are we here?' I asked, turning around. But he wasn't looking at me. He was staring at the charred remains.

I had an ill feeling in my gut. I didn't like this place. There was something about the way the blackened structure was set in the shadows of the woods that made it appear haunted, like there was a dark tale to be told if you listened carefully.

'What are you afraid of, Emma?'

'What?' I practically jumped, convinced he'd read my thoughts.

'What is it that keeps you up at night? What is the source of all of your nightmares? What are you afraid of?'

The ill feeling in the pit of my stomach spread, and I didn't want to be there any more. This was the place where bad things happened and nightmares took root. I shivered with the realization of where we were.

'This was your house, wasn't it?' I asked, barely audible, disturbed by the distant gleam in his eye. He continued to scan every inch of the ruins like he was putting it back together in his head. 'What happened here?'

'I thought I would feel different. More afraid, I guess.' Jonathan contemplated out loud, not really talking to me. 'It's so much worse in my dreams. Fire's coming out of every window. Smoke blacking out the stars. And I can't get close because it's so hot; it feels like my skin will melt off.' He walked closer, holding out his hand like he could feel the flames.

I watched as his nightmare unfolded in front of him. He wasn't here with me. He was in the presence of his past – reliving it again. I was too stunned to save him.

Jonathan crouched in front of the stone steps and reached out tentatively, prepared to pull back if they were hot. He ran his hand across the bumpy surface and shook his head.

'I just sat in the woods and watched. Watched it all burn away. But the screams . . . their screams all sound the same.'

'What?' I questioned in shock, my chest tightening with his words. 'Did someone die in the fire?' Then I remembered. 'Your father. This is how he died.'

'So did my mother and younger brother,' Jonathan murmured, sitting on the bottom step and running his hands through his hair.

I cautiously walked towards him and sat next to him on the cool stone. 'Did he set the fire?' Jonathan shook his head.

'Is this why you brought me here? To show me your nightmare – the one you keep having over and over again?'

'Actually, this was for me,' Jonathan admitted, glancing at me. 'I thought we should face our fears together. Especially since we're both leaving soon. Then we can officially start over, without our fears following us. But I'm not afraid. In truth, I'm angry.' He clenched his fists and pressed them against his thighs. 'That man took everything away from me the night of this fire, and there's nothing I can do about it. He's dead, and so are they.' Jonathan's face was hard, his eyes cold and distant. Then he bent forward, covering his face with his hands.

I barely heard him say, 'They shouldn't have been in the house. This shouldn't have happened to them. I keep hearing their screams over and over again. Reminding me I couldn't save them.'

'It's not your fault,' I soothed softly. 'You didn't do this to them. Maybe that's what you have to do. Forgive yourself.'

Jonathan lifted his head, a line creasing his brow. 'Forgive myself.' He repeated it like the words were unfamiliar to him. He took a breath, pushing away the distance in his eyes, returning to me. 'I bet you're wishing you hadn't skipped school right about now, huh?' He grinned faintly, trying to rescue us from his nightmare.

'Let's get out of here and do something much more interesting. My fear doesn't exist here.' Jonathan turned towards me, delving into me like he did, 'Okay, Emma. What are you afraid of?'

'Oh no.' I shook my head firmly. 'We don't need to conquer my fear today. I'm sure there's another way to spend our day.' He continued to wait until I finally buckled. 'Fine. I'm afraid of heights.'

'Done. But I know this has nothing to do with your nightmares, so don't think you're getting out of it that easily,' Jonathan warned, standing up and walking towards the motorcycle. I remained on the steps, unmoving – not sure I was ready to follow him to my fear. *Knowing* I wasn't. I took a breath and pushed myself off the stone, conceding, as I always seemed to do when I was with him.

I climbed on the back of the bike and watched Jonathan's past disappear behind us, swallowed up by the surrounding trees as we drove away. Then I gripped him tightly and hid my face against his back, trying to prepare to face my fear. Which was not at all possible.

We didn't have to go very far to confront my fear. Within twenty minutes, Jonathan pulled off the road into a gravel inlet that could easily be missed.

'Where are we?' I asked, taking off my helmet and sweatshirt, starting to register the eighty degree heat that had been promised.

'You'll see,' Jonathan grinned slyly. I followed him as he led us along a path into the woods. Soon the rush of water reverberated through the trees, and I caught a glimpse of rapids twisting over rocks before dipping out of sight.

The air was a little cooler within the shadows of the

trees as we followed the turbulent water that continued to evade full view. It sounded like it was running beneath our feet. And pretty soon, it was.

Jonathan stopped on a flat ledge that opened up in front of us. About twenty feet below was a pool of water, capturing a small cascade pouring into it from a little further up. The path continued down to the water's edge where a cluster of boulders rested in the water.

'This is a favourite swimming spot in the summer,' Jonathan explained, and I could easily picture it – sitting on the smooth surface of the boulders to soak in the sun and cooling off in the clear water. I peered over the edge without getting too close – my pulse thrummed through my body. Angled slabs of rock lined the bottom of the crystal pool.

'Ready?' Jonathan asked from behind me.

I whipped around. 'What? Ready for what?' Fear captured my breath; I knew what he was expecting.

'Do you want to keep your jeans on? They may weigh you down. But I would keep your sneakers on because the water can hurt from this height if you hit wrong.'

'You're not serious,' I challenged, my words coming out in a rush. 'You can't be serious.'

'I have a knife if you want to cut your jeans into shorts,' he continued casually, ignoring my panic attack.

'No, no, no, no, no,' I cried, moving to get off the ledge, but Jonathan stepped in front of me, blocking the way. 'What are you doing?' I gawked at him with wide eyes, my heart beating so hard it actually hurt.

'Jump, Emma,' he commanded, his voice stern but not threatening.

'No way,' I practically yelled. 'This is so high, and the water's not that deep. You can't make me do this. I won't do it.'

'It's actually very deep, I promise you,' he continued in his even, assertive tone. 'Emma, you're either going to jump, or I'm going to push you.' He stepped closer, making me back up towards the edge.

I searched for another way off the ledge, but it wasn't wide enough for me to get past him. 'Please don't make me do this.'

'Emma, jump or I'm going to push you,' he repeated a little more firmly. He remained emotionless and calm, but from the intensity in his eyes, I knew he was serious. I wasn't leaving this ledge without going in the water.

I turned away from him and focused on breathing, since I hardly seemed to be breathing at all.

Breathing in, then out – in, then out. My chest moved up and down. In, then out. I swallowed hard and let my eyes fall over the edge to the water below.

Jonathan remained silent behind me. I didn't look at him.

I inched closer until I was about a foot from the edge. Becoming dizzy, I quickly looked up. I focused on the trees along the cliff on the other side of the water and grounded myself again. I closed my eyes and my heartbeat pulsed through my head. My breathing quickened and my stomach rolled with nerves, and then a shot of adrenaline streaked through me.

Before the adrenaline could slip away, I took the step and leapt – just as I felt his hand press against my back. My stomach opened up, becoming hollow as the air rushed by me and my head buzzed with fear and excitement.

A second later my feet slammed into the water, and I was consumed by the frigidity.

I kicked to the surface and expelled the small amount of air in my lungs, my chest frozen from the shock of the water. My muscles tightened as I gasped for air. I focused on swimming to the boulders. My jeans were heavy and slowed my progress. A spray of water hit me from behind with a loud splash.

I knew it was Jonathan, but I was too focused on getting out of the icy water to look back. I clambered up on a small rock and then over to a bigger one, my jeans sliding down a bit as I crawled into the sun, shivering uncontrollably.

I pulled my knees into me and wrapped my arms around my chest, trying to control the convulsive tremors – waiting for the sun to warm me up.

Jonathan emerged from the water and pulled himself on to the rock next to me. I didn't acknowledge him, tucking my head into my arms. My muscles began to ache from shaking so hard.

'Whoa, that's frickin' cold.' I glanced over at him and realized he'd stripped down to a pair of black boxer briefs. I darted my eyes towards the water, my cheeks warming quickly. He didn't look as miserable as I did with his legs out in front of him, propped up with his arms behind him. 'The sun feels good though.'

I eased my legs out and realized my jeans were the reason I was so cold, keeping the water pressed against my skin. 'Can I borrow your knife?' I requested.

Jonathan narrowed his eyes. 'Why? You going to stab me with it for making you jump?'

I smiled deviously, allowing him to think I was contemplating it. Then I laughed lightly. 'No.'

'It's up with my jeans,' he nodded. He didn't show any inclination to get up, so I stood and faltered my way back to the ledge, my heels catching on my sopping wet jeans with each step.

I picked up his jeans and found the black-handled knife in the front pocket. I unfolded the blade and it snapped into place. I pulled the fabric from my skin and carefully stuck the tip through to make a hole, then began sawing around my thigh, letting the jeans leg fall to my feet. I instantly felt better as the warm air soothed the goosebumps.

I crouched to slide the knife back into the jeans' pocket, and my eyes drifted towards Jonathan lying on the boulder with his hands behind his head and his eyes closed, absorbing the sun – he appeared completely at peace. The muscles along his broad chest were relaxed, but the definition of his body was still evident, pressed against the stone. I quickly looked away and found myself inadvertently staring back over the ledge, at the water below.

I waited for the panic to set in. But it didn't. My heart beat harder, but it was adrenaline, not fear, that pumped through my veins. And it felt exhilarating.

I didn't give myself time to think before I leapt and braced for the cold that I knew awaited me. The thrill of the fall caught my breath before I was swallowed up by the heart-stopping water.

I let the adrenaline course through my body with a smile as I kicked towards the rocks – which was much easier in shorts. I picked a dry boulder and eased myself up, the warmth radiating through the hard surface and into my legs. I removed my shoes and socks and set them next to me.

I noticed Jonathan watching me with a comical grin.

'What?' I demanded impatiently.

'You're not afraid of heights.'

'I know. You cured me, right?' my voice was heavy with sarcasm.

'Emma, your fear was never of heights.' I scrunched my eyes, not following. 'What were you thinking when you were looking down at the water. What was going through your head?'

'That there was no way I was going to jump.'

Jonathan chuckled. 'Besides that.'

'That I was going to –' I stopped. He saw it in my eyes as the unspoken words caused my heart to falter.

'Emma, what are you afraid of?' Jonathan asked again, studying my face.

'I'm afraid of dying,' I breathed. Hearing it out loud made my chest hurt and my eyes sting with tears. I blinked them away. Jonathan pressed his lips together and bowed his head.

The falls crashing into the pool in the distance filled the silence. Neither of us said a word. We both knew where this fear stemmed from, and I wasn't convinced there was anything that could be done about it. *She* was never going to let me feel safe again, even if she couldn't reach out and kill me.

33

Consequences

'WOULD YOU LIKE A CHERRY ON THAT?' THE
girl asked in a low flirtatious voice.

'No, that's okay,' Jonathan answered, not fazed by her
ogling.

I stifled a laugh as I sat on top of the picnic table with
my feet on the bench, watching the entire transaction.
Jonathan returned with the two sundaes in his hands, and
I could hear giggling behind him. Two of the girls working the ice-cream stand couldn't keep their eyes off him,
whispering and laughing as he walked away.

'You have a fan club,' I teased, taking the sundae he
offered to me. 'They must recognize you from *the ads*.'

'Funny,' Jonathan retorted with a sideways glance as he
sat on the bench beside me.

'Or maybe they think you wet yourself,' I laughed, nodding towards his jeans where the wetness from his boxers
seeped through.

He smirked. 'That's probably it. You know you're going
to leave a wet ass mark on the table when you get up, right?'

I leaned to the side to reveal the dark wood mark under my damp jeans. 'Oh well.'

'What time do you have practice today?' Jonathan asked before spooning in a mouthful of ice cream.

'Three-thirty,' I told him after pulling the spoon out of my mouth.

'We'll head back after this.'

It was the first time I'd thought about returning to Weslyn, and a swell of nerves enveloped me. I should've at least texted Evan before I left. My phone was in my car, so that wasn't possible now.

'Are you worried?' he asked, reading my tense expression.

'I'll have some explaining to do,' I sighed.

'To Rachel? She won't even be home.'

'No. To Evan,' I explained glumly. 'He's probably been freaking out all day since I didn't show up at school.'

'Oh,' Jonathan pursed his lips and nodded. 'What are you going to say?'

'I don't know,' I shrugged. 'The truth I guess.'

'And he'll be okay with that? That you spent the day with me?' Jonathan appeared shocked.

'Why wouldn't he be?' I responded, not at all concerned. 'He trusts me, and it's not like you and I have a history or anything. I mean, we're . . . friends.'

'Yeah,' Jonathan smirked. 'You're right. I guess I probably wouldn't be as okay with it if I were him. But I don't trust very easily either.'

His last sentence echoed through my head, and it all suddenly became clear. 'You have a hard time getting close to people, don't you?'

'Yeah,' Jonathan answered, contemplating my question,

'I suppose I do. No one really gets me, and I guess I'm afraid –' He froze. I waited for him to admit his fear, knowing it was on the tip of his tongue. His eyes slowly hardened and his jaw tightened. He wasn't going to say it.

Jonathan stood up and tossed his sundae in the trash before striding towards the motorcycle parked on the far end of the lot.

'Jonathan!' I called after him, but he didn't slow down. I threw my ice cream away and ran after him. 'Jonathan!'

I caught up with him and grabbed his arm. 'Jonathan, stop.'

'We should get you back so you're not late,' he said dryly.

'Look at me,' I coaxed, still holding his arm as he kept his back to me. 'Come on, please.'

He took a deep breath and turned towards me with his eyes on the ground.

'You can tell me,' I said, but Jonathan remained silent. 'Jonathan, what is it? What are you afraid of?'

'You *know* what I'm afraid of,' he countered defensively.

'Did you?' I questioned him. 'I mean before now, did you know that's what it was?'

Jonathan raised his eyes to meet mine. They were soft again, but edged with pain. He shook his head. I realized my hand was still on his arm and I slid it down to his hand and squeezed it gently. He looked down at the gesture and smiled faintly before I let go.

Instead of stopping at the bike like I thought he would, he continued to the wooden fence that lined the parking lot and leaned against the top beam.

'It makes sense,' he murmured, resting his hands on the

418

wood on either side of him. 'I mean, I haven't been in a real relationship since Sadie, not until Rachel – and that wasn't supposed to happen the way it did. I mean, it was never supposed to be a relationship. That's probably why we couldn't stay together after she told me she loved me. I couldn't do it.'

'You didn't love her?'

He shook his head, lowering his eyes.

'What happened with Sadie?' I enquired cautiously.

Jonathan didn't raise his head. 'I proposed to her towards the end of our junior year at Penn State.'

My heart skipped a beat, not expecting this revelation. 'She said no?' I probed when he stalled for a moment.

'She said yes.' His dark eyes rose to find mine. The sadness in them captured my breath. 'Two weeks later, I walked in on her and another guy.'

I didn't know what to say. But it was all making sense; this was the reason he couldn't get close to anyone, and for his need for a simple and predictable life. He feared loving someone and being hurt again. It explained the impenetrable confident facade that kept him at a distance.

'I'd lost my mother and brother. Sadie was the only one who knew how much it destroyed me. And after what she did to me . . . I never let anyone else in. I've never trusted anyone to get that close. Well, except . . .' Then he looked at me, and my cheeks reddened. 'I mean, it's different,' he corrected himself quickly, 'You and I have this weird connection, it's not like . . .' He didn't finish.

'Of course,' I said, nodding adamantly. 'We get each other. That's all.'

'Right,' he agreed with a crooked smile. 'Well, it looks

like we *are* pretty pathetic after all. We've spent a gorgeous day dwelling on unconquerable fears. You're never going to want to do something with me again.'

'Sure I will,' I laughed. 'As long as you don't try to cure me again.'

'Done.' He smiled in return. 'Wait. Will the school call Rachel about where you were today? I don't want to make things worse for you with her. I know how she can be.'

'I can handle her,' I told him. 'She's kind of avoiding me right now anyway.'

'Why do you put up with it? I have to be honest, I don't really understand your relationship.'

'Neither do I,' I answered truthfully.

'Emma, has she ever said anything nice to you, you know, like she's proud of you or that she loves you for that matter?'

'I don't want to talk about her,' I muttered, picking up the helmet. I was still confounded by all that I'd learned in the past twenty-four hours, and I preferred not to think about her until I had to. 'We should get going so I'm not late for practice.'

Jonathan nodded and picked up his helmet.

The closer we got to Weslyn, the harder it was to push away the questions that my mother had left unanswered. I still didn't understand what she meant when she'd said she didn't leave me with Carol and George. I was always told, and thought I remembered, that she shoved all my things in a black garbage bag and dropped me off on their doorstep in the middle of the night. If she didn't do it, who did? And why didn't she come back for me?

That brought me back to Jonathan's question – did she ever tell me she loved me? It should've been easy enough to remember, being told I was loved, especially by my own mother. Mothers told their kids how much they loved them all the time. Even Carol would gush over Leyla and Jack with affection, letting them know they were loved.

I may have had a hard time recalling my childhood, but I always knew my father loved me. I never doubted that for a second of my life. But did my mother?

By the time we arrived on Decatur Street, I couldn't think of anything else. Thoughts of who my mother was in my life and why I was trying to build any sort of relationship with her, swirled in my head. I knew my efforts were driven by guilt. I didn't understand why she was set on trying.

Jonathan slowed drastically right before the house, causing me to look up. Rachel's car was in the driveway. My chest spasmed in panic.

Jonathan pulled to the sidewalk and stopped for me to climb off. 'I'm so sorry, Emma,' he offered as I took off my helmet. 'Do you want me to come in with you?'

'No,' I replied, hoping she wasn't looking in our direction. 'That will just make it worse. You should go.'

'Are you sure?' I nodded.

'Call me if you need *anything*, okay?'

'I told you, I can handle her,' I stated calmly, despite the churning that was devouring my insides. I wasn't sure what was going to happen, but I'd soon find out. I stepped back and watched him pull away. Then I took a deep breath and walked towards the house.

Rachel was sitting on a chair on the porch, and when I got closer, she stood and accosted me.

'Where have you been?! Who was that on the bike? Why didn't you call us? Do you have any idea what we've been going through all day?!' Her voice was elevated and her hands were on her hips.

I slowly climbed the steps and gathered myself to try to explain, hoping she'd understand why I'd needed to get away for the day. I clasped my hands in front of me and looked from the boards up to her reddened face and opened my mouth to speak . . .

Her eyes grew wide and her mouth dropped open. 'Omigod, you were with him! That was Jonathan, wasn't it? I was right. There is something going on, isn't there? How could you do this to me?! Do you even care about me?!'

I pulled my brows together in disbelief. I took long drawn breaths to control the fire erupting inside me.

'It's none of your business where I've been all day, or who I was with,' I snapped, causing her to pull her head back in shock.

'What are you talking about?' Rachel countered. 'Of course it's my business. I'm your mother.'

'No you're not,' I scoffed, feeling the tendons along my neck tighten. 'You never have been. Don't think you can be now.'

'Why are you talking to me like this? What did he say to you?'

'This has nothing to do with Jonathan. This is about you. It's always been about you – what you want, how you feel, who you want to be with. Have you ever once thought about me and what I'm going through? Do *you* care?'

Rachel's mouth opened in shock.

'Do you ever consider what I go through every time you drink too much, or disappear to a bar to come home whenever you want with whoever you want?'

She stumbled back at my attack. The angry fire spread through my veins, consuming me. I remained unaffected by the stunned look on her face or the tears forming in her eyes. My voice grew louder. I was blinded with fury, and I couldn't have held back even if I'd tried.

'You've never thought about anyone other than yourself my entire life! Do you even love me? You probably never wanted me. That's why you left me with *them*. Do you have any idea what she did to me? Do you ever think about it? That would mean you'd actually have to stop thinking of yourself for one minute!'

I took a step towards her and she shrank beneath me. The fear in her eyes fuelled my rage. My hands shook as I clenched my teeth. I was unable to reel my anger back in.

My entire body was engulfed in flames when I yelled, 'I don't understand why I'm here! You're not a mother, you never have been! I don't need you!

'Besides, you're too consumed with my father's death to care about anyone else. Why do you keep obsessing over a man who never loved you?'

The sound was loud, and the sting was hot on my cheek. My head rocked to the side with the force of her hand. I slowly lifted my head and stared at her, snapped out of my spiralling rage. Tears streamed down her face, and she looked like she was about to collapse.

My entire body trembled. I hadn't realized I'd been crying, but the corners of my eyes were raw from the flow of tears.

'Emma?' I heard behind me and spun around. Evan was coming up the walkway. 'What's going on?' He looked more distraught than I'd anticipated. As he got closer and saw the red mark on my face and our stunned expressions, the worry turned to anger. 'What happened? Did you hit her?' He glared at Rachel, who was still too shocked to speak.

I wiped my cheeks and faltered down the steps. 'I have to go.'

'What?' he questioned me in disbelief. 'Emma, where have you been all day? Why didn't you call me? What just happened here?'

'I didn't have my phone, and I'm so sorry,' my voice was shaky, the repercussions of my brutality starting to settle in. 'I have to get to practice.'

'Really? You don't look like you should be driving anywhere. You need to talk to me.'

I stopped and took a breath. My eyes pleaded for him to understand. 'I will, I promise, but I can't right now. I have to go. Don't you have a game?'

'Yeah, but –'

'Evan, go to your game. I can't explain right now. I'm going to be late for practice.' My hands shook uncontrollably. I glanced up at the porch, but she was gone. 'I'm staying at Sara's this weekend. Come over tonight, okay?'

I started to walk away, but he rushed up and blocked my path. 'I can't let you leave like this. What happened?'

'We got into an argument,' I explained, swallowing hard to keep the guilt at bay. I didn't want to think about it. I might crumple right there on the driveway. 'Please. Please, let me go to practice. You can follow me there if you don't trust me.'

His eyes narrowed. 'What?' he questioned angrily. 'Emma, this has nothing to do with trust. I was *worried* about you. You've been more withdrawn lately, and yesterday you started questioning whether you should exist or not. I was afraid that something had happened to you today. That you . . .' He couldn't finish. The pain on his face expressed what he felt.

I bit my quivering lip and closed my eyes. 'I am so sorry,' I muttered softly. 'I can't believe I did this to you. I just needed to get away for the day, to figure things out. I should have called you. I'm so, so sorry, Evan.' I wanted nothing more than to touch him, to wrap my arms around him and hold him against me. But I was afraid to reach for him, because it would've destroyed me if he'd pulled away.

'Okay,' he said to himself, nodding, not making any move towards me. 'Okay,' he repeated, looking me in the eye, nodding again like he was trying to accept my words and figure out what to do next. 'Go to practice. I'll see you at Sara's tonight.' He turned around and strode towards his car without another word, and without touching me.

I continued to my car, shutting everything off. I couldn't think. I couldn't feel. I just needed to get away from this, and I knew practice would distract me long enough to calm me down.

I backed out of the driveway before Evan was in his car. I glanced at the rear-view mirror to see him standing by his door, watching me drive away.

I swiped at the tears and wrapped my fingers tightly around the steering wheel. This was my fault. This was all my fault. And now I had two hours to figure out how to fix it.

34

Confessions

'EMMA, WHAT THE HELL IS GOING ON?!' SARA demanded fervently from the other end of the phone. 'What happened to you today?'

I sat in my car coated in sweat, having pushed myself to the extreme during practice – to distract and punish myself. I'd emerged prepared to make amends.

'I know, I was completely stupid today,' I responded with a heavy breath. 'And now everyone's angry with me. I just got out of practice and will be over after I pick up clothes for the weekend. I promise I'll tell you everything, okay?'

'Yes, you will,' she stated firmly, letting me know that she expected the extended version of the story. 'I'll see you in a little while then.'

I hung up and found a text waiting from Jonathan, *You okay?*

I have some major damage to fix, I answered.

I pulled out of the lot and headed to the house, not sure if Rachel would be home or not. I wanted to prepare myself either way, unsettled by the thought of both scenarios.

My phone beeped while I was driving. I glanced over at it to find, *It was my fault. I can try to explain if you want. I am really so sorry Emma. Mad?*

When I pulled into the driveway, I responded with, *I knew what I was doing, not your fault. Not mad, but need time to make things better. Talk soon.*

Just as I was about to open the door, my phone chimed again. My heartbeat picked up when I placed the phone to my ear, 'Hi.'

'Hi,' Evan said so quietly I could barely hear him.

'I'm at the house picking up clothes for the weekend. I'll be at Sara's soon,' I told him, my voice soft and cautious.

'I don't think I'm going to Sara's.'

My heart twisted and I closed my eyes.

'Why?' I breathed.

'I think I need time away too,' he explained in a quiet, even tone. My eyes filled. 'Emma, I know you haven't been honest with me.' A lump lodged in my throat. 'I don't understand what's going on and why you can't tell me, but I know that you've been having problems with your mother. I knew when she called in the middle of the night at Sara's, and I saw how upset she was with you over that sweater. I saw what she did to you the night of her birthday, and I knew she was the reason you left Jill's party. And now this.'

My breath shook as I listened to him, his insight crushing me.

'Emma, you're not letting me in . . . again. I can't . . . If I'm part of your life, then you can't keep shutting me out.'

We were silent for a moment. Guilt strangled me, and I choked on every word that attempted to surface.

'I'll be back next Saturday. We'll talk then.'

'Evan,' I implored. But there wasn't anyone on the other end. I swallowed my tears and clamped my mouth shut to keep the hurt trapped. I couldn't contemplate an entire week without talking to him – and I still didn't know how to explain my motives.

I got out of the car and dragged my body to the house. Anything Rachel said to me now would never be as painful as Evan's silence.

I reflected on how this day had begun with promises of the summer to come. The warmth still lingered, and there was even the scent of a fire pit in the air. It was unfortunate that the most gorgeous day of the year had become the darkest.

The front door was unlocked and the lights were off. The gold hues of twilight filtered through the windows and cast shadows along the floor. I walked to the stairs, deciding *time* might be what we all needed, and that I'd just get my things without seeking Rachel out.

'I tried,' she murmured from within the living room. I turned towards her voice, and hesitated. 'I really tried to like you. I wanted to.'

I took a step closer, recognizing the signature slurs of her tongue. I was too broken to be wounded by her words, but decided I needed to hear them anyway.

Light from the front window spread along the floor to the coffee table, leaving the couch in the dark. Rachel lay on her side, supporting her head on the arm of the couch.

A depleted bottle of vodka stood on the coffee table next to a glass filled with ice.

Rachel grabbed the bottle and dumped the contents over the cubes, filling the glass to the rim. She picked it up, sloshing the vodka over the side on to the floor. She took a large sip and placed the tumbler back on the table.

I stood in the entrance of the room, watching her. Truly wondering if the vodka took away her pain. It seemed to always amplify her emotional state, not mask it. It released her secrets, unfiltered, brutal and honest. I awaited the truthful assault.

'I thought he would love me more because of you. He was so happy when you were born. But you took him from me.' She picked up the glass and took a larger sip before setting it down, half consumed.

'You can't take them all away from me, Emily.'

I wasn't sure what she meant. At first I thought she was talking about his death, but I didn't know who else she meant . . . Then it hit me. Jonathan. She thought he'd chosen me over her.

'Why didn't they love me? Why wasn't I enough?' she choked, raising her voice. 'Why you?' Her head lolled slightly as she shifted to face me. Her eyes were heavy, but the hatred in them was unmistakable. 'You.' She shook her head lazily, closing her lids with the motion. 'You. You should never have been born.'

And just when I thought I couldn't hurt any more, her words left me incapacitated. I leaned against the doorway for support.

'Sharon left you, not me.'

I was confused again, until she clarified. 'I didn't leave

you. Was in the hospital. Took too many pills.' The more she talked, the harder it was for her to form words. The vodka was completely taking over. 'Said I couldn't have you. But never wanted you. I can't,' she breathed heavily, the effort to speak draining her. 'Can't love you.'

My head spun, and each breath was excruciating. She took another sip from the glass and almost missed the table when she set it back down with a hard thump. She laid her head on the arm of the couch and closed her eyes.

I stumbled out of the room, then stopped before I reached the stairs. I turned back around and realized there was something wrong. I scanned the living room in a panic. Where was it? What had she done with it?

Then I remembered the smell of burning wood when I came home, and spun around towards the back door. I rushed out into the small yard and practically collapsed on the stairs. It felt like someone had thrust their fist through my chest and was squeezing my heart.

In the middle of the yard was a heap of embers still glowing red. A few spindles were recognizable among the ashes, but it was gone. She had set the rocking chair on fire and now there was nothing left.

I clumsily lowered myself down on the steps while holding on to the railing, staring at the remains and shaking my head in grief, lost in the wafts of smoke.

Pulling myself up, I returned inside, empty and broken. My insides felt like they'd been ripped out and burned as well. I couldn't see straight. My eyes were glazed over as I made my way to the stairs.

I trudged up to my dark room without glancing in the living room. Flipping on the light, I mindlessly filled my bag with random clothes. I zipped the bag and the room fell back into darkness when I shut off the light. My hand slid along the railing as my legs numbly carried me along.

I gripped the doorknob to leave and hesitated, searching within the shadows of the living room. I couldn't see her. But I could hear her breathing.

Compelled, I walked to the love seat and sat down across from her. I folded my arms and stared at her silhouette, listening to her breathe.

I knew. I'd always known she didn't love me. I didn't know why I'd thought I could change that, even after all this time. It would never change. She couldn't even look at me for most of my life, forget about love me.

I knew. But I didn't understand why she'd kept trying. She'd shown up at my sports games. And the letters she'd written . . . why? I guess that had been her effort – she said she'd tried. She couldn't convince herself to love me any more than I believed that she did.

I looked away and my eyes fell upon the glass leaving a wet ring on the coffee table. Painkiller. Really?

I leaned forward and picked up the half glass of vodka. The ice cubes were melting into tiny stones. I brought it to my nose and smelled it. My mouth filled with saliva and I cringed. I pressed the rim to my lips and tipped it back, taking a large sip.

I coughed and grimaced in disgust. The liquid set my stomach on fire as it crashed against its empty walls. I took a deep breath and shuddered. It was horrible, but so was aspirin if you let it touch your tongue – and that was supposed to take away pain as well. I held my nose and swallowed again, emptying the glass – wanting it to work, to take away my pain.

I held the empty glass in my hands and my eyes filled with tears. What had I done? I clenched my jaw and breathed heavily through flared nostrils. What had I done? I shook my head, horrified.

I slammed the glass down on the table and stood up to leave. The sight of the vodka bottle filled me with so much fury, I wanted to scream. I picked it up and clenched it so tightly, I thought it might shatter in my hand. Shaking with rage, I threw it into the darkness. The glass shattered against the wall on the far side of the foyer.

I breathed a sob and rushed to leave. Grabbing my bag, I slammed the door behind me.

I didn't remember driving to Sara's. I probably shouldn't have been driving at all, blinded by tears, my head hazy. I pulled myself together as best I could when I turned into her driveway. Anna and Carl didn't appear to be home, thankfully.

Gripping my bag, I climbed the steps to Sara's front door. Sara opened it before I reached the top. 'Where have you been? I've been . . .' Her sentence trailed off. Her aghast expression indicated that I was a bigger mess than I thought.

She held the door open for me and I walked in, lowering my eyes as I passed her. I continued up the stairs to her room without a word.

I dropped my bag on the floor next to the bed I usually slept in and sat on the edge with my shoulders bowed. My head felt light and was spinning slightly.

Sara sat next to me and waited, knowing I would tell her once I found the strength.

After a few minutes of silence, I took a deep breath and said, 'I wasn't supposed to live.'

'What?' Sara gasped, sitting perfectly still.

'She killed me, Sara. I was dead. Why am I still here?' My voice was heavy. Tears filled my eyes.

'Oh, Emma,' Sara breathed. 'Don't think like that.'

'I don't want to feel like this. This pain. I shouldn't have to feel it. I was supposed to be dead.' A tear rolled over the rim of my lid and slid down my cheek.

'Emma, please tell me what happened,' Sara begged softly. 'You're not making any sense.'

I took a stuttering breath and revealed, 'My mother told me she never wanted me. That I was the reason my father never loved her. He left me everything, Sara.' I connected with her large blue eyes. They glistened with sadness. I had to look away, unable to bear her pain as well.

'What do you mean he left you everything?' she asked patiently, trying to understand.

'A lawyer came to see me yesterday. My father had a trust set up for me. The lawyer told me the truth about my parents. They were never married, and my father only stayed with her for me. She blames me. She hates me. I'm pretty sure she even tried to kill herself because of what happened.'

'What are you talking about?' Sara's brows tilted in confusion.

'That's how I ended up with Carol and George. She was in the hospital after taking too many pills. I think she tried to commit suicide.' I spoke without connecting with my words. My whole body was a whirl of incoherence. I could no longer feel or think.

'When did she tell you this?' she asked, shaking her head like it was incomprehensible.

'Tonight,' I stated flatly. 'I should have told you. I should have said something about what was going on . . . her drinking, but I thought I could handle it. I thought I could fix her. But I can't.'

'It's not your fault,' Sara consoled me, taking my hand. Her words echoed through me, and I focused on her, drawn back to my exact words to Jonathan earlier in the day. In that moment, I recognized the impossibility of forgiveness when my thoughts were tangled in culpability. Guilt was lonely and isolating. I wondered how Jonathan had lived with it all of these years.

'I'm so tired,' I told her, the ache in my chest sucking the will out of me. 'I don't want to do this any more.'

'Do what?' Sara whispered, helping me up so she could pull back the covers.

'Hurt,' I muttered, tears seeping between my quivering lips.

'You don't have to,' Sara soothed, guiding me down on the bed. 'Emma, it's going to get better. You don't have to do this alone. I'm here, okay?'

Sara lay next to me on top of the blankets and smoothed my hair away from my face. 'You don't have to hurt any more,' I heard her whisper again as I closed my eyes.

35

Everyone Hurts

I THOUGHT I'D BE UP MOST OF THE NIGHT, unable to sleep, but when I opened my eyes it was mid morning and Sara's bed was empty. I lay under the covers for a while, not sure what the point was of getting up. But I couldn't suppress the need to use the bathroom, so I forced myself out of the bed.

Since I was already there, I decided to shower. I realized I'd never showered after my day trip with Jonathan or practice last night, and I desperately needed it. I remained hollow as I stood under the water, unable to feel anything stirring inside – not an emotion or a single thought. I was tempted to go back to bed when I came out of the bathroom wrapped in a towel, but Sara had already made it and was lying on top, reading a magazine.

'Hey,' she greeted me with a smile. 'Are you hungry? My mom's making pancakes.'

I shrugged and started to dress, not caring if Sara saw my scars – she'd seen them at their worst anyway.

'So, where were you during school yesterday?' she asked

casually, keeping her eyes on the magazine as she turned the pages.

'With Jonathan,' I admitted softly, my voice hard to find.

This got her attention. 'Excuse me? You were with Jonathan? Why . . . Uh, what did you do?' It wasn't often that Sara had difficulty finding her words.

'We went for a ride on his motorcycle,' I told her. She waited, but I didn't continue. There wasn't much more I could say without revealing his secrets, and I couldn't do that.

'What's going on between you two?' she questioned. 'Anything I should be worried about?'

'No,' I answered simply. 'We get along. He understands what I'm going through, that's all.'

'What does that mean, *what you're going through*?' She sounded worried. I suppose I would have been if she'd said it.

'About Rachel's moods and stuff,' I attempted to explain. 'We talk. He understands. I mean . . . he dated Rachel, so he gets it. We've become friends through all this.'

'Okay,' Sara contemplated. 'I think. Did you explain this to Evan?'

'I didn't get to,' I breathed sitting next to her on the bed. 'Sara, I totally screwed up. He's so upset with me he wouldn't even see me before he left.' The misery of his call stirred in my chest.

'Yeah, I know,' she comforted. 'He was so freaked when you didn't show up at school yesterday. Then when you didn't answer your phone, I thought he was going to lose it completely. I gave him Rachel's number when he asked, not like she was any help or anything. You really should've called or texted him or something.'

'I know,' I sulked, feeling ill. 'I left my phone in my car. I wish I had called. But I was hoping we'd get to talk, so I could explain. I really never meant to worry him.'

'What are you going to do about Rachel?'

I was quiet for a moment. 'I can't live with her any more.' My voice cracked slightly, the emotions escaping despite my efforts to bury them.

'I know,' Sara agreed, her voice sympathetic. 'Want to go to Florida with me this week?'

'I can't,' I answered automatically. 'I really need to be here for soccer.'

'I knew you'd say that, so I talked to my mom and I'm flying down on Thursday with my dad instead of leaving with her on Monday. I want to be here with you.'

'Thanks,' I smiled faintly. 'I want that too.' And I did. I needed to be with the one person who wasn't angry with me, and didn't force me to explain every feeling that was coursing through my body.

'Can you tell me about last night a little bit?' she enquired gently. 'It was a little confusing, but you were upset, so I decided to wait.'

'Like what?'

'Who's this lawyer, and what did he tell you?'

I recounted my conversation with Charles Stanley and what he had revealed about my parents and my grandparents, and the trust I'd inherited.

'Wow,' Sara mused after I was done. 'That's crazy. That must be where Leyla and Jack are, huh? In Florida with your grandmother.'

'I think so,' I replied with a slight nod.

'Em,' Sara began cautiously, 'you said that you thought your mom may have attempted suicide. Why would you say that?'

I crossed my arms and bowed my head, picturing her on the couch, barely coherent and confessing what no mother should ever admit, no matter how true. Sharpness cut through my chest just thinking about what she'd said.

Somewhere among the slur of words she had mentioned not being the one who'd left me with Carol and George. She said Sharon had left me. She was in the hospital. She took too many pills. I shared this with Sara along with my deduction that she had overdosed.

'Maybe it was an accident,' Sara suggested.

I shrugged, thinking it over, but I doubted it. My mother had been so grief stricken by my father's death, I suspected she may have done it on purpose. I recalled my cutting words to her on the porch, and my eyes stung with shame. Regardless of her lack of feeling for me, I should never have said what I did. I had been cruel.

Anna called up to us when the pancakes were ready. I followed Sara downstairs, although I didn't feel much like eating.

I could tell by the way Anna looked at me, full of sympathy and concern, that Sara had told her. I couldn't expect Sara to keep anything from her parents after what had happened last year. I wasn't upset, but I wasn't sure I could talk to Anna about it.

But I also knew she wasn't the type of mother to leave it alone. She waited until after breakfast, when Sara was in the shower. I was sitting in the rec room, aimlessly searching the channels. Anna sat next to me on the couch, and I shut off the television. I waited for her to begin.

'Sometimes people hurt more than they can handle,' she soothed, observing me. I had a hard time meeting her eyes. 'And sometimes they don't know how to ask for help. They're so caught up in their own pain, they end up hurting everyone around them. I wish you didn't keep getting hurt.'

I didn't respond, but she knew I wouldn't.

'I know you have commitments here and won't be coming to Florida with us. We'll help you get your things next week when we return.' Anna placed her hand over mine. It was warm and soft. I tried to smile, but it never truly formed on my lips.

When she left the room, what she'd said kept floating through my head. I thought of Evan and everything I'd put him through. I began to wonder if I was the one being hurt, or the one doing the hurting.

'I want to call him,' I told Sara while sitting in the mall restaurant. She had somehow coaxed me into shopping with her. I must have been completely distracted when I said yes.

'It's only been a day,' Sara countered. 'Give him some more time.'

'I just . . .' I pushed the fries around on my plate, not eating them. 'I want to apologize. He won't even have to say he forgives me. I just need him to know how horrible I feel.'

'I'm not so sure that's what he's looking for, Emma.'

I knew she was right. An apology was just words. Evan wanted me to trust him, to confide in him. That's all he'd ever wanted. He wanted to be the one I turned to when everything was falling apart. He wanted to be . . . Jonathan.

I had no idea when this had happened. When Jonathan became the first person I thought of, the first person I called when everything was miserable and complicated. He was the one I reached out to when I couldn't sleep at night, or couldn't carry Rachel to bed, or when I needed to escape her completely. He knew me in a way that Evan didn't, but in a way that Evan had always wanted to.

'Why does he want to know?' I pondered out loud. 'Why does he want to know all the bad things, the things most people pretend not to see? Why does he want to know I hurt, or that my mother's never loved me? It's almost more important to him than knowing I'm safe and happy.'

'That's not it at all,' Sara countered with a crease between her brows. 'Emma, Evan wants to know you and all that makes you, you. The good, the bad and the horrible. He needs to do some fessing up himself and not keep running away when he gets his feelings hurt. But you can't keep him in the dark when everything starts falling apart. You're not protecting him, you know. You're pushing him away.'

'I guess I wasn't sure he'd understand,' I confessed with a sigh.

'Like Jonathan does?' Sara finished the thought. I nodded. 'Give him a chance.'

My phone chimed. I looked at the screen and then to Sara with wide eyes.

'Who is it?'

'Rachel,' I said, stunned. 'Should I answer it?' Sara shrugged with a grimace of uncertainty. I missed the call.

She followed up with a text, *Where are you?*

I showed Sara the text. 'She doesn't know you're staying with me?'

'I don't remember if I told her, or she may not remember. But why does she care?'

'I don't know,' Sara answered, just as perplexed.

I decided to text back, *At Sara's*.

I left it at that, and she responded, *OK*. I shook my head in confusion.

'Okay, enough doom and gloom.' Sara stood up. 'We're going to check out prom dresses,' she declared with a vibrant smile. She observed the dread on my face. 'Don't worry. He'll forgive you before prom. Come on. I'll make it fun.'

Sara pulled me from my seat. She excitedly led the way through store after store. She picked out the most obnoxious dresses and modelled them for me, determined to make me laugh. And I did. Exactly as she intended.

Sara jumped on the couch, attempting a split in the air while striking the electric guitar. I knelt on the ground, leaning back with the guitar raised above my head, letting the ear-splitting sound reverberate through the amp. The song we were supposed to be playing along to blared over the speakers.

Out of the corner of my eye I saw movement, and I turned to find Anna at the top of the stairs, screaming, 'Emma!'

I stood and removed the guitar strap from around my neck. Sara noticed my change from rock star to worried girl before catching sight of her mom. She hopped down from the couch and shut off the amp and the music.

442

My ears were still ringing when Anna announced, 'Your mom's on my phone.' I froze mid-step. 'She's worried about you. My phone's downstairs in my room.'

I followed Anna downstairs, glancing back at Sara's concerned face before I disappeared. We entered Anna's bedroom, where her suitcase lay open on her bed. She'd been interrupted while packing for the trip that she was leaving for in an hour. The cell phone was next to the suitcase.

Anna picked it up and said, 'She's right here,' to Rachel before handing it to me. She walked past me, closing the bedroom door behind her.

'Hi,' I said cautiously.

'Emily?' Rachel asked in relief. 'Are you okay? I didn't know you were staying all weekend. I haven't heard from you.'

My brows crumpled in confusion. 'What?'

'Did you tell me you were staying there?' she asked in her nervous rush. 'Did I forget? I'm so sorry. I probably forgot.'

'What's wrong with you?' I demanded. 'Why are you all of a sudden worried about me?'

'Oh,' she sighed, sounding disappointed. 'Are you still mad at me? I'm so sorry I overreacted on Friday. I shouldn't have thought that you would ever do anything to hurt me. I was upset. Are you really mad?'

I pulled the phone away from my ear and stared at it, completely speechless. Who was this woman? Even if she didn't remember what she'd said to me that night because she was so drunk, she had to have remembered what *I* said to *her* – how much I hurt her.

443

'Emily?' she called out to me.

'I'm here,' I answered, devoid of emotion. 'I'm staying here this week. It's vacation anyway, so ... I'm staying here.' I couldn't tell her I was moving out. I wanted to. I meant to. But I didn't.

'Okay.' Her voice sounded strained. 'Well, I guess I'll see you next week.'

'Yeah,' I breathed before I hung up, too confounded to say anything else.

'Well,' Sara demanded when I appeared at the top of the stairs. I didn't acknowledge her, too baffled by what had just happened. 'Emma,' she urged impatiently, 'what did she want?'

'I have no idea,' I murmured in a daze. I sat down on the couch next to Sara and told her what had happened.

'So she doesn't remember?' Sara questioned sceptically. 'I really doubt it, Em. I bet she wants you to think that so you'll move back in again.'

'But why would she do that? She doesn't even want me.' It didn't make sense, but I'd come to the same conclusion as Sara.

'I have no idea,' Sara agreed. 'Maybe you should talk to her.'

'You mean I should *break up* with her,' I corrected. 'I can't believe I need to have the *we're over* talk with my own mother. How depressing is that?'

'She can't keep hurting you and using you like an emotional punch bag. It's messed up. How many times do you have to forgive her before she destroys you?'

I knew she was right. It was only a matter of time before she got drunk and did something devastating again. I just

444

didn't understand why she kept pulling me back in, making me feel like she wanted me when, during her vodka-induced proclamation, she'd confessed that she wished I was never born.

'I'll come with you,' Sara said from beside me. 'I'm not going to let you do it alone.'

Sara drove us to the house the next evening after my soccer game. I still hadn't figured out what I was going to say when we pulled in behind Rachel's car.

'You don't have to come in,' I told Sara as I slowly unbuckled the seat belt, my heart beating so fast I couldn't think straight.

'Uh, no,' Sara countered adamantly. 'I'm coming in with you.'

I took long even breaths as I approached the door, trying to remain calm. It was useless. I was a wreck. Sara stayed by my side and opened the screen door for me. The front door was locked, so I used my key to let us in.

We hadn't made it very far into the foyer before we both stopped. The house was a disaster. Sara and I scanned from the kitchen to the living room speechlessly. Plastic red cups and glasses were abandoned on just about every surface. Bottles littered the floor, along with bowls of chips and empty boxes of pizza. The stench of stale beer and old pizza made our noses scrunch in disgust. It was ten times worse than Sara's house had been after the anti-Valentine's party.

'Looks like Rachel had a party,' Sara observed, stepping carefully over the cluttered floor and into the living room. 'Or two.'

'What the hell?' I muttered in disbelief, wondering when this had happened. I ran up the stairs, expecting to find her passed out in her bedroom – but it was empty. I turned to head back downstairs and my mouth dropped open. 'No way.'

My door was open and my bed was unmade. 'Oh please, no,' I shook my head. 'I can't believe she let –' I was afraid to finish the sentence.

Sara appeared behind me. 'We are so burning those sheets.'

'It doesn't matter,' I said with a heavy sigh. 'I can't live here any more.'

'Uh, of course not,' Sara scolded. 'When between the car and entering the house did you decide that you were going to do that?'

'I didn't,' I fumbled. 'I just –'

'Live in a world of denial,' Sara finished sternly. 'Em, look around and open your eyes. She's not going to change.'

'I know,' I breathed, the disappointment heavy in my voice. I sank down on the top step and pressed my elbows into my knees. The little bit of hope I'd held on to after the conversation with Rachel yesterday had slipped away as soon as I'd opened the door.

'I'm sorry, Em.' Sara sat next to me and leaned her shoulder against mine. 'I don't mean to be so harsh. I just don't want you to get hurt any more. She doesn't deserve you.'

My eyes welled and I nodded. I knew this was it. We weren't fixable. The disappointment made my chest ache as I swallowed hard. Giving up went against my nature, having never done it before. I could faintly hear the hopeful

446

thoughts forming, that maybe she could change. I pushed them away before they got too loud.

'Let's go,' I finally declared, standing with Sara.

The front door opened, and Rachel appeared in the doorway, laughing, with her arm wrapped around the waist of a guy with blond hair and a large smile.

She looked up to see us. 'Uh, I thought you were going to be away this week.'

'I am,' I said, moving past her with my shoulders pulled back – barely giving her a glance. 'I'll be back next week to get my stuff.'

'Emily!' she called after me from the porch. 'What do you mean? Don't be angry with me. I'll clean up, I promise.'

Without looking back, I got into Sara's car. I held it together while Rachel could see me. Once we'd pulled out of the driveway and started down the street, I crumpled in half and cried. I knew I never was, and never would be, someone she loved. And whether she deserved me or not, it was still painful to admit.

36

Restless

'I was just thinking about you. Can't sleep?'

'No,' I answered softly.

'I didn't want to wake you, so I was waiting to call you tomorrow.'

'Well, it *is* tomorrow,' I said with a slight grin.

'Barely,' he laughed lightly. 'I'm glad you called.'

'I was afraid you wouldn't want to hear from me.'

'Emma, I always want to hear from you. It's when I don't that makes me worry.'

'I'm sorry. Really, I'm so sorry for not telling you what was going on with my mother. But I want to. I want to tell you *everything*.'

'We'll talk when I get back, okay? For now, I just want to know you're all right.'

'I'm better.'

'The two a.m. call is convincing,' he replied playfully.

A smile crept across my face. 'I'll be able to sleep now that I've talked to you.'

'So will I.'

'Will you still call me tomorrow?' I requested, not wanting to sound too desperate.

'Yes, I will. You should try to get some sleep now.'

'Okay,' I whispered. Before I hung up, I called, 'Evan.'

'Yes, Emma.'

'I love you.'

'I love you, too.'

I hoped I hadn't dreamt the call when I woke the next morning. It stirred, faint as whispers in my head, not seeming real. But when I looked at my call history and found his number at two eleven in the morning, I exhaled in relief.

'Wow, is that a smile I see on your face, Emma Thomas?' Sara teased when she walked into the room. 'Did you actually have a nice dream for once?'

'Uh, no,' I countered. 'I talked to Evan last night.'

'Really? What did you talk about?'

'Nothing much. It was late, but he promised to call me today.'

'That's good,' she replied with a smile. 'He can't stay upset with you. He's kind of pathetic that way.'

'Sara!' I balked. 'He's not pathetic.'

She smirked and continued to her closet.

'I can't wait for the next two months to be over,' I sighed, lying on my back and looking up at the skylights with a pillow hugged to my chest. 'Are you coming out to Santa Barbara with Evan and me this summer before school starts? I'm pretty sure Jared knows the guys we're staying with.'

I waited, but Sara didn't respond. 'Sara?'

She emerged from the closet with her mouth contorted. She couldn't look me in the eye, so I knew she had something that she didn't want to tell me. 'Sara, tell me.'

Sara took a deep breath and pressed her knees against her bed, her face already apologizing for whatever it was she was about to say. I braced myself.

'I didn't accept the offer to go to CCA in San Francisco.' My eyes widened in shock. We'd been planning to go to college in California for what seemed like forever, and her acceptance by California College of the Arts was perfect. We'd be near each other while I was at Stanford.

'I'm going to Parsons.'

'New York?' I said as my mouth dropped. The disappointment left me speechless. I'd never been without Sara since I'd met her, and being so far away from her for college was impossible to wrap my head around. I didn't respond for a moment, needing to get over the blow. Then I took a step back and released the part that was about me.

Parsons was closer to her family . . . and Jared. And it was one of the best fashion design schools in the world. She watched me carefully, waiting for my full reaction. I finally looked up at her with tears in my eyes and a proud smile on my face. 'I'm going to miss you. But Sara, I'm so happy for you.' The worry disappeared, replaced by a stunning smile that lit up her eyes.

'Really?' she asked, walking around the bed. 'You're not mad?'

'Mad? I'm not going to lie. I'm sad we won't be together, but I want this for you. Parsons is amazing, and you deserve to go there.'

Sara sat next to me and gave me a hug. It surprised me at first, but I wrapped my arms around her and held her with my face buried in her hair. She squeezed me tight, not making a move to release me. A tear escaped down my cheek as I kept holding on, almost afraid to let go. I couldn't imagine my life without her.

Her voice heavy with emotion, she murmured in my ear, 'I'm coming out to California for the summer, until school starts.' We slowly separated. Her eyes glistened with tears. 'We'll see each other every break. And I'll email you and text and Skype every day; it'll be like I'm there with you. And you'll have Evan, so you won't be alone.'

I grinned at her assurances. 'I know. We're always going to be friends.'

'No. We're always going to be *sisters*.' Sara smiled and wiped away the tears that moistened her cheeks.

'Besides, there's so much to look forward to in the next two months,' she said jubilantly, trying to laugh away the sadness. 'We have prom, senior week, graduation. Emma, I know right now it sucks for you, but everything's going to get better – especially now that you're moving back in with me. I know it doesn't feel like it, but you'll get through this – you always do. And you may even enjoy the last couple of months of your senior year.'

I nodded, running my hand along my damp cheeks with my lips pressed into a smile. A mixture of emotions fuelled the tears. I'd lost my mother (again). And now Sara . . . She truly was my sister in every way, and I was so proud of her. Everything was changing so fast. I hoped it wasn't going to change too much.

*

'That was quick,' Sara noted when I returned from speaking with Evan, after having anxiously awaited his call all day. I sat down next to her at the kitchen table.

'He just wanted to say hi before it got too late,' I explained quietly, using the tongs to lift the fettuccine out of the bowl and set the small mound on my plate. 'They were on their way out to surf, so the guys were waiting for him.'

'He's still a little off, isn't he?'

'A little,' I admitted, poking at the pasta with my fork – not even considering taking a bite.

'He'll be back in a few days,' Sara said encouragingly. 'I'm sure it's hard over the phone. It will be different in person.'

'I hope so,' I sighed, playing back the awkward strain in our conversation as we searched for anything positive to say. There wasn't much to talk about until he heard what I hadn't told him over the past couple of months. The missing conversations separated us further than the physical distance between Connecticut and Hawaii.

'What should we do tonight?' Sara asked, trying to distract me.

'Don't you have to get up early to go to the airport?'

'We can make it an early night and just watch a movie,' she suggested. 'Besides, you could use the sleep.' She smirked teasingly. There was no denying the repercussions of sleep deprivation, especially with Sara. She just had to look at me to know how long it had been since I'd slept – and it had been a while. With the build-up of drama and anxiety, sleep was a turbid mirage.

'Are you going to be okay staying here by yourself?'

'I was thinking about asking Casey if I could stay with her since we have soccer together,' I told her. 'Evan's back Saturday, so it would only be for two nights.'

'That won't be bad,' Sara mused. Then she grinned wickedly and added, 'You seem pretty positive that you're staying over at his house on Saturday night. You're not all that worried he won't forgive you, are you?'

I shrugged sheepishly. 'I'm hoping I can convince him.'

'Oooh, Emma,' she chuckled. 'I *have* rubbed off on you.'

'Sara,' I gaped, 'I'm not going to seduce him so he'll forgive me. Besides we're not having sex until next month.'

'What?' Sara laughed in disbelief. 'You've *planned* it?'

'Yeah,' I admitted, my cheeks reddening. 'We have a sex date for the night before prom.'

Sara laughed harder. 'You two kill me. How in the world can that be romantic, *planning* to have sex? Where's the lust and passion?'

'You don't know Evan,' I replied without thinking, then turned crimson when Sara's mouth dropped open. 'Okay, what movie are we watching?'

I closed my eyes and listened to the rhythm of her breathing from the bed next to me, hoping it would lull me to sleep. Sara inhaled and exhaled in long easy breaths. I could predict the next draw of air. But then it stopped. I waited, but she didn't breathe in again.

I opened my eyes and rolled over on to my back, listening intently. I inhaled quickly when the silhouette appeared next to my bed.

'Sara?' I questioned. 'Is something wrong?'

She didn't move. Maybe she was sleepwalking. I propped

myself up on my elbows, trying to focus on her and asked again, 'Sara?'

When my eyes adjusted to the light, I realized it wasn't her. I kicked my legs to remove the blankets, but the more I kicked, the more tangled they became in the bedding. Then I couldn't see. I'd sunk beneath the blankets and everything was dark. I pushed at the sheets but they pulled tighter around me. Then she gripped my neck.

I choked and coughed, trying to pull her hands away, but they were too strong. I kicked and shook my head from side to side to get out from under her claws, but it was no use.

'You don't deserve to live,' she grunted.

I grabbed on to her wrists and pried them loose, screaming, 'You've already killed me!'

My hands were on my throat when I woke. My breathing was heavy and my heart was pounding fiercely. The room was dark and I could hear Sara breathing in the bed next to me. I pulled back the blankets and crept out of the room. Sleep and I weren't going to find each other tonight, and there was no point lying there, staring into the dark.

I had my phone in my trembling hand when I sat on the couch in the rec room. I thought about calling Evan, but I knew it would just be another awkward conversation, and I didn't want to go through that twice in one day.

I clicked on the television and turned down the volume so Sara wouldn't hear it. I started scanning the channels and stopped on an infomercial for a microfibre cloth that claimed to be able to clean a car, computer or boat by just adding water, *streak free*. I almost laughed out loud. After a minute of being sucked into the enthusiastic sales pitch, I picked up my phone.

'I saw your infomercial,' I said as soon as I heard him pick up.

'Just needs water,' he replied, a smile in his voice. 'Been wondering how you've been sleeping. Thought you might be cured after all.'

'Hardly,' I responded. 'How about you? Been out on any dates lately?'

'Not yet,' he chuckled. 'Where are you?'

'At Sara's.'

'That's good. You're not going back, are you?'

'No,' I replied quietly. 'I'm not. Some things aren't fixable.'

'I thought when I didn't hear from you that he may have made you stop talking to me.'

I was puzzled by his assumption. 'Evan's away right now. We haven't had a chance to talk yet.'

'Oh,' Jonathan replied. 'Then, should you be talking to me?'

'Yeah, why not? We're friends,' I replied, bewildered. 'Evan has girls who are friends too. You're not the reason things are off between us anyway.'

'Do you want to talk about it?' Jonathan asked hesitantly.

'No,' I whispered.

After a moment of silence, he asked, 'Do you want to hang out again?' Then he added quickly, 'No cliffs this time.'

I laughed. 'Sure. We could do something tomorrow if you want. I have practice in the afternoon, but maybe after that.'

'Yeah, I should be home from work by six. How about . . .' he paused for a moment. 'How about we get dinner or something? And I kind of have something to share.'

'Really?' I replied, intrigued. 'Sure, just text me where to meet you.'

'Okay. I'll see you tomorrow.' When I hung up, I realized my lips were turned up into a smile and my heart was beating a little faster.

37

Into a Nightmare

'I THOUGHT YOU SAID YOU WEREN'T VERY good,' Jonathan teased as we walked out of the pool hall and into the cool drizzly night.

'I'm not,' I retorted, pulling my hood over my head. 'You're just worse than I am.'

'Thanks,' he shot back with a smirk. 'So what next? Do you have to get back to your friend's?'

I checked my phone. Casey had promised to text me when she was on her way home from the party. In case she'd forgotten, which was definitely possible, I sent her a text asking where she was.

'I think she's still at the party,' I told him. 'Do you mind if I hang out for a while longer?'

'No, you're welcome to stay as long as you'd like,' Jonathan assured me. 'But I'm not sure what to do that's not a bar.'

'I'd like to check out the band you were talking about, if that's okay.'

'Oh, yeah, sure,' Jonathan fumbled.

'We can do something else if you don't want to go back to your apartment,' I suggested, his response making me feel a bit awkward.

'No, it's fine. I've honestly never had anyone at my place before. I'm trying to remember if I left it a mess.'

'Really? You've *never* had anyone over?' I repeated in surprise. 'Why not?'

Jonathan shrugged. 'Umm, I don't really know. I usually meet people out, I guess. But yeah, let's go there.' I followed Jonathan across the intersection and down a side street. The reflection of the water shimmered at the end.

'So, Rachel's never been here?'

'No,' he stated adamantly. 'I needed to take a break every once in a while. But she asked, trust me.'

I nodded, imagining her agitation with not knowing where he lived. But I also remembered him disappearing a few days each week, and she probably wouldn't have let that happen if she knew where to find him.

We crossed the street at the end of the road and followed the water towards the marina.

'Why did you stay?' I decided to ask, considering how long he'd put up with her, and recognizing how often he'd needed to be away from her.

'Uh, what?' Jonathan questioned in confusion. 'You mean with Rachel?'

'You had every right to get out way before you did. What made you stay?'

'I thought we agreed not to talk about her or anything else depressing.' Jonathan replied, avoiding the question as we approached an old white brick building along the wharf.

'You're right,' I conceded. I eyed the worn structure warily as Jonathan slid his key in the black metal door.

'Don't judge it by the outside,' Jonathan advised. 'They completely gutted it.' When he opened the door, he flipped on the lights, illuminating a metal grated staircase that led to an opening above.

'I guess they did,' I said, admiring the contemporary space at the top of the stairs. White walls stretched about twenty feet to an exposed beam ceiling. An entire wall was lined with brick and mill-sized paned windows that over-looked the water. The floors appeared to be original, but the thick planks were newly varnished. 'This place is amazing.'

'I was lucky to find it,' Jonathan admitted.

I walked over to the small black table set in front of a window to view the few boats rocking on the water below. Across the wharf was a boatyard where more boats awaited warmer temperatures before returning to the seas.

'Want something to drink?' Jonathan asked from the kitchen area of the studio. It was sleek, with stainless everything and tall wooden cabinets above a marble countertop.

'No, I'm fine.'

Jonathan removed a beer from the fridge and flipped it open. He approached the entertainment unit set on a long black table against the wall. I found a seat on the sofa that was perpendicular to the kitchen and the windows, offer-ing a perfect view of the entire room. The beige sofa was linear and modern in design, but more comfortable than it appeared.

As I sank into the cushion, I peered up at an open plat-form suspended next to the kitchen wall. Metal stairs led to what I assumed to be his bedroom, but it was too high to see from this angle.

His studio was so . . . clean. I didn't know why he was worried. It was almost *too* clean. That's when it struck me that there wasn't anything in it other than the furniture. No artwork or decor of any kind. Nothing . . . personal.

'How long have you lived here?' I asked, thinking that maybe he was still working on it.

'Since I graduated,' Jonathan revealed, scrolling through his downloads to find the band he'd told me about while we played pool.

'Two years?' I confirmed, scanning the room again.

'Just about,' he agreed. Acoustic guitar strums echoed through the room followed by a woman's smooth voice. 'I know. It's pretty . . . minimal. I wouldn't even know how to begin decorating it.'

'Don't you have any girlfriends who can help you out?'

'I've discovered that having girls as friends just leads to complications. So, no, I don't.'

'Complications?' I questioned curiously.

'Yeah. Someone eventually wants more, and it gets . . . *complicated*,' he explained with a shrug before taking a sip of beer.

'Oh,' I nodded, understanding. 'Yes, that is true.'

'So, you've experienced this?' Jonathan sounded interested as he sat in the chair next to the sofa.

'First hand?' I considered for a moment, then continued, 'Well, yeah. That's what happened with Evan. We started out as friends, but that didn't take.' My cheeks warmed as I reflected upon our 'friendship'.

'I have a feeling you weren't really *friends*, even at the beginning,' he noted at the sight of my flushed face.

My cheeks became hotter. 'No, probably not. But I do know what you mean. He has a girl right now who's supposed to be a friend, and she definitely has a thing for him. It's, as you said, complicated.'

'You don't care that he's friends with other girls, right? I mean, you have me,' Jonathan countered.

'No, I don't mind. But you and I are different,' I argued. 'We're *not* complicated.'

Jonathan challenged my words with a raise of his eyebrows. 'Right. We're just messed up.'

I laughed and nodded. I pushed off my shoes and curled my legs next to me on the couch. My phone beeped, and I pulled it from my pocket.

Still at party. Wanna come? Its a good one.

I grinned at Casey's message and texted back, *No thanks*.

'That your friend?' Jonathan confirmed. 'Do you have to go?'

'No. She's still at the party.'

'Good,' he replied, making me look up from my phone. He tipped back the bottle to avoid my curious expression.

'I like this,' I said, commenting on the band and letting his remark slide. 'They have a nice sound.'

'Yeah, it's just a guy and a girl,' Jonathan explained. 'They're pretty incredible.'

Their voices chimed in unison. I was enchanted by the lyrics as we sat quietly, letting them speak for us. I closed my eyes, allowing the music to float through me.

'Emma?' Jonathan called to me. I pulled my lids open,

which was harder than I expected. I must have started to doze off. 'Are you okay?'

'Sorry.' I shook my head and sat up straighter to ward off the bout of sleep. 'I'm just tired.'

'Really, are you okay?' he asked again, studying my face intently. I shifted away from his delving brown eyes and nodded.

'I haven't been sleeping much.'

'Or eating,' Jonathan reproached me.

I shrugged guiltily. 'That obvious?'

'Uh, yeah,' he confirmed with a firm nod.

'It's been a crazy week,' was my feeble defence.

'That's an understatement,' he said with a wry grin. 'I know we said we weren't going to talk about it, but we can if you want. I'm really sorry about everything that happened. I still feel like it's my fault.'

'It's not,' I stressed. 'It really had nothing to do with skipping school and spending the day with you. In the end it was about the truth, and I just didn't want to see it.'

'What do you mean?'

'She doesn't love me. She never did. There's nothing that's ever going to change that.'

Jonathan didn't respond. We were quiet for a moment before he asked, 'What about you?' I glanced over at him. His voice was quiet and smooth. 'How do you feel about *her*?'

I let his eyes search mine as I considered his question. 'I don't know. I always thought I loved her. I mean, she's my mother. But . . . I don't know.'

'What if you didn't think of her as your mother? Just as a person you know. How would you feel about her?' he coaxed.

'That I don't like her,' I answered without hesitation.

'She seems funny and nice on the outside, but when you get close enough, you realize she's selfish and manipulative, and well, a bit unstable. So I guess . . . maybe I don't love her either.' I lowered my eyes as my words took hold. 'Wow. That's messed up.'

'Tends to be our unavoidable theme,' Jonathan noted with a guilty grin. 'Sorry. We can't seem to avoid the depressing, can we?'

'I think it's because we both understand what it's like. It's not easy to talk like this with other people because they don't know. They don't know what it's like to be hated by the people who are supposed to love you.' I sank further into the couch and allowed the bleak mood to settle within me, drawing on my weariness. I thought about leaving, but I just needed to rest for a moment. I laid my head on my arm.

'What is it like?' Jonathan asked, calling me back to meet his dark eyes. 'For you I mean, what's it like?'

I breathed out a humourless laugh and allowed the honesty to slip through. 'It makes me stupid.'

'What?' Jonathan questioned in alarm. 'I don't understand how you can say that.'

I focused on a distant light on the water, trying to find the words to explain what was starting to become apparent to me – having thought incessantly about what I'd done wrong over the past year. I had my mother to thank for clicking it all into place for me with her bouts of drunken candour.

'I close my eyes to the truth. I refuse to see what's happening, convinced that I can handle whatever it is – believing that I'm strong enough and will recognize when I'm not.

'But in order to really see it, the truth, I have to admit how much I'm hated. And who wants to think they deserve that much anger? To be despised so much . . . to have someone wish you'd never existed.' I paused to take a breath.

'I shut it out. I *choose* not to see. I never ask for help. I even try to convince everyone that it's not a big deal. They don't know. No one really knows how bad it is because I won't let them.' I paused and repeated, 'It makes me stupid.'

Jonathan silently absorbed my whispered words. Exhaustion rolled over me and my head became as heavy as my heart. I felt outside of myself as my eyes burned with fatigue.

'How do you do it?' Jonathan asked. He sounded so far away. I tried to focus on him, but I couldn't. 'How do you get through it?'

'By not feeling,' I murmured, blinking heavily, lulled by the voices crooning in the background. This wasn't difficult to explain, since I'd done it so easily all those years living with Carol. 'I shut it off. And I guess if it's really bad, I block it out completely. I didn't realize I did that until my mother showed me what I'd forgotten.'

I shut my eyes. 'She thinks I'm strong because I can push everything into the dark. But it leaves me empty. And the dark always ends up finding me in my sleep.'

I felt the weight of a blanket being pulled over me. I opened my eyes and found him propped on the coffee table in front of me. He smiled gently, holding a pillow in his hands. I sat up enough for him to place it beneath my head and lowered myself down again.

'Sorry,' I whispered, my eyes sliding shut again. 'I'm so tired.'

'I know,' he replied gently. 'You can sleep here if you want.'

'I'm just gonna rest before I go,' I muttered, blinking. My eyes were so heavy; it almost hurt to keep them open. Jonathan stood up.

'Jonathan?'

He squatted down in front of me. 'Yes, Emma.'

'Do you think you'll ever love again?' I murmured, not fighting against my lids any longer.

'I think so,' he whispered, brushing the hair from my cheek. I shivered against his touch. 'I'll see you in my sleep.'

I pushed my eyes open one final time to find him walking away. 'What did you say?'

'I said I'll see you in the morning. Get some sleep.'

'I'm just going to rest for a bit,' I slurred, closing my eyes again. I couldn't have kept them open if I'd tried.

My screams still echoed through the room when I sat up in a panic, trying to breathe.

'Emma?' Jonathan called out. The clang of the metal stairs echoed sharply in the dark. It took me a moment to focus on him when he crouched in front of me. 'You're okay. It was just a dream.'

I nodded and my lips trembled. 'I can't do this any more,' I choked, my eyes filling with tears. I was too exhausted and shaken to hold them back. 'I'm so tired.'

'I know,' Jonathan said soothingly, sliding next to me on the couch and rubbing my shoulder.

I released a quivering breath and wiped my eyes with my sleeves. 'I don't know how to make it stop.'

Jonathan's brow creased with empathy.

'Can I please have a glass of water?' I requested, trying to recover from my emotional meltdown.

Jonathan nodded and stood to retrieve it. I sat up with the blanket wrapped around me and took a deep breath to calm the shaking. He turned on the lights above the island, providing enough light for me to look around.

'Where's your television?' I asked, not finding the post-nightmare distraction.

'Oh, it's in my bedroom,' he nodded towards the loft in the corner. 'You need something to clear your head?' he asked.

'Anything,' I begged. 'I can't keep thinking about her trying to kill me any more.'

'You can't let her control you. Emma, you're stronger than this. You just have to believe it.' He handed me a glass of water and sat next to me. 'Do you know what happened that night? Or did you block that out too?'

'I died,' I answered bluntly. 'So, I have no idea what happened.'

I felt the warmth of his hand encapsulate mine. The strength of it wrapped around my thin hand comforted me, but it also made my heart pound. I eased it away to hold the glass with two hands. He pretended not to notice.

'Emma,' he said, making me look at him as I sipped the water. 'Do you want to sleep better?'

I scrunched my eyes warily. 'What do you have in mind?'

'Do you trust me?'

'Are you going to try to cure me again?' I questioned sceptically.

'Yeah,' he grinned. 'I think this might work, or at least help you. Will you let me?'

I paused a moment in deliberation. Jonathan's eyes were big and pleading, begging for me to trust him. I sighed in defeat and threatened, 'If it doesn't work, I swear I will keep you up every night I can't sleep.'

'I can handle that,' he grinned in triumph. 'Get your jacket.'

'What?' I questioned in alarm. 'We're leaving?'

'Did you think I was going to try to hypnotize you or something?' he chuckled.

I sighed in resignation and slipped my shoes on as he tossed me my jacket.

'So how's your triathlon training going?' I asked, cutting through the tense silence that had encapsulated us upon entering the truck.

'Really?' Jonathan laughed in disbelief at what I was asking him.

'Well, I need to talk about *something*,' I defended myself with a groan. 'From the looks of it, we're heading back to Weslyn. And if we're going where I think we're going, then we'd better start talking before I make you turn the truck around.'

'Training's going great,' Jonathan burst out. 'I haven't been cycling lately because the weather's sucked, but so far –'

'Okay, that's not helping,' I interrupted, glancing over

at him apologetically. 'Sorry, I do want to hear about it, but I'm about ready to have a heart attack, or anxiety attack, or something.'

'Breathe, Emma,' he urged. 'Slow, deep breaths. Just breathe.'

I tried to remember how. My heart continued to convulse, and breathing was becoming more challenging.

'Wait.' It suddenly struck me. 'How do you know where to go?'

I thought I heard him laugh. 'It's not hard to find anything in Weslyn. All you have to do is ask, and people talk. Don't worry. Nothing's going to happen to you,' he assured me. 'I promise.'

I buried my face in my hands, as the world spun out of control. I couldn't watch as we turned down each road. The closer we got, the more I had to fight the urge to jump out of the truck.

'Come on, Emma.' I was too wrapped up in my anxiety to realize we'd stopped.

'I can't,' I whimpered, unable to uncover my face.

'Yes you can,' he cajoled. 'I'm here. Nothing's going to happen.'

My hands shook when I lowered them. I kept my eyes closed and tried to calm the panic that was overtaking me. 'I don't think I can get out.'

His door opened and closed behind him. I stayed within the dark cab, paralysed. My door opened, and his warm hand wrapped around mine. 'You can do this.'

I opened my eyes and looked into his. 'Come on, Emma.' I concentrated on his face. It was so sure and

468

confident. I held tight to his hand as if it were a lifeline. I suddenly felt so small.

'Just look at me,' he encouraged, as I stepped down from the truck. 'Keep looking at me.'

I nodded, unable to find my voice. I continued to focus on him, his eyes assuring me with every step.

'Okay, close your eyes,' he advised, 'I'm going to turn you towards it.' My knees buckled, but he kept me upright with his hands gripping my shoulders.

'Why are we doing this?' I whispered, feeling the warmth of the tears on my cheeks.

'Because I can sleep,' Jonathan answered softly in my ear, still holding me upright.

'What?' His words distracted me from my anxiety, and I tilted my head towards him. 'What did you say?'

'I don't know if it was facing it, or sharing it with you, but I've been sleeping through the night. And I want you to be able to, too.' He gently ran his thumb along my cheek to wipe away the tears. 'Go ahead and look.'

I reluctantly moved my eyes from his face to the house in front of me. It felt like there was a stone in my chest. I leaned against him.

'This is where it happened,' he said in a hushed whisper, wrapping his arm around my shoulder. 'This is where you died.'

I nodded, unable to see clearly through the tears.

'Do you remember now?'

I blinked the tears free and stared at the grey house, sunk within the shadows of the neighbours' trees. A 'For Sale' sign hung in the miniscule front yard. It looked so much smaller than I remembered. I got lost in the dark windows. So much pain lay hidden behind them.

'Where did it happen?' he asked, his voice faint like a whisper in my head.

'In my room,' I rasped, my eyes shifting to the side of the house. Jonathan took my hand and guided me closer. My pulse raced with each step. He led me along the wooden fence that bordered the neighbour's yard.

'Where?' he asked again.

I pointed to the second window. 'Here.' I trembled beneath the white framed window, her voice seething from the other side, *I am not losing my family because of you.* I shivered.

'Emma, what happened to you?' he probed, not letting me go.

Staring into the dark, I was swallowed by my nightmare. *Tugging at the restraints around my wrists.* 'I couldn't move,' I murmured. *The fabric upon my face.* 'And I couldn't see.' Jonathan's arm tightened around me. *Struggling beneath her weight.* 'I tried to get away, but I couldn't. Then . . . then I felt her hands . . .' I blindly touched my neck, still able to feel her cold claws. I shuddered. 'I fought so hard. There was . . . pain . . .' I breathed in quickly as it streaked through my body, 'my ankle . . .' I clamped my eyes closed. *Banging and muffled cries.* 'But then I just . . . I just gave up.'

I bowed my head with a gasp and tears ran over my nose.

'But you didn't, Emma. You didn't give up. You're here.'

'I don't want to be here any more,' I whispered.

'Okay,' he said, his lips next to my ear. 'Okay, we'll leave.'

I stepped away without looking at him, and he let me go. I walked back to the truck with my head down, trying to release the crushing pressure in my chest. I'd just stepped into one of my nightmares. And I was fighting so hard to get back out.

38

Covering Up

'GOOD MORNING,' JONATHAN SMILED FROM the chair across from me with a blanket over his lap. 'You slept.'

I took in a breath and blinked. 'Have you been there all night?'

'Do you mean, all morning?' he teased. 'But you slept.'

'You didn't sleep?' I questioned, pushing myself to sit up, the weariness still lingering despite the few hours of rest.

Jonathan shrugged without answering, but continued to wear a smug grin.

'Oh, don't start thinking you cured me or anything,' I said, suddenly realizing what was behind the grin. 'Just because I slept for a few hours, it doesn't mean the nightmares have vanished. We'll see if you deserve the pat on the back when I go to bed tonight. Besides, they don't happen *every* night, and you know that.'

'You *are* really good at this denial thing, aren't you?' he laughed. 'You have no idea what's going on until you can't ignore it any longer.'

'Yeah,' I huffed. 'I *love* not sleeping at night, and just want to prove you wrong.'

'That's not what I meant,' he grinned wider, but before I could question him, he stood up, leaving the blanket on the chair. 'Are you hungry? I have . . . cereal.'

'Thanks, but I should get to Casey's,' I replied, standing to stretch my legs with my arms extended above me – feeling the ache in my neck and back. 'Your couch isn't very comfortable to sleep on.'

'It's not meant to be slept on. I offered you the bed.' He shrugged. I didn't respond. I hadn't exactly been comfortable with that offer.

I picked up my phone and slid on my shoes. I scanned through my missed texts from Casey, and the one response that wasn't actually from me. 'Thanks for texting Casey for me last night.'

'I didn't want her to worry,' he replied, pouring cereal into a bowl. 'She thought it was you. I don't think you'll have to tell her where you were.'

I nodded, not sure how that explanation would've come out anyway. I still didn't know what I would say if she ended up asking. But then again, Casey wasn't the curious type, so I hoped to avoid the enquiry altogether.

'I have to stop by Rachel's to get my shirt for the game tomorrow,' I remembered out loud with a groan, sliding on my jacket.

Jonathan paused, appearing concerned.

'Don't worry,' I assured him. 'She should've left for

work by now. Speaking of which, aren't you going to be late?'

'I'm working from home today,' he explained. 'You have a game tomorrow?'

'Yeah.'

'Would it be okay if I watched it? I've never seen you play, and I kinda want to see what the scholarship's all about.'

'Umm, sure,' I fumbled. 'I'll text you where we're playing. I can't remember where it is right now.'

'Great. Thanks.'

I was about to leave when he called, 'Emma.'

I hesitated.

Jonathan leaned back against the island. His dark hair was dishevelled but the way the waves twisted, it looked like it was on purpose. His wrinkled T-shirt clung to him, hinting at the broad muscle beneath. Taking in his casual stance against the counter, I could actually picture him in the magazine, and recognized why he drew so much attention.

'I like this,' he confessed. 'Us. Being able to talk. I've never been able to do it before. Not even with . . . Sadie. I've needed it . . . you. And now you're here, and well . . . thank you.'

A chill ran through me when I found myself caught in the depth of his eyes. I blinked away and nodded. 'I like this too.' My voice came out small and broken as heat spread across my cheeks.

Jonathan smiled. 'I'll see you tomorrow then.'

'Yeah,' I replied with a faint smile. I suddenly wasn't so sure if his coming to see me play was such a good idea.

Something felt different this morning – like my vulnera-bility last night had allowed him to get too close, closer than he'd already been. 'I'll see you tomorrow.'

When I turned on to Decatur Street, I slowed to a crawl, just in case. I came to a sudden stop when her car appeared in the driveway, and quickly put my car in reverse. I huffed in frustration as I backed away, knowing I needed my shirt by tomorrow morning. But the last thing I wanted was another confrontation, or a *Twilight Zone* conversation where she pretended nothing was wrong.

As expected, Casey hadn't thought twice about where I'd spent the night. Instead, she went on about the great party I'd missed. I'd only had a few hours of sleep on Jonathan's couch, so I was pretty out of it most of the day. She didn't seem to notice.

I had every intention of returning to Rachel's that night, in hopes that she'd be out doing what she did best on a Friday night – but I never made it that far.

'Emma, you can sleep in the guest room,' Casey's voice cut through my head. I opened my eyes to find her standing above me with the movie still playing in the background.

'Sorry,' I said. 'I'm so pathetic today, I know. I'm just really tired.'

'It's okay,' Casey replied. 'I didn't expect us to go to a party or anything. Besides, I'm pretty tired from last night too. I'll see you in the morning?'

'Yeah,' I told her, dragging my feet to the guest room. My phone chimed as I was about to slide under the covers. I didn't look to see who was calling as I put it to my ear. 'Hello?'

'Hi,' Evan said from the other end. My heart skipped a beat at the sound of his voice.

'Hi,' I returned in joyous relief. 'How are you?'

'Good,' he responded, sounding a little surprised. Maybe I'd come across a little *too* happy to hear from him. 'I'm at the airport in LA for my connecting flight and I wanted to hear your voice. It's been really hard not talking to you.'

'You have no idea.' I exhaled. 'When will you be home?'

'Tomorrow afternoon. Can I see you? I'll come straight from the airport.'

'Um, why don't I meet you at your house? Will your parents be home?'

'My mother might be,' he said, considering, 'I don't think my father will be around. She mentioned a meeting in DC. I'll see you at my house. I should be there between two thirty and three.'

'That's perfect,' I smiled.

'I should've called you, Emma. I'm sorry,' he quickly added; the regret in his voice forced my pulse to quicken.

'You needed time,' I stated quietly. 'I deserved it.'

'No. I should have called. That wasn't right, to do that to you. I'll see you tomorrow, okay?'

When I hung up the phone I was filled with both elation and dread. I missed him so much I ached, but I knew what was going to happen when we saw each other, and I wished it was already over. I couldn't fast forward to the inevitable, so I accepted that we were about to have a long and difficult conversation and collapsed into bed where exhaustion pulled me into a dreamless sleep.

*

I left a little early for the game so I could pick up my jersey on the way. I anxiously tapped my fingers on the steering wheel the entire drive, hoping she'd stayed at *his* place, whoever that might be.

'Shit,' I grunted, when I saw the two cars in the driveway. I pulled up along the street and closed my eyes while gripping the steering wheel. Focused on running in to get my shirt and back out, I didn't bother to remove my keys from the ignition. I wouldn't acknowledge her if she said anything to me.

My heart beat frantically when I approached the front door. I hesitated before opening it, thinking I'd heard her yell. When I didn't hear it again, I continued inside.

Her agonizing cries stole the breath from my lungs. I stared in horror at the large man pounding his fist into my mother's side as she cowered on the floor in front of the couch with her hands over her head. She hollered in pain with each blow, trying to shrink away from him without anywhere to go.

'What are you doing?' I yelled, without thinking about anything except making him stop, despite the fact that he had a good five inches on me and looked enraged enough to take down a bull.

'This is none of your business,' the guy growled at me. 'Get the fuck out of here.'

'Emily,' my mother gasped. She tried to pull herself up on the coffee table. My mouth opened in shock when I saw the blood gushing out of her nose and the swelling enveloping her right eye.

He wasn't about to let her come back up, turning towards her as she stumbled to her feet. He raised his bloodied fist just as I screamed, 'No!' The collision spun my mother around, and she teetered over the top of the coffee table. It collapsed upon impact. Her crumpled body didn't move, sprawled awkwardly on the splintered wood.

He turned to intercept me when I rushed to her, shoving me out of his way with virtually no effort. I landed hard on my side with a grunt.

'You want to make this your business?' the guy threatened from above me. I shrank into the floor. He snarled down at me as he breathed heavily through flared nostrils. His black eyes threatened to bore right through me. 'Then you're going to get hurt, little girl. This is between me and Rachel, so I'm only going to warn you one last time. Stay the fuck out of it.'

I tensed, prepared for him to hit me. But he moved past me, slamming the front door behind him. I scrambled to my knees and slid over to the collapsed coffee table where my mother was starting to moan.

'Mom?' I called to her with tears in my eyes. 'Can you hear me?'

She groaned louder and squinted with her good eye. 'Emily? Is he gone?'

'Yeah, he's gone,' I assured her, tenderly sitting her up. She whimpered with the slightest movement. 'Can you get up? We need to get you to the hospital.'

'I think I broke my wrist,' she cried, holding her left wrist, the one she'd held out to break her fall.

'Easy,' I coaxed gently. My voice was steady as I supported her to sit, but my entire body was shaking.

'I'm sorry,' she gasped, fresh tears streaming down her face. 'I'm so sorry.'

I consoled her, dismissing her pleas. 'Now let's see if you can stand.' Supporting her under her arm, I helped her up.

She was crying uncontrollably by the time we reached the car. I took a deep breath when I sat on the driver's seat and tried to remember how to get to the hospital, needing to remain calm so I could think clearly.

'It's okay,' I breathed to myself. 'Everything's going to be okay.' I flipped my eyes towards my sobbing mother and said it louder for her to hear, 'Everything's going to be okay.'

Her cries dwindled to spasmodic breaths and sniffles as we neared the hospital.

'How are you doing?' I asked, afraid to take my eyes off the road, strangling the steering wheel.

'I'm sorry,' she choked again.

'Okay.' I dismissed her apology anxiously. 'But how are you feeling? Can you see out of that eye? Does anything else hurt?'

'I think I'll be fine,' she murmured, wiping the blood from her face with her sleeve-covered hand.

'Who was that guy?' I asked, now that she was starting to sound more coherent.

She just shook her head.

'Rachel,' I demanded forcefully. 'Who was that guy? Why did he do this to you?'

She swallowed audibly and released a quivering breath. 'I owe him some money,' she whispered faintly.

I pulled my brows together. 'For what?'

She wouldn't answer. I didn't ask again.

I tried to remember if I knew what he looked like, for

when the police asked. Besides being big and sleazy-looking, I couldn't remember anything about his face. Then I knew. There was only one reason my mother would owe a guy like that.

'He's your dealer,' I concluded out loud. Rachel remained silent. I couldn't stand to even look at her. I clenched my teeth together and stared at the road as the anger built up in my gut, tightening every muscle in my body.

When we arrived at the emergency room entrance, I demanded, 'Give me your phone.'

'What?' she squeaked. 'Why?'

'I'm calling Sharon to pick you up,' I told her, my voice edged with fury. 'You should probably stay with her anyway until you can fix your mess.'

'Emily,' she pleaded desperately. 'Please don't leave.'

'I'm not staying here with you,' I snapped coldly, unable to look at her. 'I'll go back to the house to pack you a bag, and I'll leave it on the porch for Sharon to pick up.'

'Don't,' she sobbed, 'don't say anything, okay?'

I turned towards her with my face pulled tight in disgust. I couldn't believe she was actually asking me to lie for her. I shook my head in anguished disbelief.

'Please,' she begged, 'I'm just going to tell them I was robbed and he took off before I could see him.' Her eye was practically swollen shut, and congealed blood lined her nose. Her one good eye continued to tear up as she breathed in spasms. She looked horrid. But I couldn't pity her. As she gibbered in front of me, desperate for me to protect her with another of her lies, I loathed her.

I seethed through clenched teeth, 'Don't worry. I won't tell the police that your drug dealer beat you because you owe him money. It's none of my business, remember?'

She gasped in a sob and turned from me, carefully letting herself out of the car and leaving her phone on the seat. As soon as the door was closed, I pulled away without looking back.

The impact of what had happened sank in as I turned onto the main road and I pressed my lips together to keep them from trembling. The anger kept back the tears, but my body shook despite my efforts.

I parked along a residential street and picked up her phone with an unsteady hand. After I'd left a message for Sharon, my phone rang.

I took a deep breath before answering.

'Emma?' Jonathan said when I answered with a strained voice. 'Are you okay? Where are you?'

I closed my eyes and grimaced. He was at my soccer game. 'Umm . . . I had to get my shirt,' I tried to explain, my voice cracking.

'What happened?' he demanded urgently. 'Emma, where are you?'

'I had to take Rachel to the hospital,' I told him, trying to remain calm. 'Jonathan . . .' I pressed my lips together. The anger was taking over, and I was about to lose it. I breathed in through my nose to ward off the tears.

'Are you okay?'

'Yeah.' I exhaled, took another deep breath and explained, 'There was some guy looking for money. He beat her pretty bad.'

'What?' Jonathan practically yelled. 'Did he hurt you?'

'No, I'm fine. But she's a mess.' I bit my trembling lip and the tears escaped.

'Where are you now?' he demanded. 'I'm driving back towards Weslyn. Where are you?'

'I'm going back to her house,' I explained. 'I have to pack a bag so she can stay at Sharon's.'

'Emma, I don't think you should go back there.'

'He's gone,' I told him, wiping my cheeks.

'Don't go into the house until I get there,' he instructed me firmly before hanging up.

I pulled back on the road and fought for control over the nerves twisting inside me, tucking everything away as I was so good at doing. I was numb but focused by the time I pulled into the driveway. Jonathan hadn't arrived yet.

The front door was still open from our hasty exit. I scouted the street in search of cars, but none were in sight. I was confident the dealer wasn't coming back.

I walked through the screen door and stood in the foyer, listening. The house remained silent, so I continued up the stairs. I was about to walk into her room, when I thought I heard a board creak. My heart stopped. I turned towards the stairs, but there wasn't anyone there.

I exhaled, realizing I was holding my breath and started towards her door. I caught sight of my open door out of the corner of my eye and froze. Something was wrong. I turned back, my heart racing. Lying on the floor inside my room was a small blue gift box – the gift box that held the necklace Evan had given me. The necklace that was supposed to be tucked under my clothes in my top drawer.

He *had* come back.

I raced across the hall. I was shaking my head, yammering, 'No, no, no, no,' when I slammed into his chest. Rocked backwards, I cautiously stepped away while he continued out of my room. He revealed a snarky smirk. My eyes widened, fearing he'd hurt me as he had my mother. My heart thrust against my chest – I braced myself to run. That's when I saw the necklace in his hand.

'Oh no,' I cried in a breath. Without considering the consequences, I lunged towards him and reached for it. He grabbed my hand before I could touch it, shoving me away.

'You should have listened,' he grunted. The hardened glare in his dark eyes sent a chill through me. I knew that look. I instinctively began to raise my hands to protect myself, but the punch knocked me to the floor. Pain flooded through my jaw, and my eyes filled with black dots.

I scrambled to my feet, trying to find my focus, needing to reach him before he could make it to the stairs. I pulled at his hand. He turned back around, snatching the necklace out of reach and exclaimed, 'You little bitch. What the fuck are you thinking?'

'You can't have it,' I cried. 'Please, I'll pay you. But you can't take that from me.'

He laughed and shoved me hard. I collided with the wall and grunted.

'Who the fuck do you think you are?' he sneered. He swung his arm and backhanded me across the head, knocking me to my hands and knees. My head pounded, but I willed myself to get back on my feet. Before I could, his boot crashed into my ribs.

I screamed out and fell to the floor, my arms wrapped around me as I curled into a ball, unable to catch my breath.

'Emma!' I heard from the bottom of the stairs.

I couldn't find my voice to warn him, to tell him to leave. Immobile in my curled position on the floor, I heard scuffling and grunts. I rolled over to see Jonathan shoving the guy against the wall and thrusting his fist into his stomach. The guy buckled over.

I used the wall to help me up, and leaned against it with an arm across my ribs. Every breath was agonizing. I wanted to yell out, but I could only gasp in broken breaths. I fumbled for my phone, but it wasn't in my pocket. I searched for it on the floor but couldn't find it.

The sparkle of the diamond caught my eye on the floorboards at my feet. I wrapped my fingers around it and clenched it tightly in my fist, feeling the stone digging into my palm.

Jonathan landed a punch to the side of the guy's head, causing him to stagger back. Before he could regain his balance, Jonathan followed with another to his jaw, and the guy teetered over, landing hard on the floor. Jonathan kept hold of his shirt, propping him up, and slammed his fist into his face. The guy's arms went limp by his sides, but Jonathan was relentless, swinging over and over again.

'Jonathan!' I screamed as blood smeared the man's face. The tendons in Jonathan's neck strained as he continued to pummel the mangled face, blood spraying out of the mouth and nose. His rage was insatiable.

I staggered over and grabbed the arm that was holding the guy up. 'Jonathan!'

Jonathan's head snapped up. His eyes were dark and

feral. I didn't recognize him with his lips pulled tight in a hateful sneer. I stumbled back, inhaling sharply.

It took him a moment to focus on me, for his eyes to soften. The stony look disappeared from his eyes. I stood with my mouth open in abhorrence. His face contorted painfully when he saw the horror on my face.

Jonathan slowly lowered the guy to the floor and stood up, not taking his eyes off me.

'Emma,' he breathed desolately. I shook my head, unable to comprehend what I'd just witnessed. I backed away and stared down at the unrecognizable figure on the floor. He wasn't moving. I couldn't even tell if he was breathing. His face was deformed and drenched in blood; he didn't look human.

'Emma, look at me,' Jonathan instructed, no longer dazed. 'Don't look at him, look at me.'

I pulled my eyes away from the blood-spattered face and focused on Jonathan. 'Emma, keep looking at me. Are you okay?'

He moved to touch my cheek. 'Your face.' I pulled back sharply, forcing him to withdraw his blood-covered hand. I absently raised my hand to my mouth and winced at its touch. When I pulled it away, my fingertips were covered in blood. At first, I wasn't sure if it was mine. But then I tasted the tang of it in my mouth. I ran my tongue along the cut on the inside of my lip where my teeth had punctured the tissue.

I was too numb with shock to recognize the pain. Everything moved slowly. I couldn't think. I couldn't breathe. I just stood in that spot and stared at Jonathan's concerned, blood-speckled face.

'Is he . . .' I rasped, but couldn't finish the question, my eyes drifting back down to the blood covering the floor.

'Don't look at him.' Jonathan stepped towards me to block my view. He guided me to the stairs with out-stretched arms, without touching me.

'What did you do?' The intensity in his hardened face flashed before me, and I shuddered. 'You looked so . . . angry.'

'I'm sorry you had to see that. But he hurt you. And I will never let anyone hurt you.' There was a quiet strength in his voice. 'Sit here, okay.'

I grabbed the banister and slowly lowered myself onto the top step. I was still stunned, unable to form a coher-ent thought. I kept seeing the man's face explode, and feeling the spray of blood across my cheeks. But what truly disturbed me was the image of Jonathan, so cold and rigid with fury. I smudged the drying blood off my cheek with the back of my hand.

Jonathan sat down beside me and blotted my face with a wet towel. I stared at him blankly. His face was clean and smooth. He appeared calm and alert, although he kept examining me uneasily, like he was afraid I might fall apart.

I pulled back with a quick breath at the touch of the cloth to my mouth. 'We'll put some ice on that when we get back.' His brown eyes connected with mine and he spoke to me softly, 'Just sit here and look straight ahead, okay?'

I nodded. This didn't feel real. I started to wonder if I was dreaming. I couldn't move. This had to be a dream. But then the pain seeped through my ribs, and the side of my face throbbed. The taste of blood ran over my tongue.

I heard Jonathan shift the unconscious body, then the

486

jangling of keys. I kept my eyes closed as Jonathan brushed past me down the stairs. My entire midsection screamed with every breath. I let the agony writhe through me, desperately needing it to keep me grounded.

'Emma,' Jonathan called to me, redirecting my attention. I opened my eyes to find him next to me. 'I need you to get in your car. You're going to follow me, okay?'

I searched his calm face, slowly becoming more alert. 'Where are we going?'

'Don't worry about anything. You just need to follow me.' His dark eyes beseeched me to trust him, and I nodded.

I pulled myself up and let out a pained breath.

'Are you okay?' he questioned in alarm, putting his hand on my arm to support me. 'How bad are you hurt?'

'I'll be all right,' I grunted breathily, moving away from him down the stairs. I didn't want him to touch me. The unrelenting rage that had overtaken him still haunted me.

My car wasn't in the driveway. In its place were Jonathan's truck and a dark blue Charger. I looked around in confusion before locating my car on the street, closer to the neighbour's house on the corner. I slowly made my way to it, panting in pain with each step.

I sat with the engine running and waited, staring straight ahead. Eventually, the Charger pulled in front of me.

I drove behind him in a trance, focusing on the licence plate with my right arm folded across my ribs, squeezing the diamond into my palm. We pulled into the parking lot of the bar outside town where we'd picked up Rachel. Even though it was the middle of the day, there were still a few cars in the deserted dirt parking lot.

I watched Jonathan wipe down the handle of the car door before walking over and getting into my passenger seat.

'Drive,' he ordered. I pulled away and merged back on to the main road.

When the bar disappeared from sight, he offered to drive.

I shook my head, needing to concentrate on something other than what we'd just done. We drove in silence until I pulled into the driveway. I shut off the engine and didn't make a move to get out.

'Jonathan, is he dead?' I asked in a whisper, turning my head to look at him.

'No,' he assured me. 'He needs to go to the hospital, but he's not dead. Someone will find him.'

'Will he come after us?'

'No. You don't have to worry about him ever again. I promise.' His eyes shone with conviction, and I knew he was confident in his words. I wasn't.

I got out of the car and Jonathan followed me to the house. He reached for the screen door to pull it open for me, and I stopped at the sight of his raw bloody knuckles. 'Your hand,' I gasped.

'Don't worry about it,' he replied dismissively. 'We need to get some ice on your face to help the swelling.'

I shook my head. 'You need to wrap that. I think we have something in the bathroom.'

I climbed the stairs with Jonathan behind me and continued to the bathroom without pause, past the blood that still covered the floor. While Jonathan rinsed his hands,

I rummaged through the closet and pulled out ointment and gauze bandages.

He blotted his knuckles dry. I gently balanced his hand on my closed fist to inspect the scraped skin that shone with blood. I was about to squeeze the ointment on his knuckles when he pulled it away. 'I'll be fine.'

'Jonathan,' I implored him, looking up at him. My words were lost when I realized how close we were.

His dark eyes pulled me in. I couldn't move. He raised his hand, gliding his fingertips across my bruised face. I inhaled with a shiver at his touch. He slowly leaned forward. I held my breath, lost in his penetrating gaze. I closed my eyes just before his lips gently brushed against mine.

I squeezed my hand and the diamond cut into me. With a shake of my head, I pulled away, my breath coming in gasps. Jonathan creased his brow in pained confusion. I rushed past him.

'Emma!' he called out as I scurried down the stairs. 'Emma, please!' he called again, his voice urgent. I pushed through the door, leaving him behind.

39

Breathe for Me

'EVAN?' I CALLED INTO THE KITCHEN AS I pushed open the door, my eyes frantically scanning the room. I paused, but only heard my wavering breaths.

'Evan?' I called out again more desperately as I continued down the hall.

'Emma?' His eyes tightened in confusion, then widened when I came into full view from where he stood at the bottom of the stairs. 'Emma!' he exclaimed. 'What happened to you?'

The pained shock in his blue eyes incapacitated me. I opened my mouth to speak but only gasped, unable to find the words. His face twisted in panic when I faltered, sinking to my knees with my arms wrapped around my ribs.

I closed my eyes at the touch of his arms sliding around me and collapsed against his chest. I didn't cry. I didn't say a word. I just breathed jagged bursts of air. He gently rocked my quaking body with his cheek pressed against my temple. I could barely hear him say, 'Oh, Emma, what happened to you?' I remained quiet and just let him hold me.

I couldn't keep the blood-soaked face from my thoughts, or Jonathan's hard glare as he'd continued to punch it. The dark look in his eye when he finally turned towards me, then the shock when he saw my horrified reaction. His touch on my cheek, and the brush of his lips.

My head shot up, and I searched for Evan, gasping frantically.

'Emma?' His eyes darted across mine, tight and intense. 'No one can hurt you now. Okay?'

I nodded and my chin quivered. I couldn't do anything except breathe in spasms as my eyes blurred with tears. But I still didn't cry. I couldn't. My entire body felt like it was about to burst apart, and I was doing all I could to hold it together.

'Can you get up?' he asked with his arms still encasing me. I shook my head and rested on his chest, closing my eyes and concentrating on the quickened beats against my ear. 'You won't stop shaking, Em. Please tell me what happened to you.'

I exhaled in a rasp, unable to speak. I felt like I was breathing under water. I pressed my nose into his shirt and inhaled him, trying to fight my way back to the surface.

'Evan?' Vivian questioned in confusion. 'Why are you . . . Emily? What's happened?'

'I don't know,' Evan replied quietly.

I opened my eyes at the touch of her cool, soft hand sweeping against my cheek. Her bright blue eyes examined me sorrowfully. 'We're going to take care of you.' I pressed my lips together to hold in the ache and nodded.

I closed my eyes again and Evan cupped the back of my head and squeezed me gently.

I heard her heels click on the floor as she said, 'I think that will be all for today. Thank you for your help, Analise. If you wouldn't mind calling your mother to let her know that we'll reschedule that meeting for another day.'

Evan slowly pulled back to examine me. I met his troubled gaze reluctantly. He gingerly tilted my chin to get a better look at the side of my face. 'Let me get some ice.'

He started to move away and my eyes widened in panic. 'No,' I pleaded, grabbing his arm. 'Not yet.'

Evan drew me back into him, kissing the top of my head. 'Okay,' he agreed.

'What do you need?' Vivian asked from behind me.

'An ice pack,' Evan told her calmly, not letting me go.

'Do you think she needs to go to the hospital?' Vivian asked.

'I don't know. She hasn't said more than a few words since she got here.'

'Emma?' Vivian soothed. I opened my eyes at the use of my preferred name, never having heard her say it before. Evan loosened his hold. 'Emma, what happened to you, dear?'

I looked into her sharp blue eyes as she patiently waited for me to explain. 'He tried to take it.' My voice came out quiet and shaky.

'Take what?' she coaxed gingerly.

Evan released me carefully when I moved my hand out from between us, unfolding my fingers to reveal the necklace. I heard her breathe in sharply at the blood coating my palm. I'd squeezed the diamond so tightly it had torn open my skin. I closed my hand back around it, numb to the wounds.

'Who was it?' she asked, her voice strong but tender.

'I don't know,' I told her. 'He was in my room when I got home.'

She nodded and stood back up. 'I'm calling the police.'

'No,' I begged, turning towards her. The pain in my ribs seared through me and I screamed, folding in half.

'Emma!' Evan called out, his arms back around me. 'Where else did he hurt you?'

My chest tightened against the panting breaths, tears streaming down my face.

'Emma, we need to look, okay?'

I slowly sat up and carefully lifted my shirt. My side was dark reddish-purple where his foot had made contact. Evan winced and squeezed my hand. I quickly looked away, unable to witness his aggrieved reaction.

'I don't want to go to the hospital,' I pleaded to Evan.

'Then I'm calling Michelle,' Vivian retorted from beside me, drawing my attention. 'We'll go to her office, and the police will meet us there.' By the set look in her eye, I knew this wasn't a choice. She bent down next to us and put her hand on the side of my face, smiling affectionately. 'Let us care for you, Emma.'

It was difficult to face myself in the fogged mirror after stepping out of the shower. The right side of my jaw was deep red. My lower lip looked like it was still packed with gauze, even though I'd removed it a while ago, once the bleeding had stopped. A small cut ran over my lip where my tooth had torn into it.

I gingerly spread the clear gel over the swollen, discoloured skin, cooling it instantly. I turned the tube over in my hand, wondering if the homeopathic medicine would really get rid of the bruising as quickly as Dr Vassar said it would. There was no way I was going to school, or anywhere in public for that matter, until it went away.

I eased Evan's T-shirt over my head, holding my breath against the sharp pain triggered by simply raising my arms. Four to six weeks. That's how long it would take for the two fractured ribs to heal. I hoped the pain would subside in less time than that, considering breathing was a form of torture.

I walked into the guest room feeling as broken as I looked. I stopped at the sight of Evan pacing next to the bed, staring at the floor with his hands on his head, unaware that I was there.

Evan strode back and forth, lost in whatever torturous thoughts had overtaken him. He'd been so calm all day – holding me, comforting me, quietly watching as Dr Vassar examined me. He listened silently while holding my hand when the police asked questions. Remaining by my side, strong and supportive, he'd hardly said a word.

But now he looked like he was coming apart. He flexed his hands, breathing in exaggerated breaths. Seeing him this disturbed paralysed me. He raised his head and stopped abruptly when he noticed I was watching.

My brows twitched at the sight of his glassy blue eyes. He hid the despair under his lids and tried to regain his composure, but his jaw only became tighter and the tendons along his neck rigid.

'Evan?' I whispered, not moving.

He opened his eyes. They glistened in agony, and the line between them deepened when he looked at me. We remained still for a moment. His torment ripped through me.

'I promised no one would ever hurt you again.' Despite his strained appearance, his voice was calm and strong. I looked into his eyes and was suffocated by the weight of their despair.

'What?' I shook my head in confusion.

Evan remained still, not moving towards me – the muscles along his arms remained taut, like he was in physical agony just saying the words. 'That night, when you were lying there, broken and barely breathing, I promised. I promised to always love you and that no one would ever hurt you again.'

My mouth opened in shock, but I was too stunned to speak. I moved to the bed, still trying to understand, and lowered myself to sit on the end of it, staring blindly at the floor. I spoke my first thought: 'What did I do to you?'

Evan knelt before me. It felt like the air was being crushed from my lungs.

'You were there?' This was one of the details I'd never heard, because I'd refused to learn what had actually happened to me that night. And he'd never told me.

Evan swallowed with a slow blink and nodded his head. 'I knew I couldn't convince you to leave, so I stayed. I waited in my car, making sure nothing happened. But I fell asleep, and when I woke up, she was there.'

'Oh my God,' I gasped, having a hard time accepting what he was telling me, shaking my head. 'No.'

'George was already in your room, trying to get her off you, but he couldn't. I pushed him out of the way and threw her off, but –' He stopped and closed his eyes. I watched his chest rise with a heavy breath before he continued. I wanted to make him stop. I didn't want to hear it. He wasn't supposed to be there, in my nightmare.

But I was too overwhelmed to ask him not to continue. I watched his lips move. 'I couldn't believe what she'd done to you. You were cuffed to the bed, and there was tape over your mouth. You'd been crying, the tears were still running down your face. But . . . you weren't breathing.'

'Evan,' I gasped, my eyes blurred. I placed my hand on his cheek and my body ached with every word. 'You shouldn't have seen that.'

He looked up at me with his eyes tight, shaking his head fiercely. 'I was supposed to protect you, Emma.'

A tear slid down my cheek.

'But I didn't.' His eyes closed, he struggled with the words. I knew he was still tortured by the image of what he'd seen.

'You were so still and pale,' he continued. His smoky blue eyes connected with mine, and he whispered, 'I breathed for you.'

'You?' The shock of his confession devoured me.

'I begged for you to breathe with every breath I gave to you. I kept pleading for you to breathe over and over again. And then . . . then you did.' He blinked away the tears that flooded his eyes. 'I promised –'

'Evan,' I interrupted, 'this isn't your fault.' I couldn't even begin to imagine what he'd gone through that night. What he'd seen. What he had been forced to do. And then had had to live with while keeping it from me for nearly a year.

'I'm so sorry,' I softly cried.

'Emma, don't,' he urged. 'You don't have anything to be sorry for.'

'But you,' I stumbled, 'but you shouldn't have . . .' I couldn't find the words to explain that he wasn't supposed to have been there. I chose to stay. It was my silence, my denial, my decision that put us there that night.

'I shouldn't have what?' he challenged. 'I *should* have called the police, or told someone long before that night. I know that now. And I have to live with that. But wanting to protect you, loving you . . . You will always be my choice.'

His words pierced me, and I closed my eyes, letting the tears slip under my lids. Evan lowered his head on my lap and wrapped his arms around me. I ran my hand over his hair, comforting him.

I'd never wanted to hurt him. To damage him. But I had. And even now, my choices continued to destroy him – all I had to do was look in his eyes to see it.

Vivian didn't say anything when he stayed with me that night. We lay facing each other, with his hand covering mine. It was difficult to lie on my broken ribs, but Dr Vassar had explained that it would help me breathe better, and it did. Until I observed the tortured look on his face. Then I found it difficult to breathe.

'Will you please tell me about Rachel and why you spent the day with Jonathan?' he asked softly, not taking his eyes off mine.

'You knew?'

'Of course,' he replied. 'What happened in that house, Emma?'

I wanted to look away, but I couldn't. His impassioned blue eyes held me captive. My voice was soft and strained with emotion. 'I thought she would be different. But she hasn't changed. When she started drinking, I was convinced it was my fault – that I reminded her of my dad and I upset her. I wanted to help her, but she just kept drinking. And got worse. Each time she'd hurt me more. In the end . . . she doesn't love me. She never has.'

Evan was quiet, gently running his hand over my cheek.

'And Jonathan?' Evan coaxed.

My eyes flickered, fearing he could see into me. 'He was there. He knows how unstable she is, so he understands. He's become . . . a friend. We went for a drive that day, to get away from her. It wasn't planned. He just wanted to be there for me.' I couldn't say more. It was evident from the tightness around his eyes that he was trying to understand, but that this was hard to hear. I kept the rest of what we'd shared to myself.

'Now I'm here for you,' he whispered, holding my hand and kissing it gently. 'Close your eyes, Emma. I'm not going anywhere.'

I closed my eyes. But I didn't sleep.

When I opened my eyes again, it was light and Evan wasn't next to me. Sara was.

'Hey,' she greeted me with an endearing smile. 'You slept a long time.'

'I did?' I responded in surprise since I didn't remember sleeping at all. Holding my breath, I gingerly pushed myself up and noticed it was almost noon. 'What are you doing here? I thought you weren't coming back until tomorrow.'

'Jared called,' she explained. 'I came back on the earliest flight I could get.'

'You didn't have –'

'Don't even start, Emma,' she scolded. 'You know I'd do anything for you. Even sit next to an annoying guy who snored on my shoulder the entire flight.' She grinned. But her grin couldn't mask her troubled eyes.

'Thanks, Sara,' I replied sincerely. 'Where's Evan?'

'Cooking something,' Sara explained. Moving closer, she raised her hand to my cheek, careful not to touch it. 'That's going to take some great make-up skills. Good thing you have me.'

'Good thing,' I agreed with a wry smile, wincing when I pulled myself up to sit, moving the pillow behind me. Sara's eyes tightened.

'Oh, I have these for you,' she said, handing me two ice packs. 'Evan has strict orders.'

I took the packs to set on my bruises. Sara opened her mouth to say something, then stopped. Her brows pulled together and she listened intently. She walked to the door and opened it. I watched her curiously, and then I heard it too. It sounded like someone was calling my name.

Sara moved out the door quickly and I scooted off the bed to follow. I couldn't make out who was saying it, but they kept calling for me.

'I know she's here,' the muffled voice declared. 'Emma!'

Sara was standing in the open doorway of the kitchen when I rounded the corner.

'Sara, don't let her out here, okay,' Evan instructed from the porch.

'What's going on?' I asked, my pulse picking up when I caught sight of the hardened look on Evan's face.

Sara closed the door, and I could hear Evan continue sternly, 'She's fine. You don't need to be here.'

I looked out the window in the sitting room and saw Jonathan standing in the driveway. My heart faltered. He was clenching his fists and his face was reddening.

'Just let me see her, Evan,' he demanded, becoming more agitated and taking a step towards Evan. 'At least tell her I'm here.'

'Why *is* he here?' Sara asked from behind me.

'He just wants to know that I'm okay,' I told her, heat rising to my cheeks. With Evan stonewalling him, I knew he was on the brink of losing his patience, and I couldn't let it escalate. I moved past her towards the kitchen.

'Where are you going?' Sara demanded urgently.

'He just wants to know that I'm okay,' I repeated with my heart beating harder against my chest.

I opened the door and Evan glanced at me quickly without realizing it was me. He turned back, stunned, when he did. 'Emma, don't.'

'It's okay,' I assured him with forced calmness. 'He just wants to make sure I'm okay.'

Evan tensed when I walked past him, but he didn't stop me.

Jonathan's face softened when I approached, the confrontational glare instantly replaced by a subtle smile, but the anxious look in his eye remained.

'Hey,' he greeted me quietly when I neared him. I stopped

in front of him with my arms crossed protectively over my ribs.

'Hey,' I replied timidly. 'What are you doing here?'

'I'm sorry,' he began. 'I've been trying to call you. I was going out of my mind worrying about you. You left so fast after . . .' He paused, and my heart faltered at the remembrance. 'I didn't know how badly you were hurt. I needed to see you.'

'Oh,' I responded, my cheeks reddening. 'Um, I don't even know where my phone is. I should've called. I'm sorry I didn't.' I could feel Evan watching us, and knew Sara was probably next to him as well. I didn't dare look.

'How are you?' he asked, but it was a loaded question, and I didn't answer until he clarified. 'How badly are you hurt?'

'I'll be okay,' I replied softly.

'I scared you, didn't I?' he said, his voice faltering. I looked up into his eyes, having avoided them since I stepped out of the house. I was struck by the sorrow in them. 'I promised never to do that. I'm so sorry, Emma.'

I swallowed hard, and nodded, unable to speak.

'I care about you,' he explained. 'I couldn't –' He glanced towards Evan without finishing – recognizing we weren't alone. 'What does he know?'

'Um,' I faltered. 'I didn't say anything, really. Just explained how everything was a mess with Rachel. And I didn't tell the police you were there either. I told them I walked in on the guy and couldn't remember what he looked like.'

'Okay,' Jonathan accepted with a nod. 'So he doesn't know about the nightmares, or your fears, or . . .'

I shook my head, dropping my eyes to the ground guiltily. I gripped my hands as the tension crashed in on us. I couldn't breathe. Jonathan reached to touch my arm and I backed away with a shake of my head.

'I know,' he said with a defeated sigh. 'It's not right to put you in this situation.'

I lifted my eyes to his. The remorse in his glistening gaze caused my heart to falter.

'Emma, please don't give up on me.' His words spilled out in a desperate rush, leaving me speechless.

'Please,' he begged again.

'I won't,' I whispered. 'I just need some time.'

'I understand,' he replied, bowing his head. 'I'll go. But I'll hear from you . . . when you're ready?'

I nodded, evading his eyes. I turned away, my shoulders bowed, crushed with guilt. I continued past Evan and Sara, who were standing on the porch, watching our every move. But I knew they hadn't heard a single word we'd said.

Sara followed me inside while Evan waited for Jonathan to back out of the driveway.

'How'd he even know where you live?' Sara asked Evan when he closed the door.

'I don't know,' Evan replied, his eyes following me carefully.

'It's not difficult to find anything in Weslyn,' I found myself saying. 'You just have to ask.' They peered at me curiously.

'What was that about?' Sara demanded as I moved to leave the room. 'He seemed so upset.'

'He was there,' Evan said before I could utter a word. My heart skipped a beat, wondering how he knew.

'What?' Sara spun towards him. She flipped her eyes from Evan to me. I looked down. That's all she needed. 'He was. Why?'

'Why did you lie to the police?' Evan demanded on top of her question.

I took a deep breath and began. 'The guy was my mother's drug dealer. I didn't want the police to know.' I looked from one to the other for a reaction. They appeared surprised, but remained quiet. I shifted my gaze back to the floor and continued. 'He beat her pretty bad because she owed him money. I found her when I went to the house to get my soccer shirt. I ended up having to take her to the hospital. Jonathan found out and didn't want me to go back to the house, but I figured the guy would be gone. I was wrong.' I paused, deciding how to continue. 'Jonathan showed up, and fought the guy off.'

'That's what I thought. I saw his knuckles,' Evan said with a slight edge to his voice. 'So, he protected you?' I raised my head, struck by his tone. I nodded and pain shot across his face, knowing Jonathan had done what he'd vowed to do – to protect me.

'So why did he come by here?' Sara asked, breaking our tense connection.

'I ran out,' I explained quickly. I couldn't tell them how badly Jonathan had beaten the guy, and that I thought he might be dead. Or the true reason I'd left in such a rush. I took a quick breath and repeated, 'He just wanted to know that I was okay.'

'That's it?' Evan asked sceptically, examining me. My face flamed up, fearing he'd seen more between us. I nodded, unable to hold his gaze for more than a second.

'I know you explained that you and Jonathan are friends and that you can talk to him about Rachel. I get it. But why do I get the feeling he knows more than I do?' His voice became stronger as he spoke, more agitated. I opened my mouth instinctively to defend Jonathan, but stopped when I saw the challenging look on Evan's face. 'Then the way he was out there . . . The way he was looking at you . . .' I shifted my eyes. He released a breath, and lowered his voice. 'I'm sorry, Emma, but I just don't trust him.'

And maybe he had good reason not to.

40

Honest Truth

No matter how hard I tried not to, I kept thinking about what I'd witnessed. His dark eyes were so compelling and trusting, yet could turn instantly cold and hard. There was more hidden in their darkness than pain and torture. More than anger and loathing.

It seemed impossible that the same man who stayed up with me in the middle of the night, laughing at infomercials, was capable of bludgeoning someone into a grotesque, bloody mess. I shuddered at the remembrance, hugging the pillow against me tighter.

'What are you thinking about?'

I turned my head with a start. Evan stood in the doorway of the sun room, the warm rays lighting up the breathtaking angles of his face. There was no darkness hidden in his steel-blue eyes. The disturbing thoughts were instantly brushed away at the sight of him.

'Hi,' I greeted him happily. 'How was school?' I closed the book that was resting on my lap and set it on the wicker table beside me along with the pillow I was mangling.

'The same.' He shrugged, sitting down and resting my legs across his lap. 'How was your day?'

'I helped stuff envelopes,' I told him. '*So* exciting.'

Evan laughed. He leaned towards me and ran his fingers over the vanishing bruise along my jaw, inspecting it. Then he leaned a little closer and gently kissed me.

'Aren't you supposed to be at practice?' I suddenly remembered when he pulled away.

'The coach had an appointment, so we have practice tomorrow instead.'

'On a Saturday?'

'Unfortunately,' Evan grimaced.

'Oh,' I sighed. 'I was hoping we could get my things tomorrow. Anna hired some guys to move the furniture out this weekend, so I need to pack up before they arrive.'

'Is Rachel back?'

'I have no idea,' I answered with a shake of my head. 'I haven't heard from her, but I don't really expect to either. I'm hoping she's not.'

'Do you want to go there this afternoon?'

A jolt shot through me just thinking about going back to the house. I knew we'd have to eventually, but I wasn't expecting it to be this afternoon. I thought I'd have more time to prepare.

'Okay,' I answered, 'let's do this,' realizing there wasn't any way to prepare for it, no matter how much notice I had.

'You don't have to,' Evan reassured me, picking up on my anxiety. 'Sara and I could go when she gets out of track practice. Besides, she said she wanted to help.'

'No,' I countered, trying to sound confident, 'I can do

it. I'll text her and tell her to meet us there when she gets out.'

'Are you sure?' he queried again, eyeing me sceptically. 'What if she's home?'

I didn't know how to tell him that it wasn't Rachel that made me dread going back to the house. It was the fear that there would still be blood on the floors. But the police hadn't returned to question me further after searching the house, so I was fairly confident that Jonathan had cleaned it up and disposed of the broken coffee table. I had a feeling I'd see the blood even with my eyes closed.

'I can handle it,' I assured him. Evan stood and offered me his hand. I took it and eased myself from the wicker chaise that was layered with pillows for my comfort. It didn't matter how many pillows it had, they didn't keep the pain at bay every time I had to breathe.

'I wonder how bad it's going to be,' I thought out loud as we weaved through the back roads of Weslyn.

'What?' Evan asked with uncertainty.

'My room.'

'How come you didn't go back with the police to see if anything was taken?'

'Because I knew there wasn't,' I replied flatly, knowing the only thing he'd tried to take was hanging around my neck.

'Do you think he'll come back?' I could feel him watching for my reaction.

I shook my head and stared out the window, not wanting him to see the look on my face as I closed my eyes and tried to push away the bloody image that induced a shudder. *What did we do?* I mouthed to my reflection, resting my head against the glass, replaying Jonathan wiping away his prints on the car door. I wondered how careful he had been when ridding the house of evidence.

I was so wrapped up in preparing myself to face the mess, that I really didn't give much thought to what it was going to be like to see my mother – if she was home. Her car was still in the driveway when we pulled in. But it had probably been there since I took her to the hospital. When we neared the house, music reverberated through the front door, confirming that she'd returned.

Evan stopped on the steps and turned to me. 'Do you want to do this? We don't have to.'

Despite the nausea in my stomach, I nodded. He eyed me warily, but didn't try to talk me out of it. Evan opened the screen door for me. I took a deep breath and walked into the house.

I didn't look for her. I continued up the stairs and Evan followed. I kept my eyes on each step and veered into my room without looking at the spot where his battered body had lain motionless. By the time Evan closed the door behind us, my heart was beating so hard I thought I might fall over.

We waited for her reaction. The music continued in the kitchen, allowing us to relax and breathe easier. I was just beginning to think we'd be able to leave without incident when I heard the door beneath my bedroom slam shut. She must have been out back. Evan stopped and looked towards me, awaiting my reaction. I shook my head with a shrug, trying to appear unaffected.

'Oh, Emma,' Evan said under his breath.

I snapped my attention back to the room and my mouth dropped open. 'What the . . .'

It was completely torn apart. The mattress was pushed off the bed. The bureau drawers were dumped and tossed in a heap. The clothes in the closet were strewn across the floor. The only things left untouched were Evan's pictures on the cloth-covered bulletin board and the stacks of clothes on the top shelf in the closet.

'My laptop's gone,' I noticed, deflated. I walked closer to the desk and discovered the hard drive on the floor beneath the desk. I eased myself under to pick it up. 'At least I still have this. I guess I can always buy another laptop.'

'True,' Evan responded, trying to sound optimistic. Then he questioned in confusion, 'But I thought you said he didn't take anything?'

'He didn't,' I confirmed. 'She must have, or someone from one of her parties maybe.' I absorbed the disaster with a disheartened sigh. 'Okay, let's do this.'

Evan set the suitcase and a large duffle bag on the bed base. He scooped the clothes from the floor and tossed them next to me so I could stuff them in the bags. There was no point in folding them.

The music stopped. Evan and I hesitated and looked at each other just as Rachel called out, 'Emily, are you here?' We'd driven my car since it had more space than Evan's two-seater sports car. She must have spotted it in the driveway.

My heart sped up at the sound of her voice.

'What do I do?' I asked him, not ready to face her.

'She knows you're here, Emma,' Evan said. 'You don't have to answer. Or you just say yes and leave it at that.'

'Emily?'

I breathed out through pursed lips and then hollered. 'Yeah, I'm here.' Evan and I stared at each other and waited, but she didn't say anything. I swallowed and tried to relax my shoulders.

Evan picked up armfuls of clothes at a time and shoved them in the bag. I knew he was trying to hurry, since I was unable to mask the escalation of my anxiety. I tried to convince myself that she didn't bother me. That I could get through this without having to face her. But she *did* get to me, and I didn't see how we'd avoid her when we left my room.

'You don't have to talk to her,' Evan advised quietly, probably reading the fretful thoughts that flickered across my face. 'We'll just leave. You won't have to say anything.'

I nodded and mindlessly tucked the clothes in the duffle bag that was already stretched to its limit. Evan struggled to zip the suitcase.

'I'll bring these to the car and get the boxes and my duffle bag. The rest should fit in them, and then we'll go.' He hesitated. 'Are you going to be okay while I'm gone?'

'Yeah,' I murmured.

I didn't move as I listened for Evan to walk down the stairs. The bedroom door didn't close all the way behind him, so I heard when she said, 'Evan! I didn't know you were here too. What are you doing?' She sounded surprised. My jaw flexed at the sound of her voice.

'Just getting her things,' he answered casually and continued out the front door.

'Emily, what's going on?' she called up to me, her voice heavy with concern. 'What are you doing?'

I didn't answer and remained motionless – hoping she'd give up.

'Emily!' she yelled louder. 'What's going on?!'

I closed my eyes and clenched my teeth. The angry storm began to rouse in my gut. I breathed deep, trying to control it. The boards creaked on the stairs.

I focused on remaining collected when I stepped out of my room, stopping her mid-step. 'I told you I was coming back to get my things.' My voice came out even and controlled, but my hands were clenched by my sides.

She appeared confused. I stood stoically at the top of the stairs and took her in. Her right eye was encircled with a greenish-blue bruise, and her left hand was in a black splint. I could tell there was more damage to her body as she leaned into the railing for support.

She didn't react to the sight of the bruise on my face. But I didn't expect her to.

'You're leaving me?' she whimpered with big eyes.

My pulse quickened, spreading the anger into my muscles. I couldn't control it.

'Am I leaving you?' I repeated, my teeth grating with each word. I pulled my brows together and scoffed in disbelief. 'Am *I* leaving *you*?'

Her eyes watered as she pleaded, 'Please don't leave me.'

Evan appeared behind her in the doorway. I caught sight of him as he assessed our positions. 'Emma.' I focused on him, trying to push away the fury that was overtaking me. He flipped his eyes to my room, and I nodded. Without looking back at her, I returned to the bedroom.

Evan entered a few seconds later, closing the door behind him. 'What happened?'

I shook my head and started pacing. 'I can't believe her. I seriously think she's delusional.'

'Emma, what did she say?'

'How could she be surprised that I'm leaving?' I fumed, staring at the floor as I continued to pace.

'Emma,' he said calmly.

'She didn't even say anything about the bruise. Does she even care what happened to me? Of course not!'

'Emma!' Evan bellowed loudly, standing in front of me. I stopped and looked up at him as he set his hands on my shoulders. 'She doesn't matter.'

I pressed my lips together to stifle the emotion and nodded. 'You're right. I'm sorry.'

'Don't be sorry,' he soothed, pulling me into him. 'I know this is hard. We don't have to stay.'

I took a breath. 'It's okay. We're almost done.'

Evan kissed the top of my head before releasing me. 'We'll be fast, all right?'

I nodded.

Evan handed me a box, and I started taking down the pictures on the board and placing them and the other items from my desk into it while he finished packing the clothes from the closet.

It was uncomfortably quiet as we rushed to gather my things. I tried to shut everything off as I finished with the box, not wanting to feel anything. But I couldn't. I couldn't quench the anger that burned in my chest every time I heard her voice asking if I was leaving – like *I* was the one abandoning *her*.

'Emma, you're shaking,' Evan noticed, taking hold of my hand.

'Sorry. She got to me,' I grimaced with my face scrunched.
'Maybe we should just go.'

'Everything's pretty much packed anyway,' I agreed, taking a look around.

Evan slung the duffle bag over his shoulder and picked up the box I'd packed. 'I'll just come back in to get the last box.' He nodded towards the one containing my sweatshirts and the pictures of my father I'd hidden beneath them.

In my final scan of the room I noticed something was missing, my heart skipping a beat.

'Are you coming?' Evan asked as he opened the door.

'I'll be down in a minute,' I told him, searching desperately. 'I want to look around one more time.'

'I'll be right back,' he said, his way of telling me not to leave the room without him.

I carefully knelt down and peered under the bureau and then the bed. I picked up the duvet that was on the floor. The framed picture of me and my father that had been on my bureau was gone. There was no reason anyone would want that picture, except for her. The one thing she thought I had left of my father, and she had taken it.

Anger engulfed my entire body. My heart pounded so hard, it was difficult to breathe.

I didn't wait for Evan. And I didn't walk out the door to his car. I sought her out in the kitchen where she sat at the table, slicing a tomato while listening to the radio.

'Do you want to stay for dinner?' she asked with a warm smile when I appeared in the doorway.

'What the fuck is wrong with you?' I snapped vehemently.

'Excuse me?' she asked in shock. 'I thought you might want to stay for dinner. I thought we could talk.'

'About what?' I shot back. 'How much you don't want me? How much you miss my father and that you blame me for his death? Or the fact that your drug dealer beat the shit out of us because you have *serious* issues? Yeah, that's great dinner conversation. I think I'll pass.'

'Why are you acting like this?' she questioned quietly, standing up and walking to the counter.

'Are you serious?' I shouted incredulously. 'Are you *that* delusional?'

She picked up a prescription bottle, emptied a few pills into her hand and tossed them in the back of her throat, rinsing them down with a glass of water.

'Oh, or maybe you're just high,' I accused her spitefully.

'What? It's medicine for my wrist,' she said defensively. 'But why should you care? You're leaving me. You don't care about me.' Her voice broke. I felt a slight twinge in my chest. There had been a time when it hurt to see her this upset, and I would've done anything to console her. Not now. As quickly as the empathy surfaced, it was swallowed up.

'No, I don't care about you. Just like you don't care about me,' I fumed, my voice cold and inhuman. 'You can take the entire bottle. I don't give a fuck.'

'I don't understand what's wrong with you.' She shook her head, tears seeping down her cheeks. 'I'll try harder. Don't leave me alone. Please, Emily. I'm so sorry.'

'No you're not,' I screamed, making her flinch. I lowered my voice again, and shot each word at her with lethal precision. 'The only thing you're sorry about is that

I was ever born. Or don't you remember telling me that in one of your drunken stupors? You conveniently forget how much you hurt me over and over again. And I'm stupid enough to keep letting you. Well, I'm done.

'You never wanted me, and I never wanted this life. So as far as you're concerned, I *am* dead. And you won't ever see me again.'

Rachel sank to the floor sobbing inconsolably. I turned my back to her.

Fury pulsed through my veins, blinding me. I almost ran into Evan who stood frozen with the screen door open, silently watching. He avoided my eyes, and my shoulders slumped in disgrace.

I hurried past Evan towards the car. My entire body trembled. I released a broken breath as the tears flooded my eyes.

'Emma,' Evan called after me, rushing to catch up and grabbing my arm.

'I can't,' I pulled away. 'I can't be here. We need to go. Please. We need to go.'

I turned away from him and climbed into the passenger side. I closed my eyes to hold back the tears, taking long drawn breaths. My chest tightened with each pass of air, trying to release the rage that possessed me.

Evan slid in beside me and pulled the keys from his pocket.

'I don't ever want to see her again,' I choked, shaking my head. I pressed my fingers into my forehead, rubbing it hard with my eyes closed. 'I can't . . .'

'I know,' Evan said, starting the car. 'Try to calm down, Emma. Breathe.'

The shame of what he'd seen hit me as we drove away. I pulled my brows together in distress. 'I'm so sorry, Evan. I don't know what just happened. I was just so . . . angry. I couldn't stop.'

'I've never seen you like that before,' Evan said quietly. 'You always keep everything locked up. It was hard to watch, but you'd reached your limit.'

I looked over at him, perplexed. 'Evan, I was awful. Worse than awful. You should be disgusted with me.' The weight of what I'd done crushed me, and I felt wretched.

'I was shocked,' Evan admitted, glancing over at me quickly. 'I mean, you were . . . enraged, and I hope to never see that side of you again. But, Emma, after everything she's put you through, you had every right to be furious. Except for you wishing away this life. That . . . that bothered me.'

'I was upset,' I whispered, still unsettled by his reaction, or lack thereof. 'You know I didn't mean it.'

'I hope so,' he returned, flashing me a worried glance.

'Where are we going?' I asked, looking around as he turned onto a street that didn't take us back to his house.

'Somewhere that will help you,' Evan answered, reaching for my trembling hand.

Then I recognized where we were headed. 'We're going to the high school?'

Evan just grinned.

I eyed him curiously when we pulled into the school's parking lot. 'I don't understand.'

'Just come with me,' Evan requested, getting out of the car.

The school was practically deserted. A few voices could be heard through the halls, but most clubs had disbanded, and the sports' practices dispersed.

When we reached the second-floor corridor, Evan turned to me and instructed, 'Close your eyes.'

'Are you serious?' I asked dubiously, not really in the mood for one of his surprises.

'It's not what you think,' he assured me. 'Just close your eyes.'

I let out a resigned breath and did as he directed. Evan kept hold of my hand and guided me further down the hall. We stopped and he released me. I heard the jangling of keys and the click of a lock.

'Keep them shut,' he ordered, taking hold of my hand again and leading me forward.

With the slightest inhalation, I instantly recognized the scents swirling in the air.

'Breathe, Emma,' he coaxed, squeezing my hand. 'It's okay.'

'How'd you know?' I asked, overcome with emotion. I breathed deeply and eased the air through my chest, searching for the release I'd always sought in this room. I opened my eyes and found Evan gazing at me affectionately.

'Because I know you.'

I closed my eyes and consumed the faint traces of paint, glue and cleaner, releasing the darkened fury with each cleansing breath.

I moved to him and put my arms around his chest, pressing against him. 'Thank you.'

He held me tenderly, being careful not to squeeze too tight.

'Hold on to this life, Emma,' he whispered. 'You're so much stronger than you think you are.'

I looked up at him with glistening eyes. Evan bent down, and the warmth of his lips captured my breath, helping me find the calm I was unable to find on my own.

41

Power of Suggestion

'WHERE ARE YOU?' SARA ASKED WHEN I picked up the phone. I groaned, instantly realizing we'd forgotten to tell her that we weren't at Rachel's.

'Oh, Sara, I'm sorry,' I replied. 'We're driving back to Evan's. Rachel and I got into a horrible fight, so we left. Are you there?'

'Yeah. Did you get everything?'

I considered, then recalled, 'There's one box left, but we can get it another day.'

'Why don't I just grab it now since I'm here?' she offered casually.

'You may not want to do that,' I cautioned. 'She was a mess when we left. I was . . . I was pretty ruthless.'

'And I'm sure she had it coming,' she responded, unaffected. 'I don't care. I'll just run in, get it and leave.'

'You were warned. Call me if you need to, otherwise just come to Evan's.'

Evan raised his eyebrows when I hung up. 'She's going in?'

I shrugged. 'Guess so.'

'Wow,' he grimaced. 'This should be interesting.'

Before we reached Evan's, my phone rang. 'Uh oh,' I groaned when I saw Sara's name on the screen.

'Emma, you need to come back to the house,' she said urgently.

'Sara, what's wrong?' Fear paralysed my heart.

'Rachel. She's not moving,' she said in a rush. 'The ambulance is coming but . . . Oh God.'

'Sara?' My eyes flickered as I listened, but it was silent. I pulled the phone away from my ear to find that we'd been disconnected. 'Evan, we need to go back.'

Without me realizing, he'd turned around as soon as he heard the stress in my voice.

The car sped up. 'What did she say?' he asked, keeping his eyes on the road.

'That Rachel wasn't moving, and an ambulance was on its way. But then . . . then something happened and I lost her. Evan, if anything happens to Sara . . .' My mind was racing, fearing that the drug dealer had returned to collect the debt, despite his injuries. Or maybe someone else was doing it for him. I couldn't sit still, wanting us to drive faster, although Evan's acceleration through the vacant residential streets meant we were travelling at easily twice the speed limit.

'We'll be there soon,' he assured me, as I gripped the handle above the door.

My chest hurt from holding my breath as we turned onto the street. An ambulance, fire truck and two police cars were out front – their lights flashing brightly against the black backdrop.

'Oh no,' I breathed. A thousand horrifying images rushed through my head, making me falter on weakened knees when I rushed out of the car.

'Sara!' I yelled, running towards the house. I was intercepted by a police officer, demanding that I stay outside. He questioned me about the people who lived there. I wasn't listening. I tried to see around him, frantically searching for her, but I was restrained and couldn't move forward.

I just about collapsed when I saw the paramedics exit and rush to the ambulance to retrieve a stretcher.

'What's going on? Please, you have to tell me if she's okay!' I pleaded in a desperate sob. 'Sara!'

'Emma?' I heard her rasp. She sounded like she was right inside the door. I tried to get to her, but the police officer held up his hand, and I was pulled back.

'Miss, you need to stay outside until they've removed her.'

'What?!' I demanded frantically. 'What do you mean?'

The paramedics and firefighters came into view through the open door, carrying a board.

'No,' I gasped, tears pouring down my face. 'No.'

But then I saw the dark hair, not Sara's fiery red. I froze.

I watched unblinking as they transferred Rachel to the stretcher and wheeled her past me with an oxygen mask over her face. All the emotion drained out of me. I stared after her in shock.

'Emma!' Sara called, rushing out of the house. Her face was red and streaked with tears.

'Sara!' I exclaimed, hugging her tight. I knew my ribs were supposed to hurt. They should have hurt a lot today, but I couldn't feel anything. Sara sobbed into my shoulder.

That's when I realized Evan was behind me. He'd been holding me back, helping the police officer restrain me. 'Sara, what happened?'

'I found her in her room,' she choked. 'Her door was open, and she was lying on the floor. There were pills and a bottle of vodka. She wouldn't move. Then she stopped breathing.' She took a quivering breath, and burst out, 'I tried, Emma. I really tried.'

'It's okay,' I said soothingly, my heart aching at her distress. 'It's okay.'

Then the realization slowly began to sink in, and I heard myself say, 'It's okay.' But I wasn't really sure who I was talking to. Everything slowed down, and I felt like I was looking through a tunnel.

The police officers asked us to come into the house to answer some questions. I responded without really connecting with what I was saying. I doubt I was coherent, and felt dazed through the entire interview. They said something about the ambulance and a hospital and I nodded, not understanding.

'Thank you,' I heard Evan say, and I watched the police officers return to their cars. There were people outside on the sidewalk. Neighbours gathered to catch a glimpse of my nightmare. That's what this was. I was trapped in a never-ending cycle of nightmares. Voices echoed around me, and I tried to focus on their faces.

'Emma, we should go,' Evan said above me. My head felt heavy as I nodded. 'Want to come with us?' He was talking to Sara, but I just kept nodding.

'Emma?' Sara called to me, taking my hand. I could still

hear her sniffling. 'She's going to be okay. I mean, she has to be.'

Who? I wanted to ask, not following. Then understanding rushed in on me all at once, I was punched in the stomach by the flood of information, my brain translating it in an instant.

'No,' I said strongly, drawing Evan and Sara's attention with a start. 'No. I don't want to go to the hospital.'

'What?' Sara questioned in confusion. 'Your mother just overdosed . . .'

'I know,' I interrupted. 'I don't want to see her.'

'Don't you want to know if she's okay?' Evan asked, his voice careful.

'No,' I replied adamantly. 'I don't want to see her. She did this. She did this because of me, to hurt me. I won't let her. I won't let her.'

'Emma, what are you talking about?' Sara demanded fervently.

Evan crouched in front of me and met my eyes. 'Are you sure?' I nodded. He studied me intently for a moment and then nodded. 'Okay. We don't have to go.'

'Evan, what the hell are you talking about? What if she –'

'Sara,' he cut her off before she could finish. 'You weren't here earlier. It's probably not a good idea to go to the hospital. We should get you home anyway. It's been a crazy night for you too.'

Sara shook her head, aghast. 'I don't understand.'

'I'll explain later,' Evan told her. 'Emma, let's go.'

I was still a bit dazed. I took his hand and allowed him

to guide me. He and Sara shut off the lights along the way, and he found the key on my keychain to lock the door. We continued to the car, and Sara crawled into the back while I sat in the passenger seat. We drove to Sara's in silence, or maybe I just couldn't hear them talking.

Anna was a wreck when we arrived. She'd been contacted by the police, since they knew Sara's father. She fretted over us when we entered, hugging each of us, running her hand over our tear-stained cheeks to examine us more closely. Evan did most of the explaining since he was the only one composed enough to make sense.

My entire body ached and my ribs burned with pain. I didn't want to talk. I didn't want to listen. I yearned to shut it all out, and crawl under the blankets. Eventually, once Anna and Carl were satisfied with what they were told, we were released upstairs.

Evan stayed with me as long as he was allowed, lying quietly in front of me on the bed, watching me drift off. Sara ended up crawling into bed with me sometime in the night, probably unable to sleep. I'm not certain I slept much either. My eyes searched in the dark – blinking in and out of consciousness.

'I told her to do it,' I whispered to Sara when she opened her eyes across from me, the dawn softly glowing above us.

She blinked wider, trying to understand.

'I told her I didn't care if she took the entire bottle. And she did.'

'Emma,' Sara breathed in shock, finally understanding what I meant. 'You didn't make her do it.'

'But I don't know if I would've stopped her either,' I confessed in a flat tone.

'Don't say that. You would have.'

'I hate her, Sara,' I rasped, my eyes blurring with tears. 'I hate her so much.' My voice broke, and I swallowed against the truth. Tears ran over my nose and onto the pillow. 'I didn't want to see her, because . . . because I don't care if she's dead.'

'Oh, Emma,' she cried, her blue eyes seeping in pain. 'I don't believe that. You're angry. But I don't believe you'd want her dead.'

I didn't say anything more. We lay silently, absorbing the torment in the other's eyes, eventually falling back into a restless sleep.

I felt responsible for what Sara had endured because of Rachel's selfishness. But I didn't feel remorse for what I'd told her. I really didn't care if my mother lived or died.

'Are you sure you don't want to come?' Sara asked again with the bag in her hand.

I looked at Sara and her mother from my kneeling position on the kitchen floor, scooping up the congealed tomato and placing it on the cutting board on the table. 'I'm sure. I'll finish picking up. I still need to throw out the food in the fridge.'

'We'll see you back at the house after we've been to the hospital,' Anna told me with the last box from my bedroom in her arms.

'I won't be much longer.'

After I'd picked up the salad ingredients Rachel had

thrown all over the kitchen, I mindlessly washed the dishes and emptied the refrigerator.

I didn't look around when I left, just shut the door behind me and locked it. I tossed the trash bags in the cans on the side of the house and dragged them to the kerb.

Instead of returning to Sara's empty house, I kept driving. I knew exactly where I was going, even though I wouldn't let myself consider why I was going there, or what might happen once I arrived.

I rang the buzzer and half hoped he wasn't home. My heart skipped a beat when the black metal door opened.

'Emma?' Jonathan scanned my face and instantly asked, 'What happened?'

I took a breath. 'Can I come in?'

'Oh, yeah, of course.' He backed up to let me pass.

I climbed the stairs with him behind me. I sat on the couch and he took a seat in the chair, anxiously awaiting my words.

'Rachel tried to kill herself last night,' I revealed without any intonation in my voice.

Jonathan slowly nodded his head and lowered his eyes. He looked back up at me and told me, 'Don't feel guilty.'

My eyes scrunched in confusion, not certain if I'd heard him correctly.

'For not caring . . . you shouldn't feel guilty.'

My eyes instantly filled with tears, knowing the real reason I'd driven here – because he understood. My throat tightened.

'I feel so horrible. What kind of person am I? I mean, she's my mother –'

'No she's not. She never was,' he countered softly. 'Emma, she wasn't even close to being your mother. You have every right to hate her.'

I bowed my head in my hands and sobbed – each gasp sending a wave of pain through my body. I wrapped my arms around my ribs, to no avail. I couldn't stop crying.

Jonathan moved next to me and wrapped his arm around my shoulder. 'You didn't do anything wrong, Emma. It was her choice, not yours. You didn't make her do it.'

'I told her to,' I choked, tilting my head up at him.

'So,' he responded, wiping the tears from my cheeks. 'It was her pain, not yours, that made her do it.'

'But I wish,' I faltered, 'I wish she were dead. Then maybe she'd stop hurting, and stop hurting me.' I tried to continue but couldn't catch my breath. 'That's so horrible. I'm so –'

'No,' he soothed, pulling me to rest my head on his shoulder, gently rubbing my back. 'She hurt you, Emma, over and over again. You can let her go now. Don't let her hurt you any more.'

I fought for my breath in the crook of his neck, letting him comfort me in his arms. It wasn't until I was calm enough to think straight that I realized it was not where I should be. I lifted my head, and his hand was on my cheek, wiping my tears. And then his soft lips were on mine.

I jumped up and stumbled back, shaking my head. 'I can't.'

Jonathan bent his head with a slow exhale. 'I don't understand.'

He looked up at me, and his eyes connected with mine,

so exposed and vulnerable. My heart ached at the intensity of their emotion. I wiped my cheeks, and shook my head again. 'I can't.'

'You should ask yourself why you can't, Emma,' he said calmly, pulling his eyes away, making me want to crumble in misery. 'Is it because you don't feel it? You're here, so you must feel something. You can't deny that, no matter how hard you try.'

I shook my head, not in denial, but in confusion – not knowing why I was compelled to see him. I thought it was because I knew he'd understand. But I could have just called him. I didn't have to be here, to see him in person.

I couldn't think straight.

'You've been through a lot in the past week,' he whispered, his dark brown eyes peering through me, seeing more than I ever intended. 'So you should just wait. Wait until everything settles. Okay?'

I didn't say anything, not certain what he was asking of me.

'We have this connection, and it's crazy,' he explained. 'I don't know how to give it up, do you?'

I shook my head, unable to speak because I knew it was true.

'It's going to be okay, Emma, I promise. We'll figure this out.'

'Okay,' I whispered. I released a quick breath and said, 'I should go.'

'I know.'

I approached the stairs, my knees weak. I turned back

towards him and said, 'Jonathan, thank you . . . for under-standing.'

'I'm always here for you, Emma,' he smiled gently. I groped my way down the stairs, barely able to stand, not feeling much better than when I'd arrived. Then again, I wasn't sure what I was feeling at all.

42

Something To Hold On To

YOU ASKED WHY I STAYED WHEN I HAD every reason to leave – I stayed for you. I was drawn to you almost instantly without really understanding what was happening. I will always be here for you, Emma.

I thought I'd caught a glimpse of his blue pick-up truck in the bustle of the parking lot – amid the cars trying to position for spots and bodies not getting out of their way. I stretched my head around a group of guys to get a better view.

'What are you looking at?' Sara asked from a few feet ahead of me, stopping when she realized I wasn't beside her. The guys began walking towards the school, and what I'd thought was his truck was a Tahoe. I released my breath and turned away.

'Nothing,' I said, catching up with her.

Sara tightened her eyes sceptically. I tried to smile, but it felt foreign, having not done it very much in the last couple of weeks.

'Do you know what we need?' Her eyes lit up at just the thought.

'What?' I asked, not certain if I should encourage the mischievous glint in her eye.

'We need a senior skip day,' she exclaimed as we spotted Evan a few rows ahead of us. He raised his chin in recognition when he saw us and waited for us to reach him.

'But don't we have one in two weeks?'

'That's *planned*. The entire senior class is skipping that day. What's the fun in that?' Sara scoffed with a shake of her head. 'Emma, you're in need of some serious spontaneity. We have to pick a day sooner, to get rid of the distractions and just have a good time. A *much needed* good time.'

'I could use that,' I sighed. I'd been fighting with more distractions than I could handle, including the Sunday I'd gone to see Jonathan – which I couldn't stop thinking about. Or the text he'd sent the next day, that I'd read every day since. I was desperate to rid myself of that distraction in particular, and clear my head.

'What do you need?' Evan asked overhearing us. He slid his hand into mine.

'A skip day,' Sara declared proudly. 'Just the four of us!'

'Four?' I questioned.

'Jared,' Sara explained. 'How about this Friday? It's supposed to be so nice and Jared will be here for Evan's birthday. We'll go to the beach.'

'I don't know if it's quite beach weather,' Evan replied.

'Who cares,' Sara shot back, already beaming at the idea. 'We don't have to wear bathing suits. We'll have a picnic and build sandcastles and play catch or whatever. Don't try to ruin our skip day, Evan!'

Evan chuckled and held up his free hand in self-defence. 'Okay, Sara. Friday is our skip day. It'll be great.'

'Of course it will.'

I grinned at her enthusiasm as she almost bounced her way to our lockers. I turned to Evan as he was about to part ways towards his. He bent down and kissed me briefly. 'Will you come over after my game today?' he murmured in my ear.

'Sure,' I smiled, letting go of his hand and watching him walk away.

I was still relishing the tingle of his breath against my ear when I opened my locker to gather my books.

'I don't think you should wait until prom,' Sara mused, eyeing me with a smirk. 'The two of you *need* to have sex more than any two people I know.'

'Sara!' I exclaimed, looking around in a panic to see who may have overheard.

'Just sayin',' she smirked again and walked away.

My cheeks flushed, I rolled my eyes and turned back towards my locker.

'I'm going to shower,' Evan told me as we parked in his driveway. 'Where do you want to wait for me?'

'I'll meet you in the barn,' I replied, opening the car door. My phone chimed as I reached the steps leading to the rec room. I was about to press the ignore button, as I had for the previous three calls that day. Then it beeped twice indicating the missed call, followed by a text.

Emma, please talk to me. Please.

I stared down at my phone. His plea felt like a weight in my chest. I hadn't stopped thinking about him since I'd left him that day. But I didn't really know what it was I was thinking . . . or feeling. I kept avoiding him, afraid of the emotions his voice would conjure up. But I couldn't keep doing this to him . . . or to myself.

I sat down on the couch and took a deep breath, listening to the phone ring on the other end.

'Hi,' he answered quickly.

'Hi,' I replied, my heart beating profusely. 'I'm sorry I haven't called.'

'I'm sorry I keep calling,' he replied. 'It's just hard, not hearing from you, especially after talking to you almost every day.'

'I know. It's been hard for me too.'

'I got a little scared. I thought maybe . . . maybe you didn't need me any more. You know, now that Rachel's not around and –'

'Don't say that,' I interrupted. 'I've wanted to call, to talk to you, but . . . I didn't know what to say. What you expected me to say.'

'Emma, I don't expect anything. I just want you to be honest, that's all.' After a pause, my mind trying to understand what he was asking of me, he filled the silence with, 'How have you been sleeping?'

I laughed lightly at the question. 'Pretty well actually. Maybe you did cure me, or I just don't care any more. How about you? Is the nightmare gone?'

'It comes back every once in a while.'

'So you've been sleeping too,' I concluded.

'I wouldn't say that,' he countered. 'I keep waking up, afraid I missed your call. So . . . not sleeping that great.'

'I'm sorry,' I repeated, my voice heavy with guilt.

'It's okay.' He dismissed it easily. 'When can I see you? I think we should . . . talk. There's so much I need to say to you, and I don't want to do it over the phone.'

'Uh . . .' I delayed answering as a streak of nerves shot through my chest. 'I'm not sure.' I jumped at the sound of the door closing at the bottom of the stairs. 'I should go. Someone's coming.'

'Emma,' he called to me. I stared at the stairs waiting for Evan to appear, still listening. 'I know you're confused right now, but I've missed us, you know, our talks – being able to share what no one else understands. I don't want to lose that, to lose you.'

'I don't either,' I murmured, watching the stairs. Then I heard the door close again. 'And we will talk. I promise. But I should go.' I hung up and sank into the couch, having a hard time catching my breath after hearing his voice. I missed talking to him. But I'd known ever since he kissed me, it wouldn't be the same between us. I never wanted this – for him to feel this way. It scared me.

After everything we'd been through, all the nights sharing and revealing what no one else knew, I couldn't deny that there was something between us. I'd felt it the first night he stayed up with me. Our horrific lives and recurring nightmares bonded us in a way that was difficult to explain.

But I also believed there was something more to what kept him up at night. Something he couldn't yet face himself. The source of all the fury that waited to be unleashed with the slightest trigger. The thought of it made my pulse race.

I closed my eyes to try to calm my thoughts and push it all away – the intensity in his eyes, the confidence in his words . . . the touch of his lips.

'Emma?'

I opened my eyes with a start to find Analise in the doorway. I hadn't heard her coming up the stairs. Her lips were drawn tight; she was not her usual bubbly self. I remained frozen, cautious of her serious expression. From the grim look on her face, I began to wonder if she'd overheard our call. My face flushed at the thought.

'Evan's in the shower,' I said, trying to sound composed.

'I know,' she replied simply. 'I wanted to talk to you.'

I held my breath.

'I never told anyone about what I saw, you know,' she revealed, taking a few steps into the room but not getting any closer. My eyes flickered in confusion, so she explained, 'That night you were hurt. I was at the house, helping Vivian.' I nodded, not wanting her to recount the entire story. 'That was when I realized how much he loved you.'

I swallowed hard and glanced down at my phone. I quickly shoved it in my pocket, as if it were branding my hand with guilt.

'I'd hoped he didn't,' she stated flatly. I puckered my lips to ask what she meant, but she didn't let me speak. 'You're not the easiest person to like. You're pretty depressing most of the time. I didn't think you deserved him.'

Shock bolted through me; I had not expected her brutal honesty. I'd never considered she had it in her. 'What's

your point, besides letting me know how miserable I am?'
I asked coolly.

Analise didn't seem fazed by my tone. 'My point is . . .
he loves you. I mean it's obvious to everyone how much
he cares for you, but I was hoping he didn't really *love* you,
not like that – not like I saw when he held you that night.
Like your pain was his and he would do anything in the
world for you, to protect you.'

I looked down, biting at my lower lip.

'All I have to say is that he's the most amazing person
I've ever met, and I'd give anything for someone to love
me like that, so you'd better deserve him, Emma.'

I looked up at her with my mouth open, speechless.
She turned away and walked downstairs just as the door
was opening at the bottom.

I heard Evan's voice. 'Hi, Analise.'

'Hi, Evan,' she chirped happily. Not a hint of the threatening tone she'd had a few seconds before.

I was still shaking off her words when Evan entered.
He tightened his eyes at the sight of my stunned expression and asked, 'Is everything okay? Did something
happen between you and Analise?'

I shook my head, still recovering. I tried to smile and
finally said, 'No, she was just asking how I was feeling.'

'Oh, that's nice of her,' he replied sceptically. 'You're
still okay that she and I are friends, right?'

'Of course,' I answered lightly, but for the first time,
actually meaning it. 'She cares about you, and everyone
needs a friend looking out for them like that.'

Evan drew his brows together like I'd just spoken in a
foreign language. 'Okay,' he said slowly. Then a breathtaking

smile spread across his face. 'So I have something to show you.'

My lips turned up at the excitement flickering in his blue eyes. 'What is it?'

'Come with me and find out.' He took my hand and pulled me from the couch. I released Analise's words of warning, and Jonathan's words of want, leaving them behind as I followed after Evan.

'Close your eyes,' Evan requested.

I scrunched my face. 'Do I have to?'

Evan released a breathy laugh. 'No, you don't have to.'

He held my hand and led me along the back of the house, eagerly awaiting my reaction. I wasn't sure what I was supposed to be seeing until we neared the large oak tree that sat on the edge of the property.

My eyes glistened as a slow smile spread across my face. 'Evan,' I breathed.

'I wanted you to have something good to hold on to. Something that would remind you of him, but also let you know that you'll always be here with me.'

I smiled wider and turned to him, engulfing him in the tightest hug. 'Thank you. I love it,' I choked in a gasp of emotion.

I pressed up on my toes to reach him. He breathed into me, his firm lips sliding over my mine making my entire body hum.

Evan pulled away and asked, 'Aren't you going to try it?'

'Yes,' I answered enthusiastically, turning back to the tree. 'Did you make it?' I wrapped my hands around the ropes and pulled my body up onto the board, balancing myself as the seat tilted beneath me.

'I did,' he revealed proudly. 'Not sure how steady the board is though.'

'It's perfect,' I glowed, pumping my legs as I leaned back. My healing ribs tweaked uncomfortably as I gained momentum, but I dismissed the tenderness. Nothing was going to keep me from enjoying this moment.

I couldn't release the smile on my face as the branches above me grew closer with each extension of my legs. I closed my eyes and felt the rush of air on my face and the flitter in my stomach as I swung back and forth. My throat closed, and I captured the tears beneath my eyelids. I was so overcome with emotion, my chest felt like it might burst.

I opened my eyes and searched for Evan when I couldn't find him in front of me. He was leaning against the tree with his arms crossed, watching. A tear rolled over my smiling cheek as his eyes danced with glints of light.

I knew how much Evan loved me. And I knew I didn't deserve it. But I also knew he was the only one I loved. The only one I would ever love.

43

Spontaneity

'THIS IS A PERFECT BEACH DAY!' I DECLARED sarcastically as we walked against the whipping wind that brought my skin out in goosebumps.

'It's not *that* bad,' Sara said defensively, her arms folded around several blankets. 'The sun's out.'

'Wish I could feel it,' I griped, carrying a bag of food and another of beach toys that the guys had packed. Sara rolled her eyes and kept walking.

We were somehow able to spread out the blanket. The guys lowered the cooler on one corner to keep it from blowing away. I set the bags on two other corners, and Sara tucked the fourth in the sand.

I ventured towards the shoreline to take in the rolling waves with my arms tucked against my body, warding off the cold wind that blew my hair from my face. Evan wrapped his arms around me and spoke in my ear. 'Want to get under a blanket with me?'

I turned towards him and smirked. 'Are you propositioning me?'

'Maybe,' he replied coyly, bending down to kiss me.

Evan grabbed one of the blankets and sat down with his arms spread wide, waiting for me to lower myself in front of him. I leaned back between his knees and he wrapped the blanket around us. My body temperature was elevated instantly.

'Much better,' I smiled, continuing to watch the waves crash before us.

'Really, it's not *that* cold.' Sara shook her head at us.

'Do you know what would be great right about now?' Jared proposed. 'Hot chocolate.'

'Yes!' I exclaimed enthusiastically.

'Too bad,' Sara shot back. 'I didn't pack any.'

'Want us to go buy some?' Evan suggested.

'No,' I replied quickly. 'You're keeping me warm.'

'Fine,' Sara huffed, 'if you really want some, we'll go.' She stood up and waited for Jared before heading towards the boardwalk in search of a coffee shop.

Evan held me against him, and I got lost in the waves, mesmerized by their rhythm. Every once in a while I could feel the heat of the sun on my face, fighting through the gusts.

'It really isn't that bad,' Evan said in my ear.

'Yes it is,' I countered, 'but I'm good as long as you stay here.' I pulled his arms tighter around me and snuggled under his chin.

'So I have the perfect night planned out.'

'Really?' I questioned, knowing he meant the night before prom. 'And why do you get to do all the planning? Maybe I wanted to.'

'Umm, okay,' he responded hesitantly. 'How about we

split up the weekend? I have the night before, and you have prom night.'

'That's not exactly fair,' I argued. 'Your night is already going to be better than mine since we're having sex.'

Evan laughed. 'We don't have to.'

'Oh yes we do,' I insisted. 'Okay, fine. It's probably not going to be that great anyway, so you have Friday, and I'll have Saturday. And *mine* will be better.'

'You're making this into a competition?' he mused with a chuckle.

'Yeah,' I grinned. 'And wait until you see me in my prom dress.'

'But my night, I get to see you without anything on at all, so I'm pretty sure I'm going to be the victor of this competition.'

I jabbed him in the ribs with my elbow. Evan released a groaning laugh and tilted me back so I was looking up at him. He wrapped the blanket tighter around us and kissed me. His cheeks felt hot against my cold nose. I slid my arms around his neck, and he enveloped us in the dark, pulling the blanket over our heads.

The sand shifted under me as he laid me down. Evan lowered himself beside me with his leg between mine. I pulled him closer, finding his lips again, the heat of his breath swirling through me with the touch of his tongue. My heart beat erratically as he pressed closer, his hand sliding across my stomach, underneath my layers.

I ran my fingers through his hair, releasing an excited breath as his mouth trailed along my neck. I could feel his body tense as I held him tight against me, breathing heavily. He pulled up, but I couldn't read his face.

'What is it?' The sun blinded me as Evan pulled back the blanket to peek out.

'I thought I heard them,' he said, dropping the blanket again. He lowered himself back down to kiss me.

Before we could get too worked up, I interrupted with, 'They will probably be back soon.' The brief interlude made me realize we were in the middle of the beach, and despite how secluded it felt under the blanket, I could only imagine what it looked like to anyone walking by.

'Yeah,' Evan groaned reluctantly, folding the blanket back.

I sat up and smoothed my hair into a ponytail. Evan ran his hand along my back as he remained lying on the blanket with his arm under his head.

'Two weeks,' he sighed. I grinned.

'We don't have to wait until then,' I suggested. 'It doesn't have to be planned.'

'But I *have* a plan,' he returned. 'So, I can wait.'

I smiled. 'You're funny.'

'Why?' he questioned, smiling too.

'All of your surprises,' I explained. 'You come across as spontaneous, but the truth is you plan out *everything*. And Sara thinks *I'm* bad.'

'I can be spontaneous!' he argued.

'Okay, then let's have sex right here, right now,' I proposed.

'Here?' Evan scanned the beach. It was practically deserted, since any sane person would deem it too cold. But there were still a few crazy people walking along the shoreline, bundled up. 'You want to have sex right now?' He watched for my reaction, to see if I was serious.

I caved in. 'Fine. No. But I was trying to make a point.'

'I can be spontaneous,' he repeated. 'You wait.'

'You can't plan to be spontaneous,' I teased.

'Hey,' Sara said, drawing our attention as they neared us. She set the tray of hot chocolate on the blanket. 'It's not that bad out if you move around.'

'Thanks for getting these,' I replied, taking a hot chocolate. 'But I'm still staying under the blanket.'

Jared looked at Evan 'Football?'.

'Sure,' Evan agreed, leaving me with a quick kiss. The heat escaped with his departure. I pulled the blanket around me with a shiver.

'Your hair's a mess.' Sara eyed me suspiciously. 'What were you two doing while we were gone?'

'Keeping warm,' I answered, my cheeks igniting as I took a sip of hot chocolate. We watched the guys toss the football and chase after it as it got carried away in the wind.

'Do you swear Evan doesn't know anything about tomorrow?'

'No, he has no clue,' Sara promised. 'He still thinks he's spending the day with his brother, hiking.'

'Good,' I smiled.

'I think you're going to pull it off.'

'I hope so.' My stomach churning with nervous energy just thinking about what I had planned for his birthday.

We turned our attention back towards the guys.

'Emma, if you ever want to visit your mother in the hospital, I'll go with you,' Sara offered suddenly.

'No,' I shook my head. 'I don't want to see her. I can't.'

'All right,' she replied, her voice low and careful. 'Em, are you okay?'

I heard the weight of concern in her question. 'I'm getting there,' I assured her with a small smile. 'Can't say my life's boring.'

Sara let out a sharp laugh. 'What? That's kind of a twisted thing to say.'

I shrugged, accepting that it was true. But her comment made me think of Jonathan, and my shoulders sank. I hadn't talked to him since the day I'd called him from Evan's. We'd texted a few times, but each text felt strained. I knew I'd need to face him eventually. He'd said he wanted me to be honest. But I wasn't so sure that he was prepared to hear the truth, and I was afraid to tell him.

Sara pulled a blanket around her, giving in to the fact that it really *wasn't* warm. The guys jogged back to us, their faces red and hair dishevelled.

Evan cuddled in under the blanket. 'Omigod, you're freezing.' I tensed away from his frigid touch.

'I know,' he said, pulling me closer, 'I need you to help warm me up.'

I squirmed under the blanket with a yelping laugh when he tried to put his cold hands under my shirt.

'Okay, fine,' Sara conceded with heavy breath, 'let's go back to my house where it's above seventy degrees and we can go swimming.'

'Thank you.' I jumped up to gather our things, wanting more than anything to get out of the relentless wind. We packed up and headed to the car.

'Do you want to come back to my place instead?' Evan asked me when we were in the back seat, on our way back to Weslyn. 'I was hoping to spend some time with you before Jared and I head off for the hike tomorrow.'

I grinned and nodded, unable to face him – afraid my grin would give away that I was hiding something. 'I like that idea. Do you mind if I shower first, to get the sand and salt off?'

'Sure. You can just meet me at my place when you're done.'

Sara didn't have an issue when I told her I was going to spend the rest of the day with Evan. I was pretty certain she wanted some alone-time of her own with Jared. I found Evan in the back yard when I arrived, sitting under the oak tree, waiting for me.

'I can't believe we spent most of the day freezing,' I said, pulling myself up on the swing. I soaked up the warmth of the sinking sun as I swayed back and forth. 'It was beautiful here all day.'

'The day's not over yet,' Evan said, leaning in and gripping the wood to give me a push. 'We can enjoy it till it's over.'

'What does that mean?' I questioned. 'Isn't that what we're doing?'

Evan laughed. 'It is. But, how about you stay the night? It's supposed to be pretty nice tonight. We can sleep outside.'

'Like camping?' I clarified.

'That's a better idea. I think I have a tent in the garage. We can sleep in the back yard, or we can go to the meadow. The sky will look incredible out there, away from the lights. What do you think?'

'Evan,' I grinned accusingly, 'did you plan this?'

He started laughing. 'No, I swear. It just came to me when you were talking about missing out on today. I'm going to be gone all of tomorrow, so let me spend the rest of today with you.'

'So you're being *spontaneous?*' I teased. He smiled and intercepted my swing, placing his hands on the board on either side of my hips. He leaned in and kissed me gently.

'Will you please stay over?' he whispered, brushing his lips across mine again.

'Yes,' I replied in a breath with my eyes closed, leaning in for another touch that made my head spin. He kissed me a little longer, and I thought I was going to fall off the swing.

He pulled away. 'C'mon, Emma.' He held out his hand and I jumped off the swing to take it.

We gathered sleeping bags and the tent, along with firewood and other essentials from the barn. Evan packed us sandwiches and drinks. I grabbed marshmallows, making Evan smile. We strapped everything into the trailer on the back of the all-terrain vehicle.

'I like spontaneity,' I announced as we headed into the woods. Evan grinned as he drove us further along the trail towards the meadow.

As the sun tucked behind the trees, we set the tent up in the clearing, closer to the brook where the grass wasn't as long. Evan pulled out a small shovel and dug a fire pit.

While he stacked the wood near the pit and prepared a fire, I set up the interior of the tent.

'You brought an air mattress?' I questioned when I pulled the sleeping bags out of the trailer.

'I thought it would be more comfortable,' he explained. 'I know you're still a little sore.'

'Thanks,' I grinned.

Evan lit the fire as the hues in the sky transitioned from orange to dark purple. The lingering warmth teased that summer was right around the corner, but still far enough away to make me yearn for it. Evan laid out a thick blanket in front of the fire where we sat to eat.

'I really do like it out here,' I said with an easy smile.

'Me too,' Evan agreed. 'Does Sara know you're staying over?'

'Ooh, no,' I said with a grimace. 'I left my phone in my car. Do you have yours?'

'No, it's in my room,' he said. 'Do you want to go back to call her?'

'She knows I'm with you, so she'll cover for me. Anna and Carl trust you.'

Evan grinned. 'I'm sure they might hesitate if they knew we weren't sleeping in separate rooms tonight.'

'No, I think they would still trust you.'

After we'd finished eating, I lay back on the blanket. The sky was filling with stars as the darkness spread.

'Everything seems so possible when I look up at the sky and see the universe gleaming before me.'

'It is,' Evan replied, lying next to me to take in the same view.

'Wanna know something I've realized?' I continued without waiting for Evan to respond. 'I've spent most of my life trying to make it to a future that still hasn't happened, or avoid a past that won't let me go. I don't remember when I've ever just stopped to live in the present, to hold on to the seconds I'm in.'

'Well, your future's still unfolding, you'll just have to let it happen as it intends to. But what's keeping you from being free of your past?'

I thought for a moment. 'Forgiveness.'

'Do you forgive *me*?'

I shifted my head towards him with my brows knotted. 'Why would I need to forgive you?'

Evan tilted his head to the side to look into my eyes. 'Because I kept it from you . . . what happened that night.'

'But I didn't want to know, so you did what you thought I needed.' I turned back to the stars. We listened to the crickets chirp in the stillness.

'Evan?'

'Yes.'

'Can you tell me one thing that I still don't understand?'

'I'll try.'

'How did my ankle shatter?'

Evan was silent. I zoned in on a single star above me and waited. 'She had a hammer. I saw it on the bed next to your foot.' His voice was low and strained. I closed my eyes, the strangled words overtaking me.

'That's why you couldn't do that Art project, isn't it? Why you had to leave the room that day?'

I reached for his hand. It was hot and tense. I laced my fingers through his and he gripped them tightly.

'I forgive you,' I breathed. 'Now you have to forgive me.'

'For what?'

'Not listening. For staying when both you and Sara begged me not to. For not telling anyone and convincing you to remain quiet too. For not asking for help. For –'

'That's enough,' he cut me off. My heart pounded hard, thinking of the many reasons I needed to be forgiven that I still hadn't named. Evan raised my hand to his lips and kissed it. He rolled on his side and intercepted my view, his eyes glassy and full of emotion.

'I forgive you,' he whispered. My throat closed and I swallowed against the tears that pooled in the corners of my eyes. 'I forgive you,' he whispered again, running his hand along the side of my face. My eyes shut with the tenderness of his touch. 'I forgive you,' he breathed, his voice wavering. I opened my eyes to see the tear glisten as it rolled down his cheek.

I opened my mouth to speak. My lip quivered and the words remained choked in the back of my throat.

'Now, Emma, you need to forgive yourself.'

I pressed my lips together and closed my eyes, the tears caught in my lashes. Before I could open them again, my breath was captured by the firmness of his lips. That kiss said every word left unspoken. It filled me with more emotion than I thought possible to contain.

I leaned towards him and he wrapped his arms around me, fusing us together. His heart beat against my chest, thumping so hard it reverberated throughout my entire body. His mouth slid over mine. I could taste our tears, the salt lingering on his lips and over my tongue.

My heart ached with each kiss. I couldn't get close enough to him, pulling him into me. I needed him more than I needed to breathe.

I pulled back and slid my shirt over my head. His warm hands ran along my back, unclasping. Our mouths collided with such frenzy, we couldn't catch our breath. Evan lifted his shirt over his head. His taut muscles pressed against my bare skin. The heat of our flesh melded us.

Evan rolled me on my back and trailed his mouth down my neck and over my skin, triggering a swirl of heat that rushed through my body. We slipped out of our clothes, only separating long enough to toss them aside. I knew him, every inch of him, but never like this.

The tenderness of his touch captured my breath. My heart thumped with each burst of air escaping my lips. I pressed my eyes closed, my brows pulled together. He intercepted my breath, his mouth engulfing mine. I could feel everything and nothing all at once, my body tensing. I clasped his hand, locking my fingers in his, arching up to meet his mouth again before exhaling and floating back to the blanket.

I lay motionless, caught in the recovery with my pulse thrumming. Evan reached into his pocket, removed the wrapper and returned to me. My heart stammered as he lowered himself, watching me intently.

I took in a sharp breath when he found me.

'Are you okay?' Evan asked, looking into my eyes.

'Yeah,' I exhaled, wrapping my legs around him.

His rhythm was gentle and slow. My breathing became faster and I closed my eyes. I ran my hands along his back, gripping him as his pace quickened.

I opened my eyes. His lips were parted and his breaths erratic. I reached up to taste him, his tongue slipping into my mouth. He pulled away with a rush of air. Looking into me. Seeing more than I ever thought possible. Vulnerable and exposed. Love and desire. My chest swelled with every imaginable emotion.

His chest was slick with sweat as he slid against me. I ran my mouth along his salty skin, my entire body pulsing. Evan clenched his eyes shut and his body became rigid, slowing until he melted on top of me. His chest thumped against my stomach as we surrendered to the calm. I kept my arms wrapped around him as he recovered in slow breaths, with his head on my chest.

'Am I hurting you?' he asked, and then clarified, 'Your ribs?'

I shook my head, having completely forgotten about them.

'I like listening to your heart,' he said, holding my hand. 'It's beating so fast.'

Evan lifted his head to inspect me, sweat trickling along his sculpted face and down his neck. 'Are you cold?'

I shook my head.

'Can you talk?'

I shook my head again. He grinned, reaching up to kiss me softly. He eased away. The cool air wicked the sweat from my body with a shiver. He leaned over and grabbed the edge of the blanket, folding it over us, positioning me so I was on his arm as we both lay on our sides, facing each other.

'Are you okay?' he asked, his eyes twitching slightly in concern.

'Yes,' I smiled brightly, making him smile in return. Then I started laughing.

'What's so funny?' he questioned, his eyes twinkling.

'I love spontaneity.'

Evan smiled wider. He leaned over and brushed his lips across mine. 'I love you, Emma.'

44

In the End

THE SUN WOKE ME EARLIER THAN I USUALLY rose, but the melodic chirping and filtered light were a welcome transition into the day.

I smiled when his breath tickled the back of my neck as he slept with his arm draped across my stomach. I shifted back, to cuddle into him. His arm instinctively tightened around me. I breathed in at the touch of his skin along my back, firm and warm. A swirling heat roused in me and I took long drawn breaths, pressing against him. Evan began to stir.

The rhythm of his breathing deepened, and I knew he was awake. His hand slid along my side, over my hips. Although the feel of his fingers tickling my skin elevated my heart rate, my body was still in a bit of shock from last night, and I knew I wasn't prepared for it again this morning.

I gently eased forward and reached over for the back-pack on the tent floor. I dug in the front pocket and pulled out the packet.

'Gum?' I offered, popping a piece in my mouth.

Evan laughed. 'Yes, thanks.' After he'd taken a piece, I rolled over to face him.

'Good, now I can kiss you,' I declared and pressed my lips against his, the burst of cinnamon filling my mouth with the touch of his tongue. 'Happy birthday,' I breathed, my head swirling. His steel-blue eyes were vibrant and reflective. My heart stuttered at their intensity.

'Thank you,' he smiled and then added, 'for the perfect present.' My cheeks warmed. Evan ran his finger along my blush, brushing the hair from my face.

'You're beautiful,' he whispered, making my cheeks even redder. He swept his finger over my lips and followed the touch with a kiss, barely touching – stealing my breath.

'I love you,' I murmured, lost in the depths of his eyes as they flickered in front of me like he was silently listening to my every thought. Evan pulled me against him and held me. I inhaled the sweet scent of his skin. 'Do we have to leave here?'

'We should probably think about it.'

My stomach growled, and I placed my hand over it. Evan grinned. 'And it sounds like you need to eat.'

'Fine,' I conceded reluctantly, 'we can get up.' I sat up, holding the sleeping bag over me. 'You know, I've never slept naked before.'

Evan laughed lightly. 'And I bet you've never roasted marshmallows naked either.' He leaned over and kissed my shoulder.

'No, that was a first too,' I nodded, making him smile. 'Do you have any idea what time it is?'

'No, but I'm sure Jared's looking for me.'

'That's right,' I grinned, trying not to blow the surprise. 'You're going hiking.' I began searching under the sleeping bag. 'Where are our clothes?'

'I think they're still outside,' Evan noted.

'Oh,' I responded with wide eyes. I unzipped the tent and a breeze of cool morning air swept in. The grass still glistened with morning dew. I spotted our clothes tossed in a small pile next to the abandoned blanket. I contemplated how cold the grass was going to be on my bare feet.

'I'll get them,' Evan offered.

'No.' I sighed, wrapping the sleeping bag around me to fend off the chill. 'I'll get them.'

I ducked out of the tent and scampered across the chilled, wet grass on the balls of my feet. I scooped up the pile and rushed back to the tent, tossing the clothes in before climbing in after them. 'Oooh, it's cold out there,' I shuddered. Evan laughed as he sorted through the articles of clothing.

'Well, you're not going to love this. Our clothes are kinda wet.' He slid his jeans over his hips, fastening them.

'Great,' I groaned, feeling the dampness against my skin as I pulled on my shirt.

'How are you feeling? I mean, are you . . . okay?' Evan asked cautiously as we dressed.

'I feel a little . . . different,' I tried to explain, not sure how to describe the post-first-time sex discomfort. Evan hesitated, not exactly following, so I added, 'But I also feel amazing.' And that wasn't at all an exaggeration.

'Good,' Evan said, accepting my answer and giving me a quick kiss. 'Let's go back to the house, and I'll make us breakfast and figure out what Jared has planned. And I can give you a dry sweatshirt to wear.'

Jared was waiting for Evan in the kitchen when we walked in. He looked from one to the other – I could only imagine what we looked like, wearing damp, wrinkled clothes, our hair unkempt. He arched his eyebrow slightly, but then redirected his attention to the bowl of cereal. 'We're leaving in twenty minutes.'

'Cereal sounds good to me,' I said, sitting on the stool next to Jared. He remained unresponsive to my discombobulated state. I was certain Sara wasn't going to have the same lack of reaction.

'Where have you been?!' she demanded when I called her from my car, having just left Evan and Jared to pack for their hike. 'I've been trying to get hold of you for forever.'

'I was with Evan,' I explained, completely baffled by her overreaction.

'I *know* that, but I needed to talk to you. My mother's having a dinner at the house tonight.'

'What?' I practically shouted, my pulse quickening. 'Sara, what am I supposed to do?'

'*That's* what I needed to talk to you about,' she said, stressed. 'Just get to the house and we'll figure something out.

My phone beeped as I said, 'Okay.' When I looked at the screen, my battery light was flashing. That was the least of my worries as I dumped it on the passenger seat and continued to the McKinleys' house.

When I entered, Anna was in the sitting room with

a woman in a suit, reviewing some papers. She stood when she saw me. I was hoping to sneak upstairs, fearing *just had sex* was written all over my face.

'Emma, I am so sorry about tonight. I knew about the party at Evan's, but I didn't realize you were planning to have dinner here first.'

'Oh, it's okay,' I said lightly, creeping up a step at a time before she could get a good look at me. 'We'll figure something out.'

'If you want to take him to a nice restaurant, I would be happy to pay for it.'

'That's very nice of you,' I assured her, taking another step. 'But it'll be fine.'

'Emma?' Sara bellowed from the third floor.

I smiled awkwardly at Anna and turned to run up the stairs. 'I'm coming!'

When I reached her, I found Sara folding the flaps of a cardboard box full of decorations.

'I have an idea,' she burst out, standing up to face me. 'You can . . .' She stopped. 'Omigod. You had sex.'

My entire body flushed, and no matter how hard I tried to stop it, a huge smile spread across my face.

'I can't believe it,' she gaped, rushing over to hug me. Then she unleashed a barrage of questions, 'Did it hurt? Did you . . . uh, bleed? Are you sore? How do you feel?'

'Um,' I stared at her in shock before I fumbled, 'Just a little . . . no . . . *yes* . . . and . . .' I smiled wide with my cheeks aglow; I didn't even have to answer the last question.

She squealed proudly, 'I can't believe you had sex! This is so amazing. It gets better, I promise.' Then she rolled her eyes in frustration. 'And I'm so mad at you right now because we don't have time for you to tell me all the details.'

'I think I just told you more details than I ever expected to,' I admitted, leaving out that it was probably the most incredible night of my life and that I wasn't sure how much better it could get. 'Anyway, what's your idea?'

'Okay, here's your grocery list. Go shopping now. Then come back here. You can shower, and I'll do your hair before we leave to decorate the barn,' Sara rattled off instructions, barely taking a breath.

'Jill, Casey and . . . Analise,' she said her name with a snarl, which made me laugh, 'are meeting me here in a couple of hours, and then we're going to the Mathews' to decorate.

'You can bring the dress with you and change right before Evan arrives at seven. That should give you time for a couple of tries, in case you burn anything.'

'Thanks,' I shot back with a mocking grin, 'but where am I going?'

Sara hesitated with her lips pressed together. 'Decatur Street.'

'What?!' I stared at her, certain she hadn't just told me that I was supposed to surprise Evan with a romantic dinner in the same house where I'd seen a man get nearly pummelled to death, and where my mother had tried to kill herself. I shook my head. 'No way, Sara.'

'I'm sorry,' Sara said with a grimace, 'but there isn't another choice if you really want to cook for him. Otherwise, you'll have to go to a restaurant. I mean, it's only a house, Emma. She's not going to be there. She was admitted into that program for the next six months. There's no one there.'

'Oh, you've got to be kidding me,' I groaned under my breath. I'd been planning this dinner all week. The logistics had been sorted out carefully. We were supposed to have dinner on the deck overlooking the pool while Sara and Jared set up the barn for the surprise party after. It was my turn to actually do something for him, but this wasn't part of the plan.

I considered just scrapping the dinner and taking him to a restaurant. But every time I thought of this night, it was more about the look on his face when he discovered I'd actually cooked for him than anything else. I didn't want to lose that over a . . . technicality.

'Fine,' I huffed, 'I'll cook there. But where should we eat? That kitchen is the least romantic place on earth.'

'How about the back yard?' Sara suggested. I shook my head, feeling nauseous at just the thought of being near the ashes of the rocking chair.

'Umm, I can put the kitchen table on the porch, I guess,' I suggested with a shrug.

'That's perfect,' Sara exclaimed. 'Let's look in the closet downstairs. I'm pretty sure my mom has a ton of table-cloths you can use to cover it up.'

'How many people are coming?' I asked, following Sara down the stairs.

'Uh, everyone,' Sara answered with a sarcastic tone. 'You put me in charge of inviting, so of course they're all coming.'

'But you just invited them yesterday,' I stated in amazement. 'That was the plan – to invite last minute so no one would ruin the surprise. We figured maybe half would come.'

'Well . . . we figured wrong,' Sara shrugged. 'It probably has something to do with seeing the Mathews' place. No one's really been there before.'

'True,' I agreed. 'But that's *a lot* of people.'

'Yes, it is,' Sara smiled. 'And everyone is arriving at eight, so you and Evan should arrive at eight thirty.'

'Okay,' I replied, anxiety churning in the pit of my stomach.

Everything was going as planned when I left Sara's with my hair in soft waves down my back and the pink dress hanging in the back seat. I kept replaying my strategy for when I arrived at the house over and over in my head.

Move the kitchen table to the porch. Cut up the salad and fruit. Season the steaks and keep them wrapped in the fridge. Mix the brownies and stick them in the oven before I change. Then the finishing touches after, like set the table, light the candles and . . . oh yeah, take the brownies out of the oven.

I could do this. It was going to go perfectly.

And despite the palpitations that made me fearful I was about to have a heart attack, and the jitters that kept my hands shaky, it was going exactly how it was supposed to. I kept glancing at my phone on the counter, hoping the battery wouldn't die before Sara called to tell me he was on his way.

In order to get him here, he'd have to know I had a surprise waiting for him. Sara was supposed to send him to me after he'd dressed at his house. Jared would make certain he didn't go anywhere near the barn. I could only imagine his reaction when he was told where he was to meet me. Sara's call was supposed to give me a twenty minute heads-up.

I was mixing the brownie batter in the bowl, reading the back of the box for the hundredth time to make sure I hadn't missed anything, when my phone chimed. My stomach fluttered with nerves, fearing he was ahead of schedule.

I picked up the phone, sucking the chocolate off my finger.

'Hello?'

'Emma?' Jonathan responded. My heart stammered. Without giving me time to react, he asked, 'Where are you?'

I took a breath and tried to sound as casual as possible. 'I'm at Decatur Street unfortunately, but it's the only place I –'

'Emma,' Jonathan interrupted, 'there's some –' A beep from the phone signalled in my ear at the same time as the smoke detector blared loudly.

'Shit!' I exclaimed, forgetting the stove had a tendency to smoke. 'Hold on. I can't hear you.' I set down the phone and the bowl I'd tucked under my arm, and proceeded to fan the alarm with the dish towel until it turned off.

'Stupid stove,' I muttered, clambering up on the sink to push the window open with a grunt.

I picked up the phone again and said, 'I'm sorry about that.' But he didn't respond. I pulled back the phone and the screen was blank; my battery was dead. 'Great. And just when everything was going so well,' I grumbled.

I opened the front door and allowed the smoke to filter through the screen. It was a good thing we were eating outside. I continued back into the kitchen to pour the batter into the greased pan. I placed it in the oven and set the timer before I made my way up to the bathroom to get dressed, knowing Sara would be trying to call me any minute – although I wouldn't be able to answer. I wanted to shoot myself for forgetting the charger.

I tried to calm my nerves as I zipped the dress along my side. My hands were sweaty, and I needed to dry them off in order to seal the last inch. Closing my eyes, I took a deep breath, unable to get rid of the flutters overtaking my stomach.

I stepped out of the bathroom, disappointed I no longer had a full length mirror to double-check the sun-dress for the chocolate that seemed to be everywhere.

I skipped down a few steps and stopped at the sound of a car door closing. He was early, and I wasn't ready.

'Shit,' I breathed, rushing down the stairs in search of my shoes. Then I saw the mess I'd left behind in the kitchen and tried to decide what was more important. I picked up the chocolate-lined bowl and dumped it in the sink, filling it with water while I scraped the scraps of vegetables and fruit from the countertop into the trash.

I slid the trash can in place and rinsed my hands just as the screen door slammed shut.

'Emma?'

I froze, my heart hammering in my chest. I shut off the water and slowly turned around, wiping my hands on a paper towel.

I opened my mouth, but nothing came out.

Jonathan's eyes widened at the sight of me. 'Wow. You look beautiful.'

'Thanks,' I choked.

But then his eyes tightened as he looked to the stove, the chocolate aroma filling the kitchen. 'Are you *cooking*?'

'Um, I wouldn't really call it cooking,' I laughed nervously. 'It's just brownies.'

'But you're cooking . . . for Evan.' Jonathan appeared disturbed by his conclusion.

'It's his birthday,' I explained feebly. 'So . . . what are you doing here?'

Jonathan remained contemplative for a moment, unable to move past the scene he'd walked in on. 'I need to talk to you. It's important.' He turned towards the living room as the timer for the brownies sounded.

I removed the pan and shut off the oven. After seeing the perplexed, yet disappointed, look on Jonathan's face, I wasn't concerned with how the brownies had come out. Without inspecting them, I set them on the cooling rack and fretfully followed him into the living room.

Jonathan was staring out the front window with his arms crossed when I entered.

'What did you need to tell me?' I asked, tearing him from his thoughts.

'I understand why you're still with him,' he began, turning towards me. 'He really cares about you, and he's a good guy. It doesn't mean I like it, but I understand.'

I needed to sit down for this. I slowly lowered myself on to the couch, preparing for where this conversation was headed.

'But, Emma, you and I have both admitted that we have this inexplicable connection between us, right?' He paused for me to respond. I could only nod slightly. 'We trust each other with secrets no one else knows. I can be completely honest with you about everything. I've never been able to do that, not even with Sadie. Have you ever told Evan about your nightmares? Your fears?'

I swallowed audibly, knowing he was right. I'd never shared the darkest part of me with anyone other than him. I never wanted Evan to know that side of me. I shook my head, shifting uncomfortably.

'I've been where you are, remember? I thought Sadie was it. But in the end, they don't understand people like us. They never will, because they've never had to go through it. You and I are the same. We share a bond that's stronger than what you think you have with Evan.

'So . . . I'll wait. I'm not going to force you to decide, because in the end, I know you'll see it, too. I'll wait because I love you, and I promised to always be here for you – for whenever you need me.'

The air seeped from my lungs. His words rushed through my head in a dizzying blur.

'Is that why you're here?' I rasped. 'To tell me you'll wait for me?'

Jonathan approached the love seat and sat across from me. He pressed his elbows on his thighs, shortening the distance between us. I knew he wanted to touch me. He grasped his hands to contain himself as I subtly leaned away.

'No, I didn't actually intend to tell you I loved you,' he confessed, averting his eyes. 'I wanted to wait until I knew you'd be able to say it back.' He took a deep breath. 'That's not the reason I'm here.' His intensely troubled expression distracted me from his confession.

'Why are you here?' I asked, but was suddenly afraid to know. My gut twisted in nervous anticipation.

'The police came to see me today,' he revealed, forcing my heart to skip a beat.

My body responded before I could completely comprehend what he was saying. 'What? Why?'

'They found a partial print on the car, and matched it to me.'

'Wait. What car?' I drew in a sharp breath when I realized. 'Oh no. But why would . . .' My words were lost with the conclusion, 'He's dead.'

Jonathan eyed me carefully as I took it all in. 'Yeah.'

'Oh no. Oh God, no.' I shook my head, still in shock. 'What did we do?'

'You didn't do anything,' he replied adamantly. 'He was hurting you, Emma. I'm not going let anything happen to you, I promise.'

'I can't believe . . . he's dead.' I kept shaking my head, unable to accept it. 'Can't we just tell the police the truth?'

'We covered it up,' Jonathan explained patiently. 'I cleaned away any trace that he was here. So no, we can't tell them the truth. They haven't charged me with anything; they're just asking questions right now. And I've spoken to a lawyer. It sounds like they don't have much to go on.'

'What did you tell them?' I asked, the panic subsiding enough to allow some coherent thoughts to surface.

'That I noticed his car at Rachel's party the night before he was found, and that I'd stopped by here to talk to her so I may have inadvertently touched it.'

I nodded slowly, consumed by a thousand thoughts

and images all at once: what we'd done, the lies we'd told, the bloody mess left behind, what could happen to us if the police ever discovered the truth. And above all else, I couldn't stop thinking about the battered body we'd abandoned in the parking lot. A cold sweat ran down my spine with a shiver.

'Just stick to your story about not seeing the face of the guy who broke in, and they can't connect him to being here after the party.'

'Okay,' I breathed, my thoughts reeling. Something he'd said left me unsettled. I paused a moment to reflect, and then it occurred to me. 'Wait. How did they have your print on file to match it?'

Jonathan's face dropped. When I peered into his dark eyes, I saw a vulnerability that made my heart ache.

'Jonathan, what did you do?' I asked fretfully, not taking my eyes off him.

'Emma, I've wanted to tell you,' he began, running his hands through his hair, 'but I was waiting until I knew you could handle it. Since I can barely live with myself, I was afraid you would –'

'What?' I begged. 'Please, just tell me.'

The distress in his eyes made my pulse thrum.

He stood up and began pacing in front of me, rubbing his hands together. I watched him anxiously. For a moment, I thought he wasn't going to speak, but then he stopped in front of the window. 'They took my prints after the fire.'

My eyes blinked in confusion. Then my mouth dropped. 'No,' I gasped, forcing him to face me.

'You have to understand. They weren't supposed to be

home. They had been at a basketball tournament, but Ryan got sick. I thought my father was home alone.' He absorbed the shocked look on my face. I couldn't utter a sound, horrified. Jonathan quickly looked away and began pacing again.

'When I moved away to college, my father took everything out on Ryan. I couldn't let that happen. He wasn't as strong as me. I needed to protect him.'

'They were your family,' I breathed in abhorrence. Jonathan stopped mid-step. 'How could –' I shook my head, the words stuck in my throat. Tears filled my eyes as the black skeletal remains of the house invaded my thoughts. My stomach turned to ice, imagining their screams as they desperately tried to get out.

'You can't hate me any more than I hate myself.' I looked up at his glassy eyes. Their tortured depths made my lip quiver. 'They weren't supposed to be there,' he repeated, consumed in grief. 'I'll never forgive myself. But I want you to know everything, to know the truth.' Jonathan bowed his head and pushed his palms into his eyes.

I closed my eyes, trying to understand what could've driven him to want to murder his own father. Then I recalled the twinge of envy I'd felt when he'd revealed that his father was dead, and how I'd wished that upon Carol. But I could never bring myself to do it. To kill her. Could I?

Then again, hadn't I just cried on his shoulder, wishing my own mother was dead? After encouraging her to end her misery with a bottle of pills? How different was I, really? Just because they weren't dead, didn't make me wish it any less.

'I don't know what to think,' I told him honestly, running my hand across my forehead with my eyes squeezed shut, a tear escaping down my cheek.

'I know,' he exhaled heavily. 'It's a lot and I'm sorry.'

My head snapped up at the sound of the screen door slamming shut.

Evan looked from Jonathan to me. 'What's going on?' I brushed away the tear. His eyes flickered in confusion then alarm. 'What did you do to her?'

I opened my mouth to answer, but Jonathan stood in front of me before I could utter a word.

'This has nothing to do with you, Evan,' Jonathan explained. His voice was low, and it was heavy with warning. 'You're not a part of every moment of her life.'

'What is that supposed to mean?' Evan demanded in the same tone.

'Jonathan, don't,' I begged, fearful of what he would say next.

'Did something happen to Rachel?' Evan enquired, keeping his eyes on Jonathan without a glance in my direction.

'No,' Jonathan laughed humourlessly. 'This is between me and Emma. You're not the only one she confides in. You don't *need* to know everything.'

I'd opened my mouth to interrupt the conversation when Evan returned with, 'And she confides in you?'

'She does,' Jonathan explained simply.

'Evan,' I called to him in a rush, needing to ease the suspicion that gleamed in his eyes.

'No, I want to hear this,' he interjected sharply. His harsh tone drove me back a step.

'Yeah, she tells me things that you wouldn't understand,' Jonathan explained coolly.

'Please don't do this,' I beseeched, reaching for Jonathan's arm. But he moved towards Evan, blocking my path. I was drowning in desperation, but neither of them responded to my pleas.

'What does she trust you with? What wouldn't *I* understand?' Evan enquired, clenching his jaw. Jonathan stepped over the threshold into the foyer. I tried to position myself next to him, to calm the growing tension that hummed between them, but it was as if I were invisible. My heart pounded against my chest.

'Don't worry about it,' Jonathan returned cockily. 'As I said, this has nothing to do with you.'

Jonathan's arrogance was getting under Evan's skin, and the taut muscles along his arms made it evident.

'Evan, I can explain,' I interjected passionately.

'I'd rather hear it from him,' he snapped, making my stomach flip.

Jonathan produced a snide grin. 'You really want to torture yourself, huh? Just let it be. I'm not taking her away from you or anything.'

'Then what is it? What is it about you that makes her want to tell you things she can't tell me?'

Jonathan shrugged dismissively. 'I get her in a way you never will. It's not your fault. You just don't understand. And I do.'

Evan's shoulders drew back as if the words were razor sharp.

I knew Jonathan was walking along a dangerous line,

but neither of them would listen to me. I couldn't keep him from pushing Evan over the edge.

'Jonathan, knock it off,' I warned him, without effect.

'I'm there for her when the nightmares wake her in the middle of the night. I'm the one she calls when she needs someone to confide in about Rachel. She reveals the secrets you can't handle because she trusts me. And she knows I will always be here to protect her.'

I screamed out in surprise as Evan's fist collided with Jonathan's jaw, knocking Jonathan back a few steps. I quickly sidestepped him as he stumbled for balance.

'You don't know anything about protecting her,' Evan seethed. Jonathan straightened, wiping his mouth with the back of his hand. A streak of blood stained his skin.

In a sudden movement, Jonathan charged Evan, ramming him against the wall. The house shook around us, as though it was vehemently protesting about the attack.

'Don't!' I yelled, rushing towards them. The violence of the exchange mounted as they grappled and threw each other around the foyer. Guttural groans escaped with each punch thrown. Blood spattered their faces.

I couldn't find a way to get between them. Their movements were so quick. They were oblivious to my presence, and I could easily have been swept up in the brawl. I begged them to stop over and over again, but they showed no signs of relenting.

My entire body shook as I shuffled around them, desperate for their attention. My cheeks were slick with tears as I fought to breathe. I felt each punch as if it were thrust directly into me, bludgeoning my heart.

I knew I'd done this. I'd created the tension between them that had erupted into this moment. Their anger and frustration had nothing to do with the person they were fighting. It had everything to do with me, and what I couldn't give them. Which was all of me. I felt my insides implode as they fell against the groaning walls.

I caught a glimpse of Evan's face and drew in a sharp breath at the sight of the gash above his right eye, blood trailing down his face. I couldn't stand any more.

'Jonathan, don't!' I commanded loudly, grabbing for his arm. Impervious to my presence, he jabbed his elbow back and collided with my jaw, sending me sailing back. Unable to keep my balance, I collapsed with a cry.

Evan redirected his attention to my stunned face just as I landed on the floor. 'Emma!'

The distraction left him open to a vicious blow to the temple.

'No!' I screamed, my voice echoing through the house. Evan's eyes left me and tilted back as his head lolled to the side like a ragdoll's. He crashed against the wall and Jonathan pinned him upright, landing a ferocious blow to the side of his face.

I scrambled to my feet, driven by the adrenaline that accelerated through me. I squeezed in front of Evan and closed my eyes, bracing for the pain of Jonathan's crushing fist. My whole body tensed, pressed against Evan's slouched form.

Nothing happened.

Evan started to slide and I quickly turned towards him, attempting to ease him to the floor. But his dead weight was too much for me to support, and he toppled over with a reverberating thump, his head knocking against the wood.

I collapsed beside him, and my chest shook with jagged breaths. 'Evan!' I bent over him to examine his bruised and bloodied face. 'Evan, can you hear me?'

I tried to reposition him, sliding him from his awkward angle against the wall, struggling to turn him on his back.

'Let me take a look,' Jonathan said from beside me. He bent down and grabbed Evan's shoulders to lay him flat.

'Don't touch him!' I shouted, bending over Evan's body as if to shield him. '*You* don't get to touch him!'

'Emma.' His voice sounded pained. He placed his hand on my back. I thrust against him forcefully, causing him to pull away with a jerk.

'Don't you dare,' I threatened. My muscles quaked; I was fuelled with rage. My eyes bored into him.

'Emma, please,' he begged, his voice breaking with emotion as he swiped at the blood trickling down the side of his face. 'I lost it. I didn't mean it. I'm sorry.'

'No you're not,' I shouted back. 'Don't even say it. This is what you do. This is what *we* do. We hurt people.' I choked on the words, forcing them out of my mouth.

The tendons along my neck strained as I screamed, 'Look what we've done!' Jonathan flinched, a tear escaped from his swollen eye. I hunched over Evan with a sob and gasped, 'We've hurt so many people.' I sniffled and gently caressed his bruised cheek. Evan remained still under my touch.

'Don't say that,' Jonathan implored me desperately. 'We're the ones who've been hurt, Emma.'

I released a vicious laugh. 'No, Jonathan. We're just

as bad as they are, with our lies and deceit. We destroy people's lives.'

Jonathan opened his mouth to stop me, but I pierced him with my vile tongue. 'And you. You've *killed* people. You're not any less of a monster than your father.'

Jonathan's bruised face turned ashen as he released a strangled gasp, like he'd been stabbed through the heart.

'It was anger and pain that drew us together. That's our *bond*. Not love.' My words shot out with lethal force, ripping his protests from his opened mouth. 'I don't love you.' His eyes flitted across mine, begging me to stop – but I continued, relentless. '*No one* could ever love you.' Jonathan's chest caved. He took several staggering steps before faltering to his knees, his confidence decimated.

Loathing corroded my veins and shrivelled my heart. I watched as he cowered under my words, relishing his silent torture. 'Don't *wait* for me. I don't want you to *be there* for me, not ever. Stay out of my life, and I won't breathe a word about what you've done.' Jonathan closed his glassy eyes and bowed his head, clutching his chest.

I turned my back to him, unable to watch his devastation. I hid my shame behind my lids, tears continued to cascade down my face, dripping from my chin. My words wielded as much destruction as Jonathan's fists. I tore people apart with my lies and secrets, unleashing a verbal wrath that could alter a person's conviction. I wasn't worthy of being loved any more than he was.

I tensed when the screen door slammed shut behind me. I knew he was gone, and that I'd never see him again.

My chest spasmed in pain as I released heaving sobs, bending over Evan's unconscious body. I placed my hand on his chest, and he shifted slightly. I sucked in broken breaths, trying to relinquish the pain, but I knew that would never happen . . . not after today.

Evan moaned below me. My body shook in agony and my insides began to splinter. It was excruciating. I could barely breathe.

'Emma?' Evan murmured, his lids twitching.

'I'm so sorry.' I released an impassioned cry, a tear dropping on his cheek. I leaned down, breathing him in with a brush of my lips against his – savouring his clean, sweet scent and the warmth of his firm lips before pulling away. 'I don't know if you'll ever forgive me, but I won't destroy your life too.' My heart fought for each beat as the pieces began to fall. 'I love you,' I breathed.

Easing his head onto the floor, I rose. My legs were unsteady as I balanced my broken frame. I faltered to the screen door and pushed it open. It took every ounce of strength I had to walk away.

'Emma!' rang through the darkness, shattering me into a thousand pieces.

Epilogue

I SLID INTO THE SILENT VEHICLE BESIDE Sara, and Carl backed out of the driveway. I stared out the window the entire drive, allowing Anna and Carl to converse in the front without comprehending a single word. Sara's presence pressed in beside me, but she made no attempt to speak.

When we pulled up to the airport drop-off, Carl removed the suitcases from the trunk while Anna awaited me on the kerb.

'I'll ship the rest of your things once you're in your dorm,' she told me, smiling kindly. She examined my face and gently brushed my cheek. 'You don't have to do this, Emma. You deserve to walk down that aisle on graduation day with everyone else. I wish you'd reconsider.'

I smiled lightly, knowing she only wanted to console me, but I was beyond reaching now. Everything was still and quiet inside me, impervious to the emotions that showed on her face. There was nothing left. It had all shattered, leaving me hollow.

'I should get going,' I replied, sliding one arm through the strap of my backpack. Anna hugged me and handed me my boarding passes.

'Call if you need anything,' she urged and I nodded.

'Your advisor will be contacting you after you arrive to

arrange for your final exams,' Carl explained, rolling the suitcase over to me and setting the duffle bag next to it.

'Thank you,' I said sincerely. He hesitated before giving me a brief, firm hug.

'You know where we are,' he said to me before getting in the car.

Sara remained still, leaning against the SUV. I paused, but she hadn't said a word to me since I'd booked my flight two days ago, and I wasn't expecting her to speak now.

I picked up the duffle bag and rolled the suitcase after me, headed towards the check-in counter.

'Emma!' Sara yelled, jogging to catch up. I closed my eyes and exhaled in relief, stopping to wait for her. Her eyes were glassy as her brow scrunched in agony. 'Don't do this. Please. This isn't what's supposed to happen.'

I remained unaffected and smiled at her reassuringly. 'It'll be okay.'

'Emma, please!'

'I'll see you in a few weeks, right?' I confirmed, my eyes soft.

She swallowed and pressed her lips together with a nod. Then she grabbed my shoulders. Her words poured out passionately, 'You're making the biggest mistake of your life. Don't do this. I know you're going to regret it.'

I waited for her to let me go, and replied in an even tone, 'I'll see you soon.' I turned from her and walked away.

I pulled the key out of the door and tossed my backpack on the bed. I opened the small refrigerator to get water, trying to ignore the fact that Lyle was in the room. Unfortunately, he was hard to ignore.

I froze with the door in my hand, recognizing the box on his bed as he shamelessly rummaged through its contents.

'What the hell?' I demanded, furious, slamming the fridge shut. I pulled the box off his bed and inspected it.

'I was looking for a sweatshirt,' he explained feebly. His invasion of my things wasn't new. He'd done it a lot in the past few months, but this was crossing the line.

'You're not going to find one in here,' I scowled angrily. 'Give me those.' I snatched the pictures from his hands.

'Relax, Evan,' he countered, flopping back down on his bed. 'Who's the girl anyway? She's pretty hot.'

'None of your business,' I snapped, placing the photos back in the box, on top of the camera case I hadn't touched in months. I hesitated, removing the square envelope from the stack. I ran my fingers over my mother's name written in her distinctive hand. A cold current filtered through me at the touch of the thick paper between my fingers.

The letter that was once sealed in this envelope had changed everything. I never got to read it. But whatever she'd written to my mother kept me from following her, forcing me to stay on the East coast while she escaped to California. No explanation. No goodbye. That letter had changed my life, and I never saw a single word of it.

I set the envelope back in the box and paused before closing it, taking in the image of her laughing. Her laugh was infectious, lighting up her caramel brown eyes, creasing them around their edges. She reminded me of the picture of her father she used to have on her dresser.

I had to look away. I knew I was only torturing myself. She'd left. She'd left me here.

Just before I closed the box I realized something was missing. I looked around the room and spotted the sweatshirt hanging on the back of the chair at Lyle's desk.

'What the fuck, Lyle!' I bellowed, grabbing it.

'What would I want with a Stanford sweatshirt?' he said defensively with a roll of his eyes.

'If you touch my things again, I'll break your hand,' I threatened. He didn't look up from his textbook, but I knew he'd heard me. The colour flushed across his face.

I shoved the sweatshirt in the box and folded the flaps, hiding the image of her laughing at something I'd said. I slid the box into the bottom of my closet, next to the others.

'I don't get it,' he muttered. 'What's up with the boxes anyway?'

I closed the closet door, shutting away all the reasons I was compelled to say, 'I don't know if I'm staying.'

Acknowledgements

Writing may be a solitary venture, but publishing is not. There are so many people who are a vital part of the entire experience, whether it's providing emotional support and words of encouragement, or reading it through and freaking out when the ending is so far off the mark they virtually have a meltdown, or examining each sentence and every word until they are perfectly constructed. I may create on this tiny island, but I am surrounded by a vast ocean of friends whom I love, and I am in awe of their magnificence.

First and foremost, I must thank my ever patient and brilliant assistant, Elizabeth. She has been the perfect partner, polishing my words until they gleam with pride. We complement each other so well, my words became hers and hers mine. She has the kindest soul I've ever had the privilege to be touched by.

Faith, my ever present voice of reason. If I ever doubt, she is always there to provide her much valued honesty and insight. I will follow her advice down the darkest roads, knowing I will end up exactly where I belong, safe and sound.

Emily, my sunshine and warmth when I need assurance that all is truly wonderful in the world. And the one to reel me back in when I've veered too far off the path. I will never get lost with her in my life.

Courtney, my bright eyed and brighter smiled friend, who can come up with the best one-liners that will keep me laughing for days. Attitude will get you everywhere, and by her side, we will conquer the world!

Amy, modestly brilliant, and I am thrilled that she was a contributor to our team, giving the story that something extra to make it spectacular.

The fabulous team at Trident Media Group for believing in me, especially my wonderful agent, Erica Silverman and my UK agent, Alex Slater.

Lindsey Heaven, for embracing my words, and the entire editing team at Penguin UK Razorbill, for making them that much better.

There were a select few who read *Barely Breathing* in varied stages from its infancy to its nearly finished progression. But there were plenty of others who were there to listen, praise, encourage and celebrate with me along the way. I thank you all!

Lastly, I want to thank my truly incredible fans who have enthusiastically embraced me since I released *Reason to Breathe*. Your enthusiasm will forever inspire me to create words worthy of being read by you!

'Emotionally intense
and heart-achingly beautiful'
– Tracey Garvis-Graves,
New York Times bestselling author of *On the Island*

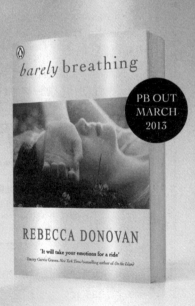

When Emma unexpectedly finds love, it challenges
her to recognize her own worth – but at the risk of revealing
a terrible secret . . .

 www.facebook.com/thebreathingseries

He just wanted a decent book to read ...

Not too much to ask, is it? It was in 1935 when Allen Lane, Managing Director of Bodley Head Publishers, stood on a platform at Exeter railway station looking for something good to read on his journey back to London. His choice was limited to popular magazines and poor-quality paperbacks – the same choice faced every day by the vast majority of readers, few of whom could afford hardbacks. Lane's disappointment and subsequent anger at the range of books generally available led him to found a company – and change the world.

'We believed in the existence in this country of a vast reading public for intelligent books at a low price, and staked everything on it'
Sir Allen Lane, 1902–1970, founder of Penguin Books

The quality paperback had arrived – and not just in bookshops. Lane was adamant that his Penguins should appear in chain stores and tobacconists, and should cost no more than a packet of cigarettes.

Reading habits (and cigarette prices) have changed since 1935, but Penguin still believes in publishing the best books for everybody to enjoy. We still believe that good design costs no more than bad design, and we still believe that quality books published passionately and responsibly make the world a better place.

So wherever you see the little bird – whether it's on a piece of prize-winning literary fiction or a celebrity autobiography, political tour de force or historical masterpiece, a serial-killer thriller, reference book, world classic or a piece of pure escapism – you can bet that it represents the very best that the genre has to offer.

Whatever you like to read – trust Penguin.